**He knew the moment he first saw her that she wasn't some
ordinary wench...**

With her long flowing hair and doll-like features, she had the
air of a pixie. So guileless, and with a look of expectancy on her
pretty face. "What's your name, lass?"

"Felicity." She gave him a broad smile, and he felt his heart
crack.

Felicity. Was it a cruel joke? He'd not felt true joy in decades,
and in his lap he held a woman with the name *Felicity*.

Come for him? He couldn't fathom it...

Berkley Sensation Books by Veronica Wolff

MASTER OF THE HIGHLANDS
SWORD OF THE HIGHLANDS
WARRIOR OF THE HIGHLANDS
LORD OF THE HIGHLANDS

Lord of the Highlands

Veronica Wolff

BERKLEY SENSATION, NEW YORK

THE BERKLEY PUBLISHING GROUP
Published by the Penguin Group
Penguin Group (USA) Inc.
375 Hudson Street, New York, New York 10014, USA

Penguin Group (Canada), 90 Eglinton Avenue East, Suite 700, Toronto, Ontario M4P 2Y3, Canada
(a division of Pearson Penguin Canada Inc.)
Penguin Books Ltd., 80 Strand, London WC2R 0RL, England
Penguin Group Ireland, 25 St. Stephen's Green, Dublin 2, Ireland (a division of Penguin Books Ltd.)
Penguin Group (Australia), 250 Camberwell Road, Camberwell, Victoria 3124, Australia
(a division of Pearson Australia Group Pty. Ltd.)
Penguin Books India Pvt. Ltd., 11 Community Centre, Panchsheel Park, New Delhi—110 017, India
Penguin Group (NZ), 67 Apollo Drive, Rosedale, North Shore 0632, New Zealand
(a division of Pearson New Zealand Ltd.)
Penguin Books (South Africa) (Pty.) Ltd., 24 Sturdee Avenue, Rosebank, Johannesburg 2196,
South Africa

Penguin Books Ltd., Registered Offices: 80 Strand, London WC2R 0RL, England

This is a work of fiction. Names, characters, places, and incidents either are the product of the author's imagination or are used fictitiously, and any resemblance to actual persons, living or dead, business establishments, events, or locales is entirely coincidental. The publisher does not have any control over and does not assume any responsibility for author or third-party websites or their content.

LORD OF THE HIGHLANDS

A Berkley Sensation Book / published by arrangement with the author

PRINTING HISTORY
Berkley Sensation mass-market edition / November 2009

ISBN: 978-0-425-23113-5

BERKLEY® SENSATION
Berkley Sensation Books are published by The Berkley Publishing Group,
a division of Penguin Group (USA) Inc.,
375 Hudson Street, New York, New York 10014.
BERKLEY® SENSATION and the "B" design are trademarks of Penguin Group (USA) Inc.

PRINTED IN THE UNITED STATES OF AMERICA

10 9 8 7 6 5 4 3 2 1

For Kate Perry,
who never fails to remind me what it's all about.

Acknowledgments

Heartfelt thanks to my usual posse of bright and talented women: Cindy Hwang, Leis Pederson, and Stephanie Kip Rostan. It's an honor to be in their company.

And to the stalwart Kate Perry, who truly is one in a million. To have a critique partner who's also a black-belted, cane-fighting, kung fu master? A girl's dream come true.

Many thanks to Monica McCarty, fast friend and coconspirator, for far too many and varied things to list here. And to the man who so fearlessly led us through the Highlands, Iain Watson, for sharing wisdom, wit, whisky, and one Roman road.

A shout-out to Tawny Weber for the Tarot expertise. And to Kristen Lane for just generally helping me keep it all together.

As usual, love and thanks to my Mom, my primary and most encouraging reader. And to Dad, for the enthusiastic support, and for all that printing.

And finally, as ever, everything I've got goes out to Adam and our two glorious wee houseguests, with special props going to the O-man for insights into musket loops that only a little guy could have, and to "Jane," my mommy-movie buddy.

Cha duine duine 'na aonar.

"A man alone is no man."

Prologue

Duncrub Castle, Perthshire, Scotland, 1622

It was the most beautiful creature he'd ever seen. Not slight like the ponies of other boys, but braw, with a chest like a great cask of ale, and a coat that shimmered dark gray, like a sword, or the dreadful eye of the Corryvreckan itself, a whirlpool so immense as to draw even the most magnificent of ships to a terrible fate far below.

His pony.

Young Will cradled the oval-shaped currycomb in his palm, gingerly scuffing circles along the animal's neck and shoulder, even though there wasn't a speck of dust left to dislodge.

He'd need to choose a name. Something reminiscent of the great heroes of old. Something suitable for kings.

"Don't think you're better than me just because Da gave you some old hack."

Will's hand froze. Though his heart jolted, he forced himself to stillness. It was best to suffer his older brother's taunts in silence.

He waited for the inevitable cuff on the shoulder, or along the side of his head, but it didn't come.

Slowly Will resumed his currying.

"Naggy old swayback old hack." Jamie was at his shoulder now, singsonging his insults. His voice had just begun to change, and the awkward cracking seemed to enrage the already volatile youth.

Will felt his cheeks redden. He concentrated on the comb, making intent circles, until his pony's skin shivered.

"Oh, are you going to cry?" Jamie's hand reached over Will to slap the beast sharply on the neck.

Ears flicking impatiently, the animal gave its tail an abrupt swish.

"Don't cry, little Willie."

He stilled. It was his seventh birthday. He'd not see this day ruined like all the others.

"Are you sad I don't like your wee naggy beast?"

Not this day. It was already so much more special than any he'd known. The most special of his life. His father had woken him early, leading him to the stable at dawn, where his birthday present had been waiting.

"This old hack isn't that great." Jamie began to pace a slow circle around them.

Will used the opportunity to slide the halter from his pony's head, wanting to replace it as quickly as he could with his bridle.

The leather was tacky in his fingers, just polished, and the scent of oil gave a twinge in his nose. The pony took the bit placidly, and Will nearly crumpled with relief. He'd not have to struggle in front of Jamie, and in that moment, he thought surely that he and this animal were destined to be as one. Will eased the straps of the bridle over his ears, thinking it impossible to love an animal more.

"All the lads get their own mounts." Jamie squatted at the pony's rear, as if examining the legs. "He's not so special."

Anger swelled in Will. His brother dared pretend to inspect his pony, when all knew the boy knew next-to-naught about them.

It was *Will* who knew horses. Will whom their father had singled out, time and again, for special instruction. *See this,*

Will, this is how to mend a split hoof. See here, Will, how this beast was lamed.

It was Will who'd been given his own pony well before any of the other boys had.

It was time to stand up to his brother's bullying. He would fight back this time. He would.

Will's breath came quickly, shallow panting high in his chest. He overturned a bucket and kicked it to rest beneath the stirrups. Taking both reins into his left hand, he relished the feel of supple leather sliding through his fingers. He stepped onto the bucket, placed his foot in the stirrup, and hauled himself over.

His pony made a low chuffing sound and the mass of him felt so right beneath the saddle.

Though there was a quiver in his voice, Will turned his head and said, "You're just sore Da thinks me the better horseman." A small smile pursed his lips, pleased at how the words had come out.

The answering silence made him look, finally, at his brother.

Jamie was twelve and the meat on his bones had yet to catch up to the scrawny length of him. Will recognized bits of their Da on his brother's face, but it was the look their father wore when he was riled. As if the Rollo features had settled sharp and angry onto his brother: the precise nose, but thinner and hooked almost to a point. The edge of cheek and chin turning Jamie's face gaunt instead of fine.

Exhilaration and fear both spiked in Will's veins. It was a heady feeling, looking down from the saddle, watching Jamie's face pale, that mouth sputtering, for once speechless.

His response, when it came, was deathly quiet. "Horse-*man*? You're a boy. A *baby*. Not a horse*man*."

Jamie's hand was swift, darting at the pony's rump like the lash of a whip.

Will didn't have a moment to contemplate the jostle of the saddle beneath him before his mount took off with a start, tearing through the stable like a rabid animal.

Jamie's laughter and the startled whinnies of the other

horses flashed like a thunderclap, then were gone as Will's pony burst out, taking the pasture at a full gallop.

"Whoaa." His voice was unsteady. Will tugged at the reins, his breath loud in his ears.

"Ho . . ." He pitched his voice low, trying to soothe the animal.

"Ho," he tried again, and this time he gently snugged his legs tightly around the pony's belly to settle him. The animal answered with an outraged shriek. It was a hideous sound, a demon sound, not a noise a creature should make at all. The pony squealed again, a possessed thing, baring his teeth, rearing up and down, and up and down, hooves skittering madly at the air.

Will held tight. Leaning forward, he twined his small fingers in the pony's mane.

He began to slide.

He wound his hands more tightly into the coarse hair. Dirt and leather oil had darkened his nails into black half-moons, and his fingertips began to go blue.

He couldn't hold on. He needed to let go.

Will released one foot and was ready to leap off, when he realized his left side was caught. His foot had slipped all the way through the stirrup. He wriggled madly, terrified now. The heel of his boot caught.

He'd have to ride it out.

Swinging his free leg back over, he found the right stirrup. Again the pony took off like a bullet.

He saw the rise in the ground before him and tried once more pulling on the reins. Will leaned back hard now, using the whole of his small body to coax the animal to slow, to stop.

The pony shrieked again, and Will's skin crawled. He realized it was his shifting weight that caused the pony's cries. What had Jamie done? He remembered his brother jostling the saddle just before the pony went mad.

Carefully, he reached back. His hand fumbled along the hard stretch of leather while his eyes remained pinned on the hill before him.

The small scree-covered slope grew closer by the second. Before, it was an innocent thing, and now it loomed, threatening.

Will's fingers gingerly probed along the back of the saddle, down to the pony's coat, now slicked warm and wet with sweat. He pulled his hand back. A thin smear of blood stained his fingertips brownish red.

Jamie. Curse him.

It would be the last rational thought Will had for some time.

His pony reached the rise. He reeled away in last-minute panic to careen along the base of the hill. But not before the hooves on his right side hit gravel, slid. Still galloping, the beast faltered.

Will wriggled, his terror at fever pitch, trying desperately to dislodge his trapped left foot.

The pony fell, rolling onto his right side. Will heard the sound of his leg being crushed. An all-consuming pain blanketed him. Smashed him.

He felt his left calf bone snap, his foot finally loose.

In an unnatural, awkward movement, the pony heaved back up and charged away.

Leaving Will lying there. Broken. On his seventh birthday.

Chapter 1

San Francisco, present day

"Jerk!" Felicity slammed her sangria onto the table, sending her bangles clattering to her wrists. "Evil, nasty, two-timing jerk."

"I warned you about Scorpios," her Aunt Livia said. "They'll sweet talk you, then turn around and *sting*." She pulled an orange slice from her glass and snapped a bite from it to underscore her point.

"Do you realize he actually called himself a *feminist*?"

"No!" Livia grimaced. "Put a man in a protest march and all of a sudden he's freaking Gandhi." Her aunt nodded sagely, tucking her long, unnaturally red hair back behind her ears. "I met the same in my day. Trust me, sweetheart, I'm much happier living in my little cottage all by my lonesome."

"But, Livvie . . ." Felicity deflated. "I love your place, but I'm sorry, I just can't give it all up and live in a canyon somewhere with a bunch of coyotes."

"I've only had trouble with the one coyote, and my little cottage was good enough for you when you came to live there as a child."

Felicity picked a big, green olive from her plate, taking a moment to think. The last thing she wanted to do was inadvertently offend her aunt. Livia had taken her in when Felicity's parents died in a car accident, and her aunt's eccentric lifestyle had been what pulled young Felicity through her grief.

"I'm sorry, Livvie. Your place was, *is* wonderful, but I'm not eight anymore."

"Would that you were." Livia looked around the tapas joint. It was in San Francisco's Mission District, and it was packed with the gamut of city dwellers: the pierced and the straitlaced, nonnative speakers mingling with middle America. "I do without you for a whole year so you can see the world, and then you move all the way out here. I hate having to come all this way just to see you."

"I was only in Central America, it was only nine months, and it was your idea, as I recall. Anyway, your trips to San Francisco would go much faster if you flew instead of insisting on the bus."

Livia ignored the jibe. "I see why the city beckons, sweetheart, but I wish you were back where you belong."

"I belong *here*," Felicity said. "And it's not as though you're living on holy ground. I mean, come on, Livvie, you're in LA."

"*Outside* Los Angeles, dear." She eyed the table full of tiny plates thoughtfully, and speared a bit of quiche with her fork. "Did you do that online dating thing you were telling me about?"

"The one in the TV commercials?" Felicity shrugged. "Yeah, I did it."

"I wish you would stay away from that Internet stuff. I told you, Tarot is better for this sort of thing than that w-w-w business. Who knows what kind of characters—"

"Everyone is screened." Felicity smiled patiently. "It's scientific. There's a formula. Fill out a questionnaire and they match you to your 'Perfect Mate.' *Find your true love with Formu-LOVE!*" she added brightly.

"Mm-hm." Her aunt sipped her drink, looking skeptical.

"You should use the cards like I taught you. And don't forget the candle. The candle is the key. You need to find yourself someone better than that . . . that guitar-strumming . . . person."

"I thought you liked those crunchy hippie-dude types."

"I used to. But times have changed." Livia gazed at her a moment, her eyes softening. "Honey, I've just seen one too many of those *types* screw my little niece over."

A shocked laugh burst from Felicity, and she raised her nearly empty glass in a toast. "To hypocrites. Good-bye to the lot of them."

"Hear, hear," Livia said. "You need yourself a real man."

"Yeah! A real man . . ." Felicity nodded enthusiastically, refilling her glass. "Someone who pulls grandmothers from burning buildings."

Her aunt let out a tipsy giggle. "That's the ticket, honey."

"Who'd jump into icy water to save a stranger. A big Viking of a man. Who'd fight to protect *me*. Who does things like . . ." Felicity thought for a moment, then slamming her hands onto the table, announced, "Fish."

"You want your man to fish?" Her aunt's exuberance momentarily waned.

"Yeah." Felicity shrugged. "I want a man's man, but I don't think I'm ready for any hunters yet."

"Ha!" Livia's shriek drew a few pairs of eyes to their table. Ignoring them, she declared, "Then here's to fishing."

They both tossed back the rest of their sangria.

"Ugh." Felicity grabbed the table edge to steady herself. "We should get the bill and go." Scowling, she reached across the table to pluck the last mushroom cap from its puddle of oil. Her stomach roiled in preparation. She always forgot what a bad idea tapas were. Sangria flowing from long-spouted jugs, with only some garlic prawns and bits of quiche to absorb it all.

She gestured to the waitress, then put a hand to her head. She lived only a short walk down Valencia Street, but she'd rather wobble home before all that cheap wine hit her any harder. And she still needed to make up a bed for her aunt. "Do you want the futon or the mattress?"

"Futon's fine, honey."

Felicity reached for her bag, but her aunt stopped her with an exaggerated frown, tossing a couple of twenties on the table before she had the chance to. "But first I'd like to walk off my sangria." Livia glanced at her oversized men's watch. "There's just too much to see for me to be going to bed this early."

Felicity stood abruptly. Normally she'd put up more of a fight, but the sangria had begun to burble in her belly. "You sure?" She pulled on her brown suede jacket and tugged the long length of her blonde hair free.

"Absolutely. I may be long of tooth, dear, but I'm not dead yet." Livia shooed her toward the door. "Go, go. You're looking green around the gills, as your lovely mother would've said. Go get some rest."

Felicity pulled her into a quick hug. *Mom.* Livvie's sister.

She swallowed back a pang of grief. Though it was still sharp, the passing years had dimmed her memories. Now the occasional washes of melancholy were less about her mom and dad in any specific way, and came more from the vague sense of what she'd been missing.

She made it home to find a letter waiting for her. She'd almost walked right past it. It must've been delivered to the wrong mailbox, and someone had slipped it under her apartment door.

Felicity picked it up and frowned. It was from Formu-LOVE. Scrunching her brows, she focused on the pink and purple envelope. *Based on Scientific Research! Find your true love with Formu-LOVE!*

She'd been waiting for it, and now that it was here, she was afraid to open the thing.

Felicity had answered pages and pages of questions, covering everything from "Ketchup or mustard?" to her thoughts on religion, birth, and death.

Could this be it? Would there be a name and a little mug shot of her "perfect mate" inside?

Her hands trembled as she tore it open. She looked at the front and back of the single sheet, then peeked in the envelope to make sure she'd gotten everything out. Shouldn't there be more?

It was just a form letter, with her online nickname and pertinent details filled in with an elaborate, loopy font.

"The least they can do for my two hundred bucks is send me a real letter," she muttered.

Dear *Mellow Yellow*,
We are sorry but the profile you provided
Formu-LOVE! was **UNMATCHABLE**.
But don't be discouraged. Scientific research
has proven . . .

She stopped reading, crumpled the paper, and flung it across the room, where it fell short of its mark. She stared angrily at the trashcan, a grimace holding back her tears.

Staggering to the couch, Felicity curled into a fetal position. "Unmatchable."

Stupid online formula. Nobody is unmatchable.

She bit her knuckle. What if she was?

She didn't want to end up alone like her Aunt Livia. Felicity adored the woman, but she just wasn't a nomad like her aunt. Traveling had been exciting, but now she was ready to nest, to build a life. Find that one true someone she knew her father had been for her mother.

"Alright, Liv." She popped back up, striding to the cabinet where she kept her Tarot cards. "You win." She lit her candle and flicked off the lamp.

She plopped onto the rug, spilling the deck out before her. It had been a gift from her aunt, not long after her parents had died. Felicity had felt guilty when she'd first contemplated those intricate and old-fashioned images. The brightly colored Hanged Man and the ominous Devil seemed like such transgressions.

But they never failed to pull her in, the cards alternately majestic, ominous, triumphant. Each suggesting a mysterious and unexpected tale, where a smiling countenance could bode ill and a dying man meant rebirth.

Felicity spread them out wide before her, rummaging them under her palms in a sloppy shuffle. They were reassuringly cool and waxy under her fingers.

"Where's the one man who's right for me?"

She gathered the cards back into a stack and did one more quick shuffle for good measure.

Unmatchable.

No, she wasn't without a match. There was one man in the universe just for her. She shut her eyes and tried to visualize him. "Where is my great big Viking of a man?"

The candle flickered, and a shiver crawled up her skin. Taking a deep breath, she gave a shake to her sangria-fogged head. It was only the candlelight, she told herself.

Still, Felicity grew somber. Alone with the cards in the darkness, it was impossible to avoid the sense that she was tapping into some great, unknown energy.

She slowly began to deal out six cards. It was an arrangement her aunt called The Great House. A simple spread, but powerful.

Taking a deep breath, she whispered, "Show me where you are."

She put her fingers on the first card, what her aunt called the Querent. It was *her* card, the one that represented Felicity's situation. She rubbed it between her fingers before turning it. "I need you," she whispered again. "How do I find you?"

The crisp flip of the card resonated in the silence of her apartment.

She drew in her breath. The Chariot. "Cool," she said quietly. She loved this card. A conquering hero, bearing a spear, in armor decorated with stars and moons, riding in a chariot drawn by sphinxes. In the dim light, he seemed to be riding straight for her.

A small smile touched her face. It was a Major Arcana

card, representing success. Turmoil, conquest. Possibly an imminent voyage, or a life-changing event.

She'd be off on a new venture soon. "Are you saying I have to come to you?" she mused, her smile growing.

She turned the next card quickly.

The Lovers. "Yesss . . ." she hissed, grinning outright. It was a man and a woman. Some sort of glorious, celestial being watched over them, his hands outstretched in a beneficent gesture.

Lovers. Her optimism swelled. There was her Viking right there. "Doesn't get much clearer than that."

Felicity flipped the next one more quickly than the last, and her hand froze. "What's with all the Major cards?" It was the Wheel of Fortune.

She tried to remember what that one meant. A profound realization taking place? But it also meant twists of fate. She studied the spinning wheel and gave a shrug. "Round and round she goes, where she stops nobody knows . . ."

Felicity held her hand poised over the fourth card. "Come on. Give me something nice and easy."

The Two of Cups.

"Oh yeah!" She patted the card triumphantly. "Yeah, baby." She studied the image. Two people gazed at each other, both ready to share their oversized golden cup. Partnership, marriage, commitment.

Placing her fingers over the back of the next card, she rubbed it into the rug with the anticipation of a Vegas blackjack dealer. "Love and marriage, love and marriage, go together like a . . ." She flipped it.

The Five of Pentacles.

"Shit."

Adversity and loss. This card pictured another man and woman, but this time they were trudging through snow, looking cold and hungry. The man's leg was bandaged, and he struggled with his crutch in the snow. "What's *that* about?"

Her excitement left her like air from a balloon. In a Tarot

reading, each new card added meaning to the last, and she had no idea what this was all telling her.

She'd just wanted to find her true love. Just a quick, fun reading. But now she sensed she should've waited for Livia to do the reading for her.

Should now wait for her to finish it.

Felicity rubbed the edge of the last card with her fingertip. She had to know. She could ask her aunt what it all meant later. She needed to see what was hidden beneath this last card.

She turned it before she could chicken out.

"No . . ." Her voice was tiny. She looked at the hideous card in front of her and groaned. This last card, the one that defined the entire reading. And it represented a total breakdown in one's life and world.

Lightning struck a great spire into flames. There was a toppling crown, and people falling to the earth. "No, not that."

The Tower.

Only a fine thread of anger stopped her despair from turning to tears. Why couldn't she have happiness? For once, something simple and pleasant. Felicity had always been dealt the bad hand.

Her parents had died when she was still in elementary school, and she'd never been the same. She'd never been quite a part of things, something always just slightly off as she made her way through the world.

All she wanted was for the loneliness to go away. For a decent boyfriend, someone who was who he said he was. It wasn't so much. A *good* man.

Felicity abruptly raked her hands through the cards, sweeping them before her on the shag rug. "I wish . . ."

She plucked the Chariot card from the pile and rubbed it between her fingers. "Where are you?" The glowing, triumphant warrior. "I wish . . . I wish I could meet *you*."

The dying light drew Felicity's eyes. Her candle was guttering out. She looked back down at the cards, and the movement set her head to whirring. *Please no nausea.* She pursed her lips. *Damned sangria.*

Her hands still on the cards, she slid down onto the rug. She'd lay there a moment, waiting for the spinning to stop.

Waiting, and wishing for her one, true man. Her Viking.

Chapter 2

London, 1658

Not again, Will Rollo thought sourly. He'd saved his friend Ormonde from many a scrape, but the Tower of London? Frowning, he pulled his cowl further over his head. An escape from the Tower far exceeded the obligations of friendship.

He nodded to his companion, and they pulled the oars up to skim near the surface of the water, dragging the small boat to a stop. Traitor's Gate loomed just ahead, connecting the Thames to the moat that encircled the Tower complex.

"Who goes there?" the guard shouted, jangling his keys as if to stress the gravity of his position.

It was early evening, and though there were hours yet before the gate would be locked for the night, traffic that time of day was uncommon.

His hired man shifted nervously at his side, and Rollo put his hand out, gesturing for calm. Coin bought men, but it didn't always buy composure.

Truly, he thought, *this is the last time*.

Rollo cleared his throat, trying his best to shed the Scots from his voice. "I've come wi' ale, gov'ner."

He frowned at the answering silence. He had one shot to get Ormonde out and needed to think quickly.

"It's for his lordship," Rollo added. He'd grown up on the other side of the servant–lord relationship, and knew invoking the wrath of an angry nobleman—even an anonymous one—was good for getting results. "He says I deliver it before the gates is locked for the night, or it's all our hides."

Rollo let out a quick, sharp cough. Keeping up the false accent was a struggle and an annoyance. Ormonde might thrive on these sorts of intrigues, but Rollo much preferred fighting his battles in the light of day. Preferably on horseback.

There was a pause, then a strained, "Be on your way then."

Rollo's shoulders eased. *Without question, the last*, he thought, giving the guard a nod as they rowed past.

He noted the man's greedy eyes paused on the cask, and fought the urge to heave a visible sigh of relief. The thing was empty, but for a stretch of rope, over twenty fathoms long. It was his ticket in and Ormonde's ride out.

Rollo spared a quick, satisfied smile. The barrel and its promise of drink had been just the thing. Only a painted French whore would've bought him swifter passage.

They cut a sharp right, rowing into the moat toward Cradle Tower, which jutted out along the southeastern side. Long ago, Edward III had built it as his own private water entrance. The days of such niceties were long gone, and Cradle Tower was now filled instead with prisoners from the Civil Wars. Cromwell's enemies all.

The fortress rose high above them, its beige and brown stone an ominous gray in the night's growing dark. As they glided in and toward the Galleyman Stairs, he contemplated the thin arrow slits along the façade. The small openings offered no help—he'd have to get Ormonde out from above.

Even though it was his crippled legs that were stiff, Rollo rubbed his shoulder, remembering his long-ago wound. He'd been shot on the field at Philiphaugh, and left for dead. But it was Ormonde who'd found him. Ormonde's boyish persistence that had pulled him from the field to safety.

He rolled his shoulders, eyeing a second guard coming into view. *The last time, Ormonde.*

"What have you there?" The guard was a beefy man, and it was at times like this that Rollo was glad of his cane.

"Ale." He stood, his cramped legs trying to find balance in the wobbling boat. His hired man pulled them close to the stone landing, and Rollo used the cane to make his way from the craft. "For you guards, mayhap?"

Rollo tried to wrench his face into a smile, but his thoughts were only for the blood that flowed too slowly back into his limbs. *Damned boats.* He despised them.

"What's this then?" The guard laughed. "You're lame!" He shook his head in wonder. "Can't be an easy job of it, hauling ale on feeble pins."

Rollo found his footing. He tossed his cane up, catching at its midpoint, and swung. He caught the guard behind his ear, and the man fell in a solid heap. "Not feeble," he gritted out.

Taking the man by the heel, Rollo dragged him under the wooden staircase. He patted down the guard's coat, plucking a ring of keys from his inside pocket.

"He'll wake," he said, returning to his companion. "But we have time."

Rollo noted the heavy length of rope that his hired man had hauled onto the landing. "Good work. You're earning your coin, and a bit besides." He looked back out to the moat, almost completely shrouded in darkness. "Be gone now," he told him. "Wait on the far side. You'll see us."

The sound of Rollo's shuffling step echoed off the dank stone as he made his ascent. The thick loops of rope cut heavily into his shoulder, but he dare not risk the noise of dragging it.

He headed straight for the end of the hall, knowing exactly where he'd find Ormonde. The Sealed Knot was a clandestine bunch, working anonymously to topple Cromwell and reinstate the true king. But they weren't so secretive as to watch in silence as one of their own was imprisoned. When alerted that Rollo planned on freeing his friend, an agent had sought him out, pointed him to trustworthy hired help, detailed Ormonde's position, and all but escorted Rollo to the Tower.

Ormonde was a nobleman, and his cell was actually quite an accommodating affair, with a settee, fireplace, and small desk. "How'd you know where to find me?" he asked the moment Rollo found the right key and slipped in.

Rollo chuckled at his friend's exuberance. Ormonde's bright red hair was in a tousle, and could use a fair spot of barbering besides, but these things only heightened the man's boyishness. Though Ormonde was in his forties, Rollo expected he'd never lose his bright-eyed zeal.

"Your Sealed Knot men seem to have much information at their disposal."

"But how . . . ?"

"Later." Rollo eyed the windowless room. They'd have to continue up, making their escape from the roof. "Let's away from here before your guard wakes sore and angry."

"Give me that." Ormonde gestured to the rope.

"I can manage," Rollo said coldly.

"You never change, do you? I know better than most how well you can manage"—he reached for the heavy mass—"but I've been cooped up here for weeks, and if I don't set this nervous energy to something, I swear—"

"Fine." Rollo shrugged the rope from his side. "Let's just be gone."

They made their way up a cramped spiral staircase to the rooftop. Rollo had read of a Jesuit priest who'd made this same escape not one hundred years prior, and he figured if a man of the cloth could do it, two battle-hardened soldiers could manage as well.

"What mission do you risk your head for this time?" Rollo placed his hands on the cold stone of the battlements and peered down. The moat—and he hoped his boat—waited for them in the blackness below. "Hand me that," he said, pointing to the rope.

"The same as ever. I'll see the true Stuart king reinstated before I die." Ormonde helped Rollo secure the end of the rope around one of the battlements. "Cromwell and his Parliament may have beheaded King Charles I, but they dare not behead his son. I vow, Charles II will be restored to the throne."

"They do call it a *kingdom*, after all," Rollo said dryly, tugging the rope tight, testing his knot. "There now. Who shall be first to give it a go?" He spared Ormonde a smile.

"I need to tell you something, Will."

Rollo's face grew stoic once more, waiting in silence for what his friend had to say.

"Your brother." Ormonde looked into the distance, weighing his words. "It's Jamie. Jamie's the one who orchestrated my capture."

"I knew . . ." Rollo inhaled sharply. "I anticipated this day. I knew, when he traded wives. To go from Graham's sister to Campbell's. Aye, getting in league with Cromwell himself wasn't far behind."

"So you're not . . . surprised?"

"There's no ill my elder brother could conceive that would give me surprise." He glanced quickly at his legs before he gave the rope one more tug. "Up and over, you."

Ormonde smiled, shaking his head, and clapped his friend on the shoulder. "I thank you for this, Will."

"Aye," he muttered, watching Ormonde's descent. "And it's the last time, for certain."

"Good evening, *cripple*."

Rollo turned sharply, though he knew from the voice whom he'd find. "Jamie. So happy you could join me. 'Tis a lovely wee fortress you have here. Though it does seem to have sprung a leak."

"Did you think I'd not hear your clopping about?" Jamie eyed his brother with disdain. "The years pass, and still you trudge around like a one-legged fishwife."

"Aye." Rollo smiled broadly. "The years pass, and still you talk to me as if you're the same twelve-year-old in our father's stable yard."

The hiss of Jamie's unsheathed broadsword cut through the night.

"Dear Jamie, you surprise me." Rollo laughed softly, tapping his cane lightly on the toe of his boot. "You're fighting your own battles now? Or is it that Cromwell doesn't have a sister for you to bed?"

Jamie leapt for him, but Rollo was ready. Tossing his cane up, he grabbed the curve of the pistol-handled grip in one hand and pulled his sword free of its wooden sheath.

"Hiding a weapon in your walking stick." Jamie slashed hard, and their swords crossed with a sharp clang. "Not fair, little brother."

"You speak of fair?" Rollo cut his sword in the sharp diagonal slash he'd perfected in years of cavalry fighting, and his brother's blade caught it just before it bit into his shoulder. "What's not fair is destroying an innocent seven-year-old simply because you don't like his pony."

Jamie unleashed then, thrashing with rapid but sloppy strokes. Rollo's legs prevented him from bobbing and weaving as another swordsman might, and he suffered the onslaught, meeting each thrust with his own block and parry.

He recognized his brother's style, though, and planned to let Jamie flail himself into exhaustion. He was younger than Jamie and, ironically, it was Rollo's injury that had kept him fitter than most men, regardless of age.

Jamie bobbed forward for what he clearly thought would be a killing lunge, and Rollo saw his chance. Though he refused to kill his brother, he found he was quite eager to bruise the lout.

Rollo stepped forward, meeting Jamie's lunge. Their swords crashed, blade sliding down blade, until the brothers' hands were inches apart.

"You always"—jutting his foot forward, Rollo grabbed his brother's wrist and flung him over his extended leg—"make this same blunder." As Jamie fell, his sword came loose and clattered across the timber roof.

Rollo put the tip of his blade to Jamie's neck. "Don't forget, *brother*. My injury makes me stronger than you. You can't admit that you gave me that strength?"

"Never." Jamie grabbed the blade in his palm, and a thin

trickle of blood seeped from his fist. "You will never be the stronger man."

He rolled from beneath the sword, shouting at once for a guard.

Rollo looked for a split second from the sword in his hand, to its wooden sheath tossed halfway across the roof, then to the battlements. With a curse, he tossed his blade down. The cane had been a fine little treasure, but he had neither the time nor the hands to spare.

He heard his brother's shouts and the scrape of his broadsword as he retrieved it.

Rollo pulled himself up between the battlements, the stone scraping his back and arms as he wriggled through. Fumbling in the dark, his hands found the rope. The rock scored his knuckles as he eased down into the blackness below.

"Will," Ormonde hissed. "Just here. Hurry now, I hear the guards rallying."

Rollo dropped the last foot, landing clumsily in the boat, and his hired man set at once to rowing them back toward Traitor's Gate.

"What are you doing?" Rollo sidled toward the empty cask, still waiting in the prow of the boat. "You were supposed to hide in there."

"Someone has beat me to it." Ormonde's voice had a peculiar edge.

Rollo swung his gaze to him. "You sound amused."

"Have a look-see," the hired man said, offering his dagger.

Rollo took the knife and pried the lid free, revealing a woman. She was curled up, fast asleep, her heavy breath echoing in the tiny chamber. "What the devil?"

He peered in. It was impossible to make out any details in the dark. "Help me," he said to Ormonde. "I'll get her"—he put his hands under her arms and pulled—"you steady the barrel."

"Good Lord," Ormonde said, turning his face away. "Is that her or the cask?"

Rollo grimaced at the smell of stale wine. "I think mayhap . . . it's both?"

He laid her down gently, staring for a moment in dumbfounded silence. She was a small, fine-boned thing, with pert little features and hair that flowed long and loose down her back. The moon had risen and illuminated her face with an unearthly light, making her seem like some sort of wayward fairy princess.

Rollo spied something on her, and he carefully took her bare arm in his hand. Her skin was warm and smooth, and he couldn't help but run his thumb over the delicate bones of her hand, her fingers longer and more graceful than he'd have expected.

He turned her arm to see what had stuck to her and peeled a strange card from the thin skin of her forearm. It pictured a man, walking blithely along, the sun at his back and a bloom in his hand. The man in the drawing gazed up at the sky, heedless of the cliff from which he was about to step. Beneath the image was written, The Fool.

Rollo quickly pocketed the peculiar thing, his skin prickling to gooseflesh.

The distant rumble of talk floated over the water from the direction of Traitor's Gate, calling him back to himself. "Hurry," he said to Ormonde. "In the cask. Now."

"What of *her*?" Ormonde pointed to the girl with a mix of bemusement and panic.

"I'll give her my cloak." Rollo slipped his arms from the blanket of dark wool, eyeing her strange and colorful skirt. "Something to cover the clothes she wears."

"But they'll recognize you. You can't risk so much for some drunken wench."

"What would you have me do? Drop her in the moat?" He settled the strange woman on his lap, leaning her against his neck as if she nuzzled him. "The guard's eyes will be on the lass, not me."

Ormonde stared at him as if he'd lost his mind. Rollo glared back, and his friend simply shrugged, climbing awkwardly into the barrel.

"Make it fast." Rollo angled away from the guard's side of the boat, draping the woman's hair over his face. The smell of lavender filled his senses, and an unsettling feeling seized him, something visceral, both foreign and yet somehow dimly remembered. He swallowed hard, reminding himself where he was. "We approach the gate."

His hired man began whistling with affected boredom as they rowed closer, and Rollo thought he had well earned his keep.

Just as he'd predicted, the guard had eyes only for their drunken passenger. The man shot Rollo a rakish and congratulatory wink, nodding them through the Traitor's Gate and out to the Thames.

But Rollo gazed sightlessly in the distance, breathing the scent of lavender and thinking he'd wager anything that this lass was more than a mere wench.

Chapter 3

She gradually came to, her body swaying back and forth. The cheery chirrup of birdsong twittered around her. The rustle of greenery under . . . *hooves*?

Horseback riding?

Where am I?

Events of the previous evening played rapid-fire in her brain as she tried to place when and where. Tapas with Aunt Livia. Sangria.

Ugh . . . sangria.

Felicity peeled her eyes open. They were gritty, courtesy of all that alcohol. Her tongue, tacky and thick in her mouth.

She took in the countryside. A patchwork of green farmland and the darker green fringe of dense trees stretched into the distance, lush and fragrant all around.

She tried to make sense of it. She was on a horse. There were *two* horses.

She glanced at the man riding the horse next to hers. Frizzy red hair. An elaborate goatee and moustache pointed about his mouth. He was oblivious to her. Concern furrowing his brow, he seemed focused only on the path ahead.

She'd never been one for elaborate facial hair.

Wait. How drunk had she been?

Where had she been? But she knew—she'd been in her apartment. In the Mission. In San Francisco.

And now she was on a horse.

She'd had sangria, but not *that* much sangria. She'd been in her apartment, wishing on a star for her true love. Or rather, on a deck of Tarot cards and Livvie's trusted candle.

She stared at the horse's neck in front of her, damp and rank with sweat, and hoped she wasn't *that* unfortunate.

Felicity glanced down. A pair of arms encased her.

Could it be? Adrenaline dumped into her veins, making her feel tingly all over. Had she done it?

She was sideways on a saddle, curled into someone's arms. Someone's *strong* arms.

Her heart gave a sharp kick in her chest.

Her eyes grazed down further, at the very masculine legs cradling her. They were encased in tight, muted blue, green, and yellow plaid. *Weird.*

But kind of . . . hot.

Slowly, she turned her head. Her neck was stiff and her eyes dry. *Forget that.*

All she knew was that the chest she leaned into was manly. She was being swept away on a horse. She'd made a wish on a star and was being swept away. *Just like in a romance novel!*

Had Livvie set this up? If so, she was going to thank her aunt for this fantasy for the rest of her life.

She turned. Velvet was soft along her cheek. Velvet, the color of brandy.

Ooh! On the romance covers, their shirts are always open. Will his shirt be open?

Slowly she lifted her chin. A dozen tiny buttons marched up the broad, flat plane of the man's belly and chest. A collar rested just below his throat, its points draping long and loose.

A strong chin. Dark stubble on a strong chin.

Oh God, oh God.

The man holding her looked down, and time stopped.

Hazel eyes pinned her. They were steady and bright, the color of his velvet jacket.

Thick waves of chestnut brown hair rested over his collar. Just then the wind tousled it from his brow. A high brow framing . . .

Oh my. So handsome.

His features were fine, chiseled into clear skin.

Felicity felt a zing, like a single firework crackling through her belly.

"You're awake." His voice was low, accented.

Felicity let her head sink back, relaxing onto his arm. She felt a big, stupid grin spread like molasses over her face.

His brows furrowed as he contemplated her. Still she couldn't wipe the dumb smile from her face.

"Are you still drunk, lass?"

Lass. He called me lass!

"Let's hope not," she murmured. Exhaling something like a dreamy sigh, she nuzzled into his arms.

How strange, though. Were they somehow at the Renaissance Faire, in Golden Gate Park? Nothing really looked familiar.

Hmmm. She studied him. Ren faire guy. Made sense. His accent could use a little work, though. But, man, he was *hot.* She could play along.

Something struck her, and she glanced around. There were no roads. "Where are we?"

"Ah!" the man at their side exclaimed. "Our fair maiden has decided to join the land of the living."

"We are currently trying to get our hides safely out of England," the man holding her said evenly.

"England?" She scrunched her brow. "Is that part of the fantasy?"

"If only!" The red-haired man barked a laugh. "A fantasy. That's rich . . ."

"No," her guy said, "'tis England indeed."

England? She stiffened, her heart kicking up a notch. He couldn't be serious. How the hell could she have landed in

England? Unless they'd kidnapped her. But how? Her apart-ment had actual *bars* on the windows.

"How'd I get here? Did Livvie set this up?"

"I think she's still feeling her wine," the red-haired man said.

"No," she protested. She'd been mustering outrage, but confusion made her voice small. "I'm not drunk." She in-haled deeply, and trying to gather herself, focused on the rhythmic sway of the horse's gait.

Horse. What was up with the horses, anyway? *Clearly* these guys weren't kidnappers. Two horses weren't exactly the fastest getaway. A kid on a skateboard could pass them. If there'd been any roads. Which there weren't. Here in *England.*

But of course there were roads in England. So why weren't there any roads *here*? Even in those British movies where everyone hied to their country manors by carriage, there were roads.

But this? This looked like . . . like the land of Robin Hood.

Her heart slammed harder in her chest as she tried to make sense of it.

She'd made a wish. She'd made a wish and ended up *here*.

She just needed to figure out where *here* was. She craned her head. Bucolic fields stretched gently before them, like paradise. He'd said England, but there was nothing modern, as far as the eye could see. She'd traveled to some pretty re-mote spots in her life, and still, you could always see some-thing. Distant cars, power lines, *something*.

But here there were just horses, and men in fancy velvet coats, and lush landscape all around. Just like Robin Hood. Or like a fairy tale. Some strange world offering a snapshot from the past.

Could it *be* the past? She gave a breathy laugh. *No way.*

She couldn't have been transported from the real world, from *her* world. She was supposed to show up for the morn-ing shift. She'd waited *weeks* for that cute coffee shop to have an opening. And who'd water all her plants?

Maybe her mind was playing tricks on her. She could only manage shallow breaths now, as though her chest had shrunk. She did another scan of the countryside. *Impossible.*

No cars, no airplanes, no telephone wires. No modern world. *Anywhere.*

"Hang on," she said suddenly. She was losing it. People didn't just land in fairy tales. She'd call Livvie, get a reality check. "A phone. Do you have a phone?"

"Have we a *what*?" the red-haired man asked.

"Telephone?" she asked in disbelief. "No? You don't . . . You don't know a Maid Marian, do you?"

"Tele . . ." The man holding her glared. "Is that French?"

"You've never heard of a phone," she muttered, her heart thundering now. "But you speak English, right? Here in . . . England? Where you don't have phones?"

England. She studied the sword dangling from the red-haired man's hip. *Old* England.

What had she done? That crazy candle. How would she ever get back? And what about Livvie? Livvie would be so worried.

Holy crap. Could it really be the past? Didn't they have all kinds of wars in the past? And plagues? *Oh God, plagues.* Why hadn't she paid more attention in history class?

Okay, be cool. Maybe it wasn't what it seemed. She didn't seem to be in any immediate danger. How to handle it?

She strained eyes and ears for some sign of life, but there was nothing. Hell, there weren't really even any *sounds*, apart from the horses. And the breathing of the men.

Of the *man*, behind her.

She finally managed a deep breath. The man behind her. He sure was hot.

Calm down. The universe was telling her something. She just needed to open herself to it.

Those matchmaking dummies had told her she was un-matchable, and the universe had proved them wrong. She apparently did have a true love. He just happened to be . . . medieval dude. *Hunky medieval dude.*

Maybe it *was* the past. How bad could it be anyway? People had survived it. No phones, no television. It seemed kind of nice, actually. Simpler.

Surely she could find a way to get word to Livvie—somehow. She'd figure that out later. Her aunt would be *so* mad if she found out that Felicity had spun out worrying about *her* instead of just relaxing into the experience.

She tilted her head back for another look at the man behind her. She knew one thing—she couldn't do any better on the One True Love front. He sure was good-looking. Seemed like a gentleman. Intense, intelligent eyes. Clean and well-dressed.

Maybe he had a castle. Maybe he hung out with princes and stuff. Maybe he *was* a prince.

"Wow," she said breathily. "Do you have a castle? In England? England . . ." She shook her head, marveling. "Will we get to see stuff like Big Ben, and the Tower of London?"

"Let's pray not," the red-haired man muttered.

The man at her back frowned. "I hadn't counted on needing three, not two, mounts." He pinned her with narrowed eyes. "'Twould be a long journey to Scotland, with you riding pillion."

"I told you, Will," the other man said. "Riding is folly. Our journey is too long. One month in which Cromwell can sniff us out with his dogs? I think not. A boat it must be."

"Scotland?" She pushed up and away from his chest, craning her neck. "I thought you said England. I've always wanted to see Scotland too."

"In time," he said brusquely. "For now, it's England. At least until we sort our transportation."

"So you're Scottish?" She glanced down at his tartan-clad legs and smiled. "Do you have a kilt too?"

He stared blankly.

"You know," she said gesturing to his legs, "one of those hot . . . man . . . skirts."

His eyes narrowed. "Aye, I'm a Scotsman, and aye, I've a *breacan feile*." He spoke slowly and with great effort, as though moderating his patience. "Now, tell us where to bring you."

His companion only chuckled.

"Bring me?" She had nowhere to be except right where she was. San Francisco was probably still just a stretch of waterfront wilderness.

"Aye," her handsome man said. "We'll do that much, lass."

Their eyes locked. *Lass.* He'd said it again. *He'll wear his kilt and call me* lass. Butterflies danced in her belly. "Can you ride horses when you wear your kilt . . . whatchamacallit?"

A low growl escaped him. "Where should I—?"

"Oh, that," she said, coming back to herself. "I've got no place to go. I think . . . I think I'm supposed to be *here*. What's your name?" she asked innocently.

The red-haired man cleared his throat. "Dare we—"

"Rollo," her man answered, "William Rollo."

"Rollo," she repeated, sounding the name slowly. "What kind of name is Rollo? It doesn't sound Scottish. Shouldn't it be something like MacRollo instead?"

"'Tis an old name," he clipped out. "A Norse name."

"Hail Rollo the Viking!" the red-headed man jested. "Your forefather became none other than the Duke of Normandy, was it? That would've been, what, eight hundred years ago?"

"My Viking . . ." Felicity sighed. She would never mock Livvie or her candles ever again.

"I'm not a Viking," Rollo snarled.

His companion laughed. "Oh, but you seem quite barbarous to me."

"Enough." Rollo nudged their horse into a brisker walk. "Who are you, woman? And where do I deposit you?"

Ignoring him, Felicity turned to the red-headed man. "Are you Scottish too, then? Or do you live here?"

He stared, amused, as if she were nuts. "Good luck with this one, Will." He chuckled. "The name is Ormonde, dear lady. James Butler, the Marquis of Ormonde, so pleased to make your acquaintance. And, if you're one of Cromwell's lackeys, I'm afraid I'll have to kill you now."

"Quit your jesting," Rollo snapped. "Truly, lass. Tell me with whom I should—"

"No, really." Felicity tried sitting up in earnest. "I'm supposed to be here. I'm not from . . ."—she pitched her voice for his ears alone—"I'm not from here. I was sent to you. I'm sure of it. Hold on!" she said suddenly. "What year is it?"

She studied his coat and lace-edged collar. Maybe she'd get to wear some lacy getup too. And she couldn't wait for her first carriage ride. "I can't believe this is really happening. It's so exciting."

There was a strained pause, and then Rollo said simply, "No."

Will eyed the lovely creature in his arms, disbelief snaking through him. His gaze took in the clattering armful of bracelets, the strangely ruffled skirt. Her feet were bare and delicate, each toenail painted a cheery pink.

"Oh no," he said again.

Their eyes met, and she grinned at him, raising her brows in exaggerated innocence.

"No," he said flatly. "No, it couldn't . . ."

But it could, he thought. *Time travel*. It could, and did happen, with a frequency that had him doubting his own sanity. Rollo scowled.

Because damned if each time he didn't find himself in its very nexus. Some great, dumb insect trapped in a web.

In what manner of dark era did they find themselves, in which witchcraft burbled and roiled as matter-of-factly as the clouds above? What was the meaning of it?

First, there had been his friend James, whose bride fell through a portrait, landing in his very own bed.

And then that great brute of a man MacColla. It made sense that the only woman with backbone enough for Alasdair came from some distant future.

But now this? What was happening?

A great, dumb insect trapped in a web, though this time the beautiful spider had come for *him*.

He eyed the woman once more. He'd known, on some level. Known the moment he first saw her that she wasn't some ordinary wench.

Lovely, fragile, and open. Smiling giddily up at him as if he were Lancelot.

Some unnamed grief stabbed him. Rollo pushed it away. He flexed his legs, deadened and worthless beneath him. The riding was difficult enough. But bearing it with someone else's weight, it became a grueling challenge.

He took a hand from the reins, pounded life into his thigh.

No. He was no woman's Lancelot.

"No," he said again, baldly.

"Are you quite well, Will?" his friend asked.

"I am . . . well enough." Rollo kicked his horse into a trot. "I must away to Perthshire. To home. *With* the woman."

"But we—"

"And no boats, Ormonde. I've had my fill of water." Men spoke dismissively of sea legs, when Rollo's were barely fit for land. He'd claim some dignity in this whole enterprise. "We find a carriage to take us from England. Then away to my family's Duncrub Castle."

He looked down at the woman in his arms. With her long, flowing hair and doll-like features, she had the air of a pixie. So guileless, a look of expectancy on her pretty face. "What's your name, lass?"

"Felicity." She gave him a broad smile, and he felt his heart crack.

Felicity. Was it a cruel joke? He'd not felt true joy in decades, and in his lap he held a woman with the name *Felicity.*

Come for him? He couldn't fathom it.

Perhaps.

Perhaps for another, more like.

Chapter 4

"This is not particularly what I'd describe as fleeing London." Ormonde looked around nervously.

Felicity couldn't understand the problem. They were taking a lovely stroll around the fringes of what Will had told her was Hampstead Heath. But, despite the acres of greenery and tranquil ponds all around, the red-headed man flinched at the sight of every new person who passed by.

"We are simply three taking the air," Rollo responded flatly.

"Why did we come to this godforsaken place anyhow? A stroll in the park?" His eyes flicked to Rollo's cane.

It was pretty, carved from a stretch of honey-colored wood, and Felicity didn't understand why her Viking had been so grumpy about getting it.

"You of all people . . ." Ormonde shook his head. "We'll be three taking to the dungeons if we don't leave soon."

Dungeons? She frowned, trying to remember her history, but academics had never been her thing. She knew England and Scotland hadn't exactly been lovey-dovey in the old days. *What does he mean,* dungeons?

She eyed the two men. They acted like they were on the run. Ormonde looked nervous, impatient at the pace Rollo was setting.

But Rollo. She sighed. *William Rollo. So handsome.* And the new silver-handled cane only made him look more dashing. Her frown blossomed into a smile as she deduced that her One True Love must be some grand and misunderstood nobleman.

"I am quite capable of strolling," Rollo snapped.

Ormonde attempted good-natured reassurances, but Will cut him off. "I needed this"—he waved his cane with revulsion—"and we needed a place where we could speak safely as well. A small village Hampstead might be, but aye," he admitted, "it's true, Cromwell's ears are everywhere. You have the right of it."

"I . . ." Ormonde stopped in his tracks. "Wait. I do?"

Though Ormonde's freckled cheeks broke into a grin, Rollo's response was grave. "Three heading north in a carriage will raise too many brows. I think you should divine that boat you so long for. I shall more appropriately clothe this one"—he gestured to Felicity—"and hire a carriage."

Clothes—thank God. In a whispered exchange, Rollo had handed their horses off to some wizened villager who'd disappeared and promptly reappeared bearing the clothes she now wore. Just the mention of it had her furtively scratching at the waist of a skirt she'd swear was made of burlap.

Now if only she could find herself a rubber band. Her hair was driving her batty. Or a headband. Hell, she'd settle for an old scrunchie.

"I shall be back in Perthshire by month's end." Rollo's jaw tightened. "But I'll not join your . . . *club.* Though I long for the restoration of King Charles II as much as you, I'll leave games of intrigue to you and your Sealed Knot Society men."

Ormonde was silent for a moment, then gave a brusque nod. "I understand. Though if it's intrigues you fear, I don't see why you persist, Will. You're one of the most honor-bound men I've known, but she"—his eyes went to Felicity—"she far exceeds the responsibilities of a gentleman."

"You are saying she is not of my concern?"

Ormonde nodded vigorously.

"I'm standing right here, guys," she chimed, but they both ignored her.

"Then it is not of your concern either," Rollo stated with finality. He looked at Felicity, his eyes locking with hers for a heartbeat. Her heart swelled.

She'd *known* she'd found herself *the one*.

Okay, if she had to admit it, the whole situation was a little weird. She glanced around the park. It was like Jane Austen–land. A couple walked on the path ahead, and the woman carried a darned parasol. And it was the *fourth* one she'd seen all day.

Apparently she really was in the past. Where there were parasols. And dungeons.

Can I deal with this?

She looked back at Rollo. Tall, dark, handsome, and so sexy serious.

Would he look that intense when he . . .

She flushed.

Oh yeah, she could deal.

"I have an inkling of this woman's origins. She needs my assistance and that is what I shall give. Fear not, I'll see her soon gone from Perth."

Gone?

"No," she hesitated. "I'm supposed to—"

"Go now," Rollo told his friend, cutting her off. His hard features softened for a moment. "You've been fancying a boat. Go find one already."

"You know where I'm from?" she asked the moment Ormonde strode away. She'd been dying to ask, but had wanted to wait until she and Will were alone.

"Aye. I know enough." He took the cane from his hand to flex and stretch his fingers. "Now we must get to the clothier before he closes for his midday meal."

"But I don't think you . . ." She watched him as he turned to head back toward the village. Rollo set a slow and shuffling pace, and yet stood tall and elegantly upright. She eyed his uneven gait, marveling at the thick knots of muscle that had been carved into his physique, as if his body was over-compensating for his injured legs.

She jogged a couple paces to catch up to him. Felicity could see the pain clearly on his face, at the corners of his eyes and mouth.

He was obviously a tragic figure who also happened to have movie star good looks.

Clearly she'd been sent through time for him.

The problem was, he didn't seem too interested in *her*. Yet.

"Here"—she took his arm, giving it a warm squeeze—"let me help—"

Rollo abruptly pulled from her. "I need no help."

"I . . ." Felicity recoiled as if stung.

"Listen." Rollo stopped, the chiseled steel of his features blunting momentarily. "The future, is it? I've met others like you."

Her face widened in shock. "You—"

"Aye. Others there have been. I will help you. To return."

"But, you're not listening. I don't want to return." She gave him an earnest smile. "The universe thinks you're the one for me."

"I . . ." He stood still as granite then, his mind seeming far from where they stood. His eyes blazed a trail down, then back up, her body. Abruptly, Will gave his head a shake. "I am no woman's man. Now come." He gestured to the path that had taken them to a quaint village square. "It's to the clothier for you. Then to Perthshire. Then home. *Your* home."

The road was a mucky minefield of horse manure, puddles, and uneven runnels in the mud. She marveled how she had to struggle to keep up with him, even though he didn't have the easy gait of other men.

Breathless, Felicity caught up to his side, but before she could speak, he announced, "Here."

She looked up to see an elaborate hand-painted sign reading: Jos. Pemberley and Sons ~ Millinery and Fine Dress Making for Ladies.

"Joseph Pemberley," she read aloud. "You brought me to a . . . mill?"

"A *milliner*." He chuckled. The sound was unexpected—low and husky, it sent goose bumps rippling across her skin. She'd gathered that laughter was a rarity for the man, and yet, she thought wistfully, it utterly transformed him.

"For hats, lass."

"You're going to buy me a hat?"

"Among other things."

"Oh, fun." *And sexy*, she thought, unable to identify the hooded look that clouded his features.

The shop was dim and cool, with a bustling shopkeeper straight out of a BBC movie.

As his gaze alighted on Felicity, though, a look of such comical distaste puckered his features, she had to bite back a giggle.

She forgot the old grump at once, though, when she spotted the tables topped with pile after pile of cloth. She gasped. There were lush swaths of jewel-toned velvet, delicate fabrics in pale colors, and bolts bearing thick stripes of colors in alternating shiny and matte textures.

"This is so—" She felt Rollo's hand wrap firmly around her upper arm. Her heart gave a kick, even though the stern look on his face told her to quiet. "This is so exciting," she finished in a stage whisper.

She surreptitiously ran her fingers over a luxurious pile of satin, cascading like a royal blue spill of water across a table near the front of the shop.

She heard a clipped hiss, and looked up to see the clothier eyeing her suspiciously.

Grabbing Rollo's arm, she hastily spun to eye another table. She wasn't sure how she was supposed to act. "I worked retail for years," she whispered, "and this guy would've been *so* fired."

"Easy, woman." Momentarily switching his cane to his left hand, Rollo loosened the death grip she had on his upper arm.

"Can you get me something in that blue?" she asked him, pointing to the bright blue satin. "That is just totally—"

"Yes?" the shopkeeper asked at their backs.

"I'd like—" she began, but Rollo cut her off at once.

"The lady requires a dress." The sharp edge to Rollo's voice challenged the peevish old shopkeeper to just try and disagree.

Lady. Felicity beamed. *The lady.*

Looking as though he was holding his breath, the man eyed her dingy clothes and pulled a long looped stretch of twine from his coat.

"Measurements won't be necessary," Rollo said. "We're in a hurry and require something ready-made."

This time, the man didn't even try to disguise his contempt. "I am a clothier, sir, and an expert tailor. I do not cater to a . . . ready-made clientele."

"What is that, then?" Rollo pointed to a display in the window.

"Oh," Felicity gasped. It was a frothy rose-colored confection on a dress form.

Total BBC movie.

There was thick gold stitching along the sleeves. Real gold, she realized. *Fancy.*

"*That*, sir, is not for sale."

"Everything has a price." His voice was steel, drawing Felicity's gaze to him, and she saw the edge reflected in his eyes, cold and flat.

So intense.

It struck her that, though he might be talking about a dress, Rollo could be speaking to much more.

And deep too.

"How can you be certain it will even fit this . . . lady?"

The two men stared a challenge, and it was the shopkeeper who lost the battle. "Very well," he said on a sharp exhale. "But this is highly irregular."

As the man toddled over to remove the dress from the window, she frantically pulled Rollo to her. "How am I supposed to—"

The shopkeeper turned, the dress draped gingerly over his arm. Appalled, he stared at Felicity whispering in Rollo's ear.

"She will surely require those . . . other garments . . . as befits a lady?" He eyed the coarse and slightly soiled dress she wore.

"Surely," Rollo bit out, patting Felicity's arm.

"And a farthingale as well, I presume?" Chin trembling, the man skimmed his eyes over her skirts.

"Not necessary."

His eyes shot up. "Necessary, I think. With a dress such as this—"

"What's a—?" she began in a furtive whisper.

"*Not* necessary." Rollo peeled his lips back into a smile that looked something like a grimace. "I think the lady may be required to do some riding and so—"

"Riding?" the man sputtered. "Not in my gown."

"*Her* gown now." Rollo tossed a bag of coin onto the counter. "And if you'd be so kind, the lady will require a dressing room."

"She"—the man looked from Rollo to Felicity and back again, clearly alarmed—"she will don it *here*?"

"Here?" she whispered urgently.

"It's here or in the carriage," he told her under his breath. Rollo nudged her to the back of the shop.

"Be so good as to shutter the place," he called to the shop-keeper over his shoulder.

"Ohh," she purred quietly. He was sending the shopkeeper from his very own shop. "So . . . *alpha*."

The man began to protest, but a quick flick of Rollo's eyes to the leather coin purse lying conspicuously on the counter silenced him.

"And do occupy yourself elsewhere," Will ordered, indicating the door.

What was he planning? She shivered in anticipation.

"There's a good man. We'll let ourselves out."

He guided her toward a screen in the back corner. Cranes of crimson lacquer held graceful poses atop a shining black background.

"Oh!" a little chirp of pleasure escaped her. She could do

a sexy little striptease behind the exotic screen. Visions filled her head and brought a muzzy smile to her face.

Too bad the outfit she was about to remove was closer to a burlap sack than a silk negligee.

Though maybe . . .

"Don't these come with bustiers or something? Can we get any other clothes while we're—"

"Just dress yourself, lass," he snapped, shooing her behind the screen. "You have no notion the danger we're in. You've called enough attention to us as it is."

"But . . ." Deflated, she stepped behind the screen. "I didn't do anything."

So much for saucily rolling off a pair of stockings and swinging them over her head.

Felicity heard the tap of his cane on the floor as Rollo walked from the dressing area. She'd been eyeing the cane since he'd gotten it, and the question burst from her lips before she could think twice. "What happened? To your legs, I mean."

Unknotting the sash at her waist, she began to peel off the soiled clothing. "Were you hurt?"

He was silent for a moment. "Aye. You could say I've been hurt."

She heard him breathing heavily, sounding something like a restlessly slumbering dragon.

She gave a dramatic pout behind the screen. She really couldn't get a bead on the man.

It had been such a thrill—she'd made her wish, done her magic, and it had come true. She'd actually landed back in time—he'd said the year was *sixteen*-something—and been deposited with some Scottish hunk with a crazy Viking name.

He even believed her, which really was a sign. If someone were to plop into her life from out of nowhere, claiming to be from the future, she'd think he was nuttier than a fruitcake.

So why was he making this so difficult?

Time to try another tack.

She stood up on her tiptoes to pop her head over the screen. "Who are you running from anyway?"

Rollo's eyes quickly flicked to her bare shoulders.

She was naked. He couldn't see her, but he knew. Just on the other side of the screen, not four paces from him, this woman was bare. Utterly and completely naked but for what flesh would be concealed by that lovely, long, yellow hair.

He opened his mouth to speak but nothing came out. Licking his lips, he made as if he were formulating something of import to say. What to say?

Her shoulders were pale and delicate, covered by that fine web of her hair, the color of sunlight.

He resolutely pinned her gaze with his. "Don't you know where you are?"

"You said England. So, yeah, England." She seemed to stand a little taller.

Her attempts at temper amused him.

Better amused than aroused. The thought gave him clarity.

"I am on the run from Cromwell. Who, by the way, would have my head on a stake for supper and your fine body on a pyre for dessert."

Fine body? What was he doing speaking such phrases to her?

She'd caught the phrase too, and pink flushed along her skin like the blush of passion. He wondered if the color infused the rest of her body.

Rollo gave his head a shake.

He was not one for smooth dealings with women, his experience not extending beyond the sisters and wives in his extended circle.

If only *he* could have her fine body for dessert.

Rollo made a sound like a growl in his throat and turned to walk to the front of the shop. Would that he could do as other men and spin on his heel with haste and flair, but instead he shuffled forth.

"Wait."

He stopped. Leaning on his cane, Rollo waited for her

to finish. He kept his back to her, his hand jammed in his pocket. All these thoughts of Felicity's naked flesh had him decidedly bothered.

"I can't . . . I don't . . ."

He heard the rustle of silk.

"I need you to help me," she finally said. Her voice sounded muted, as if she spoke from under layers of fabric. "I don't know how to put this thing on."

"Simply place it over your head. Have you no dresses where you come from?"

"Of course I've worn dresses," she snapped. "Oh, thank God." Her voice was suddenly louder and clearer.

He heard her inhale deeply. She would've made her way up and through all that fabric, then.

"But this . . ." She paused, and Rollo heard more rustling. "Well, you can't expect me to do all these buttons by myself."

He'd seen the dozens of tiny fabric buttons running up the back of the dress. He just hadn't realized their import until now. Of course she'd need help. Women needed the assistance of maids to get ready.

"I . . ." he stammered. "You . . ."

"Come on, Will. I'm decent. I just need you to button this thing up for me."

Will. She'd called him Will.

Women in his acquaintance were generally more formal. And then there had been MacColla's bride, Haley, who'd called him "Rollo" with the carefree ease of one of his school chums.

But his given name, rolling from a woman's tongue with such careless intimacy? The sound stabbed him and thrilled him both.

He turned again, staring at the screen as if it were an approaching marauder.

"Uh . . . You there?" She popped her head up again. "Will?"

"Yes." He'd never buttoned a woman's gown before. But they had to make haste. He'd paid a lad to fetch a carriage from the mews—it would surely be out front by now. Waiting to put as much distance between them and England as possible.

Cromwell's Parliamentary soldiers had captured Ormonde, imprisoned him in the Tower. And Rollo had freed his friend right from under their noses.

From under his brother's nose.

His brother Jamie would be on the lookout for him. Blood or no, Jamie would not let such a slight stand.

Rollo girded himself. Tried to let thoughts of Roundheads and Royalists tamp down his unruly flesh.

He inhaled deeply, a white-knuckled grip on the head of his cane. "Buttons are buttons," he muttered, and stepped behind the screen.

Chapter 5

Why was he being so quiet?

"Are you still there?" Felicity clutched the dress to her chest. Despite the fact that she was, for all intents and purposes, almost completely covered, she suddenly felt very self-conscious.

She shook her head, amused. She wasn't usually so modest. She supposed she was getting into the spirit of the time period. Or maybe it was just in reaction to the strangely grave and proper man on the other side of the partition.

"It's okay, come in," she said, seeing that he stood at the edge of the screen.

She turned back around, offering him her back for buttoning. The dress began to slide, and she tucked her elbows to her sides to hold it in place.

"The corset thingy tied in the front"—hooking a thumb at the top, she gave a little tug to her stays—"I *think* I did it right." It was a ridiculously tight contraption, but she had to wear something, and this was all the shopkeeper had left behind for her.

Still, she thought her breasts were going to pop up and out at any moment.

"Are you there?"—she twisted to make sure Rollo hadn't disappeared—"ugh, does this need to be so tight?"

He was staring at her with narrowed eyes and a clenched jaw.

"I just need you to button me. I can't reach up the back."

He didn't budge. *He could make this a little easier.* Felicity raised her brows. "Please?"

He gave a curt nod.

Is he angry or something?

"Sorry." She shrugged. "I tried to . . ."

"No apologies, lass." Rollo's voice was ragged. His eyes grazed her bared shoulders. He cleared his throat.

The tense silence was unbearable. She shrugged again.

"Be still."

"Oh, sorry. I mean . . . Sorry I was sorry." She scrunched her face, happy her back was to him. She tried to stand as still as possible. "Okay, I'll just shut up."

Felicity sensed Rollo placing his cane down. She heard his shuffle at her back. Felt his approach. Heard his breath, suddenly close at her ear.

She shivered, and felt her skin pebble tight.

Why was he just standing there?

She fought the urge to apologize again, just to fill the silence. Could this really be her Viking? He sure was a serious one.

Why wasn't he buttoning—?

His hands skimmed along her back. The silk of her dress under his fingertips made a muted shushing sound.

Oh. A breath escaped her, and she clamped her lips between her teeth.

Rollo's fingers went to her waist, tugging the fabric together, securing the first button.

The room was suddenly unbearably hot.

"Are . . . are you sure this dress will fit me?"

"Aye." His voice had a steely, sharp edge. She felt his breath on her neck. He did the next button. And then the next.

His fingers found a rhythm. Dip beneath the fabric, pull

gently, flick the button through. Dip, pull, flick. She felt the warmth of his fingers through the linen of her corset all the while.

"Thanks," she managed. Heat rippled beneath the surface of her skin, suffusing her body. "I . . ."

He was almost done. She didn't want him to be done. She'd thought the stays were tight, but the dress snugged her even more, and it was the most erotic sensation she'd ever experienced. The feel of her breasts pressed tight, rubbing up against so much stiff fabric.

She glanced down. Her breasts were two pale, perfect mounds above the rose-colored silk.

She hoped her nipples didn't pop out.

But it looked pretty hot.

Oh, wow.

She hadn't realized her breasts could *do* that.

He froze behind her.

He was done.

She blushed. He hadn't even seen the front of the dress yet, but still the anticipation of it made her blush.

She turned slowly and his gaze was waiting for her. Simmering, and deadly serious.

Rollo ran his eyes down the length of her, pausing at her breasts.

She struggled to inhale.

He ran his eyes back up.

And this time she saw something raw there. Those hazel eyes, the color of chocolate in the dimly lit room, stared at her. Didn't budge from her.

Wanting him overwhelmed her. She leaned closer, taking him in. Taking in his gorgeous face, that thick, wavy brown hair. That perfect mouth.

So damned handsome.

She leaned closer.

He didn't move, and her heart thrilled with it.

Her Viking. She'd kiss her Viking now.

Closer.

His lips parted. She trembled, getting closer.

She brought her hand to his chest. Rested her palm lightly on him. She felt his muscles tense, so tight and hard beneath his waistcoat.

She was mesmerized. Those eyes of his, with just a little bit of gold that she could see now, up close.

Lean down, Will.

Why wasn't he leaning down? She had the bodice on, now it was time for her Viking to rip it from her.

He tilted his chin down. Brought his hand slowly up, cupped her cheek.

Yes.

A bell jingled as the front door opened, and Rollo closed his eyes as if in pain.

"Hello?" The shopkeeper sounded confused, suspicious.

Rollo brought his hand back quickly to his side.

Felicity made a tiny deflated sound, and he marveled at the endearingly feminine noise.

Had she truly wanted him to kiss her?

Good Christ.

He'd almost kissed her.

He inhaled deeply, exhaled sharply, and opened his eyes to her. What had he been thinking?

That open and guileless gaze snagged his. He held it as he called, "Aye, just here. We've finished."

They needed to go, but still, Rollo couldn't take his eyes from her.

Those brown eyes with that yellow hair. The delicate features of some fairy-tale beauty. And breasts that he wanted to free from her gown, take in his mouth. And suck. And ravage.

Those goddamned buttons had mocked him. He wanted to tear them off, to take her in his arms, and see if the rest of her was as creamy and pale as the delectable stretch of décolletage that he'd decided would surely then and there be the death of him.

"Hello?" The disembodied voice was closer now.

Rollo turned, reached for his cane, and just then stumbled. His damned legs had cramped up, so tightly wound had he been holding himself.

The shopkeeper peeked behind the screen just as Rollo cursed under his breath. Scandalized, the man's eyes grew wide. "If you'd be so kind—"

"Aye," Rollo gritted out, "you've my coin. We leave you now."

The click and drag of his cane and feet were the only sounds as they made their way, excruciatingly slowly, from the shop.

Rollo felt Felicity's eyes on him in the carriage, and he pushed himself as far into the corner as possible.

She smelled so . . . lush. Womanly and rich, her scent filled the small enclosure, driving him to distraction. Did she have to watch him so?

The wheel caught on a rut. The carriage gave a sharp jolt, and Felicity bounced closer in his direction.

"Sixteen fifty-eight," he said suddenly, his voice cracking. "The year. Is 1658."

"I . . ." She looked confused for a moment. "Oh. Okay."

"That doesn't . . . shock you?" And he'd thought Mac-Colla's woman Haley had been a peculiar one.

"Shock *me*? What about you? I'm from the *twenty-first* century, and you act as though women pop back in time every day."

"Bloody hell, but it seems you all do . . ." he muttered.

"What?" She leaned closer to hear.

"I've seen . . . *this*"—he waved his hands, gesturing to her—"before. But don't fash yourself." He glanced away from her to stare back out the window. "As I said, I will help you return to your proper place."

"I've been trying to tell you. I think *this* is my proper place. I did . . . something—"

"This couldn't possibly be your *proper place*." He sat upright to confront her. "Not very long ago, our king was relieved of his head. His son, the rightful king, Charles II, lives in exile, rallying to be restored to the throne. And Cromwell's agents comb the countryside seeking men like *me* to hang from a gibbet in the market square."

"Well, maybe I was sent back to help you."

"I don't need your help," he snapped.

"I . . ." Her shoulders fell. "Is this about your legs or something?"

He bristled. Would she not leave it alone?

"Because I wasn't saying you needed *help* help. Gosh, you're sensitive. I was just saying, I think for some reason I came back to you *specifically*." She poked her finger at his chest. "I made a wish, asked for a Viking, and—"

The laugh exploded from him, surprising them both. "You asked for a *Viking*?"

"No, not a real Viking. It was . . . a metaphor."

"You requested a metaphorical Viking from the universe?"

"Yes." She crossed her arms. "Though it didn't sound so silly at the time."

He sank back into the seat, staring fixedly at the ceiling of the carriage. Why had he insisted on hiring a carriage? Why hadn't he put her on that boat with Ormonde instead? He could've *ridden* to Perthshire. It could've taken him months.

"I am no woman's Viking," he grumbled.

"You can't . . ." She froze, a look of horror crossing her face. "Wait, you're not married already, are you?"

He swung his head to look at her, his face dark. "Do I *look* married?"

She merely stared blankly.

Rollo gestured to his legs. Was she purposely misunderstanding? He raised his brows, waiting impatiently for his point to dawn.

"What, you think because you limp, you can't get married?" Her laugh was the one to shock him then. "You have *got* to be kidding me. You're, like, the hottest man ever. Big whoop, you've got a limp."

What could she mean by *hot*?

She scooted closer to eye his legs. "They don't look *so* bad, anyhow. Not set correctly after a break—that's it, right?"

"Aye." He looked again out the window. The carriage suddenly felt intolerably small. "A horse crushed my legs when I was but a lad."

Her indrawn breath drew his eyes back to her. "That's horrible!"

He had to chuckle at the earnest look on her face.

"It's not funny," she scolded. "That's, like, the worst thing I've ever heard."

Felicity reached her hand out tentatively, then brought it back to her lap. "May I?"

"May you what?"

"I studied massage for a while. I think . . . Well . . ." She tilted her head to get a better look.

Her eyes on him were agony. And yet somehow the shame that usually overtook him at the topic of his legs remained at bay.

"I've seen you pound at your leg. Like this." Felicity balled her hand into a fist and thumped at her thigh. "But that's not going to help you at all."

"God save me, is that what I look like?" He shrugged on the familiar self-loathing like a pair of well-worn boots.

Felicity wore her frustration plainly on her face, and he thought it would've been comical if she weren't so damned pretty.

In answer, she simply reached out and grabbed his upper thigh.

"What the—?"

Losh, but her hands were strong.

"This is really . . ."

What was she doing?

"Quite . . ."

Good Lord save him.

"Inappropriate."

Oh . . . He shuddered, the breath leaving him slowly, as decades of tension unspooled and the pain that had been a constant slowly began to dissolve.

She instantly lightened the pressure. "That didn't hurt, did it?"

Rollo responded with a tight shake of his head.

"Oh, good." She redoubled her efforts, using knuckles and thumbs to ease the tightness at the front of his legs. "Because I only studied massage for a year. Well, not really a year. Almost a year."

She found a sensitive spot and he flinched.

"You sure you're okay?"

He gave a single nod, his eyes shut tight.

"Because you don't need to be mister tough guy. Just tell me if it hurts." Her hand grazed the side of his thigh.

Rollo held his breath—what was she *doing*?

She dug her thumb in hard, and everything else fell away.

This strange . . . *massage* . . . was shaping up to be one of the single most memorable moments of his life, and yet, seemingly oblivious, Felicity chattered on.

"So anyway, I was really into it," she said, making circular motions with her thumb. "Into massage school, I mean. But *boom*, my first hairy back and that was it." She laughed.

"Wait." She froze. "You don't have a hairy back, do you?"

What was she on about?

"No," he managed. "Not that I know of."

"Oh good. 'Cause that's a deal breaker. Though it'd be a shame to have come all this way . . ." She giggled.

"So anyway, I'd really thought it would be my thing. Massage, I mean. Livvie, my Aunt Livia, that is, used to . . ."

She sighed wistfully. The sudden sadness in her voice had him cracking open an eyelid to watch her. Felicity's lively brown eyes were suddenly quiet. He studied her hand on his leg and fought the urge to take it in his.

"My parents died in a car accident. I was just a little kid, but . . . I was in the car with them." She grew utterly silent, her uncharacteristic stillness jarring.

"You probably don't know what that is," she finally said. She sighed, resuming a slow, stroking motion along the side of his thigh. "A car . . . It's like a *really* fast carriage. But with no horses attached."

She worked silently then, seeming to collect her thoughts.

Rollo watched her, and wondered at the foreign emotion that stabbed his chest. The poor lass, baring her thoughts for all and sundry. And yet, in that instant, he couldn't fathom what she might be thinking.

"Anyway," she said finally, "I was hurt. My back. It was bad, for such a little kid."

She paused, using the opportunity to dig her fingertips in deep. "I guess we have that in common, huh? Getting hurt at such a young age. But I had Livvie to massage my back every night."

She slowly released the pressure and it was like a torrent of blood was released, rushing through his leg, up his spine, to the base of his neck, making him light-headed.

Groaning, he let his head fall back, savoring the feel of tendons and fibers that had long been in iron knots relaxing for what felt like the first time. Even his chest felt as if it were opening, his breathing somehow freer, his neck, his jaw, all somehow eased.

"Good, huh?" She smiled at him, then looked back at his leg. His left had been snapped in two, but it was his right that had been utterly smashed.

"It's a tragedy that this wasn't set right. I had to have a back brace myself, for a while. But it was the feel of Livvie's hands on me every night. That's what really saved me. So, I thought, maybe massage. But, no. All those hairy backs." She gave a quiet, sad laugh. "I can't really seem to find my thing. But I will," she finished, sounding an upbeat note.

All that talking had eased her, and she became immersed in the muscles around his right knee, finding knots, digging, stroking.

Rollo let himself grow easy too, shutting his eyes, savoring the feel of a pair of deft hands working his body.

It was entirely inappropriate, but he couldn't bring himself to make her stop. He hadn't felt this good since before the accident. How did she manage it with just a single touch?

And if she was capable of making him feel so good with a mere hand on his leg—?

The thought sent a bolt of heat straight to his groin.

His eyes flew open, and his first sight was Felicity doggedly massaging his calf between two hands. Deep in thought, she licked and bit at her lower lip.

He felt himself growing hard, and harder still. His eyes flew from her mouth.

But they landed on her chest. She'd had to lean down, and her dress was tugged dangerously low, her breasts rising and falling with her efforts.

Losh, but was she *trying* to pull herself out of that thing?

He tried to move away, and must have made some sound, but the effect was the opposite of what he'd intended.

"Oh gosh, I'm sorry," she said, placing her palm flat on his thigh.

Move the hand. Move the hand.

"Did I hurt you?"

He tried to answer but couldn't, and she began rubbing slowly again. "Sorry, I'll go lighter. I found a good spot—"

Her hands grew still.

Surely she didn't realize how hard she was making him. Curse his body.

At least he knew one aspect of his physique that was in strong, working order. All the good *that* did.

Of course . . . he *could* touch her.

She seemed determined that they were meant for each other. He had only to reach out. Touch back. Her thigh—would it be soft or firm beneath his fingertips?

"That's enough lass," he croaked.

"Oh." She sat back. "Enough, yes, of course."

He clenched his eyes shut tight. A woman like her would want a man whole. A man to sweep her into his arms and climb stairs. Climb mountains.

Not an object of pity. For one day she would pity him. Something, somehow would come to pass, and she'd offer him that look he knew so well. He didn't think he could bear to see *that* look, clouding the open joy that was her lovely face.

His realm would forever be one of battles and kings. Not secreted moments in dark carriages.

What she would do next, he had no idea. Rollo could only sit back, shut his eyes tight, and damn his body.

She wasn't a fairy princess. She was the devil's own.

Felicity. What a name. Joyously damning him to a hell of soothing touches and creamy skin that would be forever out of his reach.

Chapter 6

"Cool!" Felicity said, walking off the day's ride by stamping her feet and stretching her legs. She was trying her best to be cheery, even though she was sore, dirty, and hungry. And Will hadn't even kissed her *once*.

Travel by carriage had become impossible. They'd switched to horses just north of Stirling, and now she didn't even get to sit next to him anymore.

But, she was keeping it together. She'd muster a bright outlook, and soon he'd realize they were destined for each other.

"Wow," she said, looking around her. The sun had shone brightly all day, igniting the lush countryside to glowing greens, reds, and yellows. "Scotland is sooo gorgeous."

Hills rose like a promise on the horizon. The Highlands, Will had told her, with glens and heather and, she was certain, a goodly number of tartan-clad men too. Though she'd be surprised if any of them were as grimly sexy as her Viking.

"I can't wait til we're in the hills." She shaded her eyes and looked into the distance. "But, wait, what about moors? There are moors here too, right? I mean, what exactly *is* a moor, anyway? Gosh, it all sounds so *Wuthering Heights*," she added in a murmur. "And you mentioned thistle. I don't think I've ever even seen thistle. Does it smell good?"

Her question was met with silence.

They'd been traveling for weeks. Mostly, the weather was gloomy and the food was gross, but through it all, Felicity had remained what she thought was quite the chipper and easygoing travel companion. And *still*, he barely even spoke to her.

"And all these lakes, or what do you call them, *lochs*?" She studied his back, willing him to chat. She wasn't used to so much quiet. Back home there was always some sort of ambient noise—cars, distant sirens, the neighbor's television— even at night. And besides, she could usually get a person to talk. She wasn't accustomed to such a silent companion. "All these lochs are so—"

"Och," he said, the sound drawn out like a hiss in the back of his throat, "please, lass." Will gestured with his free hand for her to be quiet. "I'm trying to catch our dinner."

Rollo sat in the grass, and Felicity stilled, watching in fascination as he gently tugged and spun clumps of found sheep's wool into string, fashioning a small noose.

"What on earth—?" She clapped a hand to her mouth. "Oops, sorry!" she whispered, her chirpiness untouched by his mood.

This would be their first night sleeping outside, and she wasn't sure if the elation she felt was due more to the prospect of camping in old Scotland or to the fact that they were going to be spending the night not separated by the walls of an inn.

Maybe beside a romantic fire. With him snuggling her close for warmth.

If only she felt cuter.

"God I wish I had a brush." For what felt like the millionth time that day, she wound her hair into a thick rope, twisting and knotting it into a bun. "How do women deal with their hair here? Hey," she exclaimed suddenly, "could you rig some of that wool into a hair band for me?"

He shot her a glare over his shoulder and she shrugged, giving him a smile in return. Will couldn't step on *her* buzz. He'd changed into a kilt when they'd switched to horseback, and she just about thought she'd pass out from the now constant hum in her girl parts. *A man in a kilt—who knew?*

Her eyes were continually drawn like a magnet to bits of his exposed calf and knee. Once they'd dismounted, she kept finding excuses to walk behind him. At one point, a renegade gust of wind had almost blown the thing up, and she was desperate to see what he had on under there.

She was also eager to see what sort of shape his legs were really in. It appeared his left one had healed relatively straight, but his right bowed at an angle that made her heart pang at the thought of the boy he'd been when he'd suffered so.

She watched him work, trying to remain quiet, but couldn't bear it. She asked in a loud whisper, "What on earth is that little noose thing for?"

A dark cloud skittered across his brow.

"Okay, okay," she said quickly. "I'll shut up for real. Promise."

Despite the million questions rattling around in her mind, she forced herself to silence. But it didn't mean she'd budge from the spot, and she alternately studied him and gazed at the gorgeous panorama awaiting them.

She felt his stillness and glanced to find he was watching her. They locked gazes for a curious moment.

"See the wee den," he said finally, his voice a low rasp. He pointed to a small rise roughly twenty feet away. "Just there."

She squinted her eyes, but it all looked like brush and ragged grass to her. "I don't see it."

"A wee hole. Just there, lass." He pointed again. His exasperation of the past weeks had mellowed to something sounding like resignation. Felicity thought it was a promising development.

"I still don't see it." She stood to get a closer look. "What's in there, anyway?"

"Rabbit."

"Oh no, you're going to catch a little bunny?" He'd risen, and she joined him on his approach to the den.

"Your other option is black pudding." He stopped by the side of a shallow grassy rise, and sure enough, a small shadowy hole spoke to an animal living within.

"Ooh"—she put her hand on his arm to stop him—"pudding sounds *much* better." She was hungry, but that tiny noose was just too grim. "But how can you even make that here?"

"Black pudding? I'd find a cow . . ."

"I could do with some dairy," she said optimistically.

"I'd make a cut at the shoulder, bleed just enough from the animal to mix with a spot of our oats—"

"Oh, that is disgusting." She stopped him with a raised hand. "I wanted alpha male, but not *that* alpha." She shook her head, then gestured to a patch of loch glittering in the distance. "Surely with all these lakes you could just catch us a fish?"

"This is much faster. And besides, you could use the meat. *I* could use the meat. We've long days ahead."

"Well . . ." She *was* starving. "You'll cook it though, right?"

He gave an exasperated grunt in response and leaned down by the rabbit den. He grabbed hold of a branch from some nearby gorse, and then pulled a dagger from his sock to slice it free.

"*Ohmygod*," she gasped. "That is too hot. What else are you hiding in those socks, Will?"

Though silent, he turned a satisfying shade of beet red.

"William Rollo, you're blushing."

Scowling, he jammed the small stick just above the hole and began to wind the end of the noose around it.

"That thing is hideous. Like something from some little bunny horror movie." She eyed the elaborate pistol holstered at his waist. "Why don't you just shoot one?"

"I'm not partial to the taste of iron in my meat. In any case, bullets are a hard-won commodity."

"Yeah . . ." She grew momentarily thoughtful. "Where do you get bullets, anyway?"

"Metal," he bit out.

"Duh. But where do you get the metal?"

"Och, woman, do you ever give up?" Impatiently, he wound the string around once more, setting his trap. "Men melt it. Now let's away from here, and pray for some roast meat for supper."

"Can we take a walk?" she asked at his back. *Preferably someplace very windy*, she thought, eyeing the sway of his kilt along his thighs.

"A . . ." He stopped in his tracks, staring at her in disbelief. "You've been riding all day and now you'd like to walk?"

"Yes." She crossed her arms over her chest. She hadn't really *really* wanted to, but now she was just feeling contrary.

"Walk where?"

"I don't know. Around." She panicked suddenly, realizing that, with his legs, the last thing he'd want to do after a day of hard riding was walk. "Maybe we could find something to go with the bunny."

Felicity was a whiz in the kitchen, and made a wicked good stew. Men loved it. They always loved her cooking.

There had even been a time she'd dreamt of working in a restaurant, and had taken a bunch of cooking classes. She ended up scoring a plum job as a chef's assistant, but her first night on the job had shocked her into reality. Everyone shouted at each other, cursing and jostling around in what felt like a thousand-degree kitchen. It'd been enough restaurant work for a lifetime.

But a simple rabbit stew? She could definitely swing a decent rabbit stew. She just needed to find the right herbs. Then Will would see how clever she was. That she could take good care of him.

"There has to be something green around here that we can eat," she continued. "I'm dying to actually crunch into something fresh."

She gave him an encouraging smile.

"Och." He shook his head. "A walk. Aye, walk on, then."

"Well, you don't have to be so grumpy about it," she mumbled under her breath.

Rollo pointed out a juniper bush, assuring her that the dark berries were edible, and with a whack of his cane, sent a shower of berries raining down.

"But we need something else," she mused, walking slowly along the old drover's path. "How about this?" Felicity knelt by a thick, weedy clump of foliage. "I keep seeing it. It looks like it could be . . . I don't know, mint or something."

"Lord no, lass. Those are nettles. Don't even think about—"

She didn't know why she did it, all she knew was that the draw was irresistible. Her hand was out and gripping the nettle leaves before she knew what she was doing.

"Ow!" There was a moment of tingling, then a sharp sting flushed over her palm and fingertips. "Ow ow ow." She shook it out hard, but that didn't stop the burning, or the tiny red welts that bloomed sudden and complete on her hand.

"That was a fool thing to do." His voice cut her, and Felicity didn't know which stung more, the nettles, or the fact that his sharp words probably constituted the most he'd said to her for some time.

"Whatever. It's no big deal." She wanted to shoot him a defiant glare, but felt her chin begin to quiver, and so turned her back on him instead.

Her hand was killing her, but she wasn't about to let him see that. "Let's just see if you've successfully murdered little Bugs or not."

"Och, lass—"

"My name's not *lass*," she snapped. Felicity heard him rustling at her back, but she refused to turn and look at him. She'd not be able to bear it if his face was as cold as his words had been. "Don't get me wrong, *lad*, I dig the *ochs* and *ayes* and all that. But I haven't heard you say my name once. Do you even *remember* my name?"

"Felicity." His voice was taut, the single word containing an apology, a scold, a plea. "Of course I know your name.

It's a beautiful name. It suits you," he added quietly. "Turn around, Felicity. Please."

Drawing her features into a careful blank, she turned.

He stood there, the sharpness of his gaze blunted into something approaching tenderness. Rollo stretched out his hands, and she saw he'd filled them with fistfuls of oblong green leaves.

She looked up at him, a question in her eyes.

"Dock leaves, las—" He crooked the corner of his mouth into a gentle half smile, and she felt suddenly warmed deep down. "A docken plant, Felicity. For your hand."

He stepped carefully toward her, crushing the coarse leaves between his fingers. He reached for her, took her hand, and it was as if an electric shock arced between them. He drew a sharp breath in between his lips, and she swore he'd felt it too.

He rubbed her palm and fingers with the weed, and, mesmerized, she watched the play of bones and tendons under the skin of his hands. They were broad and masculine, just a little dirty, but not coarse, and she was desperate to feel them on her.

As he rubbed, she tried to imagine whether his touch would be rough or gentle. Would he grab her and claim her, or stroke lightly, teasing her?

She could just squeeze his hand, she thought. Right then and there, just squeeze it. Maybe give a quick, saucy little rub of her thumb on his palm. Would he glance up, look longingly into her eyes? Kiss her like he almost did in the dress shop?

Or, what would he do if she just tackled him? Simply grabbed the man and kissed him. She could jump him and they could roll to the ground in a passionate embrace. Unless, of course, they landed in that evil mint stuff. All that stinging would put a damper on things.

The stinging. She realized the sting on her palm had disappeared.

"Wow . . ." Smiling, she looked up at him. But his eyes

were shuttered once again. Feeling herself deflate, she pulled away and thanked him quietly.

"Hush," he said suddenly.

She glowered. This time she *knew* she hadn't said anything.

A brisk shake of his head and a firm grip on her arm alerted her that something was wrong. He leaned down, taking his cane where he'd laid it on the ground at their feet. He held her gaze as he listened carefully.

"What?" she mouthed, and then she heard it. The distant sound of men singing. A kick of fear hammered her heart against her chest.

Though Rollo's face was calm, Felicity sensed the shift in his posture. Tensed, poised, like a wary wolf measuring approaching intruders.

He looked from her, to the thick tangle of birch and alder that had shadowed their path, and then back again. He gave her a quick nod and, holding her arm, led her with surprising stealth into the woods.

Her breath was loud in her ears, but she felt unable to calm herself. His steady hand on her was the only thing keeping her focused.

It's okay, she told herself. She knew she was being as quiet as possible. *I am the only one who can hear my heart pounding.*

"We must get back to the horses." His whisper at her ear startled her.

Trembling now, she mustered a nod, straining to hear where the men might be, how many there were. What would they do if they found them?

The woods seemed suddenly loud around her. The rustle of leaves as birds flitted from branch to branch. The tinkling sound of a faraway stream.

A trick of the trees sent another sound bursting to them, abrupt and close. It was the men, shouting, singing, laughing. Her legs froze.

She felt Will's hand graze the small of her back. It

was warm, and she realized how fear had made her skin clammy.

"Be easy, Felicity." He gave her waist a squeeze. He gestured to a break in the trees, carefully guiding them to where he'd tied the horses for grazing. "Easy, lass."

There it was again: the "lass" thing. He caught it too and shot her a shrug and a half smile, a flash of humor to gird her. And she thought this man could call her whatever he wanted, as long as he kept doling out those rare glimpses of warmth.

The men's voices were closing in, and the sound echoed strangely underneath the canopy of trees.

"Now." Gripping her waist tight, he pulled her across the final yards. His right leg swung in a stiff jog.

A thick carpet of bracken slowed their progress, much of the fern reddened into the color of late summer. The rustle was unbearably loud, and she sensed a change in the approaching men.

Will and Felicity hurtled from the trees. The contrast between the oppressive copse and the wide-open air was dramatic, and she gulped in a lungful of fresh oxygen.

The horses were oblivious to the threat, and greeted them with vacant eyes, chomping on grass with docile focus.

Will had his hands on her from behind, and she shivered at the feel of him, powerful at her back, sweeping her up and onto the saddle in a single, fluid motion.

He was on his own horse in an instant, cane tucked between thigh and saddle, urging the animals back and away down the drover path.

"Ho there!" a voice called from behind. Rollo glanced back, and the grim look crossing his face made her afraid to turn around.

Will wore a dirk belted at his side, and he pulled it free, slapping the flat of the blade on her horse's rump, sending it careening from him.

"Will!" she shrieked, yanking hard on the reins, trying to slow the animal down. In the back of her mind, Felicity knew she needed to get out of there, but terror muddled her. She knew only Rollo, and wanted to stay by his side.

"Oh my God, oh my God," she chanted, her voice hitching, breathy and frantic. Her horse reeled and spun to an uneasy stop, and she watched the scene unfold. Three men on three burly ponies stood there, surrounding him. "Will, watch out!"

He resheathed his dirk, and she screamed again, "What are you doing?"

The cane was in his hand. He tossed it up, catching it by the base. Standing high in the saddle, he cantered past the knot of men and swung, whacking one sharply on his temple with the cane's silver handle.

A hollow noise like a golf club clocking a ball resonated to her, a grotesque sound that sent a peculiar, animal shot of elation through Felicity's veins. The man slid to the ground, his mount turning and making a wild-eyed dash into the woods.

She caught the quick, nervous glance shared by the two remaining men. Will, however, was methodical. He appeared to think nothing of the two beyond what he'd sized up, and his face was utterly still as he set to dispatching them as neatly as a farmer would till a field.

Not waiting for either of his enemies to strike first, Rollo slid the cane through his grip and, kicking his horse into an abrupt gallop, closed the short distance between him and the closest man. Gripping the silver handle, he jousted the man in the throat. The man toppled backwards, and the horse skittered away, its rider hanging limp from the side of the saddle.

"Hup, hup," was all she heard Will say as he reeled his horse about in a tight circle. The animal gave a single, brisk toss of its head, but was otherwise still.

The sight astounded her. This creature that had seemed just minutes before like a normal, perhaps slightly worse-for-wear horse, was now fit for a dressage arena.

One man remained, and, thumping his legs hard at his

horse's belly, he charged Will, a broadsword swinging wildly before him.

"Watch out!" she shrieked again, but Rollo was cool, and merely ducked, his hair wild from the near miss.

Using only his seat, Will spun his horse once more. He tucked the cane back under his thigh, swapping it for his dirk, which he had out and ready.

The men charged each other, and Felicity's heart slammed hard against her chest. There was no way Will's short dagger could be a match for the long blade of his opponent.

Rollo was like stone in the saddle, standing slightly in the stirrups, utterly calm. The other man whooped, riding hard for him. A black grin bisected the man's face, thinking he had the advantage. Felicity heard her own hollow screeching as if from a distance.

She saw Will shift ever so slightly. His left calf twitched, left foot cocking out at a sharp angle. And she gasped as Rollo's horse danced one, two, three perfect steps to the side. An elegant little prance, and Will was to the man's left.

He'd switched the dirk to his opposite hand, and leaning in, easily sliced the man's neck as he galloped past.

Felicity's cheer stuck in her throat. Sensing a body near, she looked down to see an ugly man staring back up at her. It was shocking, and surreal, this gap-toothed face gazing hungrily up at her.

He came to her as a vivid snapshot, his close-cropped hair a faint yellow dusting on the top of his head, thick beige clinging in his smile, as if he'd not sucked all the bread from his teeth. And he held her reins in his hand.

"Will?" His name was a tremulous question in her throat, swallowed at once by the clamor of hooves galloping toward her.

Her horse shied from Rollo's approach. Though the man's hand slid down the leather straps, he continued to hold them tight.

It happened in an instant, in a patchwork of impressions. Her horse dancing nervously beneath her. The dramatic whoosh of Rollo's advance.

His horse stopped short and sure, rearing up and landing with a hideous crash onto the man's head and body. His fall was hard and complete, his tenacious grip tugging Felicity's reins down with him, giving a sharp yank to her horse's head before his fingers finally slipped from the leather.

She trembled in shock, staring at the man lying still at her feet. Blood soaked his brow and one arm canted at an unnatural angle from his shoulder.

He flinched to life and Felicity screamed.

She sensed Rollo's movement at the corner of her eye. His horse hovered close to hers now, as if he could shield her from danger by his proximity alone. She felt rather than saw the sweep of his arm, and shuddered a sob to see the small dagger from Will's sock now quivering in the man's throat.

Fighting hysteria, she made a shrill giggling sound, half sob, half laugh. "Talk about going for the throat."

"Aye," he said simply.

"That's all? *Aye?*" *Do the yoga breathing.* "Good Lord, but I'm not in Kansas anymore."

She stared at him, sitting composed and grimly handsome on his horse. He wore the edge of his plaid swept up and over his shoulder—the wool was green and yellow, blue and black, and it flapped dully in the breeze.

"He just kills four men, neat as you please, and all I get's an *aye*," she muttered, feeling herself calming.

Her eyes roved his face unabashedly. He'd gotten a shave in Stirling, and stubble had already reappeared, a brown shadow along his strong jaw. His wavy hair had been tousled from his efforts, but he'd already raked it impatiently back in place.

"I mean, come on. No jaunty comebacks, like, 'I'll bet he found that one hard to swallow?' Or, maybe something about him clearing *that* from his throat." She shuddered a sigh, her breathing finally even. "Who were those guys anyway?"

"I know not. Nor will we wait to find out." His eyes scanned her, making certain she was settled.

Just that flicker of contact had her body crackling, and

her mind agitated at such a silly response. She thumped her heels on her horse's belly, nudging the beast into a walk.

"You'll want to turn your horse about." She felt herself flush a hot shade of red. She and dignity didn't seem to be fast friends these days.

"That means it's black pudding for me tonight, huh?" she asked, struggling to turn her mount on the ragged drover's path.

"Aye," he replied, his horse already ahead of hers. "But you'll find the proof of the pudding is in the eating."

And this time she could've sworn she heard a smile in his voice.

❀

Will flinched and tossed on the bed of heather. It molded to him, easing his body, yet his eyelids still fluttered with renegade dreams.

Running. The sand was packed hard and cool at his feet and it kicked up, sounding a raspy *chuff* with each step.

His arms pumped, his legs stretched and flexed, pounding out a powerful gait along the sand. The wind tasted chilled and briny in his mouth. He smiled with the joy of it.

And then *she* was there, standing on the horizon.

She wore a dress of gauzy white, and it fluttered around her legs and clung tight at her breasts. If only he could get a little closer, he'd be able to see her body through the gossamer fabric. See the rise of her breasts, the slope of her thigh.

He ran to her, calling her name. *Felicity.*

Her yellow hair whipped behind her in the breeze, and he wondered why she didn't turn to him. The water was at her knees now, yet still she stood, unmoving, waiting and watching for something on the horizon.

The joy in his heart flicked into panic. She needed to step back, step away from the water's edge. Why would she not turn to him?

He ran harder, and yet he couldn't close the gap between

them. The water rose higher, to her waist now, and he saw her stumble in its pull.

His arms pumped harder. Legs that never failed him in his dreams felt stiff, his joints popping and tendons cracking. He couldn't reach her. He tried to call to her, but could make no sound.

Felicity turned, finally. Finally, she caught and held his gaze. Ever so slowly and without a splash, she disappeared beneath the surface of the waves.

Chapter 7

He'd been sensing trouble for days, and by the time the sun crested the sky, Will knew they had a problem.

Once again the horse swung his head back to nip at his flanks. "Easy, lad," he soothed, leaning forward in the saddle to stroke at the animal's neck. The creature had grown increasingly agitated throughout the morning, and now the nipping and grunting had become constant.

"There's nothing for it," he grumbled, pulling to a halt.

"What's going on?" Felicity looked at him, perplexed. "Why are you stopping?"

"We've a problem with the horse." He scanned the horizon and pointed to a stand of trees in the distance. "We'll rest there."

"But we just ate lunch." The air was brisk, but the noonday sun glared hazy and bright, and she shaded her eyes to look at him. "What's wrong with the horse?"

Will tried to ignore the way the light picked white and golden highlights in her long, blonde hair. Pulling his eyes from her, he swung his leg over to dismount. "Colic, lass. The horse has colic, and he'll be horse*meat* if I don't tend to him."

"I just thought he was a cranky old guy." She got down, and keeping hold of her reins, reached over to pat at Will's horse. The animal swung his head to bite at her, and Felicity squealed.

"Easy," he said quickly. He pulled Felicity close, putting himself between her and the animal. "You'll do no good for the horse. Or for yourself. A horse in pain can be a dangerous thing."

She edged further from Will's horse as they walked, and he watched as she cut nervous sidelong glances their way. He hoped she'd be all right. There was no choice, though. It was imperative Will find healing herbs, and he'd need to leave Felicity behind to mind the animal.

Despite the saddle on its back, the horse dropped to a roll the moment they stopped to rest by the trees. "Och, lad," Will snapped. "Up. Up, up." With a quick swat to its rump, he urged the animal back to standing and handed the reins to Felicity. "You'll need to keep him walking. Don't let him roll."

Her brow furrowed in concern. "But rolling looks like it feels so good."

She was so guileless and sweet, and Will quickly shoved such thoughts from his mind. "He'll twist his gut," he said flatly. "It could kill him."

"Oh. Jeez. That's horrible. Wait," she said suddenly, trying to hand the reins back. "I can't hold him. What if he bites me? You said he could be dangerous."

"Just keep him moving," he said, taking the healthier of the two horses from her. "Walk him a quarter hour every hour. I'll take off the saddle, and you can lead the poor lad by the reins."

"What do you mean walk him?" She looked at the animal as if he were infected with cholera, not colic. "Where will *you* be?"

"Easy, woman." He chuckled.

"Don't use your soothe-y horse-y voice with me. Where are you going? You can't just leave me with a huge, sick animal. What if he dies?"

"He won't if I leave now." Will gave her what he hoped was an encouraging nod. He knew Felicity was nervous. And well she should be. But they needed their mounts, and the animal would die without immediate care. "He won't get well on his own. I promise to return soon. I'll need to gather mint," he thought aloud, "valerian if I can find it. We passed a wee marsh late yesterday. I'm going to double back. See what I can find."

She held the reins away from her body, arm outstretched rigidly. "But . . . You . . . What if . . ."

"Och, calm yourself, and the beast will calm too." He smiled. "Relax, and he'll not hurt you. It's men I fear more than any animal."

"Oh great." The horse looked as if he might roll again, and she hopped into a hasty walk. "That makes me feel so much better," she said over her shoulder.

"I'll return as soon as I can."

As soon as he could was well after dark. She'd spent the first hour terrified that the animal would rear up and trample her like she'd seen him do when Will was in the saddle. The rest of the time she'd worried that snaggle-toothed, sword-wielding men might pop out of the woods at any moment.

The nighttime sky was overcast, and had darkened into a uniform gray-black overhead. Being alone, in the eerily quiet night, with an enormous, sick horse had her filling the silence with an anxious monologue. About the horse, about his belly, about how Will would be back at any moment. But as she walked, her nervous chatter became low coos, and quick pats slowed into lingering strokes, until she was at ease, and the horse seemed so too.

She walked the animal in a close circle along the fringe of trees, worried that they'd trip in the shadows. The night was bitter cold, and though the walking kept the chill from her bones, it did nothing to alleviate the very urgent needs of her body.

"Felicity?"

"Thank God," she said, hearing Will's voice calling low. "We're still here. Please hurry, I really need to . . . you know . . . *go*."

He laughed quietly. "I'll be but a moment."

Will rustled in the dark, a tapestry of sounds floating to her on the crisp air. His low murmurs to her mare, the dull smack of a hand patting solid horseflesh. Stillness, and then the nascent crackle and pop of a fire.

He materialized from the shadows, tall and silent, and she gave a start.

"Here, lass," he said, tucking something in her hair.

The feel of his fingers tracing along her scalp made her breath catch. "What's that?"

"Mint. They say it keeps the midges away."

She fingered the sprig in her hair, limp and softly fuzzy. Will could be so disarmingly thoughtful. She smiled up at him. Just a silly bit of mint, and yet her impulse was to press it in a book.

He cleared his throat. "How's the lad?" he asked, taking the reins from her. He ran a hand down the flat plane of the horse's cheek.

"Okay, I think." She leaned over to stretch her legs. "I'm beat though. Do you mind if I—?"

"Aye, of course," he said quickly, with a nod to the trees.

She ducked away to relieve herself, and when she came back, the horse was lying down with Will seated by his side. The animal grunted and nipped once at the air, then rested his head in the dirt.

"I thought he wasn't supposed to roll," she said.

"Aye, rolling is bad. But rest is a fine thing. Come." He gestured to the ground. "You could use a spot of it yourself. Come bide a wee by the fire."

"I would *love* to sit by the fire," she said, plopping down next to him. Just that little bit of physical relief, combined with the promise of heat and maybe even a drink of water, had her nearly giddy with pleasure. "Now if only we had s'mores."

He met her eyes, confusion flickering on his brow, and she felt a little thrill when their gazes caught. The flames popped and crackled, casting an orange glow along one side of his face. The light danced in his eyes, and far from feeling chilled now, she thought she might melt there on the spot.

"I'm afraid I don't have much, but I do have water with herbs on to boil. We'll see if we can get some into him, and mayhap we can spare some for you too," Will told her, offering a rare smile.

"How is he? Can I . . ." She reached a hesitant hand to the horse. "Can I pet him? Would that be all right?"

"Aye." Will had replaced the bridle with a halter, and he offered her the length of rope. "'Twould be a fine thing," he told her, urging her to take hold of the animal.

The horse chuffed and flinched, making as if to roll, and Felicity scooted closer, instinctively guiding his head into her lap. She smoothed the wiry forelock from his eyes, and to her surprise, the horse eased.

"The beast has taken to you." Will used his cane to pull a small pot from over the fire. There was a hiss as hot water sizzled along cast iron, and the sharp smell of mint tingled pleasantly in her sinuses. "You did well today. Despite your worries."

It was modest, as compliments went, but still she swelled with pride. The horse did seem soothed, she thought, stroking her palm down his sleek neck. "Thanks. I never realized how nice horses were. I'm such a city girl. Before all this"— she gestured around her—"the closest I'd ever gotten to a horse was when my Aunt Livvie took me to the racetrack for my eighteenth birthday."

"But surely you'd ridden before?"

"Nope. Never."

"That's remarkable," he said, astounded. "You got on a saddle without a word, never having ridden before?"

"That's right. Wait," she amended quickly. "Scratch that. I went on a pony ride when I was a kid, but—" She stopped herself, remembering Will's horrific tale of his childhood accident. "Oh, God, I'm sorry."

"For what?"

"You know . . . the pony thing."

To her surprise, he gave a low laugh. "Don't fash yourself, lass. I remember the *pony thing* daily. It's not as though your words remind me of something I don't already know."

She stroked the horse's neck. It was pure power, silky and muscular under her fingertips. Will watched her, and she felt oddly shy, unable to meet his eyes. She hoped she was petting the animal correctly.

"Aye," he said finally. "It's remarkable how the beast has taken to you."

She smiled. "Maybe horses are my thing, huh?"

"Your . . . *thing*?"

"Yeah." She sighed. "Haven't I told you? I've tried it all. But I've never managed to find my calling. Lots of things interest me, but nothing has ever really sparked my passion."

He was quiet for a moment, and just when she began to worry that her last sentence was somehow inappropriate, he spoke. "I believe horses are *my* calling. I can't imagine never having ridden. Horses are the one thing in my life I can rely on."

"What about your family? Surely you can rely on them."

Will stiffened. "I suppose you could say their behavior is . . . reliably predictable. But I've found horses are really the only dependable thing."

"That's sad," she said at once. This was possibly the most Will had ever opened up to her, and Felicity wanted to press him, explore every little aspect of what he said to her.

"Not sad," he told her with cool finality. "It simply is."

So much for sharing.

"What is colic, anyway?" she asked after an extended silence.

"It might be a number of things. Something could be blocked. His belly," he said, running his palm along the horse's stomach, "feel how it's warm."

She brought her hand next to his. The horse's stomach felt hot, distended. Felicity felt the heat of Will's arm, so close to hers. Her gaze went to his fingers, long and strong in the firelight. Concern for the animal warred with the sudden and complete awareness of Will, in such close proximity.

"It could be as simple as gas, or as dire as a twist in his gut. Either way, the beast needs water." Will rose. Taking the rope from her, he pulled the horse to standing. "Come now, laddie," he said in a low voice. "Let's have a wee drink, shall we?"

She stood too, using her skirts to pick up the pot. The water had cooled quickly in the night air, and Rollo took it from her with his bare hands.

He held it to the horse's mouth, but the animal merely lipped it, not drinking. Will grunted.

"What's in the water?"

"Valerian, to relax the gut. Mint too. If he doesn't work it out, the colic will be the death of him." He pulled the horse into a walk. "You should rest, Felicity. I've a long night ahead."

"I won't be able to sleep." She fell into step on the other side of the horse, scratching lightly behind his ears. It killed her to see the poor thing in such distress. "And I like being able to help."

They walked in peaceable silence for some time, then Will asked, "Would you like to assist me, then? With the horses, I mean."

He pulled the horse to a halt, and steadied Felicity's hands as she brought the water once more to the animal's mouth.

"Really?" She let her heart soar over what she knew was probably such a silly thing. "You'd let me do that? Maybe show me some things?"

Their eyes met in the dark, and Will was the first to look away.

"Aye." His answer was clipped, distant once more, and Felicity wondered if she'd even heard him correctly. Will studied the night sky. "Though it's mostly stablemen who'll be minding the horses from now on. Winter is in the air, and the beasts need hay for bedding and fresh feed for their bellies."

Thoughtful, he stroked the animal's side. "We've no choice. I fear it shall be inns for us, from now on."

Chapter 8

"Not another one," she grumbled, studying the dingy sign swinging above the inn's front door. Felicity wondered just how many seedy inns with fleas and rodents and leering men there were between England and wherever it was they were headed in Scotland.

It had been so nice, that one night's respite with Will and the horse and the great outdoors. Though they'd walked in silence, his proximity had sent a warm buzzing through her body. She'd felt connected to another person in a way she'd never before experienced.

She'd also felt genuinely useful for the first time ever. Like she'd been needed, and had been able to help. And she'd loved doing it.

But the animal had recovered, and Rollo quickly receded back into himself. His retreat stung. Every day that passed left Felicity wondering even more if that night had actually happened, or if it had just been some strange and disjointed dream.

The Pipe and Tabor Inn. She scowled. "What the heck's a *tabor* anyhow?" she asked, urging her horse to catch up with Rollo's.

She'd thought old Scotland would be a real hoot, but after God knew how many days on horseback and God *only* knew how many roasted rabbits she was supposed to be grateful for, Felicity thought she might just be ready to pack it all in and head for the nearest spa.

"Oh man, I'd give anything to soak in a great big Jacuzzi tub." She sighed wistfully. "And a shampoo. My hair"—she rubbed vigorously at her scalp—"is driving me *insane*. I can't keep it out of my face."

She noticed he'd gotten ahead of her. "Hey, Will," she said to his back, kicking her horse into a grudging trot, "are there any hot springs around here? There's got to be something in, like, Italy right about now. I mean, it's only about a two-hour flight there. How long a ride could it be?"

She noted him shaking his head. Was that a *no* or just an annoyed headshake? If it was a *no*, why couldn't he just say *no*? What would it take to get a rise out of the man? Get him to chat, just a little.

"I mean, it's Europe," she continued, "it's all mushed together here. Or maybe Switzerland," she mused to herself. "Isn't there some hot mineral spring thing in Switzerland?"

She caught up to him just as he was pulling his horse to a halt. They'd walked their mounts around the inn to a barn and paddock area at the back.

"At least this getup is easier to ride in. That pink dress was impossible." She fiddled with her skirts, untangling them from the ridiculous sidesaddle he'd gotten for her. "But do *all* seventeenth-century women wear the same dress, day after day after day?"

"We've been on the road, lass."

"Finally, he speaks!"

Rollo glowered at her.

"I don't know . . . God this thing itches," she said suddenly, scratching at the drab blue-gray bodice. "I'm pretty skeptical, Will." She fought a flicker of despair. "Please tell me I'm not going to spend the rest of my life in this riding dress."

"It's called a riding *habit*."

"Well isn't *that* appropriate." She unhooked her leg from the saddle and studied the drop to the ground. "Seeing as life in a convent might just be a little more thrilling than watching your back as we ride through the never-ending countryside."

He merely shrugged, focused instead on scanning the distance, looking, she presumed, for the stableman.

His nonreaction to her peevish mood was making her even more peevish. She studied him, so in his own world. Could it be Will wasn't *the one*? She'd come all the way back in time, just for him, and he hadn't shown her one bit of emotion. Well, she'd thought there'd been a flicker of something, that night with the horse. But that had been weeks ago, and since then, *nada*.

He hadn't even tried to kiss her. *And really*, Felicity thought, *what red-blooded man wouldn't even try?* She was cute. She dusted off her skirts. Kind of dirty, but surely cute enough to kiss.

"You didn't answer me," she said. "What's a *tabor*? And where the heck are we, anyway?"

He tilted his head, looking at her with a cocked brow. "What?"

"Only that you have a strange way of speaking, lass." He slid from his custom saddle and began to loosen his horse's girth and carefully shorten and tuck up the stirrups.

Watching him, she felt a pang of sympathy. It struck her that what looked like an exercise in great care—readying his horse—was actually an opportunity for Rollo to get his blood flowing once more.

"A *tabor* is a drum," he said, catching her stare. "For pipers. And we are in a place called Muirton."

The sympathy dissolved and was replaced by peevishness once more. For a man who looked like he was in pain at the end of every day, he sure thought nothing of riding all over the country. How far away did his family live, anyway?

She frowned at him, just waiting for an excuse to snap. "I hate rabbit, you know," she said abruptly.

A rare smile cracked at the edges of Rollo's mouth. "And what has the wee creature done to invoke your wrath?"

Ignoring his question, she rattled on, "I was even a vegetarian for a while. But I do love my In-N-Out Burgers." She shivered. "With special sauce. And fries. Do you know they make their fries fresh? You can even see them chopping up the potatoes."

"You should be grateful—"

"I know, I know. *Grateful for the food.*" She sighed. "I am." Felicity began to stretch out her legs. "Hey," she added brightly, "do you think they have any oats here? I could sure use a big bowl of oats. I haven't had oats in, ohhh, *six hours* now." She giggled to herself.

"You can be facetious all you like, it won't make my home materialize any more quickly. Though Duncrub Castle is but a day's ride away now."

"Do you *really* live in a castle?" Visions of the Disney castle filled her head with turrets and flags and grand balls. She sighed.

"More manor house, truly. But generations of Lords Rollo have preferred calling it a castle." He shrugged. "A man can call a goat a horse, and he'll still have to walk to market, aye?" He chuckled to himself.

Oh . . . That sound again. That hesitant, husky laugh. She caught his gaze and felt her insides go all gooey. Surely he knew what he did to her . . . right?

"I'll secure our rooms," he said, once again hard as granite. He handed her the horses' reins. "Do not stir from this spot. These mounts would fetch a dear price this far north. It'd be a shame if harm came to them."

"I'll be fine too, don't you worry. Thanks for the concern, though."

Was that another smile she caught cracking his features?

She crossed her heart in her best Girl Scout promise. "No harm will come to the mounts," she told him, affecting a deep bass voice.

Felicity watched Rollo shuffle away, then turned her energy to the horses. "You appreciate me, don't you," she cooed, running her hand down the long, hard plane of her horse's nose.

Will's horse nudged her with his head, and she giggled, patting him hard along the neck. "You too," she whispered. "I wouldn't forget you, laddie. We need to find you two something to munch on."

She felt so at ease with the animals, and marveled at how her attitude had shifted so dramatically from fear, to apprehension, to real affection.

Which wasn't to say she hadn't fantasized a million times about riding the rest of the way to Rollo's in Aunt Livia's old Volvo.

Livvie. She sighed.

Livvie would know she was gone by now. What would she be thinking? Would she have been back to Felicity's apartment? Had she seen the candle? The cards? What would she make of it all?

Felicity reached up to scratch the mare's head, and the animal flicked her ears.

She knew in her heart of hearts that Livvie would want her to stay. Liv would miss her terribly, sure, but, more than anything, her aunt would want her to have a grand adventure with a man meant for her. Livvie, who'd sent her off to Central America so Felicity could have a "vision quest."

She laughed to herself.

Livvie most of all would tell her to grab hold of Mister Right and hold on tight.

Now if only there were a way to communicate with her aunt just one more time. Tell her she was safe.

"Such a symphony of expressions on such a lovely face."

The voice was smooth, a mellow, masculine sound the aural equivalent of velvet.

Felicity turned to find a face that matched the voice, on a man standing not five feet away, smiling at her.

"Cute," she whispered under her breath. Was the seventeenth century where all the hotties were hiding?

Acute self-consciousness swamped her. Did she have to

be such a filthy mess? She curled her hands into fists to hide her blackened fingernails.

"I must know what thoughts whisk you along such a spectrum of emotion." His smile was broad but polite, he was long and lean without being skinny, and his sandy blond hair shone in modestly cut waves along his shoulders.

"Oh," she said, mustering a big, surprised smile. She knew her teeth were whiter than anything old Scotland offered, and so she'd taken to playing it up in the past weeks.

"Well?" he purred.

"Well . . . ?"

Maybe she had it all wrong. Could *this* be Mister Right?

She gave the thought a second to germinate while she stared openly at the man.

Nope. She wasn't feeling it. Wasn't feeling that crazy *zing* thing she always felt when Rollo caught her eye. As if every molecule in her body stood to attention in Will's presence.

"Ah, I see confusion too." Beaming, the stranger stepped closer. He was a foot away now, tilting his head this way and that, admiring Felicity's face. "First mirth, then melancholy, and now hmm . . . I dare say we need another *m*."

She froze, feeling a blush creeping all the way to her hairline.

"Mystery," he exclaimed. "Yes, that's it. I see such mysterious machinations playing on your bonny mien. Was that too much?"

"Uhhh . . ." It was nice to be paid attention to, but the dude was trying *way* too hard.

"Too many *m*'s, that is?"

He gave her a wink, and something inside her drooped a little. Will never winked at her. What she wouldn't do for a wink from *Will*.

"But what am I thinking?" He playfully slapped his brow. "I have been remiss. I must introduce myself."

He pulled her hand into his, lightly kissing her knuckles, and she wasn't sure if she was more elated at such a thrillingly gallant gesture, or horrified by the stinky, horsey grime that she knew encased her hand like a glove.

"Alexander Robertson, utterly charmed to make your acquaintance."

She began to pull her hand away. *Surely* she stank like muck and dirty leather.

He only gripped tighter, giving her fingers one final squeeze.

She shivered. If only *Will* would grab her hand and give her a proper squeeze.

"And who do I have the pleasure of meeting?"

"Oh . . ." She and Rollo had discussed this. She was to give her real name. It worked out quite nicely that her last name, Wallace, not only sounded Scottish, it was also a large, relatively amorphous clan hailing from outside the city of Glasgow.

As for how to explain their travel together, Rollo had told her she could claim a betrothal to him.

Now *that* had been like pulling teeth.

"Felicity Wallace," she hesitated.

"Fe-li-ci-ty," he let the sound trip joyfully over his tongue. "A name as delightful as she who bears it."

She smiled. Will had sounded stricken at the name. This was more like it.

"And what brings you to stand so lovely and forlorn, here in this modest village, bearing two mounts? Please do not tell me you await your husband."

"I . . ." She blushed. "He's not my husband, exactly—"

"Capital!" He stepped closer. His proximity cast her in shadow, and she instinctively took a slight step back.

"Now, do tell where you are from, Felicity of not-exactly-a-husband." He smiled wider, placing his hand on her horse's back. It struck her as an overly familiar gesture.

"Outside Glasgow." She looked around. What was taking Will so long?

"And is your *almost-husband* from Glasgow as well?"

The way he referred to him made her blush, as if she'd done something improper. Were women not supposed to travel with their fiancés? Was she giving him some horrible impression of her?

"No," she said, standing a little straighter, trying to look the part of an affronted seventeenth-century lady. She took another step back.

"If he leaves you unguarded, it's his own fault I'm here to sweep in and get better acquainted." Robertson leaned closer.

"Who *are* you?"

"Ah!" he exclaimed, opening his palms up to the sky. "You do not recognize my name?"

Definitely not Mister Right.

"I am minister of the village of Dunning. If you are not from these parts and, I dare say"—he eyed her in a way she *knew* couldn't have been entirely appropriate for the time period *or* a minister—"you are not, Dunning is a cheery wee village here in Perthshire."

"Oh, how—"

He cut her off, continuing merrily, "My journey has been neither easy nor brief, but I find that to adventure through the countryside is to rouse the senses."

"How far—?"

"And 'tis well worth it too," he interrupted again, adding a knowing and self-satisfied little chuckle.

She crossed her arms impatiently. This man didn't strike her as particularly *ministerial*. "Why do you—?"

"Dunning can feel quite isolated. A *minister* I may be, but I'd not have my existence be quite so *cloistered*." He laughed outright then, pleased at his own wit.

"*You're* a minister?" The words burst from her, coming out more loudly than she'd expected. Actually, she hadn't really even expected to be able to fit them in edgewise.

"Why, yes indeed. I know I am *quite* young for my own parish," he added, mistaking her confusion for admiration.

He edged closer. Did he expect her to be wilting with attraction to him?

"But truly, I do find travel so invigorating. And, indeed, necessary!"

"Indeed," she repeated, stealing furtive glances over the man's shoulder. *Any day now, Will.*

"I am a man of enterprise! I say, if a man is to have any ambition in life, he must keep abreast of the goings on in his country, do you not agree?"

Felicity managed a little half nod. She'd thought he was cute. Talk about wrong first impressions.

"I believe my successes are owed to zeal and industry, in equal parts."

"Oh, please," she whispered, scooting back a little more.

"God gives each of us certain gifts, and I dare not squander mine."

"It's good to be so aware of your talents," she said, trying to bite back a laugh.

"Indeed," he beamed.

Indeed, another indeed. Felicity glanced around again, just in time to see Rollo reappearing, with grooms in tow.

Saved.

The two men met each other with stony silence.

She wasn't sure how a seventeenth-century woman would approach the situation. "Uh . . . Alexander," she stammered, "this is—"

"Lord Rollo," the minister said, giving a curt nod to Will. "Everyone has heard of the great exploits of the esteemed Lord Rollo."

Felicity would've sworn she saw Will's cheek twitch.

Fascinating.

Alexander turned back to her, his tone a bit more subdued. "Had I known you were thus . . . spoken for, I'd not have hoped to press my suit."

"Press your—? Ohhh . . ." *Ew. Thanks, but no.*

"She is most definitely *spoken for*." Will took her arm in his, and her heart did a flip-flop.

"Now that's more like it," she muttered.

"What were you thinking speaking with . . . *that* one?" he asked after Alexander, the grooms, and the horses had all gone their separate ways.

"What are your 'great exploits'?" she asked eagerly.

Will ignored the question. "How long were you with Robertson?"

"Are you jealous?" She perked up. Did that mean he had feelings? Maybe *jealousy* was the key to Will Rollo.

He stopped in his tracks, a black cloud darkening his features. "Jealousy has naught to do with it. Just . . . simply . . . stay away from that man. He's dangerous."

"Dangerous? He's a minister. How can he be dangerous?"

He stilled once more, and this time she stumbled slightly, catching herself.

"You are not to speak with that man," he hissed. "Ever. He travels about doing the devil's work."

"Devil's work?" She giggled at the unexpected reply.

He gestured for her silence.

"Devil's work?" she asked again, in a mockingly grave whisper. "He said he just liked to see the countryside, meet—"

"He's a witch pricker."

"Pricker?!" A loud laugh burst from her. "That's *exactly* what he was—a little pricker!" She had to wipe the tears from her eyes it was so funny.

Will glowered at her, and Felicity thought steam might whistle out of his ears at any moment.

"Listen well, woman," he said in a voice that was deadly quiet. "This . . . *minister* . . . says he does God's work, but I say he's an ambitious prig who thinks to accelerate his ambitions through sensational trials that are a mockery of justice."

She stared blankly. "What are you talking about?"

His jaw tightened. "The man claims he has a gift. For identifying witches. He kills those he finds."

Dread prickled like ice in her belly. "Do you mean like . . . a witch hunt?"

"Aye, that's precisely what I mean. He's ordered the death of hundreds of women. And this has brought him fame." Rollo looked quickly to the right and left. Gripping her arm, he began to walk them slowly toward the inn's front door. "These were innocent women. Some were sick, perhaps.

Some practiced midwifery. And others, I think, Alexander Robertson simply determined he didn't like."

"Oh," she replied, subdued. "It seemed like he liked me . . . He asked so many questions. I think I answered them all right . . ." Her voice petered out.

"You must never forget who you are," Rollo whispered urgently in her ear, and the feel of his breath sent an inadvertent shiver along her skin.

Focus. She had to focus.

"You're so guileless," he accused.

"You make it sound like that's a bad thing."

"Och, Felicity, lass, it's a bonny thing," he said with an earnestness that broke her heart. "But you betray yourself. With a mere look, a mere word."

He slowed even more to buy them more time. "Why do you think we've been taking this godforsaken route, avoiding the larger burghs in favor of these pitiable villages?" He gave a squeeze to her arm. "To keep you safe, Felicity."

He had to stop speaking, for they'd reached the door.

Rollo. Her Viking. He'd been so cold and distant. But it was because he'd been worried, trying to protect her.

Because she had more to fear than anyone.

She wasn't like those innocent women.

She'd made herself travel back through time.

Which would mean . . .

I am a witch.

❦

Rollo hesitated at her door. What he was about to do was entirely inappropriate. He looked behind him. The hallway was dim and empty. Dinner had come and gone. Folk had returned to their rooms for the night, or were drunk in the inn's common room. Nobody would see.

Or, he could simply turn and head downstairs for a mug of ale and some stew.

But Felicity had seemed so alone.

He knew he'd scared her. He was glad of it. The lass

needed some scaring. It was as if she thought she were a part of some great and merry romp.

He'd insisted she stay in her room for the night. What she really needed to do was return to her own time. To let him help her find her way home. But she seemed determined that she'd come back for *him*.

Anguish pierced straight to his heart. A woman, wanting to lay claim to *him*.

It was too much.

Too tempting.

And too risky. She needed to get away, now, far away, from Will, from this time and place.

He dared not get too close. He didn't want to know too much about her. Every day she spent with him was one day too many.

Danger simmered. Fear and greed drove men to heinous acts. Like beheading a king.

Like torturing women in the name of superstitions that should've gone out with the Dark Ages.

The thought brought the handle of his cane up, cracking a knock at her door.

He regretted it instantly.

She is likely afraid, he told himself. She would long for company. Might fear the danger she found herself in.

The door opened, and it was like a wash of sunlight on chilled flesh.

She stood there, and he knew.

Perhaps the gravest danger was to his heart.

Chapter 9

"Hi," she said in a relieved voice, stepping aside for Rollo to enter. "I'm dying in here. I'm sorry. I know you said not to leave, but I'm about to crawl out of my skin, and so I finally just ordered a bath. I heard the woman right outside, so technically I didn't really *leave* the room, and she said she'd bring the hot water in here so—"

"Hush." He touched a finger to her chin, then pulled his hand away at once.

The ghost of his touch lingered on her skin. She'd been desperate to eat, to bathe, to talk to someone, but that one moment of contact made it all fall away. Felicity stared dumbly as he clicked the door shut behind him.

"Do you think you can eat?" he asked.

"Are you kidding?" She brightened at once. "All I've had is bread and cheese. I'm *starving.*"

He gave a curt nod and turned to go.

"Wait!" She reached around him to slam her palm against the door. "You just got here. Where are you going?"

"Easy, woman." He chuckled.

Wow, how she loved it when she made him make that

sound. And calling her *woman* . . . It felt so seventeenth-century alpha male, in such a strangely good way.

She pulled her hand back, and let it graze along his side in an accidentally-on-purpose sort of way.

"I'll return shortly," he told her. His voice had grown tight, and she hoped maybe she and her hand were the ones to put the edge there.

But then fifteen minutes passed, and then another fifteen, as Felicity paced her room, waiting for Will to come back.

She heard another knock and sprang to the door, opening it with a broad smile on her face. "There you—!"

Not Will.

"Oh," she said, feeling a fierce blush creep along her cheeks. "Excuse me."

A virtual army of inn workers were assembled outside her door. A wall of smells assaulted her. Some good, others not so much.

"Can I help you?" she asked, muting a small cough.

"Aye, mum." A woman stepped forward. Faded linen clothing like something straight out of the costume department hung from her plump frame.

"Lord Rollo asked that we deliver this."

"Deliver—?"

The bodies all parted, revealing a small side table absolutely smothered in food.

"Ohh," Felicity gasped. Those would be the *good* smells.

She stepped aside to let the wave of them bustle in, setting up chairs, arranging plates and cutlery, decanting wine.

"Wine!" She grinned, her hands fisting in anticipation.

Felicity felt eyes on her and looked up to find Rollo watching her intently from the doorway. She forgot her hunger, feeling her belly fill with butterflies instead.

Her grin muted to a tremulous smile.

"Thank you," she said quietly, as the small army left.

"I couldn't let you starve." He smiled at her, and her knees buckled.

Rollo swept to her side, his cane clattering to the floor,

to ease her into a chair. "Look at you. You're famished, lass."

His hands were warm and strong on her arm and at her back. The butterflies in her belly moved south, became a hard ache at her core. "*Famished* is an interesting word for it," she murmured. "What did you bring me?"

He muttered a curse under his breath as he bent to retrieve his cane. Sitting across from her, he lifted a lid and the room filled with the smell of roast meat and wine. "You have before you beef in French claret, with bacon and onions."

"Ohmygod," she whispered, actually feeling tears prick her eyes. "That smells so good."

"Scotland has friends among the French. We learned to prepare food from the best."

She looked up, caught his eye, and his hand froze, the lid still perched over the serving dish.

Oil lamps cast a flickering, golden glow over the room. Light and shadows danced on Will's features, his sharp cheekbones, strong jaw, and those intense eyes, focused only on her.

He sat so regally across from her. It took her breath away.

"*Lord* Rollo," she mused.

"Aye?" There was a flicker of humor in his eyes.

"You're a seventeenth-century lord. Who lives in a castle. You wear your velvet coats as easily as my stupid old boyfriends wore their ratty old T-shirts."

The humor in his eyes hardened into something unreadable. "Your . . . boyfriends?"

"Yeah." She waved a hand dismissively. "None of them did it for me. They all ended up being jerks."

His brow furrowed, as if he were trying to make sense of her words. He began to slowly dish out their dinner. "There have been men in your life, and yet you've never married?"

"I've never been asked. Not that I would've said yes."

"Never been asked? Modern men must be daft."

She giggled, startled by the sentiment. "You really do care." She thought about the food on the table and the roof over her head, and grew serious. "You've been so great to me, but I feel like all I've done is gripe and moan."

He'd done so much for her. She'd doubted him, but he'd only had her best interests at heart. "I haven't exactly been the nicest companion these past days."

"You've not met my friend Alasdair MacColla," he told her with a smile. "Trust me when I say you've been a delightful companion."

She ignored the rare glimpse of humor, earnestly wanting him to understand. "But I should've trusted you more. I'll trust you, Will, from now on."

He watched her, quietly weighing her words. He cut such a dashing figure across from her. He'd shaved, and bathed, and looked so elegantly handsome in the lamplight.

He was like a prince in a fairy tale. *Her* prince. He was a gentleman, a lord, some great and noble hero.

He'd kept her safe. There was a fire in the hearth and food on the table worthy of the best French restaurant.

Of course he'd be familiar with fine cuisine, and things like claret, and brandy in cut-glass snifters, not to mention an army of butlers and maids. She'd lost sight of all that, on the road with him these last weeks.

She was suddenly nervous. "I . . . I hope I'm dressed all right. My hair's a mess . . . I've got nothing good to tie it back with. And I aired out my gown"—she looked down, smoothing the lap of what was once her rose-colored confection—"but I'm afraid this thing could up and walk away all by itself."

She felt his hand on her arm, stilling her.

"You look lovely, Felicity."

"Ugh. I look like a wreck. Plus—"

"Shh." He gave her arm a squeeze. "If you tried, you would still be nothing less that the loveliest woman in all Scotland."

Something stilled in her chest. She thought it must be her heart skipping a beat.

"And besides, I think I might just be able to send my suit of clothes off with your gown. They can take a turn about the village together, aye?"

She laughed then, a tension-relieving giggle.

Will seemed so uncomfortable himself sometimes. Maybe that's how he was so deft at recognizing her discomfort and easing it.

"Don't fret," he added, "I'll make certain you have new gowns when we get to my family's home."

"You mean when we get back to your *castle*, right?" She gave him a sly smile. "Wait. Gown*s*?"

"Aye," he laughed, "you may have a gown made in every color if you like."

He pulled his hand away, and her arm felt chilled in its wake.

"And," he said, his voice grown somber, "you can take them back with you."

"Back . . . ?" His meaning dawned. "Oh no you don't. I'm staying with you."

"And meeting Robertson wasn't enough to spur your departure? Felicity"—he gestured to the walls around them—"I'm afraid to let you leave this very room."

His tone softened. "I will protect you, bring you to my home. But the stones and mortar of Duncrub Castle won't be enough to save you if"—he scowled—"the *minister* has you in his sights."

She crumpled back in her chair. Could he be right? Was she in danger? But how could anyone think *she* was a witch? If she kept her origins a secret, they wouldn't. Felicity glanced back down at her dress. She was in period clothes. If she lay low, with Will's help, wouldn't she just blend?

Looking up, she studied him, sitting so stoically across from her. The light glowed on his thick chestnut hair.

The universe had sent her *there*, to *him*. To this man who rendered her insides to mush whenever he spared her one of his rare smiles. How could the universe be wrong?

She frowned, unwilling to contemplate leaving. "The food. It's getting cold."

"Och," he said with a start. "That was ill-done of me. The food. Of course."

"Will you show me what else you brought me?" She dug deep, trying for a smile.

"Aye," he said, readily accepting the change in topic and mood. "You've the beef with claret. A pot of auld reekie—"

"Old *what*? Old stinky?"

"No!" He barked a laugh, and her chest swelled with pleasure.

"Auld *reekie*, lass. Called thus because it hails from Edinburgh. 'Tis simply chicken soup with whisky."

"Oh, yum. My aunt made the best chicken noodle soup." She inhaled deeply. "Total comfort food. Though I doubt she laced it with whisky."

"I thought it best for your nerves. I had them prepare you a whisky toddy as well."

"Wine, whisky, whisky . . . I'm sensing a theme here."

"Indeed." He took the decanter of wine and poured two glasses. "And to crown this theme, I've unearthed a bottle of our host's finest claret."

She gave a dreamy sigh. "You have no idea how much I'd love a glass of wine. Or I guess maybe you did. Wait," she said, taking the glass from his hand, "how *did* you know?"

"Well, if your intemperate condition upon arrival was any indication . . ." He gave her a sly smile.

"Oh." She made a face. "That's *so* not like me. And it wasn't wine anyhow. *That's* the problem. I'd been drinking sangria. Wine with sugar and fruit added," she clarified, noting his quizzical look.

"Oho." He raised his glass to her. "And that is so much worse than mere wine?"

"It is," she protested, leaning over to swat him on the arm. "The sugar will get you every time."

She glanced down at the spread between them. "Speaking of sugar . . . What is *that*?"

"Ah. That, Felicity, is gingerbread. And this," he said, uncovering another treat, "cherry cake with whisky."

"More whisky," she mused. "Are you trying to get me drunk, Mister Rollo?"

"It's *Lord* Rollo," he deadpanned.

She thought that, just then, she might be lighting the room with her glow. She craved uncovering Will's sense of humor even more than she craved a hot shower.

She pulled her eyes from him, turning her focus to the bowl of beef stew he'd ladled out for her. She dug her fork in and stirred, and the most heavenly aroma filled her senses. "I think my mouth is actually, literally watering." She closed her eyes, moaning as she took a bite.

"Ohmygosh." Her eyes shot back open and she set to rifling through the bowl to spear a bit with her fork. "What is this?" She leaned over and, without thinking, held it to Rollo's mouth.

"I . . ." He looked at it, uncertain.

"Come on, just taste it," she said, hoping he'd open his mouth soon, because she was about to feel pretty silly.

His gaze met hers, and what she'd put out there as a blithe gesture became something charged, erotic.

The flickering light caught Will's hazel eyes just so, making them seem golden. He opened his mouth slowly, leaning forward, and Felicity flashed to a thousand different fantasies. Of him leaning toward her, just like that, to taste *her*. Taking her hand in his, opening his mouth just that way, to kiss her palm. Her neck. Her, all over.

He wrapped his lips around the fork. She watched them, those fine, perfect lips, slowly taking the food into his mouth.

The sensation of wet heat widening her, opening her, suffused Felicity. She tensed her thighs, suddenly aware of a maddening need she had to satisfy.

His eyes pierced her with their intensity. What would he be thinking? She faltered, began to pull her hand back.

Will touched her wrist, gently took the fork from her fingers. His touch burned her skin.

He cleared his throat. "That was a turnip. But you're doing it all wrong." His voice was husky, ragged. "The neeps are best"—he carefully dug in his bowl, snagging careful proportions of stew—"when you get just enough with the onions"—he brought the fork to her lips—"and the meat."

She opened her mouth and tasted. "Oh, yes," she groaned, and saw his body gird at the sound she made.

He wanted her. She saw it in his eyes, there in the lamplight, feeding her carefully.

"More," she urged him. She would show him how much he wanted her, how it was okay to want her. Just the thought of it had her body throbbing. "Feed me more."

Hesitating, he fed her one more bite, then grew silent. The air was electric, as if they'd crossed some invisible threshold from which there was no return.

Rollo was quiet as he finished his meal and Felicity saw his eyes flick to the door. "No way, Viking." She'd seen the sex in his eyes. They flashed back to hers, surprised. "No retreat yet."

"I . . ." he faltered.

He wanted her, and so he also wanted to flee. Will's eyes shot to the door.

Uh-oh.

He straightened, his hands shifting to his thighs.

He was getting ready to leave. She wouldn't let him. *Here goes nothing.* "You're not going yet."

Felicity rose, slinked to his side of the table, and settled onto Will's lap.

"What are you . . ." Rollo's body didn't just still, it seized, every muscle hardening to stone. His hands gripped the edges of his chair, as if bracing for impact. "What are you doing?"

"I want that cake," she said, her sultry tone suggesting a whole lot more than cherry cake. Felicity leaned forward to cut a slice, using the opportunity to nestle her rump more snugly in his lap. She knew she'd shocked him, and there was no going back now. Because she would kiss her Viking before the night was out. "There's nothing wrong with a little cake, is there?"

His eyes ran down the length of her, concealed in slightly soiled pink silk. They landed on her feet, peeking pale and delicate from beneath her hem, and he thought he wasn't so sure there was nothing wrong.

This felt so good, there *had* to be something wrong.

"I'm sorry," she said, mistaking his silence. She waggled her feet, and her shifting weight atop his thighs was pure torture. "I hope it's okay. My bare feet I mean."

He realized he'd never in his life seen a woman's naked foot before Felicity's. His mouth went dry.

"I can't bear to wear those tight little slippers. I never wear shoes inside."

Rollo couldn't move. He thought he might have actually tried, but he couldn't budge. It was a wonder he was able to breathe.

"And I totally need a pedi."

"A . . . ?"

"A pedicure." She raised a leg, wiggling her toes. Her dress shifted a few inches up her calf.

He had no idea what she was chattering about.

He couldn't imagine a more perfect foot. Surely there didn't exist toes more perfect, more adorable, than these.

He inched his hands to the sides of his thighs. He was so close to stroking her legs. He imagined sweeping his palms down to touch that sweet, pale foot.

"Look at me, Will," she whispered.

There—she'd spoken his name again. Her voice was cloaked in sweetness and innocence, and it set his body on fire. She gave him a little smile and parted her lips.

She whispered to him, was whispering such sweet things, he thought perhaps he'd died and transcended to some glorious heaven, a place of his dreams peopled only with this exquisite, lone angel.

"Do you think I'm kissable, Will?" She gently took one of his hands, studied it, then held it in hers.

God help me.

His whole body quickened.

Did he think she was kissable? God help him, did he ever.

He'd been fantasizing about it from the very first. Kissing her, touching her, nuzzling her . . .

Ravaging her.

But he'd not thought it could ever happen.

"Because," she said in the barest whisper, "I think I'd really like to kiss you now."

Chapter 10

She leaned in. There it was again, that shimmer of gold in his eyes. They were hooded. Dark and hungry.

Oh yeah. He wanted her. She could see it. Her whole body thrummed, felt poised for some great change.

He moved. She panicked for a moment, thinking that he might try to leave. But then she saw he was merely shifting. Taking his hand from the side of his leg, bringing it to rest lightly around the back of her neck. His fingers wove under her hair, found her skin.

You've got it in you, don't you, Will Rollo?

Her skin beaded tight at once, her whole body ready for him, rallying to his touch. The feel of his skin against hers was heady. It was a simple connection, yet it roused some deep-down craving, stirring her to a fever pitch.

Oh wow . . . What else could those fingers do?

"Please, Will," she whispered. She needed more.

He threaded his fingers through her hair, stroked them back out, and Felicity luxuriated in his touch.

For so many weeks, they'd been in such close proximity,

and yet miles apart. But now, *this*. Her heart hammered in her chest. *More*, she thought. She wanted more.

She still held his other hand in hers. She studied it. It was large and strong, with a thick ridge of callus from decades of gripping his cane. Felicity traced the lines on his hand, lightly ran her fingertips over the thickened skin at the top of his palm. How would that hand feel chafing over her nakedness, those powerful fingers gripping her flesh?

A sudden stab of desire made her flinch, and she gripped his hand, brought it to her chest. Just close enough to feel the uppermost swell of her breast.

"I . . . " His voice cracked. He took his hand from her and clenched it, rubbing his fingers together as if to savor the memory.

"Och," he rasped, shaking his head. Reaching a fingertip to her face, he gently traced the slope of her cheek. "You're too lovely."

"Please . . ." *Please, please kiss me, touch me, grab me.*

"You're too . . ." He leaned closer, his eyes devouring her every feature.

Now, Will, oh please, now . . .

"Och, God help me," he uttered, his voice hoarse with need. Darkness clouded his features, and she glimpsed a lust so keen and so powerful Felicity felt it would submerge her, sweep her away.

She leaned closer still. Her body hummed, desperate for him. His perfect, perfect lips parted. She felt his breath on her mouth.

"Kiss me." Her voice was the barest whisper even to her own ears.

He licked his lower lip, and sparks crackled low in her belly. Too much, he was too much, too unbearably, unwittingly sexy.

Joy filled her, expanded her. She was about to kiss her Vik—

"Mum?" There was a sharp rap at the door. "I've the hot water you requested, mum."

A pained sound escaped her throat. *Dammit. Damn damn dammit.*

"Mum?" There was another knock, louder now. "Are you all right there?"

"I . . ." Felicity cleared her throat. She pulled back, holding Will's gaze for a heartbeat. He was raw. Vulnerable, despairing. And then his eyelids slid closed, shuttering himself to her once again.

Damn it.

"I'm fine," she called testily. With one last look at him, she rose from his lap. "Coming."

Three maids bustled in, but Rollo couldn't focus. He wasn't certain if they'd just saved him, or doomed him to an eternity of anguished need.

His world swam red. He was steeped in desire. His blood boiled with it. His body, wild and hard, his every nerve, mad with it.

He'd spent a lifetime with every impulse of his flesh utterly, deliberately, painfully suppressed. But a thin fissure had begun to crack along that façade, and it was as if he could hear the hounds of hell baying on the other side. The needs of a man, *his* needs, demanding satisfaction, demanding relief, in a cacophony of raging desire.

Dark lusts, primal urges, secret desires, all focused on Felicity. Only Felicity.

"Apologies, mum. With all the food preparations, your bath slipped my mind." Rollo heard the women shuffling around, felt their curious gazes on him.

There was the sound of a metal washbasin clanging onto wood. "'Tis so late, I hope you don't mind, t'won't be a full bathing. Just a wee splash. Though we can arrange a nice hip bath tomorrow, to be certain."

He leaned forward. Gathered his feet under him. Took and clutched at the head of his cane. Somehow pulled himself to standing.

"Will, wait." Her voice was furtive, urgent at his back. But he could only shuffle forward to the door.

He shouldn't have taken it so far. What could he have been thinking to take it so far? He needed to get out of there. Tamp down his hardened groin with a bellyful of whisky.

"Please." She pleaded with him now. He felt the maids' eyes on them and knew it would be the talk belowstairs.

But he couldn't spare her a look. To glance back now would only twist the knife in his heart.

He heard the heavy slosh of water in the bucket. The slap of droplets spilled on the floor.

In his mind, water rolled down her naked body. She'd stand straight, hands combing through her hair. Her breasts would bead in the chill air. She'd cup and wash them, her palms chafing over sensitive nipples. He pictured her delicate fingers. They'd stroke between her legs, cleansing, probing.

God help him.

Gritting his teeth, he shuffled to the stairs. He'd limp his cursed body down, where he'd sit, and drink, alone.

❈

Jamie Rollo walked into the pub, ready to get soused. His family's castle was but a day's ride away, and he always required a good girding with whisky before facing his brother.

Damned William. Jamie knew the self-righteous prig would be making his way back to Duncrub.

He plopped down hard at an empty table. The rickety wood creaked as he sat, and he kicked a neighboring chair free, propping his mucky boots in front of him.

He'd make his bloody younger brother pay for the fiasco back in London. Jamie couldn't believe the cripple had managed to free a prisoner out from under him.

And now his betters doubted his commitment and competence. Outwardly questioned Jamie's ability to manage the simple imprisonment of fools.

Oh, little Willie would pay. Dearly, and for everything.

"Whisky," he called to a passing servingwoman. He'd been riding hard north all day and was in a mood to pickle himself with drink. "And whatever slop you're serving for supper this evening."

He used his heel to scrape at the mud on his boots. It was late summer, and the rain had been heavy throughout Perthshire. "I feel like a goddamned mushroom," he grumbled. "Perth. Sweet bosom of my clan. A seething heap of shit."

"Beg pardon?" the wench asked, setting the whisky in front of him.

"Bring me ale as well, woman. And now." He didn't spare her a glance as she bustled away.

He needed to think. Needed a plan.

He'd return home to wait for his lame brother. Though their father was still alive, the old man had become an imbecile since suffering a fit two years past. And so little brother Willie had nobody to protect him now.

Chuckling, he swung his feet to the floor. Their father had adored Will, but it was *Jamie* their mother preferred. She claimed it was because Jamie favored her side of the family, but he'd secretly known it was that Will's legs disgusted her.

Their mother knew how to love a strapping lad. But a feeble, broken one? No, it'd been Jamie who'd been his mother's chosen son.

Not that Will had needed any more attention. His whole life, folk attended him as if he were a bloody head of state instead of a self-righteous cripple. His series of military victories with James Graham had been the last straw. Who'd have thought a cripple could fight on the battlefield?

He scowled. Graham had been a damned popinjay who'd deserved to die. Though the way the man had been lauded, one would've thought he'd been the bloody Messiah instead of a supposed war hero.

The Graham clan. He cleared his throat and spat onto the floor. Jamie had married Graham's cow of a sister, then wisely left her for a Campbell. At the time, he hadn't cared who Campbell was fighting for; Jamie only knew it was against his brother, and that had been good enough for him.

He'd come to admire Campbell, though. Had come to respect the values that he and their Lord Protector, Oliver Cromwell, stood for.

And so he'd become a key figure in Cromwell's inner circle, chasing down fools who dreamed of reinstating a Stuart to the throne. Cromwell recognized his potential, even if his own father didn't. Jamie's duty was to snare and cage Royalists like rabbits up in the Tower. Until his damned little brother had come along.

"*I wonder at your commitment, Rollo*," Cromwell himself had mused.

Damn his brother.

Planting his elbows on the table, he scrubbed his hands through his hair. Will was a cursed bastard who continued to thwart him left and right. And no matter how exacting his planning, Jamie always ended up looking the incompetent one. Ever since they'd been lads, it had been thus.

Except . . . A smile twitched at the corner of his mouth. Except for his greatest triumph, when it was Will who'd been beaten. The terror on his brother's face when his prized pony charged . . . Jamie chuckled. It had been worth the beating their father had laid into him. His arse had hurt for a month.

The barmaid came back with a pint. She stood for a moment, waiting, but he ignored her, instead taking a big pull from his mug. She stormed off and he sneered, shaking his head. If the hag thought he'd spare her a coin for cloudy ale the temperature of piss, she was sorely mistaken.

Threading his fingers at the back of his head, Jamie leaned back to think.

Putting a burr under that pony's saddle had been inspired. He needed something *that* good, that simple and far-reaching, to get back at his brother.

For the thousandth time, he imagined killing Will. But though he fantasized about it, he wouldn't murder his brother outright. Not because of any moral compunction. He'd simply have the crippled prig alive, writhing in the knowledge that it was Jamie who finally triumphed.

He brought the whisky to his mouth, held it there, letting the fumes burn his sinuses. He needed to think, needed to come up with something that would torture Will for the rest of his days.

A burst of chill evening air had Jamie turning in his seat. A man stood at the door, scanning the room, letting his eyes adjust to the light.

He was taller than average, with hair that shone like a woman's. Jamie glowered. He didn't know what the world was coming to; there were popinjays all around.

He took a big swig from his mug and wiped his mouth on the back of his sleeve. He always acted instinctively boorish when faced with pretty lads like this one. Pretty men in pretty velvet coats were beneath contempt.

Belching, he sat tall in his chair. It dawned on him that he angled for a good fight. His brother was nowhere about, but bloodying up this pretty lad's face would be just the thing.

And he knew just the way.

Downing the rest of his glass in one swig, he watched as the man politely flagged down the barmaid, made his request.

Jamie interrupted them, bellowing, "More whisky."

The man turned and spotted him, and Jamie knew he'd approach the table. He was the only other man there not soiled by a day of hard labor.

Jamie might not be one for lace at his cuffs, but neither did he disguise his wealth. He knew his clothes showed it. Fine materials and a simple, elegant cut. And he knew fops like this one couldn't resist the company of wealth.

"A fine evening, sir," the man gushed. "May I join you?"

Jamie's only response was to kick a chair in the man's direction.

He eyed it, eyed Jamie, and with the merest of shrugs, took a seat.

"M'lords," the servingwoman said.

Jamie looked up, surprised to see the old crow had returned. "You certainly made haste for *him*." He gestured to the stranger who promptly began to dig in his coin purse.

"Oh," she cooed, accepting a copper. "Verra generous, sir." She narrowed her eyes accusingly at Jamie, plunking a chipped bowl in front of him. A charred slab of biscuit glistened on top, the aroma questionable at best.

"Ah, a filthy bowl of"—he inhaled deeply—"let's see. I suppose that's food you've brought us, correct?"

"Shepherd's pie." She crossed her arms over her scrawny chest. "I don't make it. You dinna have to eat it."

He eyed her. The sass was unexpected.

"A moment," Jamie stopped her, digging in his pocket, then flicked a coin in her direction.

Open-mouthed, she stared at him a moment, then quickly tucked the bit of silver safely at her sagging bosom. "Thank ye, sir," she muttered in surprise, scuffling away before Jamie could change his mind.

The stranger had been watching the proceedings with wide eyes, and Jamie's hand twitched with the irrational urge to gesture against the evil eye. The impulse made him more churlish than before.

"To the Lord Protector," Jamie announced suddenly, lifting his glass to his companion. A sly sneer dared the man to challenge the unpopular sentiment. *I'll have my fight before the night is through*, he thought.

A hush fell around them. To propose a toast to Cromwell in such a public spot was at best audacious. At worst, it was suicide.

He'd expected the stranger to take the bait. Rise in some grand, foolish-foppish manner to stand against Jamie. The man shocked him, though, when he merely raised his own glass, chiming, "To the cause."

Perthshire straddled both Highlands and Low, and it seemed folk were accustomed to dissenting opinions, for chatter in the pub gradually resumed.

Jamie took a swig from his whisky, following it with a deep pull from his ale. This stranger piqued his curiosity, and he found he wanted to bide a time with the man.

Jamie belched into his hand. "Where are we anyway?"

The dandy shot him a skeptical look.

"Och, man, easy. I've been on the road. I can't recall how many inns in how many villages I've seen these last weeks."

"Ah," he replied, easing visibly. He smiled and sipped his ale. "I too am a traveling fellow. And we two are currently enjoying the hospitality of *Uachdar Ardair*," the pretty man said with a flourish, using Auchterarder's Gaelic name.

"That close, eh?" Jamie's eyes grew distant.

"Close to—?"

"Och, close to my bloody family." He took a quick gulp of ale and slammed his hands down on the table as if he were turning over a new leaf, then and there. "So tell me, man, how is it you find yourself in such a dreary wee offshoot of Perthshire?"

"I am a minister and a seeker, wending my way through the countryside, sowing the seeds of God's word, nourishing myself on the gentle wisdom of the simpler folk." He sighed gustily. "Until I met a goddess."

"A goddess, eh?" Jamie chuckled.

"A god-dess, I say." He pronounced the word grandiosely, his eyes clouding dreamily. "With hair like the sunlight and the otherworldly mien of an uneasy angel."

"So where's your god-*dess* now?" Jamie tipped the last of his whisky back.

"Alas, she travels with another. And so I come to drown my sorrows on my journey home."

"Funny, we seem to have much the same goal." Jamie's voice had just the slightest slur at the edges.

"To our common aspirations."

Jamie slammed his whisky glass down and raised his ale to the stranger's toast.

"May I know the name of the man who shares my most admirable objective?"

"Rollo," he said simply, swiping his sleeve along his mouth.

The minister spewed ale from his mouth. "Any relation to the Lord Rollo?"

"I *am* the Lord Rollo." Jamie's eyes narrowed. "The eldest."

"One of the esteemed Lords Rollo of Dunning Parish? It is an honor," he said warily. "Though, you are not familiar to me. You must have been away for some time."

"Aye." His voice grew menacingly quiet. "Some time."

"Then"—his eyes flashed wide—"you are brother to the one who claims the hand of my Venus."

Jamie barked out a sharp laugh. "Surely you're mistaken. My brother's a cripple who—"

"I'd know him anywhere." It was the minister's voice that grew quiet now. "He rode with Montrose, for the King."

"Aye, that's the self-righteous prig." Jamie's face flattened, his eyes grown chill. "My brother travels with . . . a woman?"

The minister nodded vigorously, pleased to have met a conspirator as appalled by this turn of events as he. Jamie studied the man. He seemed a self-involved sort. The sort whose narcissism left him guileless, too utterly caught up in his own affairs to suspect the designs of another.

Skepticism turned to a sly sort of hope, as it dawned on Jamie just what sort of grief he could cause his brother. "What's your name, minister?"

"Robertson." He tipped his glass to Jamie. "Alexander Robertson. Witch pricker."

"Robertson of Dunning," he stated, understanding dawning.

"I see you've heard of me?" The minister's affected virtuosity curdled into something considerably less high-minded.

An ego, Jamie thought with a wicked smile. "Oh indeed. Your good works precede you."

He'd strike up an alliance with this minister, he decided suddenly. One never knew when one would need the friendship of a power hungry religious lunatic. It was gravy that the man had taken a fancy to Will's woman.

He'd meet this woman. See if she might not be the dagger he could stab into his brother's back.

Chapter 11

"Wow, it's so pretty here. Look." Felicity pointed. "There's another stream, do you see? Just over that rise."

Will gave a noncommittal grunt.

Felicity looked at him with raised brows, the smile not budging from her face. Will had almost kissed her, and nothing could get her down. Not even his grumpy mood.

Because he'd said she was *lovely*. He almost kissed her *and* he thought she was lovely. *Too lovely*, if she recalled correctly.

"So, what's the difference between Perth and Perthshire anyway? *Perthshire*. It sounds like something from *The Hobbit*." She inhaled deeply, and her breath hung like mist in the crisp air. Will had given her a tartan shawl, and she loved the feel of the chill on her face while her body was so comfortably warm. "That's us, just riding our horses down to the shire."

"It's pronounced *Perth*-sure," Will muttered. "Not Perth*shire*."

Maybe he was grumpy because he *hadn't* gotten to kiss her. Her grin grew wider at the prospect.

"You didn't answer my question," she pressed. "Is Perth—"

"Perth is the city."

"So are your parents close to the city?"

"Somewhat."

"Hey," she exclaimed. Will was no longer by her side, and realizing it, she pulled her horse to a stop. "Where'd you go?" Putting a hand at the rear of her saddle, she twisted her body around to face him. "Is something bothering . . ."

Will's reins were knotted high on his horse's neck, and he was in the process of dismounting.

"What the heck are you doing?"

"It's time for a rest," he answered in a clipped voice.

"Mm-hm." Felicity's eyes narrowed. "We're, what, an hour away from your castle, and you're resting?"

"Aye."

Visions of baths, roaring fires, and hot buttered bread had been dancing in her head all morning. She was not going to stop now. "C'mon, Will. I'm *dying* to see your place. Can't you just rest when we get there?"

"It's not quite like that."

"What do you mean, not like that?" Reluctantly, she turned her horse, walked back to him, and dismounted. "I've spent the past *how many weeks* wanting to rest, and *now* you finally decide to take it easy?"

"Please," he said simply.

She heard something in his voice, something tight, pained even, and she decided not to push it. She would get to the bottom of it, though, she decided. If it killed her.

She watched quietly as he took a woolen blanket from where it was rolled at the back of his saddle. He tossed it to her wordlessly, and then plopped down at the foot of a silver-barked tree.

"All right," she told him. With a shrug, she unfurled the blanket on the ground next to him, and sat on it. "I'm always up for a rest."

Silence.

"How long are we resting for?"

"A while."

"Good. A while." She stretched her legs in front of her, waggling her feet. "A good, long while."

She sighed, looking around. Perthshire really was ridiculously pretty. They were riding along the base of a valley. The stretch of land was yellowed with the season and bordered by grand, old trees. Soft reddish ferns, long grasses, and renegade clumps of winter wildflowers clung to the soil like a lush and ragged patchwork.

Though she missed modern conveniences, she hadn't thought of the city once. Taking in the landscape, she marveled at what she'd been missing all these years. Despite the dirt, despite the discomfort, she'd felt moments of true contentment on their slow ride through the countryside. Just her and Will, with some horses, and gorgeous land all around. It made her wonder what, exactly, she'd been searching for in her old life, when here joy seemed so ready for the taking.

A breeze caught the treetops, and leaves rustled overhead. "Wait," she blurted out, realizing what was missing. "Where are all the birds?"

"There are geese."

"I haven't seen any," she said, studying the sky. "Anyway, where are the rest of the birds? We're out in the middle of nowhere. Shouldn't there be twittering and chirping?"

"I imagine they've flown south. It is almost winter, after all."

"Oh. Of course. We don't really get winter in San Francisco. There are birds year-round."

He nodded quietly.

So much for their little nature discussion.

Was he acting so funny because of what had happened between them the night before? Either way, Will was about to arrive *home*. "Aren't you excited? When was the last time you were home?"

"Years."

"Years? You haven't been home for *years*?" She shifted

to face him where he sat, in profile, against the tree. "Where have you been?"

"At war. There's been much fighting. I'm weary from it."

"Ohhh," she said, as it all became clear. "Is that what the minister meant by your *exploits*? Are you some sort of war hero?"

"Aye. Some sort."

Admiration swelled in her. Of course Will was a hero. The way he sat on his horse, so brave and strong, clocking all the bad guys with his cane and his knife? She should've known it.

"Well then you should be extra happy to come home." She waited for a response, but he wasn't making this easy. Squaring her shoulders, Felicity decided direct was best. "Why aren't you happier?"

"Happier?" He swung his head to face her.

There was something raw in his eyes. Something deeper than pain, more complicated than anger.

She considered backing off, but plowed ahead before she lost her nerve. "You've been away fighting at war. You haven't been home in years. We've been on the road forever. We're finally almost there, and you decide to stop now. *Here*." She opened her hands to gesture to the land around them. "What's the deal?"

"The horses needed to graze."

She didn't buy it for a minute. "But aren't you excited to get home?"

"By *excited*, do you mean *agitated*?" He gave a humorless laugh. "Then, aye, I am *excited* indeed."

She studied him. The dark look on his face spoke to something more than just whether or not they'd kissed. "Is it your father? Are you worried about seeing your father? You'd said he was . . . sick."

"Aye." He raised his chin, inhaling deeply. "Mayhap that's a part of it."

"Well, your mom is fine, though, right? Aren't you looking forward to seeing her?"

Will's sharp laugh startled her. "My mother. Looking forward to seeing my mother? No, lass, that wouldn't exactly be my choice of words."

"You don't want to see your mom?" Disbelief tinged her voice.

"*Don't want to see her.* Aye, that's more the way I'd phrase it."

She looked at Will, feeling suddenly as though she didn't know him at all. "How can you say that? Do you know how lucky you are to even *have* a mom?"

Her mind went to her own mother, gone for how many years now? All Felicity had were pictures. A white-bordered and faded snapshot of her mom as a young girl, in a yellow dress, with blonde bangs and hair curled under. As a teenager, captured by someone's Kodak Instamatic, her hair angular and shaggy. Holding Felicity's hand for her first day of kindergarten, her mom wearing big, dangly earrings and a men's felt hat.

"God, what I wouldn't do to have a mom to disagree with," she said in a small voice. She thought about how hard it must be for women in the seventeenth century. For a woman whose husband was ill, especially. "Come on, Will, how bad can she be?"

"How bad, Felicity?" His voice was cool, shutting her out. Standing, he politely reached a hand down to pull her up. "Come, then. I will show you how bad."

They rode in uncomfortable silence. Will was stiff and brusque, and he acted as if he were headed for the executioner instead of on his way home.

Duncrub was much like Will had described. A grand manor house made of stone, with ivy climbing the exterior walls, and stout chimneys announcing a generous smattering of fireplaces within. There wasn't a single Disney-esque turret in sight.

She was startled by how Will was received. The household staff clearly recognized him, but they acted as if he were the taxman instead of a long-missed son.

"Can I not just go to my own rooms?" Will asked a cold-eyed maid.

"No, m'lord." She whisked them into a large room with

a marble fireplace and paneled with dark, glossy wood. "All guests are received in the drawing room."

"Ah, I am a *guest*." Leaning down to Felicity's ear, he grumbled, "It seems I am no longer welcome to wander at my leisure."

"William."

They spun in tandem, and Felicity saw at once what had made Will want to stop and rest by the roadside.

His mother was lovely. Perfect. A bun coiled tightly at the nape of her neck, not a hair out of place. Though marbled by strands of gray, her hair would still be considered brown. Her skin was just beginning to thin with age, but wasn't so very lined, and Felicity sensed immediately this woman's fury for the beauty she'd once been.

Eek.

Her gaze swept disdainfully over Felicity. Her eyes were darker than Will's, cold and flat, like shiny stones.

A young man appeared at the doorway, and his mother turned, her sharp chin darting like a striking snake. "Fetch William's father," she ordered.

"I'm sorry I doubted you," Felicity whispered quickly. She reached for Will's hand and gave his fingers a surreptitious squeeze.

The corner of his mouth twitched. She savored it, imagining it was as big a smile as she was going to get for some time.

His mother turned her attention back to them. "Who is . . . *this*?"

"*This* is Felicity Wallace." Will's hand came to rest protectively at the small of her back. It was a small gesture, but for a moment it made Felicity feel as though she could slay dragons.

"So pleased to make your acquaintance," she said, managing a smile. Unsure what she should say, she'd chosen what she considered a very old-fashioned-movie turn of phrase.

The room was uncomfortably silent. Felicity's smile felt like a grimace on her face. *C'mon Will, the hand is nice, but throw me a line here.*

Shouldn't the woman shake her hand, introduce herself, *something*? "I . . . I'm afraid I don't know what I should call you."

"I am Lady Rollo." His mother's tone spoke to confusion and just a hint of outrage.

"Oh . . ." *Jeez, lady. Give me a break.* "Of course."

Felicity was saved by a bustling at the door. A small army of household staff bore Will's father into the room on an elaborately reinforced chair.

"I thought you should see the thing your father has become," Lady Rollo said, turning her back to her husband. "I gave up waiting for you to show up, to give me your condolences."

"I've been away." Will's hand pressed harder at Felicity's back, and she wondered if he might just need that little bit of contact too. The anguish furrowing his brow made her wish she could wrap her arms around him.

Tell her, Will. Tell her you're a war hero. Tell her you've been fighting noble fights.

"Besides," he added, eyeing his father across the room, "condolences don't exactly seem in order. The man doesn't appear to be dead yet."

Her gaze went to the old man in the chair. Though the staff had faced him toward the window, she would've sworn Will's father canted his head their way.

"What did you say happened to your father?" she asked in a low voice.

"He suffered a spell," Lady Rollo clipped out.

The man's eyes appeared to track the scene in the room.

Not a spell. A stroke.

"It was quite ghastly," his mother continued. " 'Twould have been better if he'd simply died."

Felicity's eyes shot to Will at such a hideous statement, but his gaze didn't swerve from his father.

Standing tall, she strode over to where his father sat. "It's a pleasure to meet you, sir." She took the man's hand in hers and gave it a squeeze. "I've heard so much about you."

"What are you about, girl?" Lady Rollo's words burst from her like a blizzard through an opened door.

"I think . . . I think your husband's *spell* . . ."

"That man is not my husband. That is a driveling shell of my husband."

Felicity looked into the man's eyes, and she *knew* she saw a spark there. She took a deep breath.

Pissing off the future mother-in-law. Not a great start.

"I bet this . . . episode," Felicity ventured, "it probably just harmed his body, not his mind."

She'd chosen her words with care, but Lady Rollo spun on her all the same. "Are you a physician?"

"No." Felicity felt about two feet tall.

"Then you have no notion of what's transpired here."

"Enough, Mother." Will's voice was steely. "We've paid our regards. If you're through, I need to tend to the mounts."

Felicity shot him a desperate look. There was no way she could stay without him in the room. She was a people person, but this was way over her head. She wanted to get out of there too.

But Will's mother beat her to it. "A man of your station in the stables . . . Vulgar." Lady Rollo was indignant, her tone contemptuous as she stalked to the door. "This whole situation . . . *Vulgar*," she hissed, storming from the room.

Will ignored his mother and looked at Felicity instead. Ambient light struck his face just so, igniting the golds and browns and greens of his eyes. They were warm on her, and Felicity thought she saw affection there. "I truly must go and tend the horses."

"Can I—?" She stood, walked toward him.

"Best not." His eyes cut to his father. "We've enough to explain as it is. I'll return soon."

"All right," she relented. "Then I'd like to stay and sit with your dad for a while, if it's okay."

His nod was almost imperceptible, some untold emotion lining his features.

"And Will? Make sure to drape a blanket over Laddie's belly. I think it's good for his digestion."

"Aye." He pinched her chin between his fingers. "I'll make certain they walk the lad before stabling him for the night."

Chapter 12

The old wooden bucket sat just where it always had. Will nudged it with his foot. All the times he'd eagerly dragged that bucket out, flipped it over, and clambered up onto a horse for his morning ride.

In the days before.

Before his accident. Before he'd seen the flash in his brother's eyes that day. Decades had passed, but still that look haunted him. Such glee had twinkled in young Jamie's eyes, at the sight of Will's terror.

To see such malice in one's own blood was to lose one's innocence forever.

Rollo walked to the old stall. Stepping inside, he ran his cane along the floor, leaving a faint line in the hard-packed dirt.

Though raked out long ago, the whiff of hay and the faint tang of urine prickled his nostrils. The smell of the stables had once been so reassuring. It was a rich scent, of manure and leather oil, and he couldn't help but find the ghost of it reassuring now.

If only he could turn his back on everything and fill his

days with serenity like this. Since arriving home, he'd returned frequently to check on their horses, deciding he'd
give up battles, and plots, and kings to lead a life of peaceful seclusion. To have mornings spent in the stables, his
greatest concerns the baling of hay and the breeding of
mares.

He leaned against the stall door, remembering the child
he'd been. And remembering that poor, damned pony. He'd
been put down that very day. His father had put the bullet in
the beast's head himself.

Will lifted his cane, pushing open the shutters of a small
window. He'd been so proud of that bloody animal, his first
sight of it with its head out that window, greeting him with
a chuff and a twitch of its ears. Dust motes were all that
filled the space now, flashes of white floating in the dim
stall.

Aside from his and Felicity's mounts grazing in a paddock out back, the stable was empty. His mother had no use
for horses about. Caring for his feeble-minded father was
enough for her.

He sighed deeply. What would his father have made of
Will, returning with the strange and lovely Felicity in hand?
Slapped him on the back, he was certain, with an *about time,
fool lad*.

Because it was his father most of all who'd deluded himself about Will's injury. He never understood how so much
more than his son's leg had been crushed that day. Hadn't
understood why Will never chose to marry.

Their fortune would've found him any number of brides,
but it was Will's pride that kept him alone. He'd not suffer the snickers of a pretty young thing when his back was
turned. Or gasps of horror when they saw his crooked flesh.

Pretty young thing. Clenching his eyes shut, he slammed
his head back against the warped wood. What was he doing
with Felicity?

Traveling with her had become pure torture. Renegade
imaginings of the feel of her skin, or the curve of her naked

body, had intensified. His fantasies darkening into pure, torturous lust. He wanted to take her, have her. Bury himself in her.

Her teasing innuendo mocked him. She thought she wanted him. But she didn't know. She was a pretty young thing indeed, carried away on her whims, taken with the magic and the unreality of the moment.

A pretty young thing who'd surely choose the next strapping Highlander to cross her path. He was sure he'd been chosen by the universe, in some absurd stroke of cruelty, to find Felicity just that: some braw hero to sweep her away. Like James did Magda, or MacColla with his Haley.

But Rollo? Such was not his fate. His fate had been written in this very stall over thirty years past. He was a broken fool who'd best remain alone.

The pretty young thing and The Fool, he thought, reaching for his sporran. Carefully he opened the pouch. Carefully removed the strange and colorful card. He'd secured it away, and it was as clean and unbent as the day he'd peeled it from Felicity's arm. *The Fool.*

Him.

The universe didn't get much clearer than that.

Footsteps sounded at the door of the stable. Swiftly tucking the card away, Rollo marshaled his features into a careful mask.

"Will." The whispered voice was furtive, hesitant.

Rollo sighed, pulled away from the wall. Peering into the shadows, he knew whom he'd see. The figure was backlit, setting his red hair to a frizzy auburn halo.

"Ormonde." Will shook his head. "Have you ever in your life made a conventional entrance?"

"But conventions can get so tedious, don't you agree?" He strode to Will, clapped him on the shoulder. "Now tell me what has you sulking in a dank barn, friend. I've spied your woman up at the house. Not getting along with the dearest Lady Rollo, is it?"

"Oho." Will gave him a small smile. "Is that why you seek me out here? You're afraid to run into my mother?"

"No woman scares me." Ormonde gave a rakish cock to his brow. "But truly. Your brother has been spotted. And so I must make haste. You'll recall, Jamie and I weren't the fastest of friends. And though my room at the Tower was charming indeed, I quite prefer less, shall we say, *restrictive* accommodations."

"Jamie's about?" Will's tone grew hard. He was instantly on his guard, wondering just what would drive Ormonde to take such a risk. "What could possibly bring you here?"

"I suppose you'd not believe me if I said it was the pleasure of your company?"

Rollo's eyes narrowed.

"Thought not." Ormonde plucked a bit of hay from his sleeve, gathering his thoughts. "I need to ask you a favor."

"A favor."

"Aye. We need you to travel—"

"I'll not go back to London," Will stated simply.

"It would be but a brief stop on your way to Belgium." Ormonde blunted his words with a smile. "I've found a man who'll take you across the water, to Calais. You'll need to dress as a fisher—"

"Belgium?"

"Our king is in exile there."

"I know who's in Belgium," Will snapped.

"I've been ferrying correspondence between our men in London and Charles II, in Bruges. I'm afraid I can no longer make the trip. You saw firsthand what happened the last time I set foot in England."

"This is too much, Ormonde. Spy games leave the taste of cowardice in my mouth. I'm a fighting man. I face my enemies in the open. I've battled for the King, and would go to battle again. But these intrigues? I am finished with them."

Both men froze, hearing muffled sounds outside. The low chuff of a horse, an answering whinny.

"Away," Will hissed. "Quick now."

He heard boots hit the ground. A man dismounting.

Ormonde scanned the row of stalls. His eyes were bright and alert.

"There's a door," Will whispered. "Through there." Putting a hand to his friend's shoulder, Rollo pointed to an abandoned tack room at the rear of the stable. "Best not come back."

With a nod, Ormonde raced away, the dirt and dust of the old corridor swirling in his wake.

Chapter 13

Will walked forward, putting space between him and his friend. He wasn't surprised when Jamie's silhouette appeared in the doorway.

"I knew I'd find you in the barn." Scowling, Jamie used his toe to scrape a chunk of mud from his boot heel. "Still haven't grown up, have you, Willie?"

"Jamie." The name echoed cold in the deserted stable.

The last time they'd seen each other, he'd freed Ormonde from under Jamie's nose. Will imagined his brother had come seeking revenge, though it was audacious of him to appear in broad daylight. Jamie generally preferred skulking about in the shadows.

"I'm surprised you show your face here," Will said evenly.

"Are you now?" Jamie sauntered down the stable corridor, mindlessly running his fingers along the wall as he approached. "I could say the same of you. 'Tis I who find a parent here, after all. Not you. Mother never could stomach your legs, now, could she?"

Standing erect, Will adjusted his grip on the handle of

his cane, poised to fight if necessary. "Is that what you've come to say to me? My body's destroyed and there's no beast for you to maim, so instead you bait me with taunts of our mother?"

"Oh no, Brother dear. I know you better than that. I know you're happy torturing your own damn self." Laughing, he glanced over Will's shoulder to the end of the barn. "I've actually come to make peace," Jamie continued. "For Mother. Have the Rollo boys be as one once more."

Will bristled. He edged down the corridor, closer to Jamie and away from Ormonde, hoping his friend had already fled through the tack room door. "Never have we been *as one*. What is it you really want?"

"You don't believe me? I even brought your little cane with me. As a peace offering."

Rollo noticed his cane for the first time—the one he'd abandoned at the Tower—dangling beside Jamie's sword in the scabbard at his side. He'd had it specially fashioned, secreting a lethally sharp blade within a walking stick, creating a masterpiece among weapons.

His eyes narrowed. Jamie would know what it meant to him. The gesture would not be made without some hidden price.

"Take it then." Jamie pulled the cane from his side, handed it to Will. "And we can be as brothers again."

"Brothers who keep finding themselves on opposite sides of the battlefield."

Jamie shrugged. "You wound me, Willie." He glanced around, scowling, and muttered, "Christ, I don't know how you can abide this stink. You always did love the fetid confines of the stable yard."

He brushed the dust from his dun-colored britches as if all were settled. "Come now, Mother awaits." Pinning Rollo with a searching look, he added, "As does that woman of yours. I saw her, you know."

Anger erupted, molten steel in his chest. Felicity was off-limits. He'd not have her near his brother. Not have her be even in sight of him.

Will had to protect her, but carefully. If Jamie got even a whiff of jealousy, that would be it. His brother destroyed everything Will had ever cared about. Jamie had maimed his animal: what would he do to Felicity if he got the idea she were his woman?

Will kept his face a careful blank, and so Jamie continued, pressing, "Nicely done, that. She's a luscious trifle of a thing, with a sweet pair of tits."

Jamie began to walk back down the corridor, musing aloud. "Though generally I prefer a little more ass on a woman. Something to hold onto."

Will's body grew rigid, rage flexing his every muscle. *Still. Be still and betray nothing.*

"But what I'd like to know is why she's with you," Jamie went on. "I can't help but feel she's too . . . *pretty* for you. Where on earth did you find her, and pray tell, why is she with you?"

Will stood, frozen in place. His brother walked ahead, oblivious.

"It must be asked, is the girl a wee bit daft? She's up there attempting conversation with our half-wit father."

Will was seething now, imagining all the various ways in which he could murder his brother. He bore both canes now: his favorite, the one which hid his sword, and the one he'd bought as a replacement when he'd thought the other lost to the Tower of London.

He lifted them both from the ground. He'd had years in which to perfect the use of all manner of staves, rods, and walking sticks as weapons. Mapped into his brain were dozens of ways to maim, or to kill. A few swift motions and he could have Jamie cold on the ground.

Lash across the knee. The handle hooks the neck, reaps him down. A strike across the temple finishes it.

Jamie grew still. Enemies they may be, but first they'd been brothers, and brothers *knew*. He'd have sensed the change in Will, would be poised for his attack.

Will contemplated his brother's stiffened back, gathering himself. He'd not sink to Jamie's level. The man was naught more than a swine, and Will refused to roll about in the muck.

Taking a deep breath, he set the tips of his canes back in the dirt. Affecting a cavalier posture he didn't feel, Will strolled ahead.

But he didn't see the malice hidden from him, a reptilian smile that curved slowly at Jamie's mouth.

❀

The stroll back to the house had been a misery. Will hated his slow pace. Hated even more to be the object of his brother's scrutiny. Jamie walked alongside him, making idle chatter, but Will knew that his brother would've been taking great pleasure in the plodding gait.

By the time they reached their mother's drawing room, Will's simmering anger sought release. And it took aim at the most vulnerable of targets.

Felicity.

He'd spent a lifetime taking great pains to fortify himself against his brother's attacks. That she'd made him vulnerable to Jamie's scorn infuriated him.

They walked in and there she knelt, by his father at the window. They'd been at Duncrub for a few days now, and he kept finding her just there. He wondered what she could possibly be thinking of, trying to engage his father.

Sunlight canted in at an angle, pricking bright white strands in her blonde hair. Her prettiness mocked him, fueling his anger.

"Felicity." He bit her name out, hating the feel of his brother at his back. Hating the sight of his once strapping father, now drooling and decrepit, staring dumbly out the window.

But then she turned, greeting him with such a look of open pleasure, he had to grip his canes to fight his knees from buckling.

"Will," she said, smiling. Then he saw her eyes go cold as she looked to his brother.

And Will swelled with pride, in that moment feeling Felicity's beautiful smile to be the greatest victory of all.

"I'll leave you then," Jamie said with a chill in his voice, "for the family reunion. Be sure not to tip Father dear over, Mistress Felicity. He's best approached as more a decorative element than actual additional company."

"Jerk," Felicity said as Jamie left the room. She curled her upper lip in a little sneer.

Will fought not to beam at the darling sight of it. How often he'd made his own sneers at Jamie's back. "If by that you mean my brother's a scurrilous jackass of a human being, then, aye, he's a jerk indeed."

"Jackass?" She giggled. "Shouldn't you say something like, I don't know, *knave*, or *blackguard* instead?"

"What, and all seventeenth-century men must speak as though we're John Donne?"

"I don't know who he is, but William Rollo, I think you just made a joke." Her face stilled in amazement, and the light in her eyes cracked his heart as a chisel would stone.

Felicity stood, and she felt a pang letting go of the moment they'd just shared. She didn't know what it was that had just happened, but she did know she wanted to discuss Will's dad before his jerky brother came back in the room.

She beckoned him closer, but Will had gone back to looking at her as if she had the plague.

"Come on, I won't bite." She felt a little flicker in her chest, wondering what it meant that he had such a response to her. "Come here. I want to show you something. With your dad," she added, getting impatient.

As he approached, Felicity tried to see Will's father as he would see him. He'd clearly been an attractive man in his day. And he wasn't an old man by any means, by modern standards at least. She estimated he was in his sixties, with Will's thick, waving hair turned silver, and the same bright, hazel eyes.

And though his face was a frozen mask, it was those eyes that gave him away. They danced with light, and she was shocked that no one could see it.

"Will, your father's not senile."

"I'd rather not speak of—"

"Now look," Felicity said, ignoring him. She leaned in and pointed to the right side of his father's face. "See how this side of his face looks different? Your father's . . . *spell* . . . or whatever it was that your mom called it, wasn't a spell at all."

She stood and, speaking directly to the older man, said, "You, sir, had a stroke."

Will only watched her. His skepticism was so frustrating. He should be jumping for joy, but all she saw was his grief, simmering just below the surface.

"A stroke," she repeated. "It's like a little explosion that happens in the brain. Well, I don't know how it works, but Will, your father's still in there. He's just having trouble moving."

She put her hands on her knees to lean closer. "Have you ever tried asking him to blink? Like, having him blink if he understands? Seriously," she said, looking up at Rollo, her frustration growing.

Will's silence had been annoying her, but now it seemed like he was ignoring her outright. "Am I the only one who can see that the lights are on in there?" she asked, raising her voice.

"There's no cause to—"

"To yell? I'll yell if I want to. I don't know why you're not listening to me. The poor man has been left to just sit here. Will, your father—"

"Our father can't help you now, Willie."

Jamie stood at the door, chuckling. "Lovers' quarrel?"

Felicity opened her mouth to give the creep what for, but Will shot her a glare so sharp and so abrupt as to silence her at once.

"I heard the commotion and simply had to bear witness. A woman who can get a rise out of my brother?" Jamie made a lewd sneer. "Well, I doubt you could get a *rise* out of him. He is a cripple, after all."

Jamie wasn't half the man his younger brother was, and she wished Will would just walk across the room and clock him one with his cane. But Will merely stood, straight as an arrow, so still he seemed to have stopped breathing.

"Easy now!" Jamie laughed. "I jest, I jest. But I see I must guard my words." He walked to Felicity. "I'd have you believe the best of your future brother-in-law, dear girl."

"She is not—"

"Not"—he interrupted Will at once, his eyes narrowed—"your intended?"

Felicity's heart fell. Weren't they supposed to be pretending a betrothal? Didn't they kind of almost *have* a betrothal?

Jamie turned his attention to her, his eyes roving her body in a slow and overly familiar sweep.

She crossed her arms, feeling suddenly overly exposed in the low-cut gown. *Dream on, punk.*

"How could it be?" Jamie mused. He waited until his brother's back was turned to add in a voice pitched suggestively low, "Then perhaps *I'll* be the one to curry your favor."

Chapter 14

Felicity loved the *shush-shush* sound her leather slippers made along the slate-paved floor. The long corridor was dim and empty, and wearing her new gown she felt like some distinguished and mysterious lady making her way back to her boudoir for the evening.

Or maybe like an impassioned, melancholy nun. Like one of those women in *The Sound of Music*.

Well, maybe not a nun. Someone very grand, though, certainly.

The door to what Will had referred to as the solar was open, and she peeked in, gasping at the sight. Light slanted in through ceiling-high windows. An elaborately carved hearth framed one end of the room, which was furnished with a few small sofas, a card table, and writing desk.

Writing desk.

She decided suddenly that she'd love a little bit of paper. Just a sheet or two. Just enough to write a letter to Livvie. Even if it didn't get delivered for a few hundred years, it would be a way to communicate with her aunt.

She looked up and down the hall and darted inside. The

chair gave a squeak as she sat, and she grimaced, her heart pounding. It wasn't like she was doing anything wrong, she assured herself.

Just a sheet of paper.

Then why did she feel so nervous?

Gently she pulled open the door of the slant-top desk and the hinges gave a hideous squeal.

Ooh . . . fast fast fast. Just a quick peek. Just for paper.

"May I help you?"

Oh damn. She let loose an exaggerated grimace while her back was still turned. Did it have to be his mom? Felicity felt her face go twelve shades of red.

"No," she said, mustering her dignity. Pasting a smile on her face, she looked over her shoulder. "I was just looking for paper."

"But of course." Rollo's mother glided into the room, an exquisite vision in royal blue, her hair pulled back sleek and tight at the nape of her neck. She came to stand over Felicity's shoulder. "You'd be wanting to write to your family."

"Oh, yes." *You have no idea, lady.* If only she could write to her aunt and get some advice on how to handle *this* situation.

"I'll see to it that paper is sent to your room."

Felicity stammered a thank-you, then stared dumbly, waiting for conversational inspiration to strike.

Your son sure is hot, Mrs. Rollo.

Wow, you really are an ice queen, ma'am.

"You have a lovely home, Lady Rollo."

That got the frost to melt a little bit.

"Thank you." His mother gave an august nod, the queen humoring her subject.

Felicity smiled broadly. *She shoots, she scores.* The old Felicity Wallace charm could warm up the iciest of grande dames. "Duncrub Castle is so much more . . . gorgeous . . . than I expected. Will had told me it was more like a manor house than a castle. And he was right."

"Indeed?" The Lady Rollo pursed her lips.

"Oh, yes." *We'll be fast friends. Maybe she'll teach me to embroider.* "I expected turrets and flags."

"Truly?"

"Yes." Was that a flicker of humor on his mom's face? Felicity smiled hopefully. *I'll get her to warm up and she'll be like the mom I never had.* She gave a good-natured giggle. "And maybe even a moat!"

"Mm-hm."

"But this isn't like some old, cold castle at all," Felicity said, imagining her and Will's children running around the grand halls. They'd do things like play cricket, or whist.

Will's mother eyed her, then asked carefully, "Where did you say your family was from?"

"Me? Oh, from . . ." She took a moment to make sure she remembered all the details. "From outside Glasgow."

"I see."

Lady Rollo seemed frosty again, and Felicity couldn't figure out what might have happened.

"Hello dear." She nodded a greeting over the younger woman's shoulder.

Felicity's anxiety was replaced with a little thrill of anticipation. *Will?* She'd been dying to run into him. A whole day had passed since they'd last seen each other, plus she was wearing a new dress. It was the prettiest lavender color, and she'd shimmied her breasts high in the corset herself.

She was getting the hang of this period thing, for sure. *If he isn't going to take charge,* she thought with a quick perusal of her bodice, *I'll just have to drop some serious hints myself.*

Drawing her shoulders back, she tried to mimic Lady Rollo's elegance. She turned, and deflated at once.

Jamie.

His eyes were waiting for her, an oily little smile wrinkling at the corners.

Creep creep creepy.

"Jamie, dearest, our guest seems quite . . . *taken* with our Duncrub. Perhaps you'd take her for a stroll."

"Oh, it's really not—"

"It would be an honor," he said at once, striding over to help her from her seat. Jamie took her arm in his. "I fear my brother has been neglecting you."

She bristled. The close proximity was unwelcome, the feel of this man's body touching hers repugnant. "Not at all," she mumbled, wondering how she could possibly get out of it.

"Has he yet shown you our lovely Kincladie Wood?"

"He . . . no." Her eyes brightened. "But there's really no possible way I could go into woods with these shoes."

"Nonsense." Jamie used the excuse to peruse the length of her.

Creep.

"The path is dry, and you are perfectly outfitted."

"I'd really rather not. I . . . I'm feeling quite tired all of a sudden."

"Then a walk is just the thing to invigorate you. I shall show you the Roman fort. Has Willie told you about it?"

Rollo was *so* not a Willie. And why *hadn't* he shown her around more? "No," she replied, trying to hide her frown.

"Then we *must* go. Come," he said with a little tug to her arm. "I just saw Willie himself, outside. Perhaps he'll join us."

At the possibility of seeing Will, she demurred. And though they didn't run into him, the walk was surprisingly pleasant, along gentle rolls through lush pastureland, amid old trees, clumps of wildflowers, and the reddish fronds of late-season ferns.

He told her how the Roman Empire had made its way there centuries ago, and they walked among the furrows of what he claimed were an old Roman rampart and ditch.

Felicity found herself growing a little easier. Maybe Will's brother wasn't all bad.

"Scotland has so much texture," she said, unthinking.

Jamie was silent for a moment. This Felicity truly was a peculiar one. But so lovely, and unaffected, and he found he couldn't take his eyes from her.

The last woman he lay with was his wife, and she had

the jowly, tight-lipped look of a Campbell. The woman he'd married was nothing like this flower. The walk had flushed her cheeks pink, and her décolletage glowed dewy and pale. He knew she'd have dressed with his damned brother in mind, but it was Willie's own fault if he chose not to appreciate the boon he'd been offered.

"Aye, and just there"—he pointed to a low shrub—"you can see the brambles have ripened."

Jamie couldn't help but flick his gaze down, taking in Felicity's own ripened fruits. He licked his lips, studying her profile.

"Brambles? I'm afraid I've never seen . . ." She roved her eyes over the sea of greenery, uncertain what he was pointing to.

It couldn't be so easy, could it? Jamie chuckled low. "Have you not seen brambles then?"

The girl shook her head in guileless wonder, and he thought how Willie really was missing a good bet.

He walked to one of the bushes tangling the edge of their path and began to pluck a handful of small, ripe berries.

"Oh, blackberries!" she said brightly. "How funny, you call them brambles?" She looked up at him and Jamie watched as Felicity caught herself, schooling her radiant exuberance into something flatter and primmer.

Too easy.

She reached her hand out to try one, but Jamie gave a shake to his head, and brought a berry up to her mouth. Her lips parted automatically, but she blushed at once, looking away.

A small drop of juice darkened the corner of her lip, and Jamie inhaled sharply, fighting the urge to lean down and take her mouth with his.

He raised his hand instead, and, cupping her face, he dabbed his thumb along Felicity's lower lip. He'd meant to pass it off as a cavalier gesture, but his groin tightened at the silk of her skin against his roughened hand, and he dragged the tip of his thumb slowly along her mouth.

She recoiled. "Get your hands off me."

He laughed.

Hastily, she turned to walk from him. His heartbeat sped. He imagined grabbing those hips, spinning her in his arms.

She walked briskly from him, a nervous filly. "I . . . You . . ." She fumbled for words. What was that he heard in her voice? Excitement?

He watched the play of her fine shoulder blades under that creamy skin. Followed the line of her spine down to what he was sure was a tight little ass.

Giving a shake to his head, he adjusted the growing thickness in his britches.

She stopped before a crude stone monument—a cross atop a pile of gray stones. Simple white lettering declared: MAGGIE WALL BURNT HERE 1657 AS A WITCH.

"You've found our monument to dear, mad Maggie." Jamie came to stand at her side, resting his hand on her lower back. "She was burnt here, only last year. Pity."

He eased his hand down. Felt the answering rustle of layers of crisp petticoat. She hopped a step to the side.

"The more zealous of our townsfolk claimed she was a witch."

"A . . ." Felicity swung to look at him, her face blanched the color of the whitewashed letters. "A witch?"

"No need to fear." He chuckled, amused by her naïveté. "They say the flames sear the soul from the body. Maggie's spirit is long gone from here."

Felicity looked frightened, her face the picture of vulnerability and innocence. *Now is the moment to offer comfort*, Jamie thought, and he reached for her. Wrapped his hand behind her neck to pull her close.

"No," she shrieked, swatting his hand aside. "Pig."

The venom took him aback, and he felt an answering wave of hostility sweep cold through his chest.

"Saving yourself for the cripple? You need a man. I don't imagine wee Willie could get his prick hard if he tried." He grabbed her hand, brought it to his crotch.

"What the . . ." Felicity screamed, pulling her hand hard from his.

Fury flushed her cheeks red, and Jamie laughed at the sight. He should've known she'd not be up for a good game. Pathetic, just like his brother.

"I'm going home." She strode ahead, and Jamie had the sense of her being a small and weak thing.

"And by the way," she ranted, "you are such an unbelievable jerk to be hitting on your brother's woman."

His lust soured into loathing. "You're a fool if you think our Willie will marry a girl like you." He watched as she marched ahead, fighting the impulse to catch up to her and shove her faster along the path.

Until he looked over his shoulder, glimpsing once more the stone grave marker.

MAGGIE WALL BURNT HERE 1657 AS A WITCH.

And Jamie's glower eased, chilling into a slow, calculated smile.

Chapter 15

Will opened his bedroom door to find Felicity in the hallway, panting, and with her fist poised to knock.

"Finally," she exclaimed, bursting into his room. She was breathless and agitated, but it only made her look all the more radiant.

She was wearing her new gown, and the bodice molded to her body like a second skin. The light purple color set off the blonde in her hair, and the effect was like lavender flowers and sunshine.

Will scrubbed a hand over his face. What madness had him waxing so rhapsodic?

Fool. You're naught but a fool.

"Where have you been all day?" she demanded.

"Just here," he replied cautiously. Looking from her to the door, he added, "Where you should not be. It's entirely inappropriate for you to be in my rooms."

"Screw that." She stormed back, pushing the door to. "Your brother just made a pass at me."

"A . . ." He furrowed his brows, a cold knot settling in his belly. "What did Jamie do to you?"

"You left me alone all day, and he, you know, he tried to touch me."

The chill in his gut froze into white fury. "I'll kill him."

"No," she said, startling him. "*I'll* kill him. Jerk. He's a total jerk." She stormed to the window, staring out.

"Och," he bit out. "Felicity." It was all he could say. He wanted to go to her. Comfort her. And then murder Jamie.

Instead, he fisted his hands at his sides. He needed to get her out of there. His brother and mother were poison. The latter had spent the better part of the afternoon interrogating him about their guest's origins.

Will would have Felicity safe and away from prying eyes. And from roving hands especially.

"I hate how he keeps calling you Willie," she grumbled.

Rollo's eyes shot to her. The woman had a knack for seeing things as he saw them.

"And I am sorry." She rounded on him. "Your mom isn't going to win any hospitality awards either. Your poor dad. Sitting down there all by himself all the time. Jamie and your mom treat him like he's part of the furniture."

The chill in his heart warmed at her words. "Are you quite finished?" he asked patiently.

She gave him a rueful smile, then inhaling deeply, looked back out the window. "I had to get it off my chest. I feel better now."

"I'm glad of it, lass, but I don't." He stepped closer to her. She didn't see as he reached his hand to hover just above her shoulder. And then, hesitating, pulled it back. "Just stay away from my brother."

"I will." She turned, and they both tensed to realize how close he'd stepped to her. "Just don't leave me again, all right?" Her voice was small, sweetly vulnerable.

And all Will wanted to do was take her in his arms. Nestle her close. Protect her from his bastard of a brother. From any who'd dare to even look at her wrong.

"What were you doing all day, anyway?" she asked.

"Today?" It took Rollo a second to get back in the moment. "I spent the day trying to sort the best way to get you home. We must be away to Lochaber, I've decided. To Cameron lands. There is one there who can help."

"I don't want to go." She put her hands on her hips. "You can't make me go."

She stepped even closer to him, and he edged aside, bumping into the windowsill.

"You're really not getting it, are you?"

He glanced away. It was too painful to look at her, and he gazed sightlessly out the window instead.

"Will." She put her hand on his arm. "Look at me."

His body grew rigid, instantly hard at her touch. At the sound of her gentle, sweet murmurings. The muscles of his bad leg began to tremble, so focused was he on keeping himself in check.

"I want to be with you, Will. I don't know how much more plainly I can put it. Don't you get it? I was sent back for you."

"It's impossible." His voice was a tight rasp.

This is it, she thought. This was her moment. He wanted to send her away, and she had to show him she needed to stay.

"If you don't believe me . . ." Her touch on his arm curled into a steady grip. She waited. Willed him to look at her.

And finally, he did.

His eyes sought hers, and they were tender, and pained, and needful, and the sight plucked a twinge in her heart. The light from the window set his hair to a thousand shades of brown, and she wondered how it was Will didn't realize he was the handsomest, the most desirable, the best of all men.

"If you don't believe me," she said again, "I'll just have to show you."

She reached her hand up to his cheek. He was tall, she thought distantly, taller than she'd realized. The barest scruff of whiskers rasped against her palm. It was such a masculine thing, his nascent beard, and the sensation pushed her over the edge.

"Kiss me," she told him in the barest whisper.

And, finally, this time he did.

His mouth came to hers. For the merest moment he was tentative, but with a moan in his throat, he quickly deepened the kiss. He grew demanding, claiming her, opening her to him.

He was more than she'd even imagined he could be. Hard with just the right moments of gentle, tender but sure.

Finally. Finally, she was kissing her Viking. The thought thrilled through her. She felt herself open to him at once, was flooded with the need for him. Ached to have him near her, in her.

Though one hand twined in her hair, his other remained clenched at his side. As if the moment might somehow shatter, him barely holding on, bracing for some inevitable fall.

Urging him to touch her, Felicity wrapped her arms around him. Pulling him close, raking her fingers through his hair, along his back, under his waistcoat.

Touch me. She was frantic for him to let himself go. There was such passion in his kiss, but still she felt the wall he was struggling to keep between them.

Touch me touch me touch me.

Finally, she simply ran her hand down his arm. She realized he held tight to the handle of his cane. Felicity grasped his hand in hers, stroked her thumb along his wrist, and the cane clattered to the floor.

She pulled his hand up, brought it to her breast. And the groan he sounded came from deep in his soul as William Rollo finally let himself free.

His hands roved her, kneading her breasts, rubbing along her collarbone, her throat, the nape of her neck, and back down to her breast. He pinched her, rubbed the flat of his palm against her, and she thought it impossible to want a man more.

She pulled her mouth from his. "Kiss me," she gasped.

Rollo put his forehead to hers. His eyes were dark and unfocused.

"Och, woman." The husky burr in his voice brought a fresh surge of damp between her thighs. "I am kissing you."

"No, Will." She arched her back. "I mean . . ." How much more could she put her breasts in his face, she wondered distantly. "Kiss me."

He growled then, an animal sound, tight with lust and need and other dark things. Slipping his hand beneath her neckline, he freed a breast from her bodice. She felt his moan on her sensitive skin as he sucked her into his mouth.

Her nipples beaded tight, her want for him excruciating. She arched nearer to him. Threaded her fingers into his hair, pulling him tighter, closer.

There was a distant sound, and she felt him grow still. Her breast slipped from his mouth, bobbing to rest on the shelf of her loosened bodice.

Will moved his head up slowly. Reluctantly. "This is not the place for . . . us." He gave her a chaste kiss on the forehead. Tucked her back in her dress, silently, reverently.

"You'll be the death of me, woman." He gently wiped the glisten of moisture from her lips, wet and swollen from his kiss. "But I die for you a happy man."

"Oh, Will." She tenderly cupped his cheek.

"No, Felicity. Hear me. You are a gift. A wonder. And if I die tomorrow, I die complete."

"Please," she said, making a breathy sound that was barely a laugh. "Don't die tomorrow, now that you've finally kissed me."

"Och, love . . ."

Love. They caught it at the same time. The word had come lightly from his lips, but the sound of it locked their gazes, and intensity held their eyes connected. A thrill crackled through her chest, warming Felicity through.

And Rollo gave her a smile then. A full, open smile, and it was as though he'd never truly smiled before that moment.

❀

Jamie stepped away from the door in disgust. To deny him, and then offer herself to the cripple?

It was unimaginable.

Willie may have won the battle, but it'd be Jamie who'd win the war.

And he knew just the battlefield.

Chapter 16

Witchcraft was a foolish notion. But quite efficient when it came to dispatching unruly women.

The memory of his brother suckling at Felicity like some ravenous calf made Jamie's chest tight with rage. *Unruly* indeed.

He'd taken a brief detour, wanting to pass the grave marker before he got to Saint Serf's. Jamie contemplated the stone cross, the crudely painted words. Maggie Wall burnt here.

Always his brother got what he wanted. *Always ever.* And it would stop. Willie would pay, once and for all.

And Jamie would let the fine minister of Dunning do the dirty work for him.

The church struck him as a crumbling old thing, but he knew this minister would have naught but pride, and so Jamie mustered an enthusiasm he didn't feel.

He found the pathetic man strolling the gardens like some king surveying his holdings.

"Robertson." Jamie forced a genial smile. "And so I find you."

"Ah, my friend!" Alexander Robertson strolled over, greeting him with a gratified smile. "So happy you've come. 'Tis an enlightened man indeed, who chooses to acquaint himself with the pearls of his community."

Vain, self-regarding ass. "Aye, 'twould be a grave error to visit Dunning and miss the sight of your glorious parish." *Or of you in action, witch-hunter.*

"Truer words, my friend." Robertson nodded somberly. "Truer words."

The minister brightened, spreading his hands wide to gesture to the church behind him. "But I am being remiss. Would you like a tour? Our steeple tower is impressively ancient. Norman, in fact, and quite the commanding presence in our humble valley. Though"—Robertson put his hand to his forehead in exaggerated dismay—"you are from a fine tradition of Lords Rollo, you would know this already, of course."

"But of course." Jamie wrenched his smirk into something approximating glowing admiration. "From our mother's breast, we heard of the glory of your fine place of worship, and of the men who minister here."

His smile grew genuine as he realized he was enjoying himself. He only wished he weren't so impatient . . . he imagined he'd find great pleasure in toying with this man over the long term.

"Sadly, church business is not what's brought me here today," Jamie said, shaking his head in affected distress. "Or, rather, what I have to share is of the *utmost* concern for your fine parish."

Robertson stilled, and Jamie felt the early flushes of triumph. He'd known the man would crave drama like a fishwife her husband's ear.

"Pray," Robertson said gravely. "Pray tell of the news you bear."

"I met the woman you claim to love."

"You . . ." The minister canted his head, the strange turn to the conversation throwing him. "You've met her? My goddess?"

"Aye. Her indeed. One Felicity Wallace. And, my

friend"—he rested his hand amiably on Robertson's shoulder—"I think you dodged a grim fate."

"Truly? But why?"

"Well, it's . . ." Jamie mimed hesitation. He needed to hide his smile now. This was becoming quite the lark.

Be somber.

Till the soil.

"I'm certain it's nothing really. It's just that there's something . . . peculiar about her."

"Aye?" Robertson's voice was a tight whisper.

"Aye." *The seeds of doubt.* "I saw her plucking strange herbs from the woods around Duncrub. She moved with such purpose. As if . . ."

"As if?"

"As if . . . well, it was as if she were concocting a brew."

"No! A brew?"

"Aye." *I sow.* "And then there was her talisman."

"Lord protect us," Robertson hissed, raising and kissing the cross that hung from his pocket. "A talisman, you say?"

"Indeed." Jamie struggled not to laugh. The talisman was quite the stroke of last-minute brilliance.

"Is it"—Robertson lowered his voice to a frantic whisper—"witchcraft?"

"Oh no," Jamie replied quickly. "Certainly not in your fine and God-fearing parish. Though . . ."

"Though?"

"Though it is odd . . ." Jamie let his voice trail off.

"Odd?" Robertson stepped closer, an eager coconspirator.

"Well, it's only that . . ." Jamie made as if he were conceding. "I didn't see her at vespers on Sunday."

Robertson gasped. "Quite right. You are quite right, my lord. She was *not* at vespers. I know I would have seen her."

"Then perhaps we should be on our guard, Minister Robertson. Well pleased I am to have such a vigilant leader of the church among us. Well pleased indeed."

And then I shall reap.

❧

"And you're sure you're not cold?" Felicity leaned down, looking in the eyes of Will's father. A small flock of servants had helped her carry the man's chair, with him in it, outside into the formal gardens.

Perfectly squared-off hedges were softened by shaggy clumps of wildflowers and an extensive rose garden. But, at the moment, it was the privacy Felicity appreciated best of all. She wanted to try to connect with his dad without having to worry about prying, judgmental eyes. "Don't forget, it's blink once for *yes*, and twice for *no*."

He gave a slow, owlish blink.

"Wait. I'm sorry," she said with an exaggerated shrug. "I forgot my question. Are you cold, yes or no?"

He blinked twice, and she would've sworn the man was trying to smile.

"Good. Well . . . just blink a bunch of times or something if you change your mind." She began to neatly fold up the woolen blanket she'd brought outside. "I volunteered at a hospital for a while. I helped rehabilitate people just like you. I'd thought for a while that I wanted to be an OT . . . that's occupational therapist. But . . . I don't know."

Sighing, she sat down on the bench across from him. "I just never took to it. I always ended up getting too emotionally involved. All these people whose lives had been so profoundly changed . . ." She frowned. "I used to get *so* depressed."

Felicity adjusted her skirts on the cold stone. "I guess I've tried everything at one point or another. At least it seems that way. I really thought I wanted to help people, but I don't know. Maybe I'm the one who needs help!" she joked, leaning in as if sharing a conspiratorial laugh.

"Hold on," she said, suddenly serious. "Am I talking too much? I think I have a habit of—"

Will's father quickly blinked twice.

"Oh." She smiled at him. "Good. Because I was going to say, I'm a lemons from lemonade kinda gal. Wait"—she gave a little shake to her head—"I mean lemonade from *lemons*. Anyway, you get the point. My aunt—Livvie—I told you about her earlier?"

She waited for his blink and then continued, "Well my Aunt Livvie taught me to make the best of things."

She grew quiet, thinking of her aunt. What would she make of all this? Making a wish on that candle and ending up in the past? Knowing Liv, she'd probably high five her.

Felicity shook her head. "Goodness knows, my life hasn't always gone the way I expected."

She paused, looking at the garden around them. Her life sure had hit some unexpected curves. And yet, Felicity couldn't help but think it'd been all those painful twists and turns that had brought her to Will.

"And now I've met my hero, and gee, talk about mixed signals." She gave Will's father a pointed look. "I wish you could answer me. I sure would love some wisdom about your son."

She tilted her head back, looking to the sky on a lengthy exhale. "He . . . *wow* . . . where do I begin? He drives me *crazy*. And boy do I mean crazy in *all* meanings of the word." She looked at him through slanted eyes. "Well, I won't go *there*. But suffice it to say, I adore the guy. And I think he likes me. But he seems determined to get me the heck out of here. I tell you, your boy Will is breakin' my heart."

"He can't answer you, you know."

"Oh!" Felicity turned to see Rollo approaching across the lawn, and a giddy flush of anticipation made her stomach flutter. "Will. Hi."

She whispered to his father, "Speak of the devil. You don't think he heard, do you?" she asked, biting her lip.

The man blinked twice, and she squeezed his hand. She didn't have many memories of her own father, and it delighted her to feel like she had a friend in Will's.

Rollo set a tray of food beside her on the bench. "I saw you out here and thought I'd bring my father's meal myself. I've just now summoned a maid to feed him."

"What?" Felicity pulled the tray toward her. "We don't need a maid. Jeez, *I'll* feed your father." She lifted a square of linen to reveal a yellowish broth. "Gross. What is this? Is this what they feed you every day?"

He blinked once, holding his eyes shut for a beat, as if to express his misery.

"That's horrible! You poor man." She rounded on Will. "The poor man, he only gets *this*?"

"I beg your pardon, but don't tell me you truly think you just communicated with the man."

"I certainly did." She scooted to the edge of the bench, ready to spoon the broth into his father's mouth.

"Don't worry, Mister Rollo," she told him, "I'll see to it you get something better to eat. If I have to mush it up myself. *Yuck*," she added with a shudder. "You must be sick of this slop."

"So the man shuts his eyes for a moment, and you think you're having a heartfelt chat? If so, you'd best be informed that 'Mister' is definitely not the chosen form of address for my father." Will chuckled, and Felicity was torn as to whether she was more annoyed by him, or charmed by that sexy little laugh.

Deciding to ignore him altogether, Felicity squared her shoulders. "Your son doesn't think we're communicating. That means he won't mind if we talk about *him*. So tell me, Mister Rollo . . . you don't mind if I call you *Mister* Rollo, do you?"

He blinked twice in quick succession, and Felicity shot Rollo a victorious look.

"Tell me, did Will ever have a girlfriend?"

Rollo made a choking sound, and his father gave two short blinks.

"I find that shocking," she said innocently. "Don't you?"

One blink.

"He is, after all, a fairly decent-looking man, objectively speaking."

A long pause followed finally by a brief blink.

Felicity snickered. "I mean, you'd think the guy would provide you with some grandkids."

Another blink.

"I know he's all hung up about his legs, but methinks the loins are still operational—"

"Good Lord, woman," Will exclaimed.

His father's eyes grew very round.

And then Rollo laughed, from deep in his belly, and she flushed warm with the sound of it.

"That is quite . . ." He shook his head in awe. "Nay, Felicity, *you*. *You* are quite something. I dare say, you've proved your point."

"Thank you," she said primly, and resumed spooning the broth into the man's mouth.

"You know, Will." She sat back, watching as his father swallowed. "If he has enough muscle control to swallow, he can probably speak again."

Will didn't respond, and so she turned to catch him staring at her in silence.

"Truly?" he asked quietly.

"Yeah. I think so." She shrugged. "I make no promises. But from what little I know . . . I think that's how it works."

"To be given back my father . . ." Will locked eyes with him. Tears hovered in the older man's eyes. "Can you truly understand?" he asked him.

His father blinked once, and moisture spilled down his cheeks.

"Och, man." He stood, gripping his father firmly on the shoulder. He stayed there, hand clasped tight. "All this time . . ."

"You're so lucky," Felicity mused gently. "I lost my father. I'm glad for you, Will. So glad you're getting a second chance with yours."

Rollo pinned her with a searing glance, and she wondered if he weren't seeing her, truly seeing the real her, for the first time.

"Aye. I have my father returned to me." He leaned over, brushing a kiss on the top of her head. "And it's all because of you."

"You're welcome." She raised her brows impishly. "That was a thank-you, right?"

"Indeed." Her mischievous ways startled him, delighted him. Stretching out his hand, he had the strange compulsion to play along. "Now, come."

"Well, then! Excuse us, please, Mister Rollo," she said smiling and taking Will's hand. With a tilt of her head, she asked, "Are you taking me somewhere to show me your appreciation?"

He paled, sparing a quick glance at his father. "No, I'm taking you for a turn around the garden." Pitching his voice lower, he added, "Believing as I do that my father has heard quite enough for one afternoon."

He led them toward one of the garden's many flower-beds.

"Will you be regaling me with praise as we go? Like, how wrong you were not to believe me. How talented, how brilliant—"

"Och, woman. Enough." He chuckled, adding his own silent litany. *How beautiful, how adorable, how luscious . . .* He leaned down and, pulling the *sgian dubh* from where it was tucked at his calf, cut a small handful of blooms that had taken root amidst the decorative paving stones.

"Don't think you can change the subject with that sexy James Bond sock knife of yours," she told him.

"Would you still that tongue for but one moment?"

"What's that about my tongue, William Rollo?" she countered with a purr in her voice.

His unruly cock stirred in response.

"*Ist,*" he whispered, standing and stepping toward her. He moved slowly, and in the four paces to her side, he felt his heart drift from lighthearted, to focused, to somber.

Her face stilled to see the handful of humble flowers he'd plucked for her. Bright blue blooms atop long, thin stems. He felt suddenly nervous.

"Harebells," he told her, placing the posy in her hand. "My favorite. Always so sunny and upright." He tucked a loose bit of hair behind her ear, thinking he could as easily be describing Felicity as those flowers. "A tenacious wee blossom, just like you."

"Oh, Will. They're lovely." She brought them to her nose, even though he knew they held not much scent beyond the freshness of green and sky. "Just perfect."

She seemed at a loss for words, and the thought that he might have caught her off guard was surprisingly, deeply gratifying.

"They suit you." He wondered at the ease he'd found with her, this newfound comfort that had loosened his tongue, giving him words enough to quiet one like Felicity. Cupping her cheek, he lay a chaste kiss on her forehead. "My wildest wee blossom of all."

"Too bad my eyes aren't blue to match," she said with an awkward laugh.

"Your eyes . . ." He took her chin, tilted her face to his. "Never have I seen such expressive eyes. Lush and brown. Rich like the earth, like the trees. Beautiful beside your hair, yellow as the sun. Nay, Felicity, your eyes are just right."

He saw tears shimmering in those eyes, and the sight stabbed him. "But whatever is the matter?" He gave her a gentle smile. "Should I have picked you some fine roses instead?"

"Oh no. I'm definitely not a roses girl. I . . ." She was quiet for a moment, studying the posy in her hand, and he was pleased to have moved her so. "Thank you," she said finally.

She gave him a shy smile. "See, you say you're not the chivalrous knight in shining armor, but I knew you would be."

"No, lass, I said I wasn't a Viking." He tenderly kissed the moisture from the corner of each eye. "I am, however, most pleased to settle for knight."

A bright, loud laugh burst from her, such a joyful feminine sound, and he couldn't help but laugh with her. And the feel of it filled him, expanded him. So many years without joy, to laugh with this woman was intoxicating. A revelation, a rapture.

A gift without price.

❀

"I see," Robertson whispered. They watched from afar, through a break in the hedgerow. The minister trembled with some heightened emotion. "To speak so with your imbecilic father . . ."

"Aye," Jamie said. His father, communicating? He couldn't believe it. But still . . . he fought off a peculiar, discomfiting feeling.

"The physicians claim it was a spell," Jamie continued with a stiffened mouth. "But I believe it was evil spirits that overran my father's body. Dark demons, which rendered him mute. His eyes waver madly now, from the visions they sow in his head. Only a witch would converse with such a man."

"So I see," the minister said again.

And Jamie watched as Robertson's face froze into a mask. Of alarm. Of shock. And a flicker of elation.

Chapter 17

Rollo's gaze clung to the sight of Felicity on the path ahead of him. They walked among the precisely manicured hedges and stone statuary of his family's formal gardens, and he couldn't take his eyes off her.

More specifically, he couldn't tear his gaze from the sight of her hips, swaying back and forth beneath all the godforsaken layers of fabric that hid her curves from him.

He didn't know what he was doing. He needed to be paying mind to Jamie, trying to figure out what, exactly, the knave was about.

Or tending to his father, trying to connect with the man. Will had dozens of questions for him. To discover that he'd been in there, cognizant, all this time? It gave him a chill.

And then there was Ormonde. Will hoped the man was safe. His flame red hair didn't offer much of a disguise if Jamie's spies were about, and it'd be straight back to the Tower for him. Hopefully his message to Ormonde had been clear: Will wanted naught more to do with the Sealed Knot men.

No, there were many things Rollo needed to consider, and

to do, and yet he couldn't bring himself to tear his eyes from
this woman. And so, here he was, strolling. The only thing
commanding his attention, trying to imagine the curve of
what would surely be a pale, sweet backside.

Thinking on it now, he realized he'd only given mind to
how beautiful Felicity was. Lovely, with unguarded ways,
always with her innocent chatter. She was like a light shining
straight into the dark chambers of his heart.

But now he'd seen another, different facet. She was so
much more than merely pretty. Watching her communicate
with his father, Rollo realized just how special, just how extraordinary a woman she truly was.

Did *all* who met Felicity feel her light blaze straight into
their hearts? He marveled at the thought.

She'd stopped on the path, and Will let himself walk right
up along her back. He didn't touch her. Such indiscretion
would be too reckless so close to his family's home.

But still, Rollo allowed himself to hover, just against her.
Near enough to feel the heat of her through her gown. He pressed
closer. Felt the give of fabric against his hardened groin.

She was sweet torture, this woman.

"Are you even listening, Will?"

No indeed. He took a deep breath in and exhaled through
his teeth. "Apologies. You were saying?"

"These gardens . . ." She canted her head, studying a particularly extravagant topiary hedge. "This is nuts. Who takes
care of all this stuff anyway?"

"My mother has people," he replied, distractedly examining the hedge before him. "I've never given it thought. How
peculiar," he muttered suddenly. "Her tastes in topiary do
seem to run to the . . . Byzantine."

She giggled, bumping her hips back to nudge him. The
brief jostling pressure had dark thoughts furrowing his brow.
She was frisky as a kitten, and here he was, about to explode
right on the spot.

He closed his eyes, breathing deeply to gather himself.
But all that did was bring her scent more clearly to him.
She'd washed her hair with something smelling of roses.

"I mean, you already live in the most spectacular garden in the world." She waved her hand, gesturing toward the hills lining the horizon. "It's just weird to me, this whole formal garden concept."

"It . . . I . . ." What to say? What was she talking about? He needed to gather himself. His arm stretched stiffly toward the ground, gripping the cane at his side. His eyes went to her hair, the source of this scent that was suddenly driving him mad. "I see you finally sorted out the issue of your hair."

"Huh?" She tilted her head to look up at him, and he thought the sight of those bright eyes trained only on him would surely be his undoing. "What on earth are you talking about, Will?"

He cleared his throat. "Your hair. You kept saying it was driving you mad. You seem to have sorted it out," he added, his voice finally steady.

"Oh." She seemed to visibly deflate. "No, it's still making me batty."

She lifted her hands to feel the mass of it at the nape of her neck. "I thought having it always in my eyes drove me crazy enough. But then some girl helped me this morning, and"—she ran her fingers along the tight looping bun—"ow!"

She shot him a dramatic pout. "She put *pins* in my hair. She kept sticking me, over and over. I swear she was using straight pins. I wouldn't be surprised if I were bleeding under here. All I want," she muttered on, "is a barrette, or a rubber band, or a scrunchie, or a head band, or a butterfly clip, or—"

"Hush," Will whispered with a small smile on his face. "This is my home," he said, letting his cane drop to the ground. "And when you are in my care"—he slowly ran his fingers along the sweep of her bun, carefully removing each pin, one by one, dropping them with exaggerated disdain to the grass—"you may wear your hair however you like."

As he pulled the last pin free, her hair spilled down her back. Felicity shuddered in pleasure.

"Ohmygosh. That feels so . . ."

The feel of her hair loose. The feel of Will at her back. The feel of his fingers on her.

The sensations overwhelmed her. The man drove her crazy. Didn't he see? Didn't he see how good they were together? He was so caring, and gentle, and thoughtful, and he had no idea how great he was.

He was utterly silent, lacing his fingers in her hair, pulling them gently through. He rubbed her head. Massaged the nape of her neck. Traced his thumbs lightly around the curve of her ears. Brought his hands back up to scrape his fingertips lightly along her scalp.

"Oh that feels so good." Felicity didn't understand why it was that every woman in Perthshire, or wherever it was he'd said they were, wasn't all over Lord William Rollo like white on rice. "Will, you have *no* idea, do you?"

"Hm?"

"You've got no idea," she whispered, turning to face him. She pressed the front of her body against his. Feeling his arousal, her eyes widened.

"Ohh," she said with a wicked smile. "Maybe you have some idea then."

Felicity reached around to graze her hands lightly down his back, along his ass, stroked back up. He wore only his shirt and plaid, and the rough wool clung to her palms. The fabric slid over his body, and she felt each curve of muscle and flesh.

"I don't think you have anything on under here."

"This . . . this is unseemly." Breath shuddered from his body. "We must—"

"Is that your sporran, Lord Rollo, or are you just happy to see me?"

"Och, Christ, woman . . ."

"Come on." She nipped her teeth at his shirt. "Can't we duck into a . . . whatchamacallit . . . a hedgerow or something?"

"I . . ." Will brought his hands tentatively to her shoulders. "But the others . . ."

She glanced around quickly. "There aren't any others. Come on." She began to step back, away from the house, to the fringe of trees in the distance. "Take me into the woods,

Will. Your stupid brother took me into the woods," she added, a dare in her voice.

"I fear my own base impulses far more than I fear my brother," he muttered darkly.

She'd love to get a load of Will's base impulses. "Then please, by all means. Trees. Now."

She reached around his shoulders and slowly stroked down, all the way to the backs of his thighs. "Let me just get your cane." Ever so gradually, she began to squat to the ground, drawing her hands lightly down his legs.

He was erect, his kilt tented out before him, his flesh extended long and solid, just for her. It gave her a ripple of pleasure.

She let her cheek graze his cock as she lowered herself to kneel. Will groaned at her touch, and the ripple in her belly swelled into hot, wet need.

She continued to move down, slowly.

He flinched as she reached the gnarled curve of his right leg, but she flinched back, a brief, hard grip that stilled him.

Her knee reached the ground. She took his cane from the grass. Pulled back up to standing, skimming even closer to his body as she rose.

The hard length of his erection settled between her breasts. She rubbed herself along it as she stood.

Their eyes met. He was coiled, grim, every aspect of him tight and dark with desire.

"Come," he told her, his voice a low rasp. He pulled her around the corner of a boxed-off hedge into a tight cul-de-sac of shrubbery. The green walls reached overhead, punctuated by statue after statue of mythic figures, their blank marble eyes staring sightlessly ahead.

She pulled from him, turning to tug at his kilt. "You've got to get this off." Her fingers fumbled with his brown leather belt. "You can't just show me this"—she paused to stroke his thick bulge—"and expect me to ignore it."

"The plaid stays on," he gritted, spinning her back around to face one of the statues. It was some wide-shouldered goddess, her hand raised in a gesture of triumph, or judgment.

"Then shouldn't we . . ."

He wrapped his arm tight around her belly, grinding himself into the back of her skirts.

She shivered, slumped into him.

"Shouldn't we . . . ?" he mimicked her, his voice pitched wickedly low. His accent, husky and warm in her ear, shot every nerve in her body to attention. Nestling his face in her hair, his mouth found her earlobe and he gave her a light nip.

"Oh." She shuddered in a breath. "Nevermind."

He wound his hand in a swath of her hair and exposed her neck. The air was cool on her skin, and her nipples pulled tight.

"I'll not be taking you in the woods like some savage." His body still cradling hers from behind, he trailed slow kisses up her neck. "But there'll be none the wiser if we are two merely admiring the statuary."

"You are full of surprises," she said breathlessly.

He raked his hand through her hair. Cupping the back of her head, he tilted her face to him and took her in a hard kiss.

God she wanted him. Craved his hands on her, all over. Just when she thought she couldn't wait a moment longer, Will eased his other hand down the belly of her gown, pulling her closer. She moaned into his mouth.

She felt him hard and urgent at her back. His hand grazed even lower, cupping firmly between her legs.

A gasp tore her mouth from his. "Yes, Will."

Holding her more tightly, he began to knead his fingers steadily, rubbing her through the layers of fabric.

"Someday"—his voice was hoarse and hot in her ear—"someday I will see you torn from this gown."

The mere suggestion of Will, standing behind her naked instead of covered in all these clothes, made her muscles quiver. She sagged even more against the hard length of his body. "Yes. Please."

Will held her securely to him. "Hush, woman. And listen."

His hand worked faster, and the chafe of linen over her bare flesh had her body shrieking for release.

And for once, Felicity was rendered speechless.

"I will have my hands on your bare body." His palm ground against her in a steady rhythm.

Muscles deep in her core began to clench.

"I will touch you," he threatened through gritted teeth. "And I will take you."

Her knees buckled. Rollo's strong arm held fast, his hand cradling her even tighter. Need and pleasure thrummed through her, suffused her.

"And I will have you." He stroked more firmly, through all that fabric, and her pelvis rocked against his palm, urging him on.

"Yes Will," she breathed. Her whole body trembled. She felt flushed, hot, weak. "Please."

"Every inch of you will be mine."

And Felicity felt his growl of release resonate through her, as he pulled her close, pumping hard into her back, riding her climax with his own.

Chapter 18

"This is something I've only dreamt of." Will tenderly straightened Felicity's skirts and smoothed her hair, and the look of pleasure on her face had him prolonging his touches long after she'd been put to rights. "You are something I could only have dreamt of."

"Does this mean I can stay?"

Stay.

No, he thought.

Yes.

Impossible for her to stay. Impossible, too, to say goodbye.

"It means . . ." he faltered. Would he really push such joy from his life? He didn't remember anymore why he'd once tried.

"It means we can discuss it, maybe?" she asked innocently.

"Aye." He smiled and watched her bend down to shake dust from her hem. His gaze dragged over that fine, firm derriere. The feel of it through her skirts had been just as sweet as he'd imagined it could be.

And some day he'd see it bare. Grip her bare hips in his hands, and ride her completely, utterly naked.

She stood, catching him, and gave him a quizzical look. Realization lit in her eyes. "You were checking me out!"

He felt the blood rise to his cheeks.

"Admit it, you were checking me out and . . ." Pointing a finger at him, she gave him a satisfied smile. "You're blushing again. And *now* I know what it means."

Shrugging, he gave her a smile, feeling a rush at such a trivial exchange.

"Mm-hm. Don't play innocent with me." She lifted her arms, gathering her hair and smoothing it from her neck. Her breasts strained against her bodice with the gesture, and Will felt his body stir, again, already.

"You gotta take it easy on a girl," she told him, blithely chattering away, oblivious to the turn his thoughts had taken. "You men are lucky. For you, it's a onetime deal. You do it, you're done, and in my experience, you roll over and sack out."

He looked at her, perplexed. Was she discussing what he thought she was discussing?

"A woman, though. You touch me like *that*." Nodding toward the sculpture garden, she made a delicious little moan that shot life straight between his legs. "That just gets me going."

Again already indeed, he thought, sliding his sporran to his hip.

"So don't be checking me out if you have no intention of touching the goods."

Rollo's eyes narrowed, her meaning now crystal clear. "You are mistaken," he told her in a low voice. He, in fact, had every intention of handling her goods. Furtive groping in the sculpture garden had him decidedly *un*satisfied.

"Because I'm not nearly done with you," he warned. "You once told me that *I* had no idea," he continued, stalking toward her.

He'd thought climaxing would release the pressure he'd been feeling. And he'd been wrong. This hard knot between his legs that was his cock remained a constant ache. "'Tis *you* who have no idea, Felicity. No idea what I've been living with."

Her eyes flicked to his plaid and back up again. The prettiest little flush suffused her cheeks, and such pleasure, such lust raged through him, his cock jumped in response.

"I am far from satisfied," he gritted out, and there was no need for him to feign desire rekindled. The conspicuous stiffness under his plaid said it all.

A wicked smile curved the corners of his mouth. "And now see who is the one blushing."

Rollo let his eyes rove her openly now. His stolen glimpses had only whet his appetite, and he let himself linger on those breasts, those hips.

"Trees," he growled, mimicking her earlier words. "Now."

This is the moment, she thought, her heart racing. She'd been harboring this wet ache for this man for so long now, and finally, finally, she'd find release.

She didn't know how they made it from the garden, to the edge of the trees, to this small clearing. It might've taken them five minutes or fifty, she had no idea.

All she knew was she was about to be with Will. To see him, to feel him. He'd fill her. Fill this terrible, aching lack that had throbbed inside her for weeks. Her body trembled from the thought.

The woods were cool. An idyll, where green leaves glowed yellow from dappled sunlight, and dewy grass glittered, tranquil in the shadows.

The woods were cool, and still, her blood ran hot.

He stopped short. She sensed his cane clatter to the dirt, but didn't give it a thought. Her only thoughts, for him, standing before her, so intense. She stared into those hazel eyes, wondering what he might be thinking. She knew he wanted her. But would he be feeling this other thing too, this stabbing in her heart she felt when she looked at him?

He leaned down. Brought his mouth gently to hers. Kissed her, slowly, tenderly. She savored the taste of him, breathing him in. Kissing him back, slowly, until she thought her chest would burst from the need to let go. To pull him down, to take him. Be taken.

A stream trickled somewhere in the distance. A happy sound, so carefree and light, and in such counterpoint to her galloping heart.

He pulled away. His body was tense, and she thought maybe he felt it too. This raging need. But still, he kept himself in check.

Will was from such a different world, and she thought how, right then, he'd probably be concerned for her. He'd be mindful of her fears, her anxieties.

If only he knew how much she wanted him. Her only fear, the thought that he might not love her. Desire consumed her. It was a palpable thing, like a constant drone in her head, or a filter that colored her world.

If he didn't know, she would show him.

"Lie down," she whispered. She urged him lower. Seated herself next to him in the dirt, guided Will's shoulders down til he was lying on his back. She stretched her body along his, on her side.

He watched her, his eyes now gold in the light, now green in the shadow, so intent on her.

She climbed onto him, straddled him. She felt him through all that wool, big and hard, and feminine satisfaction swelled through her to know she was the cause. Felicity rocked her hips, settling him in her cleft, and heat and want suffused her.

"I've thought about this for some time," she told him, her voice husky with desire. She took his hand, raised it to her breast.

He cupped her carefully at first. She ground her hips more snugly to him, and something dark and hungry clouded his eyes. He gripped her more surely then, kneading her breast, thumbing her nipple, a faint bump through the thick fabric of her gown.

"Aye? And what did you think?"

"I wondered if you'd be gentle." She leaned over him and watched, gratified, as he ogled her nearly spilling from the low-cut gown. She rubbed her thumb along his lower lip. "Or if you'd be rough."

"Oh, aye?" His voice was hoarse, tight with lust. "And what did you decide?"

"I decided you'd be a little of both. A little gentle." She leaned down further, taking his mouth in a tender kiss. "And"—Felicity pulled away and then dipped back in, nipping at his lower lip—"a little rough. Because, Will Rollo, I want you way too much not to get a little rough."

"Och, woman." He breathed deeply, tried to master himself. Despite what she said about gentleness, he wanted to tear the clothes from her body. Free his cock from the aggravation of all this wool that had been chafing him for so many weeks now, the coarse fabric abrading his flesh til it felt raw. His every nerve, strained and ready.

He sat up just enough to wrap his arms around her back. The movement burrowed him more snugly into her cleft, the drag of wool on his skin maddening. He needed to feel her, flesh on flesh.

He wanted to rip, but instead he carefully untied each lace. Many hours had he spent studying those intricate closures, imagining all the ways in which he could tear them from her.

The gown loosened and her breasts shifted lower, fuller. He needed to feel them, would finally feel them, against his skin.

His hands found her ankles. Stroking upward, he smoothed his palms up her calves, her thighs, dragging her gown up and over her head. Felicity, naked.

His heart stopped in his chest at the sight of her. This lovely, unexpected gift. She was so pale and perfect. The dappled sunlight fell on her yellow hair, stippling shadows across the delicate curve of her mouth, her cheekbones, her brows. He forced himself to breathe.

"You're beautiful," he told her quietly, simply. The smile she gave him in response was so soft, so dear, he thought that to feel this woman's adoration was to know true joy.

"Felicity," he said, savoring her name in his mouth, thinking how truly she'd been named. "Such a joy you are. Such a treasure." He traced a tentative finger down her cheek, her throat. Brought his eyes once more to her breasts, and something stabbed at his heart. Surely he didn't deserve this. Surely it would end. "Are you certain you want a man like me?"

Mesmerized he watched those expressive brown eyes, one moment raw with desire, the next serene and sure.

"I've never been more certain."

And then something happened to those eyes. They darkened, raking over his body, avidly, hungrily.

She brought her hands to his plaid. Pushed it from his shoulder. Pulled his shirt over his head. Unbuckled his belt. Loosened the plaid at his waist.

Felicity shifted one hip up, and then the other, tugging the wool from his lap, freeing him, finally. "Oh, aye," he heard himself groan.

Still on his lap, she scooted back, devouring him with her eyes. The vision of this beautiful, perfect woman ogling his erection made his cock twitch, and Rollo thought he'd never been so hard. The need to be in her was a torture now, urgent, consuming.

She brought her hand to him. Her grip was cool, and yet it didn't soothe him. His body raged, hot and hungry for her. She brought her thumb to the tip of him, rubbed the thick bead of moisture there, his head slick and ready for her. "Och, Felicity, love," he moaned.

Easing her weight onto one knee, she tried to tug the wool from where it was still draped over his thighs.

"No," he rasped, stilling her hand with his. "The plaid stays." He'd not ruin this moment by exposing his detested flaws to her.

She froze, pinning him with an unreadable gaze. "William Rollo," Felicity said in a calm monotone. "You think too much." Pushing at his shoulders, she guided him back onto the ground and straddled him once more. "I'm not doing my job very well," she purred, crawling back down the length of him, "if you're able to do all this thinking."

He shut his eyes. He wanted to keep his legs hidden from

her, and yet he was paralyzed, desperate to know what this strange and miraculous woman would do next.

He felt her hand on him again. Felt her stroke down, then up, the head of him tacky and slick with his want for her.

And then he felt her tongue, and the world as he knew it collapsed on itself. "Oh . . ." was all he could manage.

She sucked him slowly into her mouth, deeper and deeper. "Ohh," he rasped again. He'd not have guessed such a thing could ever happen to him. "What are you . . . ?"

Felicity pulled back up and he felt a wet pop as he slid from between her lips. She stroked with both hands, all over and around him, and then spoke, her breath hot on his damp and sensitized skin. "You are still thinking too much," she scolded in a whisper.

She took him into her mouth again, eagerly now. And this time, when she finally pulled away and he felt her pulling the plaid from over his legs, he couldn't muster concern. Self-consciousness had been dissolved, relegated to some distant memory.

"You silly man," she murmured. "I don't see what the big deal is."

It wasn't until he felt her kisses trail up and down each leg that he knew what she referred to. He stilled, waiting. Holding himself frozen, wondering what she would think, what she would say. He felt her tongue graze his right knee.

His cursed knee. The last time he'd been able to stretch it, to straighten or bend it, had been the morning of his seventh birthday.

"I've told you before," she scolded. "You're hot." She nibbled down the side of his leg. "Scars . . . are hot."

He didn't fully trust what he thought he was hearing.

Until she crawled back up the length of him. The way she stalked low along his body, desire smoking her eyes, stoked his body to a fever pitch. He thought he might climax from the feel of her skin on his alone.

He couldn't bear it. Could wait no longer.

She'd reached just level to him when Rollo tangled his fingers in her hair, and took her mouth in a punishing kiss.

He flipped Felicity onto her back, his mouth ravaging hers, her neck, her breasts.

He twined his fingers with hers, pinning her hands over her head, staring at her, his heart pounding. Her lips were reddened from his kisses, slightly parted, waiting for more. "I love you, Felicity. What may come, know that I love you."

He dared not wait for her response. Couldn't bear to know whether she loved him in return, and so stole the words from her mouth with a kiss.

And then, with a shift of his hips, he stole the breath from her lungs.

Will plunged into her, sinking slowly down to the root of him. She was so wet and so ready, the feel of her body gripping him shook him to the core.

He stilled, holding himself over her, in her, catching his breath. Their gazes caught. She was panting, her eyes half lidded, muzzy from desire.

He never knew it would be like this. Had never imagined.

They lost themselves then, bodies tangling on the forest floor. Hands, mouths, hips, frenzied and consuming each other until someone's shout, someone's moan, resounded through the trees.

And Will and Felicity lay entwined, their hard breathing the only human sound amidst the peaceful rustle and burble of the woods.

Chapter 19

Felicity grinned at the roses littering her bed. Their scent had greeted her first, the moment she'd walked into the room.

She took one of the voluptuous pink blooms and pressed it to her nose. The fragrance was lush, heady. *A flower for lovers*, Will had written in his note. He knew she didn't consider herself a roses girl. Yet she was his, he wrote, his lover, like it or no.

And she was liking it. Very, very much.

Felicity sat on the edge of the bed, nose still nestled in the thick, velvety petals, looking around at this strange, new life of hers.

Her room was airy, with yellow wainscoting and quaint furniture like something from a doll's house. Her favorite lavender dress rustled along the silk of the navy blue duvet.

She'd thought nothing could be more life-changing than getting transported into the past. But that was before she'd been with Will, rolling on the forest floor like some wild thing. Hearing his words of love. Giving herself, utterly. This losing herself in him, this was the real life-altering event, profound, unexpected.

The man, quite simply, rocked her world.

Aunt Livia would've been thrilled. *Now there's a roses girl*, Felicity thought with a smile. She would've adored these thick, pink blooms, so obscene in their heavily scented beauty. Livvie always did say love may conquer all, but nothing conquers a woman's heart like a nice bunch of roses.

Felicity missed her, and allowed the sharp pangs of emotion to roll through her. She missed Livvie, but was more sure than ever that this was where she was meant to be. Positive now that she was meant to be by Will's side.

Still, she'd like to find some way to get word to her. Would find some way. Because Felicity had no doubt, if she could travel back in time, surely there was some way to communicate with her aunt.

She gave a little resolved nod, and thought, *First things first*. And first, the roses.

She carefully arranged them on the bed, separating tangled leaves, unsnagging thorns. Their pink so vivid atop the blue bedcovers.

She ran her fingers over the petals. So like suede, their touch was irresistible. A fresh burst of fragrance pervaded the room.

She'd find a small vase, she decided suddenly. She had pressed the blue blossoms Will had given her in a book. But these roses smelled just too heavenly to tuck away.

She frowned, hesitating. She didn't want to be a bother to anyone, but she dreaded going by herself to what Will called *belowstairs*, the realm of butlers and cooks and maids.

All those people scared her. She could never understand what they said, was certain they couldn't understand her, and she didn't know what to make of their curious, sidelong glances.

The roses, though. The outer petals were already beginning to look limp. Surely she could find a pitcher in the kitchen. She'd go down the stairs and follow the smell of food. She'd identify the nicest-looking cook, mimic pouring water, and hopefully they'd get the picture.

She sprang from the bed, striding from her room before she could change her mind.

She made her way downstairs, and then for the first time ever, headed lower, down the other set of steps, to below-stairs. The stairway was dimly lit, and Felicity descended slowly, rehearsing what she'd say if she ran into one of the Rollo household's many servants.

She froze, hearing shouts. Some sort of argument drifted up to her. She definitely didn't want to walk in on a fight. Faltering, she thought she could turn back, ask Will to find her a vase instead. He'd *love* to find a vase for her.

But this was her place now. If she was going to be with him, to make this place and time her own, she needed to just deal with herself—and these ridiculous anxieties.

Lady of the house, she chanted to herself. *I am lady of the house.* And, setting her shoulders, she made her way to the bottom of the staircase.

"Badly done!" Rollo's mother's voice echoed down the corridor.

Oh crap. Felicity froze, her foot hovering on the last step. Why did it have to be Rollo's mom? That's the last argument she wanted to walk in on.

But she really wanted that vase.

You can do this. Punishing servants was standard operating procedure for seventeenth-century ladies, right? *I can do this.*

"That . . . was . . . ill . . . done."

She heard a distant smack. Good Lord, was the woman beating someone? Felicity made a mental note never to let her alone with the grandkids.

She stepped out into the hallway. The floorboards creaked, and she stopped, her heart pounding.

"Naughty!"

Felicity bit her knuckle. What was his mother's deal, anyway? *Sheesh.*

If the woman was beating a servant, maybe she should do something to intervene. His mom, though—total ice queen, and Felicity was terrified to cross her.

But . . . if she was going to be with Will, she'd need to make herself at home. Be a part of the household.

Maybe she could bring some twenty-first-century sensibilities to the ways in which Lady Rollo treated her staff. She could enlighten the woman. Maybe it'd even bring them closer together.

The thought girded her. Giving herself a determined nod, Felicity walked down the hallway, in the direction of the shouting.

A knocking began to sound. A hollow *thump-thump-thump*. She hurried up.

"Bad, bad boy!"

That was it. She walked faster. Reprimanding an adult was one thing, but if Rollo's mom were beating some poor boy, she'd have to put a stop to it.

She paused just outside a darkened room. It was where the shouting had come from.

What on earth . . . ? Why would Lady Rollo be in a dark room? Felicity stood there, letting her eyes adjust.

His mom was there, facing the wall, just in front of a low shelf. There were lots of jars. A servant stood behind her. Not a boy, Felicity saw. He was tall, like a man.

How weird. Did he do something wrong to the preserves?

"Youuu . . ." his mother growled.

Felicity squinted, desperately curious now, waiting to see what jam- or sauce-related transgression the man/boy had perpetrated.

He moved, and the abruptness of it was violent, startling. Grabbing Lady Rollo's shoulders, the servant swung her to the side.

Felicity gasped. Was she being attacked?

It was when Lady Rollo landed on her elbows, leaning over a wine barrel, that Felicity realized in horror what was happening.

Lady Rollo was getting it on with one of the hot, young servant guys.

Ohhhhh shit.

The older woman's head rose in slow motion, an eagle sighting its prey. Felicity, mortified, met her gaze.

And backed out of the room, fleeing back up the stairs, all thoughts of flowers and vases shocked right out of her head.

❀

"When will you do something about this Felicity person?" Lady Rollo clinked her spoon impatiently on the rim of her teacup.

"Don't fret, Mother dear." Jamie kicked his legs in front of him, taking a slow sip of tea. He loved when his mother got nervous. Rare were the times she let that perfect ivory façade crack, and he found it eminently amusing. He watched her, stirring her tea with such menace. Biting the inside of his cheek, he told her, "The situation is well in hand."

She pinned her son with a cold stare. "Don't condescend to *me*, Jamie. You forget. I remain in control of the purse strings. And don't think that wealthy wife of yours can help you. The wars have gutted the Campbells, and their family coffers run low. That woman, pining away for you on Campbell land," she mused. "It's shameful what you did marrying her."

He bristled, and then cursed inwardly, knowing his mother had seen it. She knew him too well.

"That's right," she said, narrowing her eyes. "Until your father dies, *I* am the only one able and willing to forgive your perpetual gambling debts."

He had to look away. Studied the cup in his hand instead. It was precisely those debts that kept him under her thumb. She knew it, and always Jamie tasted a son's love curdling into resentment whenever she chose to lord it over him.

He'd thought before, in his drunken moments, that he could cut her loose. Claim that his father was as good as dead. Jamie would inherit. But he'd find himself in debtor's prison, with the Rollo fortune as forfeit.

His mother was harping on. "I am the one who looks the other way when you bring home your unsavory . . . *friends*. Or should I call them accomplices? No, Jamie, if you weren't so weak—"

"Weak?" He finally snapped. Weak he was not. He'd leave *weak* to his pathetically crippled baby brother. "Speak not to me of weak, Mother, when you seem to raise your petticoats for the nearest strapping cottar to hand."

He let the accusation hang, enjoying the flush of outrage suffusing her cheeks. His mother was indeed an attractive one, but the thought of her bedding blacksmiths and stable hands disgusted him.

"No," he said. "It seems we are a pair. If word got out that you're not a wife in truth to my father? Think you on what might happen to that precious fortune you keep harping about."

"Enough." She raised her hand to silence him. Despite her furrowed brow, she bore a smile for her favorite son.

He knew she enjoyed their sparring. He did too; he'd learned it from the best.

Shaking her head, she told him quietly, "'Tis a sad day when a woman finds the only man able to stand up to her is her own son."

He spared her a smile and raised his teacup to her as if in a toast.

"Just promise me?"

"Anything, Mother." Jamie tossed back the last sip of his tea and stood to go.

"Just promise you will deal with the woman."

He gave her a nod. He'd take care of Felicity. And convenient it would be too, seeing as it also took care of his brother.

Jamie took his mother's hand, pressing her knuckles to his lips in a formal kiss. "As you will it, Mother dear."

Chapter 20

Feeling Felicity writhe and moan her pleasure in the sculpture garden had Rollo musing she was no less than a gift from those very marble gods.

And the notion had given him just the idea.

He'd left before dawn for the journey to Perth, arriving during peak market hours, making it back to Duncrub in time for a late supper.

He wanted to give her a gift, somehow show her how much she'd come to mean to him. Though no gift on earth would be adequate to the task, Will found he wanted to buy her something all the same.

He hurried from the stables, patting the flap of his sporran over and again, making sure he'd not somehow lost the bundle he'd tucked in there. He hoped she'd like it. Rollo smiled, thinking she might.

He hesitated in Duncrub's entryway. Should he find Felicity first, or eat first? He'd not eaten since before noon—and that while horseback—and he found he was fair starved.

But he wanted to see her. Needed to see her. He'd spent

the better part of the day fantasizing about the give of her flesh under his grip and the feel of his mouth on hers.

Debating the needs of his loins versus the needs of his belly, he heard his mother approach. He'd grown up hearing the telltale elegant skim of fabric over stone and the unwelcome sound never failed to identify her.

Rollo realized he was not overly fond of that sound. He girded himself.

"You dare bring such *filth* into my home?"

"Mother," he said, facing her. "I'd expected your usual frost, but this . . . venom, this is a surprise." He forced a casual smile. "To what do I owe such an uncharacteristic display of emotion?"

"What?" she sputtered, staring trembling at her son. "Who do you think you are to speak to me so? If your father were here, you'd never dare to speak thus—"

"Father *is* here, Mother." He'd spent his life avoiding his mother. His brother. But if Felicity had taught him anything in the past weeks, it was that life was too precious not to speak one's mind and one's heart with the same single voice.

"Mostly, Mother, I speak so, because it's high time somebody addressed you truthfully. My brother has spent his life tiptoeing around you. But I never have, and there's the rub, aye? It wasn't that you couldn't stomach a broken son, it's that you couldn't abide a willful one. It's no secret you harbor few affections—"

"Affection?" Her voice was a strained hiss. "You speak to me of affection? What do you know of it, when all you've done lately is bring your . . . your witch whore into my home?"

Fury crackled through him, ice crystallizing his veins in a single, rapid wave. Rollo stepped to his mother, stopped, checked himself. He'd not threaten her. Never could he stoop to that.

Despite the vitriol, despite the twisted charade that was their family, Will would never raise a hand to one of his parents.

His free hand balled into a tight fist at his side. The feel of his nails digging into the meat of his palm gave him focus. "You will not speak of Felicity—"

"*Nobody* will speak of Felicity," she interrupted, her tone a carefully modulated chill. "And if you hope to call even a single farthing of the Rollo fortune your own some day, you will keep her presence a secret. The fact that she spent even a single hour here, a secret. You will take it to your grave, young man."

"Felicity is where she belongs now." Jamie's voice came from the doorway, where he'd been standing, hovering in silence.

"Skulking about in the shadows again?" Will sneered at his brother. He should've known. Jamie would've seen Will's attachment to Felicity, and now he'd worry it like a dog his bone.

"You may get as testy as you like," Jamie said. "It won't save your pretty little witch."

Will grew utterly still. "What do you mean?"

"She is where she belongs," his mother chirped.

But Will's eyes didn't swerve from his brother. "What are you saying?" White noise buzzed in his head. "What have you done with Felicity?"

Jamie only shrugged. "She was a peculiar bird, your woman. It was only a matter of time."

"A matter of time before what?" Will faced his brother, strode to him, but his fury seized his muscles, made him awkward, and his approach was labored, wooden.

Jamie eyed his younger brother with disdain. "Before she was imprisoned, cripple."

"Imprisoned?" Will's world went red. "What have you done?"

"I've not done a thing." Jamie casually rested his head back on the doorjamb.

"The minister and his men came for her," his mother said. "For *witchcraft*. Never have I felt such shame."

"Alexander Robertson?" The thought of the man touching Felicity, of any man touching her . . . Horror swept him, turned his belly to ice.

Foreboding followed quick on its heels. Robertson was a madman with a taste for the smell of burnt flesh, his favorite pursuit throwing women on a witch's pyre. Dozens of them. "And none of you tried to stop him?"

"Well," Jamie chuckled, "your woman tried. A wee spitfire that one. She'd scald any man." He raised his brow in a lewd smirk. "Or have you already discovered that?"

"Where did they take her?" Will's voice sounded like the edge of a knife blade.

Jamie only shrugged.

"You can't bear to see me happy, can you? Or is it you can't bear that she chose me over you?" Love for Felicity had stoked something to life in his soul. And this time, rather than weathering his brother in bitter silence, Will raged. Plainspoken words his seven-year-old self would've cheered to hear. "Horses, women . . . they all seem to prefer me, don't they, Jamie?"

"You bloody bastard," Jamie hissed, and in three great strides, he had his sword unsheathed.

But Will was ready for him. He whipped his cane, slashing at Jamie's sword, sending it clattering across the foyer.

"Boys," their mother shrieked. "You will not shed blood in my home."

Will cast a cold eye on his mother. "You'd not look ill on it spilt elsewhere, though, would you?"

He turned on his heel, away from his detested family, grateful for once that purpose gave ease to his gait.

He'd leave Duncrub, at once. He'd not have time to gather his things. Who knew what more mischief Jamie might rain down.

He'd see his father, one last time. Then leave. Forever, if need be. Fortune be damned. His family be damned.

But first he needed to find paper, pen a letter.

Rollo needed help, and he knew just the place to find it.

❧

Alexander Robertson was a creep. Felicity couldn't believe she'd actually thought he was cute at first.

She eyed that blond hair, pulled back in a little ponytail. She hated little ponytails on men.

At least she wasn't tied up. The guards had wanted to tie her up, but apparently the minister fancied himself quite the gentleman. *Creep.*

"You could marry me," he told her.

"So . . . let me get this straight. My options are to be burned for witchcraft or . . . get down and dirty with *you*?" Felicity looked around at the barren walls. Cold stone smelling of dank and urine. "I hate to break it to you, but your little pad isn't exactly a date-getter."

Aboveground it hadn't looked so bad. In fact, Keltie Castle seemed quite the spread, with tapestries on the walls and a blazing fire in the hearth. But Robertson's lackeys had whisked her, screaming, down a ladder into an underground chamber where torchlight flickered on walls too shallow for her to stand upright.

She was terrified he might leave her alone. It was so still down there, with the black shadows threatening. She was frightened to death of that darkness, that utter silence, and of the memories it stirred.

Cold, black silence was too like the inside of her parents' car, right after the accident. She'd shoved the memories away long ago, burying them down deep. But just two minutes alone in a place devoid of light or movement, and she was slammed back into the past, a terrified kid again.

And so she kept talking, because the sound of her voice was better than being left alone in this dungeon, quiet like a grave.

Robertson, unfortunately, seemed to be finding all her talk charming.

It had struck her that maybe this could be the thing that could save her: chattering on, using her feminine wiles to convince the minister to change his mind. Except she'd changed his mind *too* much, because now he seemed smitten.

She studied his features in the dim light. What she'd first thought was benign charm now seemed oily, smarmy, and just plain gross.

She just had to hold on. Will would come and save her. She *knew* he would come.

He was her Viking, after all. This whole escapade was writ in stone somewhere, on some grand tablet, kept by the fates, marking the ways of the universe.

Robertson reached for her, tried to stroke his fingers down her cheek. His touch disgusted her. Sneaky and ticklish, it reminded her of a spider.

Gross. She shuddered, flinching away.

"I'd be careful if I were you. Will is coming for me, and he won't take very kindly to this. You sure wouldn't want him to use that cane of his to open up a can of whoop-ass on your sorry minister hide."

"What a strange wee creature you are," he murmured, obviously not understanding half of what she'd said. "Like an exotic bird in a cage." He edged closer on the narrow bench. "But I'm afraid only *I* can save you now."

"Man, you are *such* a total creep." She scooted away, her bottom half hanging off the cold stone now. "You and that Jamie both. Total creeps. I gotta ask, does this kidnapping thing work for you guys? I mean, generally speaking?"

She had to keep his attention, keep chattering. Keep that torch lit until Will came for her.

"Is that what this whole witch thing is about?" she continued. "Women who you think are, I don't know, too cute, or too independent, or strong-willed, they won't date you, so you call them witches instead?"

"You silly chit. I'd watch your tongue were I you."

"Then it's a good thing you're not me," she snapped, thinking she'd found his Achilles' heel. Seems the guy probably didn't have the best track record with the ladies. "Because then you'd be sitting in a dungeon getting hit on by a nasty loser. An unattractive, unappealing, stinky dog of a man."

His eyes narrowed, and Felicity worried that she'd gone too far. She was sure he couldn't have understood all of what she said, but she imagined a phrase like *stinky dog* must resonate on some level.

"I'll ask once more," Robertson said in a menacingly tight voice, "where are you from?"

"I told you. Glasgow." Too bad she'd never been there in her life. Hadn't the faintest idea what the place was like at all.

"I cannot believe it." He peered at her, as if her features held some clue. "From which part? Who is your father?"

Uhhh . . . She and Will hadn't planned that far. She decided to wing it with the truth. "My father's dead, you jerk."

"Dead. A dead Wallace," he mused. "Your father . . . was a Royalist, I think."

"I . . ."

"He was," Robertson shouted triumphantly. "I can see it on your face. Listen well, girl. Royalists find no ally in my parish. Though I am more . . . discreet than others. Your death, should it come, won't be some tedious political commentary." His gaze grew fever bright. "My dear, your destiny will be a spectacle greeted by a cheering crowd."

He stroked her cheek with his thumb once more, and this time the grip of his hand held her in place. "I will not tell you twice. One way or another, Felicity Wallace, you shall submit to me. Or you shall perish in flames."

Chapter 21

Will stooped over the desk, weighing his words. He'd found both paper and his father in the library.

He needed to make haste now. He would turn to the Sealed Knot, that secret society of men dedicated to the restoration of the King. Though he'd sworn never again to get pulled into their intrigues, never before had he something so precious to lose.

He would leave a letter, in the usual spot. And he'd wait.

He folded his note, tucked it in his sporran. His eyes lingered briefly over the velvet-wrapped bundle tucked there. Felicity's gift. He'd see it in her hands if it killed him.

And kill him it might.

He looked to his father, and found the man had been watching him. A chill shivered over his skin. The thought that his father was trapped in his body was too much to bear.

"Da," he rasped. "Would that you had some words of wisdom for your youngest son. I'd give the use of my good leg to hear your voice once more."

Shuffling closer, Rollo pulled a chair before his father and sat.

"I must go." He looked deeply into the man's eyes. They were the hazel color of Will's own, yet rheumy. The eyes of an old man. And Will too felt like an old man. Had become an old man on his seventh birthday, so many years past.

"I hate . . ." Rollo's voice cracked. Would these be the last words he spoke to his father? He needed to weigh them carefully. "I hate to leave you. But I must go. They took her. Jamie had men come and take Felicity. Would that you could—"

"Aye," the older man croaked, and Will startled at the sound.

"Och, Da, you speak to me." A pang struck his heart, happiness and grief both.

The man blinked rapidly.

"Have you more to say?" Will sat on the edge of his chair, his heart hammering in his chest. His father—speaking.

The older man shut his eyes once, slowly and deliberately.

"Tell it," he said urgently. "Do you know something?"

"K . . ." Trying desperately to make a sound, the man's tongue flexed grotesquely, and spittle flew from his mouth.

"What?" Rollo gripped his hand. "Where? Do you know where they've taken her?"

"Kkkk . . ." The sound scudded along the back of his tongue.

"To the kirk?" Will asked eagerly. "Back to the church at Saint Serf's?"

"Mmm . . ." A despairing sound echoed in the man's throat. He shut his eyes. Opened them, trying again, his face red with the effort. "Kkkk . . . Kelt . . ."

"Kelt. Keltie?" Will asked suddenly. "They've taken her to Keltie Castle?"

His father blinked once, saw his son had understood, then shut his eyes from exertion.

"Thank you, Da," he said quietly. He hesitated a moment, then clapped a hand on his father's shoulder. Never had he shown his father affection. At least, not since the accident, which in some ways was the only measurable span of Will's life. He leaned down now, kissed the older man on the head. "I'm sorry it took me so long to see."

He straightened, overwhelmed by gratitude, love, and some other, indistinct feeling. Will thought perhaps it might be grief. For his own self.

"Keltie Castle," he muttered, picturing at once the granite specter and its famed dungeon with walls nine feet thick.

He patted his sporran one last time, hoping Ormonde was out there somewhere. His friend was the only one Rollo trusted to help Felicity find her way home.

For Will would be of no help. Because, he vowed, he'd be giving his own life to save hers.

❂

Ormonde came, finally, as Will knew he would. To place a note under a stone at Dupplin Cross was as good as putting correspondence directly into the Sealed Knot's hands.

He'd had too much time to think, though, while he waited among the Forteviot castle ruins. Rollo had decided it only fitting that it was some ancient Pictish landmark that bore witness to his despair.

Resting his back against the cold stone, he fingered his gift to Felicity, marveling at what a wretch he'd become in so short a time.

For he knew what he must do. He would save her. He prayed he'd have the chance to give her this one gift.

And then Rollo would say good-bye.

For, even if he survived—and he doubted he would—she needed to return to her own home, her own time. It was far too dangerous for her to stay.

Fool. That strange and colorful card had been right. He'd been a fool. A fool to let himself get close to her. A fool to feel the warm flicker of hope in his chest. A fool to love her.

And now he was a wretched fool.

"Och, man," Ormonde scolded. "Put that thing back in your sporran."

"Aye." Will tucked the velvet pouch away, then scrubbed his face with his hands. "We need a plan."

"A plan. Yes." Ormonde sat cross-legged across from Will in the grass and placed his hands on his knees in an exaggerated gesture of focus. "Let us assess. We are a cripple and a redheaded fugitive, come to secret a helpless waif from a castle full of religious zealots." He gave a sage nod. "No, Will, I can't see how storming this wee castle will pose a problem at all."

"I need solutions, not sarcasm." Even so, Rollo felt a glimmer of humor pierce his melancholy, and he welcomed it. He wondered if that weren't the real reason he'd called on Ormonde above all others. The man had a way of cracking Will's grim shell. "Don't forget it was this cripple who pulled your arse from the Tower."

"I'll never forget it," Ormonde said, and instead of laughing at Rollo's momentary humor, he grew serious. "But you know what this means, Will."

He gave a tight nod. He'd seen it coming. "Your letter. I'll deliver it to the King."

"You know the risk you take," Ormonde said quietly. "Cromwell's spies troll the English Channel. Many of our men have already been captured. Hanged."

"Aye." Will's voice was tight, his face hardened to planes of steel. "My life matters not. It's Felicity we must save now."

"We shall try. But you need to be realistic. We are grossly outnumbered."

"There must be something we can use against them," Rollo said. "Some way to outmaneuver them."

His friend snapped his fingers in mock excitement. "I know," he said sarcastically, "how about we set off a flurry of fireworks . . . *Chinese* fireworks! A display so grand as to convince our God-fearing witch-hunters that the wrath of the Almighty is upon them. Apocalypse is nigh, etcetera."

"Enough," Will said sharply. He paused a moment, then, "Well . . . maybe."

"Off to the Orient, are we?" Ormonde rolled his eyes.

"Quit your jesting," Will told him. "Listen. We won't storm the castle. We'll bring the guardsmen to us. Blast our way in, perhaps, with black powder."

"Impossible," Ormonde replied at once.

"And that is precisely why they won't expect it."

"Bloody hell, Will. They won't expect it because it's impossible. You'll bring the whole damned building down right atop your Felicity's bonny head."

"All right then," Rollo said. "Smoke. We smoke them out, like rabbits from a hole. Create some sort of device that releases smoke, not fire."

Ormonde stared blankly, then asked, "Where, pray tell, do you plan to find these grand stores of . . . what would we even use for that . . . saltpeter?"

"I'll let your Sealed Knot men handle that. They owe me."

"Aye, Will." His friend grew somber. "As you will owe them, and tenfold."

Chapter 22

It was the musket loops that finally convinced Ormonde. Keltie Castle was small, more a grand home than any traditional notion of a castle. Small holes called musket loops lined the front of the building, along the base, located in what would be the guardroom, from which guardsmen could point their muskets, shooting any who dared to attempt forced entry.

Will hoped Ormonde would provide enough of a distraction so that there'd be no gun barrels pointing through those loops, waiting to greet Rollo when the time came for him to toss his wee candles through.

"Hopefully we'll not blow ourselves up," Ormonde whispered, watching Rollo pour a measure of saltpeter into one of the makeshift vessels they'd fashioned from paraffin.

"It won't explode." Will tucked a strip of touchpaper in the powder, like a wick resting in lantern oil. The paper had been soaked in saltpeter and would burn slowly enough to allow Rollo to get away before his creation could quite literally backfire. "Though I'd not look askance at a good, rousing *boom*. Perfect," he muttered, smoothing softened paraffin over the top to finish. "A perfect wee candle."

"Are you certain this will be enough?" Ormonde asked him. "These will make enough smoke?"

"It's not of your concern. You know what you have to do," Rollo added, referring to Ormonde's preposterous disguise, and the men's low laughter broke the tension.

There had been much discussion over who would be forced to dress up and create a distraction. Will claimed it was his friend's histrionic nature that awarded him the honors, but really it was that he'd not put Ormonde in any danger above and beyond what he was already being exposed to.

Saltpeter did have the irksome tendency to explode when kept in large quantities.

"Understood," Ormonde said. "I create a distraction. You plant your wee smoke candles. So, tell me how is it we avoid alerting *every* guardsman this side of the Tay? The smoke will be silent, but your pistol shots won't be."

"No pistols. You leave the guards to me. I can be as silent as death."

"So dire, he is." Ormonde chuckled.

Ignoring him, Rollo studied the moon in the sky. "It's closing in on dawn. We act now, or not at all."

"Aye, aye." Ormonde heaved himself up to standing. He brushed the leaves and dirt from the rough brown cassock that was his disguise.

"Leave yourself be," Will ordered. "It's more realistic that way."

"Please tell me, why is it I have to portray the religious lunatic, when you get to be dressed as . . . let's see . . . *a high-born lord*?"

"I promise"—Will stood and clapped his friend on the shoulder—"you can play the lordling next time. And Ormonde?" he asked, growing serious. He opened his sporran to retrieve the velvet-wrapped bundle. "I'd have you give this to Felicity, in case I'm . . . unable."

"Och, lad." Ormonde put his hand up to stop him. "Put your wee pouch away already. Give it to the woman yourself. You survived how many campaigns riding by Graham's side in the wars? I think we can handle a few provincials."

A brief nod and a tense quarter hour later, Will heard the beginnings of his friend's "distraction."

It began with a distant howl. And then, in an absurd turn that only Ormonde would think of, the redheaded man crowed like a rooster.

Shaking his head, Will gathered his makeshift smoke candles. The cock's crow was a nice touch. He was certain the guardsmen would leave their post once Ormonde unleashed his mad babble of scripture.

There was a door in the rear of the building. Not wanting to leave the safety of Keltie, the guards would surely at least peer through it. Rollo hoped they'd keep it unlatched, for it would serve as Ormonde's route back in. He'd not have his friend tangled in the inevitable scuffle that'd be occupying Rollo by the front entrance.

"I come to see the witch!" his friend screeched.

Will began to light each strand of touchpaper, thinking the tattered brown mendicant's cassock had been just the thing to accent Ormonde's simulated madness. *Any moment now*, he thought, urging the guardsmen to move. The impromptu wicks smoldered already, giving him a lungful of smoke.

"Death to the witch! *'Thou shalt not suffer a witch to live!'*" Ormonde's voice grew louder as he approached the rear of the castle. "Burn her! Maggie Wall was a witch who haunts me still! Burn this evil woman as you burned Maggie Wall!"

Enough, Will thought, glowering. *Enough with the damned burning.*

Apparently his friend decided the same, for he altered his approach. "Deuteronomy saith . . ." Ormonde paused, and Rollo tensed, hoping that his friend hadn't already exhausted his battery of scripture.

"Deuteronomy saith!" he shouted again suddenly, and Will braced for what might be in store.

His friend was close now, and his dramatically lowered voice resounded through the trees. "He that is wounded in the testicles, or hath his privy member cut off, shall not enter into the congregation of the Lord. Deuteronomy saith it is so!"

Trust his friend to devote the finite resources of his mind to quotes pertaining to the male member.

"Woe betide him *and* his stones who turn a deaf ear!"

Will fought a smile, thinking *that* should get the guardsmen to move. And indeed he saw the first musket shift. A flash of moonlight on the barrel. And then it slid from the loop. And then another.

Rollo stood, pounding life into his legs. The gesture brought the image of Felicity to his mind, like a sudden blinding flare of light, so acute he flinched from it. Flinched from the memory of her scolding him about that very movement. In the carriage so long ago, when she'd first touched him, truly touched him, and changed his life forever.

With a shake to his head, he made his way to the front of Keltie Castle. For once it was the need for silence that slowed his pace, and he cursed every second that kept Felicity in that dungeon.

He stood by the first musket loop, waited a moment. Though the stone was thick, Rollo didn't sense another body on the other side, and so he leaned down. Looked in.

The glimpse through such a small hole was piecemeal, but he could see a torch sputtering on the wall. Two abandoned stools. The room, empty. *Does that mean there were two guards?* he wondered distantly, certain he'd not be so lucky.

No matter their number, the guardsmen had all gone to investigate, and Will had but a moment to deposit his wee ruse into the empty guardroom. The paraffin was hot to the touch, and he'd have it out of his hands before the saltpeter began to smoke in earnest.

He tossed one through, listening intently to the soft splat the softened wax made on the stone floor. Oxygen hit the saltpeter, and a tentative wisp of dark smoke coiled into the room.

Will smiled. *I'm coming, Felicity.*

He tossed the rest of the makeshift candles through, hearing the approaching voices of the guardsmen echo on the stone.

That meant Ormonde would be racing back into the woods by now. Safely, he hoped. For his friend needed to double back and whisk Felicity from the dungeon while Rollo occupied the guards.

He heard shouting and looked to see smoke drifting from the musket loops. Gray fingers turning a ghostly white before disappearing on the night's gentle breeze.

The guardsmen began to curse. To cough.

How many are there?

Will sidled up to the front entrance, just out of view.

The first guard burst through and was caught at once by Rollo's cane, waiting leveled at his neck. The man gagged, a hideously ragged sound, as if he choked on a bone. He stumbled forward and fell writhing, hands clutching at his throat.

The second guard was an even easier mark, for he paused just beyond the doorway, watching his fellow with a mixture of confusion and fear. Will gave a grim smile, wondering if the men might actually believe some avenging force had come to smite them.

The guard stood, and Rollo slid his cane through his lightly flexed fist, knocking the man's temple as he would a billiard ball. The man fell hard and at once.

Will didn't wait for the third and, he now knew, final man. He couldn't chance the guard's sounding an alarm. And so Rollo pivoted to face the doorway, swinging his cane as he moved, plowing up into the man's groin. The guard doubled over, and Will batted down, catching him neatly on the back of the head.

Rollo stood, panting. Waiting to hear footfalls that didn't come. *Safe.*

Ormonde should be appearing, bringing Felicity out safe at any moment. *Where are you?* Rollo allowed a few hard pounds of his heart.

And that was when he heard her scream.

Chapter 23

The feel of the minister's hands repulsed her. Where was Will? Felicity knew he'd come, she just didn't understand what was taking him so long.

Robertson had scooted closer and closer, until she found herself hanging off the edge of the bench. One more inch and she'd be on the floor, so instead she was forced to suffer the feel of his thigh along hers.

The man had gotten braver. The touch on her chin had migrated to her shoulder. Then to lingering strokes along her back.

His hand slinked lower.

"Why," she blurted suddenly, feeling his fingertips graze the curve of her bottom, "don't you take me upstairs?" She looked around at the dank dungeon. A rickety ladder led down to where she was being held. The room was claustrophobic, with low stone walls and a curved ceiling.

"I will take you upstairs when you give your word you'll come to your senses." He chucked her chin as if she were a wayward child.

She studied that ladder. Her only way out. She knew without hesitation that her Viking would find a way to manage it. He'd swoop down and save her like some seventeenth-century superhero.

"Hm?" Robertson tweaked her cheek. "I'd have your answer, sweet."

"Uh . . ." Felicity didn't tell him no, nor would she ever tell him yes, hoping that her feigned indecision bought her more time. "I need to hear more about you. Your good works." *You narcissistic wacko.*

She prayed her chatter distracted him from a fact that, to her, seemed chillingly clear: Alexander Robertson could simply take what he wanted at any time.

"Oh no, this is familiar ground, and I'm ready to"—he traced a single finger down her spine—"explore new territory." He cocked a brow, looking self-satisfied.

"Territory . . . yeah . . ." She fumbled, struggling to think of new material. "Speaking of territory, what is this place? It's gross. And cold. I'm really cold, you know."

She sniffed. "And it stinks."

"So you've said. Now it's time to stop your—"

"Wait," she said, sniffing again. "I mean, it really stinks. Like smoke. Do you smell smoke?"

"Enough," Robertson snapped. "I'm finished with your prattling. You merely postpone the inevitable."

"No, really," she said, panicked now. She actually did smell smoke, and the primitive animal instinct tucked away in the back of her brain began to sound alarm bells in response.

A man dropped to the floor, and she yelped in surprise. Relief swept her. Her Rollo had come.

And then she registered the soiled cloak and dark hood. The man approached, walking smoothly, with no limp, and she screamed. He pulled a long dagger from one of his loose sleeves.

She toppled from the bench in her terror, still screaming. Robertson had been taken off guard, and she skittered backward along the floor watching as the intruder overtook him, stabbing him in the neck. The minister dropped at once, his gushing wound making a gruesome gurgling sound at her feet.

Cold stone cut into her back as she slammed against the wall in a frantic effort to scramble away.

She'd been holding herself in check, desperate for Rollo to appear, but reality was crashing down around her. The foreign grittiness of it all made something in her snap.

What was she doing there? Did she really want to live in a world where crazy, dirty, wild people ran around, going at each other with swords and knives?

One more shrill shriek burst from her.

"Haud your wheesht, woman." He pushed back his cowl, and Felicity suffered a surreal moment, wondering who, and how, and why this man seemed so familiar. She cried out again, unable to stop herself.

"Bloody hell, would you please . . . Och, hush! It's Ormonde. Will's friend."

Her breath continued to shudder in gasps, even though she now recognized the redheaded man from when she'd first arrived.

Crazy, dirty, wild. And that, apparently, was her *friend*.

"Where's Will?" She'd tried to gather herself, but hysteria made her question come out as a wail.

"Will is—"

The slam of a body dropping to the ground behind them announced the arrival of a guard. A big bear of a man, with ragged brown teeth.

"Och, hell, woman." Guarding her body with his, Ormonde spun to face the man.

The guard stepped forward and another man dropped into the dungeon. This one had a goatee, his long sword already out and drawn.

She was terrified. Maybe Rollo had been right. Maybe she didn't belong there. *I can't do this. I really, really can't do this.*

"Did you have to caterwaul so?" Ormonde grumbled, raising his dagger and bracing himself as the bearded one went for him.

In her hysteria, Felicity focused on the second man's ugly scrap of facial hair, so pointy, so absurd, like one of the Musketeers.

I have to do this. I doubted Will before. He proved me wrong. I told him I'd never doubt him again. He'll come for me.

The other, beefier guard bolted, and her gaze shifted, watching in slow-motion horror as he headed straight for her. The guard scooped her up from the ground like a rag doll, forcing the breath from her body in a high-pitched wheeze. Wrapping his arm around her belly, he swept around behind her in a mockery of an embrace. He smelled sour, his breath panting out of his open mouth, foul like rotten meat.

His knife was at her throat.

Oh God. I just want to go home.

"Drop it," she heard the other guard say, and her attention was drawn back to Ormonde. The bearded guard was nodding at Ormonde's dagger, his blade pointed at Ormonde's chest, poised to run him through. "Drop your dirk. Now."

"Can we discuss this?" Ormonde's feigned nonchalance astounded her.

I can do this. Will is coming. He'll come save me.

"There's naught to discuss. You drop your blade, or she gets it in the throat." Ormonde followed the man's gaze, coming to rest on the sight of the dagger at Felicity's neck.

Desperate to shut out the nightmare unfolding around her, she shut her eyes tight. Tears spilled in a hot flood down her cheeks.

Hold on. He won't let me die.

She heard Ormonde's knife clatter to the ground. Did that mean all was lost? Was he dead already? She opened her eyes, terrified of what she might find.

But the sight that greeted Felicity sent relief swelling through her. Legs were emerging slowly into the chamber from above, as a man lowered himself down the ladder, stealthily, rung by rung, using only his arms.

Will. He was there. He'd come. Crazy, dirty, wild men with swords didn't matter. Not when she had Will.

My Viking will protect me. We're meant to be.

She quickly looked back to Ormonde. She couldn't spoil it by giving Will away, and fought to keep her eyes on his friend instead. If he'd also spotted Rollo, she didn't know. The redheaded man seemed only to have eyes for the blade pointed at his chest.

What could she do? She wished there were some way she could help them. Her eyes swept down, scanned Robertson's body, lying in a bloody heap. She shuddered.

She felt the man behind her stiffen. Had he seen Rollo? Should she scream? Create a distraction? Stomp on his foot? She was helpless. Powerless. The feeling chilled her.

Events slowed, her perception the sluggish click of a camera shutter.

The guard behind her was beginning to shout a warning.

Her eyes went back to the bearded man. Would he run his blade through Ormonde? She watched him, watched in dreadful slow motion, focused, absurdly, on that beard. A curled moustache atop a pointed, brown goatee. Ridiculous.

But then the man made the strangest face. A look of surprise. Then an eerie, blank sort of expression suffused his features. His eyes, deadened. His mouth, and that facial hair, all gone slack.

He crumpled to the ground. Ormonde jumped aside just in time to avoid the man's blade as it thrust awkwardly forward before dropping to the dirt.

And there stood Rollo. Tall, with eyes that were shadowed and lethally intent in the flickering torchlight. He was utter calm. Utter stillness.

His arm extended as if he'd just thrown a ball, or a dart. Or a knife.

Felicity's eyes went to his *sgian dubh*, quivering deep in the man's back.

She looked back up to find Rollo's gaze devouring her. The flex of his jaw and the hard cast to his eyes were all that marred his outward calm.

Her heart soared. She knew what the set of that strong jaw meant. He'd come for her. He'd make this all go away.

My Viking will always come for me.

The surreal slow-motion unfolding of events exploded into rapid-fire action.

Ormonde squatting to retrieve his blade.

The cold press of steel on her throat, grown urgent.

Will, a shuffled step and a quick leap toward her. He led with his hands. Hands that grabbed the guardsman's face. It was a savage gesture, without thought, like an animal pouncing, mauling his prey.

She pulled away, out from the path of Rollo's feral leap. Away from her attacker's knife.

The guardsman's neck sounded a morbid crack, a hollow echo in the dank stone chamber. His fall, a dull thud.

Rollo went to Felicity at once. Wrapped her in his arms. His hands were all over her. He felt her face, her throat. The feel of him, solid against her, was like a homecoming.

Will, her home now.

Stroking her hair, he pulled her close, and then pushed back again, to ensure with his eyes what his hands had discerned. That she was unharmed.

"You came," she cried. "I knew you'd come. I told him to watch out—that you'd come."

"How could I not?" His hands stilled, cupped her cheeks. Rollo leaned in to kiss her tenderly. One chaste and lingering kiss on her mouth, still damp from her tears.

"I hate to interrupt you lovers, but I'd rather we make haste from here, before Robertson's wee army of God discovers we've regained possession of his pretty prize witch."

"Aye. Are you fine to travel?" Will asked her gently.

At her nod, he tucked her close. Her eyes widened.

"Where's your cane?"

"I couldn't very well climb down the ladder with it, could I?" He gave her a small smile.

"You came down to save me with nothing but that little knife in your sock?"

"A man has his hands too, aye?" He squeezed her waist, emphasizing his point.

She gave a startled laugh, and spied a flicker of joy on his face in response, as if only now it was hitting him that she was safe. That Robertson was dead.

"But you're right," Rollo said, turning to his friend. "We need to be away, and at once, before my brother comes sniffing about." Lifting his arm, he said to Ormonde, "For once I'll ask for your assistance, man."

"Oh God be praised," Ormonde said, rolling his eyes. He stepped to Rollo, offering his shoulder for the short walk across the chamber floor. "Finally. The man accepts help."

"Don't gloat," Will told him, with a rare twinkle in his eye. "This will be the last thing I ask of you."

"Indeed," Ormonde said, growing serious. "From this moment on, you are the one who'll be called upon. The Sealed Knot men don't forget a debt." He looked at the bodies littering the floor behind them, some complicated internal calculation knitting his brow. "And so it is here I must say good-bye to you. For now."

They climbed back up the ladder, the red-haired man's ominous words hanging in the air.

Chapter 24

"So . . . *cool*," Felicity said, kicking at the edges of the dirt pathway. "You're telling me the Romans marched right here? Like, along this very track?"

"Aye, along this very one." Rollo stopped and turned, studying the path they'd just traversed. Some stretches were a deep and well-defined track, when all that was left of others was an eroded scar in the earth.

The Roman road was concealed by a dense thicket, which rose like a canopy around them, its mossy branches gnarled with age, dark and smelling of lush, rotted undergrowth, like some forest primeval. He'd had to slash their way in, edging carefully through and into the heart of what felt to Felicity like some long-slumbering dryad, vaguely malevolent and poised at any moment to creak into life, wrapping its woody claws around to seal them in forever.

"What you see is the ghost of the Roman Empire's northernmost border."

"Did you have to say *ghost*?"

"Don't fret, you." Chucking her chin, Rollo gave a low

laugh. "Though many know of the Roman fort in Kincladie Wood, few know this ancient road exists as well."

"That just means they'll never find us," she said with dramatic gloom, chafing her arms and walking on.

"Afraid we'll rouse the big Green Man from his slumber and he'll come and eat us?"

She nodded nervously, an exaggerated frown of fear crinkling her features. "That's almost exactly what I was thinking."

"Fear not." He wrapped his arm around her, hugging her close. "I shall protect you. I'm a valiant knight, remember?" Rollo kissed the top of her head. "And besides," he added, patting his sporran, "there's a reward for you at the end."

"A reward?" she cooed, giving him a saucy wink.

He opened his mouth to speak, and then shut it again, growing somber.

It seemed to Felicity she'd just witnessed some inner light flickering, then winking out.

"Wait." She stopped. "What's the matter?"

"There's naught that's—"

"Don't you *naught* me, William Rollo. You just thought something. Something not good, and I want to know what it was."

"It's only . . ."

"Only?" she demanded.

"It's only that we cannot . . . We should not lie together again."

"What?" She rounded on him. "That's crazy talk. Why the hell not? You didn't just save me from some deranged kidnapper only to . . . Wait." She thought she knew what this was about. Her good, old-fashioned, noble Viking. "Is it that you think we should get married first, because—"

At the mention of marriage, she saw something in him die. She saw the despair, and she knew.

"You're going to send me back, aren't you?" she asked him quietly.

He gave her a silent, grim nod.

"You bastard." She shoved him in the chest, and his eyes

widened in surprise. "You are *not* going to send me back. I belong with *you*," she said, stabbing a finger in his chest.

"I shouldn't have compromised you so," he said, his words so formal, she felt like she was being shut out. "I'd rather have you safe than—"

"Than have sex with me?" Felicity blurted. She grew still. "Are you saying we shouldn't have done it the first time?"

He opened his mouth, but didn't speak. Why wasn't he saying anything?

Tears threatened, her voice reed-thin. "Are you saying you think this was a mistake?"

"Och, love. Never." He canted his head, studying her as if for the last time. Such openness, such raw emotion was in his gaze, Felicity thought her heart would break from it. "I'll never regret it. Never regret you. But . . . it's too dangerous. I was a fool. You had me believing that you were sent back to me. *For* me. To be by my side."

"But I was," she said simply. "And now mister preacher man is dead. I'm safe. We're getting away. Happily ever after, and all that jazz."

"Your . . . happily ever after . . . can only come when you are safe. Here you are not, will never be, safe." He took her shoulders. His hands were so gentle and strong, his eyes on her so intent, so earnest. And it was as though he'd begun to pull away already. "Aye, Robertson is dead, but his followers are not. These men . . . they're like a great, ravenous beast that's scented blood. They enjoy what they do, Felicity. Some of them truly believe you *are* a witch. They want to see you burn."

"But . . ."

"No, love, let me finish." The shadow of some distant pain pinched his features. "If that weren't enough, there's my brother to contend with. Robertson wasn't in this alone. I see Jamie's hand at work. My brother will not rest until he sees you ripped from my arms."

They stared at each other in silence. Felicity's mind refused to process what was happening.

"It would be too selfish of me," he said finally. "Too great a risk. I'll not see you in danger ever again. And so I must see you gone."

Tears stung her eyes. Her throat clenched, from misery, from frustration, from desperation. She had to convince him she needed to stay. He was her hero, her Viking. He could protect her. She would *show* him she needed to stay.

"Screw that, William Rollo." Her voice was a fierce growl.

She leapt for him, and Rollo stumbled backwards. His cane clattered to the dirt as he caught her, supported her. She wrapped her legs around him, kissing him, tangling her fingers wildly in his thick, soft, chestnut hair.

It took him only a moment to start kissing her back, and she knew a brief flicker of triumph. She felt his moans hum through her, but whether they were sounds of pleasure or anguish, Felicity wasn't sure.

She craved him, completely. Wanted to take him in, feel his breath in her lungs. To feel him inside her, to feel Rollo spill himself, inside her.

Then, surely, he'd realize.

She pulled from him, cradled his face in her hands. Her voice was the barest whisper. "Please, Will. I want you. Just one more time."

She felt him between her legs, hard and wanting her in return, and she knew she had him. She'd convince him she could handle the past, and he'd want one more, and one more, and one more again.

"Lay me down, Will." Felicity trailed slow kisses along his face, his neck. "Lay down with me."

She unhooked her legs from around his waist. Nestling the hard length of him between her thighs, she did a slow slide down the front of his body to the ground.

"We shouldn't . . ." he said raggedly. "I must remain alert. I vowed I'd see you back safe."

"What better way to keep me safe than to lay right on top of me?" She tugged at his arms, beckoning him down to the ground.

The forest floor was cool and soft, a rich, mossy loam that gave with their weight. Light filtered in through the knotted thicket overhead, and what had seemed a malignant wood spirit now felt natural, some primitive homecoming, dirt and sex and trees.

He lay on his side facing her, his face a map of pain and longing.

"Don't think," she whispered to him. "Just be. Let go, Will. You'll most regret the thing you don't do, not the thing you do."

She traced her fingertip lightly along his features. The strong edges of jaw and cheekbone, his aristocratic brow and nose.

"Don't you want me?" Her soft voice mingled with the rustles and sighs of the forest around them.

"How could you even think I'd not want you?" he asked hoarsely. Will put his hand on hers, stilling it. He turned his head to kiss her palm. "Wanting you is all I've been doing since the first day I laid eyes on you."

"And so you have me." Putting her hands on his shoulders, she guided him onto his back and swung a leg over to straddle him. He nestled between her legs, hard already, and the feel of it flashed her back to their first time.

Him, familiar, a body already known by her own, as readily recognized as his heart. Her chest crackled with the joy of it.

He watched her, watched this glorious creature climb onto him for the second time in his life, not knowing how it could be that he was worthy of such a thing. Elation and grief collided in his heart with an ache rivaled only by the one between his legs.

Will reached up to unlace her. She stopped him, giving him a single slow, mute shake of her head.

With a seductive arch of her back, Felicity reached behind to undo her own laces. She was careful and silent, her eyes not shifting from his. Her hair slipped through her gown as she raised it over her head, falling in a heavy spill over her shoulders and breasts.

Compelled to touch it, to touch her, he brushed his knuckle lightly over a swath of that hair, thick yellow silk over her hardened nipple.

She inhaled sharply, and his eyes shot back to hers. They both remained silent, this moment a fragile thing, charged already with the pain of good-bye.

She was naked now, and Will clothed, and looking up at her, the watery sunlight illuminating her from above, he could almost believe she was the fairy princess he'd mused about when he'd had his first sight of her.

Felicity reached down, began to carefully undress him, and this time he let her. Her concentration, those graceful and precise movements, stabbed him with an anguish that stole the breath from his chest.

Finally he felt her skin on his, and he shut his eyes, overwhelmed by it all. His desire, his pain, both drowning him.

He felt her shift, lean closer. Felt her face hover over his, but still he kept his eyes closed. Perhaps he'd never wake from this dream. Perhaps they'd always been here, could always remain here, in this magical, dark place, alone together.

He felt her kiss him tenderly. On his cheeks, his brow, her soft mouth tasting him all over, as if he were a sweet. The notion of it unmanned him.

How had he come to feel so deeply for her? Such a delight, such a treasure, she'd changed his life. Him, a man changed.

How would he ever live without her?

The thought made his lust grow desperate, his cock straining with the need to be in her, to claim her and keep her close.

He opened his eyes, and his first sight was her lovely face still held near, lips parted and waiting for him. He kissed her, dragged his hands along her naked back, and her hair fell around them like a curtain, burying him in the smell of her, a scent like flowers and musk.

He could wait no longer. Grabbing her hips, he lifted her

up and onto him. The feel of her tight, wet heat enveloping him, bringing him home, made him shudder with pleasure. It felt too good, she felt too good.

The urge to plow into her consumed him, and he fought it, holding himself still until he could master his breath. Felicity moved first, with a moan and a rocking of her hips, and his lust exploded in response, subsuming him, blinding him, like a battle rage.

Will shifted, braced her body to flip her onto her back, but Felicity tensed her thighs, stopping him.

"No," she said, finally breaking the silence. "I want to stay on top this time."

He brought his hands, his mouth, to her breasts. Gripped her ass, her legs, clutching her closer, tighter. He couldn't consume enough of her.

She moved slowly at first, writhing over him, whispering his name, and then faster, and faster still, until he thought he might die from it. Might lose himself forever, if only he'd let go one last final bit.

And then he felt it—her movements slowing, strengthening, Felicity sat hard on him, gradually stilling.

Her hands, her thighs, and God help him, her muscles down deep, the whole of her body seized, clutching him. His cock, gripped deep inside her. He watched and felt the waves of her climax crash over her. Watched as her skin flushed pink, watched her eyes close and mouth open. Watched as she was lost to him.

And Will lost himself then too. Shutting his eyes, he let go, let himself spin into blackness, the touch and taste and smell of her the only gravity holding him to this earth.

Later, she dozed, but Will did not. He needed to savor every last moment with this woman. Stroking the hair from her damp brow, he wondered how he could ever let her go.

But how could he let her stay?

Felicity had been right on one count. He would have no regrets. He'd let himself love her.

Then he'd say good-bye.

Felicity would leave him, and he knew he would die inside. His life would be forfeit. He'd throw himself into his cause, help the Sealed Knot men, deliver their messages to the King.

Only now it wouldn't matter to him if he lived or died doing it.

Chapter 25

She woke sprawled over Will, the faint bristle of hair on a muscular chest tickling between her fingers. He'd finally fallen asleep. It was as if she'd given him a dare when she'd said men sack out right after sex. She'd dozed off right away, but every time she roused, he was there to soothe her at once, his hand caressing through her hair.

Night had fallen, and though her body was warm where it touched his, her back felt chilled and exposed. Carefully, she disentangled herself, found his plaid, and pulled it up over them both.

The thing was huge. Such a long stretch of wool, the same blue, green, and yellow of those funny, sexy pants he was wearing when she first met him. She much preferred him in the kilt.

She was wide awake, and occupied her mind with random thoughts. Like wondering how he wrapped all this wool around himself. And thinking about those troops of marching Romans. About witches, and ministers, and magic.

She filled her head with thoughts, and yet a numbing sadness persisted, looming somewhere at the edges, threatening to overtake her. He thought she was in danger, that she needed to go back.

And she knew he was right about the danger. She'd gotten a taste of Robertson's men. A demon light had blazed in their eyes, longing to tie her up and toss her in the dungeon. To burn her.

But Will thought he couldn't protect her, and there she knew he was wrong. He was her brave hero; she didn't understand why he didn't see it himself. He was strong and valiant, and would save her from any threat. And she had a limited time in which to convince him.

Knowing there was only one thing that would calm her mind, she slid her hand down Will's chest. He stirred, sighed deeply in and out, then his breathing grew rhythmic once more.

She felt suddenly wicked and free there, lying naked in the woods, the flicker of starlight making its way into their burrow, a faint patchwork shimmering through the dense thicket overhead.

Felicity traced her hand lower. Found the light line of hair at the base of that flat belly, leading from navel to groin. A little shiver of pleasure rippled through her, tracing her fingers through it. *Happy trails*, she thought with a naughty smile.

She wondered what time it was. Feeling that chest and those abs had made her eager for the sun to rise. Will's upper body was strong, compensating for his damaged legs, and she wanted to see him move in the daylight. Watch how his muscles would shift and flex. She wanted to memorize every detail.

Her hand moved lower. Brushed along his cock. It began to rouse at once. She didn't want to wake Will, but she couldn't keep her hands off of him. He was so vulnerable in sleep, all hers, there for the taking.

She touched him again. He continued to stir, stiffen. She couldn't not touch him. He swelled to life, that thin skin, fine like silk.

"I thought you said just the once." His voice was a husky rasp.

"Well . . ." She looked up and smiled at him in the dark.

She'd loved watching him sleep, but she much preferred having him awake, by her and with her.

She could've fooled herself, thinking her goal was simply to really *really* convince him she needed to stay, but Felicity knew she simply just wanted Will inside her again. To connect with him, feel his love filling her.

"As long as we're here . . ." She began to stroke him, just in case he needed her to draw a picture.

He didn't.

Will pulled her closer, careful with her body along the moss and leaves of the ancient path. He kissed her, and deepened the kiss at once. His body ready for her, at once.

He turned her away from him, onto her side, and giving his arm for a pillow, settled himself behind her. Her back had been so chilled, but the feel of that solid chest and belly on her skin warmed her, finally, thoroughly. Heated her.

She was turned on already, thought she'd probably woken that way, and she nestled her rump back to find him, urge him on.

He stroked his hand down her side, along her leg, and back up again, cupping her breast and pulling her more tightly to him. He slid into her and this time was only tender, only slow, nibbling lightly along her shoulder, nuzzling kisses and words of love into her neck.

And as they came, Felicity embraced the calm that finally smoothed the chatter from her mind.

⊗

"How do you work this thing?" She stood before him in only her petticoat, his plaid draped over and around her, trying to get a handle on all that wool.

Part of her wanted to make him get up and stalk his naked way over to her. Another part simply wanted to try the darned thing on.

"Planning to don my plaid, is it?" He grinned.

"No. Maybe." Shrugging, she smiled back at him. "I just want to see how you do it." She bobbed the fabric up and down. "Man, this is heavy."

"We Scotsmen are a strapping lot." He sat extra straight, giving a slight flex to his muscles.

"Sure you are," she said with a laugh.

"Och, you devil me." Chuckling, he gestured to the fabric. "Just lay out my plaid, love. You can help me put it on."

"Oh my God," she gasped. "It's about time you asked. The only thing sexier than your kilt is the thought of helping you into it." She billowed the wool out like a sheet, letting it fall heavily to the ground. "Strike that, actually. Nothing beats taking it off," she said, mustering her best saucy wink.

"Don't get any ideas, woman." He furrowed his brows in an attempt to look menacing. "There's only so much a man can take."

He moved opposite her, straightening the fabric's edges along the ground. Felicity guessed it was no less than five feet wide and over twelve feet long.

"This is kooky!"

"I'm not sure what that word is, love, but if you mean to say this is not always the most convenient procedure, then aye, it isn't."

She didn't correct him; Will was just too cute. He looked up and caught her staring at him with what she was certain was a dopey, adoring look.

"If I'd known the sight of my plaid would put you in such a sweet dither, I'd have enlisted your help long ago."

He sat down and began to gather the wool into folds. "Come, kneel just here. We need to pleat it. Aye," he said, seeing her pick up his belt, "we need that too, tucked so." He slipped his belt under the plaid, roughly bisecting the wool across the center.

He lay down on it, with the upper edge of the plaid beneath his head and the bottom resting just under his knees. "Then you roll right into it."

"Ooh," she purred. "Can I roll right in there with you?"

"Next time," he promised with exaggerated solemnity. "I swear it."

"Oh!" she exclaimed suddenly, watching as he wrapped the wool around his legs. "So you get on top, belt it, and the bottom half is the kilt—"

"And the other"—he sat up, pulling the two top ends over his shoulder, one from the front, one from behind—"goes like so."

She retrieved his leather cord from the dirt and tied it off at his shoulder for him. "And next the sporran, right?" she asked, crawling to grab it.

"Aye." He gave her a broad smile. "And inside that sporran is a wee token for you."

"Token? I love tokens!" She plucked his sporran from the ground to hand to him. Hesitating, she pulled it back, tucking it to her chest. "Can *I* see what's in your little murse?"

"My . . . eh?"

"You know, man-purse. Murse."

"Och, woman." He snagged it from her hands, swatting her on the behind just as she was sitting back down. "Mock me, and I'll be forced to punish you."

"Mm-hm." Waggling her fingers toward his sporran, she said, "Hand it over, big boy."

He relented, and she snatched the whole thing back.

She experienced a moment of total contentment. It felt like such an intimate thing, such a personal thing, holding his sporran. Her and Will, just sitting there looking through his stuff. She smiled.

"You still didn't answer my question," she said, stroking the sporran's flap. It was covered by something gray, furry, and somewhat matted, the provenance of which she dare not question.

"Yes."

"Yes you didn't answer my question, or yes I can look in your murse?"

"Call it that one more time and I'll withhold your wee gift."

She feigned outrage, and he barked out a laugh in response. "Careful," he warned, "or I'll kiss that scowl from your face."

"Oh I wish you would." She leaned in, offering herself to be kissed.

Her offer had been playful, but Rollo grew serious. His suddenly hooded eyes prompted an instant response from her body, warm and flushed.

"You will be the death of me," he muttered, cradling the back of her head for a slow, deep kiss. Her breath caught in her chest, and she wondered if she'd ever get over this. Ever get over the complete craving she felt when it came to Will. He pulled from her, leaving Felicity dazed.

His eyes held hers for a moment, and she thought he must have felt it too. He smudged her lower lip with his thumb. "Open it, then," he told her huskily. "As you must."

The prospect of rifling through his sporran spread a tickled little grin on her face, and she watched as it caught his too.

"Oh, I must," she said, digging in. "Let's see . . . Bullets?" she asked, pulling out a heavy pouch that clacked as she palmed it.

"Aye, lead shot."

"Aren't *you* dangerous?" she mused with a smile, continuing to rifle. "What else . . . A handkerchief, and, oh"—giggling, she pulled out a leather coin purse—"look, another murse, how cute!"

He glowered at her.

"Okay, okay," she said, stifling her laughter, and pulled out a small metal box. "What's this?"

"My tinderbox."

"What's in it?"

"My tinder," he said hesitantly.

"Yeah, but what's tinder?"

"Lord above, woman. Jamie is surely scouring the countryside for us, and you're asking *what's tinder*. I use it to light a fire."

"Ohhhh." She peeked back in the bag, muttering, "You can light my fire any day of the week, William Rollo."

She froze. There was a card stuck along the inside of the bag. "What's this?" It had wedged into a seam, and she plucked it out.

A Tarot card, just like Livvie's deck. A man walked blithely along, not seeing the cliff he was about to step from. *The Fool.*

"This is a Tarot card." A jumble of emotions rattled her. Such a small and specific memory of her aunt shot her through with grief. But she was also confused. "Where did you get this?"

"I found it. On a pretty girl." He smiled, cupped her cheek, and Felicity thought she might float away.

She must've brought one of the Tarot cards with her. And Will had kept it. She marveled. Why would he keep such a trifling thing?

She smiled back, savoring the connection of his eyes locked with hers. Beaming, she dipped back into the sporran.

"A-ha! Here's a little *somethin-somethin*," she said, pulling out the blue velvet bag. "What might this be?"

"That might be something."

"Something for me?"

"Aye. Though you've been exceptionally naughty. I don't know that you've earned it."

"You just watch me earn it," she said in her best seductress voice. "Maybe I haven't been naughty enough . . ."

"Oho!" He laughed, wrapping her hands around the gift. "If I have any hopes of walking out of here no more lame than I already am, you'll need to staunch your naughtiness for another hour at least."

"Well?" she asked.

"Well what?"

"Well can I open it?"

"And you're suggesting I could stop you?"

"Oh goodie," she said, assessing the pouch in her hand. There was something thick inside. Larger than a ring, smaller than a bracelet, though with the heft of one. "What is it?"

He merely shrugged, and she leaned in, planting an enthusiastic kiss on his cheek. "I love presents."

"Aye, so I see."

She beamed at him. She could listen to that accent for the rest of her life and she'd never tire of all Will's *ayes*.

Felicity carefully unknotted the drawstring, and made a little anticipatory gasp to see the twinkle of polished metal.

She pulled out a piece of jewelry made of hammered gold. It was shaped like a torc, an unclosed circle that bore the head of a Celtic creature at each end, with brownish gems for eyes. A thick, blunt pin was secured along the back.

"Oh, Will." Tucking it close to her heart, she told him, "I love it."

"A Viking design," he said, smiling. "I thought it only fitting."

"Viking jewelry from my Viking." She shook her head, momentarily speechless, tilting the piece to glint in the weak sunlight.

"The stones are garnet," he told her, watching her avidly. "They put me in mind of your eyes, when they're caught by the sun."

"Is . . . is it a brooch?"

"No . . ." He turned her head gently and, gathering two thick swaths of her hair, secured it at the crown of her head. "For your bothersome hair. Don't you know? My wish is to free you of even the smallest of your troubles."

"My silly hair." Tears stung her eyes as she turned to look at him. Her Will. He was gorgeous to her, sitting there looking so uncharacteristically rumpled, with a day-old beard and disheveled brown hair. "You remembered."

"Aye, Felicity. You are a hard woman to forget."

❁

They walked along the road, and Will was more certain than ever that Felicity must go.

Time alone with her was heaven. If he thought it were possible to disappear together, to run away and hide on some distant island as James had with Magda, he'd leap at the chance. But he could not let himself forget, for even a moment, the grave danger she was in.

Every minute she spent in the past, the danger only grew. Jamie was relentless; he wouldn't stop until everything Will loved was destroyed. Even now, he'd be combing the countryside for them. Even now, he'd have Robertson's followers whipped into a bloodthirsty frenzy.

He had to keep her safe. They had to say good-bye. And Will knew their parting would forever extinguish this strange new vitality, this joy, he'd discovered deep within.

She'd leave, returning to her strange and foreign world. But Will would stay. He'd pledged his help to the Sealed Knot men, to the King. He'd keep his word, and it would likely cost him his life.

But parting from Felicity? The cost of that would be his very soul.

She kept biting her lip in concentration, touching the back of her head, tracing her finger over her wee hair ornament. Will wondered if there wasn't an invisible string tied from that mouth to his heart, because every time she nibbled at it with that look of happiness on her face, he felt a tug in his chest. It was deeply gratifying to have pleased her so.

She was such a delight, always so ready to embrace pleasure, to be with her was a revelation. When he was by her side, he forgot his inclination to sink ever downward. He'd lived his life driven by disquiet, despondency. But Felicity was so easy, so light, with an inner fire that illuminated a side of himself he'd never known existed.

It was agony to think on their coming good-bye. He was leading them to Lochaber, to Cameron lands. He'd heard tell of a witch there, one who could help his Felicity.

The thought was too painful. An instant misery, like those nettles that had stung her what felt like so long ago. And so he pushed it from his mind, choosing instead to cling to this brief flare of joy in his life.

This joy that he would allow himself to feel, before he had to bid it farewell forever.

Chapter 26

"You will deliver Ormonde and your brother William to me."
Richard Cromwell flicked the ends of his hair over his shoulders, a habit that Jamie was finding particularly irritating.
"Their heads will suffice."

"Who are you to order me?" Jamie paused before the grave
of Maggie Wall. Once such an inspiration, it now served as a
bitter reminder of how Will had thwarted his plans yet again.

Oliver Cromwell's half-wit son had shown up on the
doorstep of Duncrub Castle, bold as day. Jamie promptly
whisked him to someplace more discreet. Robertson's un-
timely death had riled the minister's followers and set village
tongues to wagging, and he dared not bring undue attention
onto the Rollo household. "Is that an order from your father?" Jamie asked.

"My father is dead."

"Ah." *Oliver Cromwell, dead?* The news silenced Jamie,
his mind barraged by a thousand different thoughts. Would
Cromwell's death mean the restoration of the King? Would
Parliamentarians like him find their fates on the gallows?

"And who takes over in his stead?" Jamie finally asked.

"I," Richard said simply. He removed a large handkerchief from his pocket and fastidiously spread it over a large rock. He sat, crossing his legs primly at the ankles. "Richard Cromwell, Lord Protector of England, Scotland, and Ireland. I quite like the sound."

Could it be true? Could Oliver Cromwell truly have designated his underachieving third son as his successor? And should this half-wit fail? They'd all be hanged as traitors.

"I shall mourn your father," Jamie told him carefully. Richard gave a mute nod and another flick over his shoulders, and Jamie thought his pale hair and weak features gave the impression of a diluted version of the elder Cromwell. "Oliver Cromwell was one of the last, great men. His death must have been a shock to your family."

"Indeed. Thankfully it didn't happen before he had the opportunity to name me his successor." Dusting a leaf from his trousers, he scanned his eyes slowly over Jamie. "My father spoke of you. I was curious to meet you. The infamous eldest Rollo."

Jamie bristled. When would he be seen as his own person? He was always lumped with the Rollo men. Tiresome and self-righteous, the lot of them.

"How is it to have a crippled war hero for a brother?" Richard asked suddenly. "It must've stung when he bested you at the Tower."

Jamie was grateful his face was turned. *Tread with care.* He schooled his emotions, smoothing the loathing from his face. "I would've traveled to you, in London," he said, ignoring the jibe. "Upon hearing the news."

"But I find it illuminating to meet men in their own province," Richard said, taking in the woods around them. "There is no better way to take the measure of a man than unguarded and among his family. And your Perthshire has a peculiar . . . charm. *Maggie Wall.* Peculiar indeed," he added with distaste, studying the crudely painted grave marker. "Though I would've liked to see the actual inside of your home."

"Too much danger has crossed my mother's doorstep already."

"A dutiful son." Richard nodded. "If only we could see the same sense of duty applied to the Parliamentary cause."

Jamie was struck speechless, and Cromwell took advantage. "I too am a dutiful son," he continued. "And carry on I must. It appears our Royalist enemies have found ways to communicate. Correspondence has been making its way to the King."

"Beg pardon," Jamie said in mock innocence. Though he knew he should proceed with caution, this little meeting had him feeling decidedly testy. "But we no longer call Charles II king, correct?"

"Spare me the academics." Richard's lip twitched in a petulant grimace. The man was silent for a moment, presumably deliberate, the intention for Jamie to feel his wrath. But Jamie found it had quite the opposite effect, almost comic.

Weak-chinned buffoon.

All had heard of Oliver's attempts to discipline Richard, to train him, hammer a backbone into the man. But Oliver could lay in his deathbed and call his son a leader, and still it wouldn't make him one.

"As I was saying, the death of my father gives these Royalists fresh hope. The people have gotten the idea they need"—he scowled—"*representation* in the Parliament. More and more rally each day to restore the King."

"Englishmen do love their monarchs," Jamie muttered. *I could always flee to France. Escape the wrath of a restored king, should this half-wit fail.*

"But I'd have the people love *me*."

Or I could find myself an exotic whore and wait this out in the Indies. Jamie could barely conceal his disdain. "It's not the people whose love you require. As I understand it, you're finding few friends among the military."

"And that's where you come in, Rollo." Cromwell's eyes narrowed, and Jamie wondered where in hell this could be going. "If I were to bring down this secret Sealed Knot group, it would do much to earn confidence. Ormonde is a member, and it seems your own brother must be too. Both men were in our hands, and both *you* lost."

My damned brother. Always it comes back to damned Willie. "It wasn't my brother who was imprisoned. It was his woman."

"Beside the point. I don't understand why my father put up with you." Richard shook his head as if disappointed in a willful child. "You were asked to keep a handle on Ormonde. He escaped on your watch, and now he ferries back and forth, easy as you please, carrying letters to and from Charles as if he were a goddamned pigeon."

Jamie had to look away. He refused to suffer such scolding. Richard had been ineffectual when he was merely Cromwell's third son, and Jamie couldn't imagine he'd be any more capable now.

He glimpsed Richard's lizard smile out of the corner of his eyes. The man thought he'd scored a victory, and it made Jamie's blood boil.

"What's important to you?" Richard pressed. "Because if it's advancement, I suggest you do what you can to squash these Royalists. Retrieve your brother, retrieve Ormonde, get a handle on these things which have spun out of your control."

Out of my control?

Jamie wondered about true leaders and what special quality it was that sparked fear in the hearts of their men. For though Richard was giving him a talking-to, Jamie couldn't muster enough respect even to look the man directly in the eye.

"Your father doubted neither my commitment nor my abilities," Jamie said coldly. *No man, not even this fool, will doubt my abilities ever again.* "I will do these things for you. I will bring you my brother."

"Yes, you will." Richard flicked his hair. "As I've said, his head will suffice."

Chapter 27

"Don't get me wrong." Felicity adjusted herself on the thick blanket they were using in lieu of a saddle. When the Roman road ended and they'd emerged from the woods, Will left her to rest, and he returned having somehow procured a horse.

"I'm very happy to be off my feet." She wriggled those feet, stretching her sore calves. "And," she added, nestling her rump back along his belly, "I'm totally loving this riding with you thing." And boy, was she. Being safely encased in the hard muscle of Will's arms and legs was pure, delicious heaven. "But it seems to me you can't just take someone's horse."

"'Twas borrowed from a Campbell. Believe me, love, the Campbells have coin enough for an entire herd of horses, straight from Arabia if they wished it."

"Yeah . . ." she said hesitantly. She didn't think she'd ever really get all the various clans and the seemingly irrational hatred some of them bore each other. "But it's still stealing."

"Then would that I could have *stolen* two."

"Wouldn't that just be twice as bad?"

He sighed deeply.

"What did *that* mean?" She reached back and nudged him with her elbow.

"It means you have much to learn about the ways of the Highlands."

"Are you saying I'll be staying?"

"You know I'm not." He hugged his arms snugly around her belly in an effort to take the sting from his words.

"You'll see. You'll decide to let me stay." She took one of his hands from her belly and brought it to her breast. "How's about we take a little break so I can try to convince you again?" She wriggled her hips, grinding back in an attempt to rouse him.

"Och, woman." Will nuzzled her from behind, trailing lingering kisses and nibbles along her neck. He gave her breast a gentle squeeze. "Would that we had time. But there's no rest for us now."

Her neck was cool as he pulled from her to take in the wide-open glen around them. The riding was slow going now, headed uphill.

"They'll be after us," he said. "We cannot risk getting caught. I imagine we'll have riled my brother," Will added with a low chuckle.

"Where are we going?"

"I've told you. To Cameron country, to return you home."

"Will we be safe there?" She still hadn't gotten over the shock of being kidnapped, or of witnessing men go at each other so savagely. Though she wanted to remain with Will, her strong preference would be to stay clear of men with swords.

And ministers too, now that she thought about it.

"That's the point of this exercise, love. I'd not have you anywhere that's not safe."

She leaned her head back, flush with the feeling of being loved, of being so cared for and protected, and in such a very literal way.

"I've got to know," she heard herself ask. "Have you ever been in love?"

"As I also must know," he replied quickly, "has anyone ever told you, you ask too many questions?"

"It's the mark of an intelligent woman."

"Oh indeed?"

"Yup. Come on, just tell me. You know I won't let you rest until you answer me."

If Felicity had thought about it beforehand, she probably would've been too nervous to ask such a thing. But now that the question was out there, she had to know the answer. Reaching her hand back to tousle his head, she tried to lighten the moment by telling him in a seductive snarl, "You can run, but you can't hide."

He was silent. Completely silent and still at her back. Just when Felicity thought she'd asked a question she maybe didn't want the answer to, Will spoke.

"No," he told her quietly. "You are the first. And the last."

A part of her had known. And though something deep down had sensed how new, how novel, Will's feelings were to him, his words resonated through her. She let them hang, stabbing her, leaving her unexpectedly gutted, and sad.

It felt like such a tremendous loss. She couldn't bring herself to understand it. How could she have made such an extraordinary journey, come all this way to find love with this one man, only to have to say good-bye? She couldn't accept that it was happening, that she would be leaving him.

They rode to the top of the slow-rising hill. Will pulled their horse to a halt and loosened the reins, letting him lower his head to graze. The animal's coat was lightly damp from exertion, and it gave a twitch and shiver from the gentle breeze that swept the hilltop.

The Highlands rolled out before them. Uneven, tangled greens here, but rock there, gray and lifeless and ragged. Water like indigo glass stretched toward the horizon. There was the distant honking of geese, but an utter quiet also overwhelmed them, like the sound of stone and still water.

The view took her breath away. And it put a picture to all the emotions roiling in her. The not quite desolation, not quite loneliness that clutched at the edges of her heart.

She needed to hear his voice, and so with a nod to a far hill asked, "Is that where we're going?"

"No, love." He gathered the reins, and the horse tossed his head in protest. Will felt Felicity's sudden melancholy like a winter rain. Though it was something he'd known was on the horizon, still it chilled him, stole something from his heart. "We've a long journey yet."

Will needed only to think about moving to push his horse into a walk. He'd always felt at home on horseback. He was a cavalryman; he believed he'd been born thus.

Then the accident had happened, and great beasts like this one had become for him the strong legs he lacked. Many horses, just like this one, saving him in battle.

He let his mind drift, thinking on all those moments in his life when he'd cheated death. As a seven-year-old crushed by a pony. As a man lying broken and bleeding on the battlefield.

It had been Ormonde who'd helped him that day, when he'd been shot on the field at Philiphaugh. Ormonde had pulled him from a puddle of his own blood. Taken him to safety.

He'd been fighting by James Graham's side. Will's mind touched on his beloved friend and comrade. Graham was out there somewhere, with his Magda and a cottage full of daughters.

And now Will found himself again owing Ormonde. Will was indebted to him and Ormonde's Sealed Knot men, and never did he turn his back on his friends. Never did Will forget an obligation.

Soon he would let Felicity go and would let his life be forfeit for the restoration of a king.

But first they needed to ride. Rough, hilly riding, until they reached Lochaber. He felt exposed on these open Highland passes and would feel this nagging danger at their backs until they found themselves safe on Cameron land. Until Felicity was safely returned home.

The thought sickened him. Will felt as though he was dying from the inside, and he'd not be surprised if, in the moment of their farewell, he were to breathe his last.

Fighting his misery, he wrapped his arms more tightly around her. Pulled her as snugly to him as he could, savoring the fit of her back against his belly, her ass pressed against his groin.

He supposed he could've found them a second horse, but he'd wanted to feel her close like this. Having her astride before him felt such a wickedly improper thing, with her skirts hiked up to afford illicit glimpses of calf and knee. He savored the shift of her shoulders on his chest and the soft give of her breasts against his arms. He fantasized that he was her second skin.

They headed downhill now, and Will leaned back to balance them. Pulled her back with him. They reached the bottom of the hill and he straightened, leaning forward into her, holding her even tighter, closer.

She made a small, pleased noise, and his hands gripped, pressed under her breasts.

"Will . . ." The breathlessness in her voice had him instantly rigid. "You know," she began, shifting against him, "Will, this is giving me ideas."

"Oh aye." He was well acquainted with *ideas*. He'd been having them since the moment they'd first met. Waking dreams that plagued him, day after day. He felt like a damned schoolboy, stealing renegade glimpses of breast and hip. And now here she was, flesh and blood, pressed against him for the taking.

He cupped her breast, kneaded it, and felt a rush of blood in his head, the desire for her dizzying. The knowledge that he could just take her, have her, unmoored him.

"Lower," she said, and he recognized that husky timbre in her voice. It was the sound of Felicity's want, and his already hard body quickened even more in response. "Lower, Will."

Could she really mean . . . ?

"I know you said we can't stop." Felicity took his hand, nudged it down. "But we don't need to. Just touch me," she told him softly.

There was a moan, and Will realized it must've been his own. He didn't require any more urging from her, and brought his hand down. Nestling it between her legs, he damned her thick skirts that once again stood between him and her sweet flesh.

He was fully erect now, and the rub and tangle of his plaid irritated him. Yet again he'd be forced to ride his climax through the maddening chafe of wool.

"Wait," she said, and he froze, stopping at once. He cursed himself for being a boor. Had she not wanted him to touch her so? Had he somehow misunderstood?

She took the reins, clumsily pulled the horse to a stop.

"What—?" he began.

But Felicity swung her leg over, settling herself sidesaddle, and the words froze in his throat. She twisted her body, anchoring herself on one of his shoulders.

"What," he exclaimed, "what in God's name are you—?"

She muttered curses under her breath, struggling and hiking at her skirts. With a violent tug, Felicity flipped her gown up. With a naughty giggle, she was clambering around to face him atop the horse.

"Good Lord, woman, I . . ."

She shoved his plaid up, and cool air hit him, a shock on his burning flesh. And then, God help him, she mounted him. Took him into her, and her wetness drew him deep, and God help him, it felt like where he belonged.

"Felicity, love." Stroking up her back, his hands spanned the width of her, and he savored the feel of this strange, delicate creature in his arms. He caressed the silk of her hair, and kissed her cheeks and brow and lips. He couldn't see enough of her, couldn't taste enough of her. "You are too much."

"Trot," she said.

"What?"

"Trot, Will. Make the horse trot."

"Och, no," he managed. "You'll kill us both."

And he continued to kiss her instead, and though his body raged, he set aside a small sliver of his mind, concentrating on keeping her balanced over him, on keeping the horse calm below.

She laughed a husky little laugh he recognized, and Will knew he was in trouble. And then, as he suspected she might, Felicity kicked the horse herself. Her legs, these soft, smooth, pale legs of a woman, began kicking away, slamming her heels at the horse's belly.

Will was their only connection to the horse now, and he held Felicity firmly, bearing her weight, his arms bracing her to him. His legs holding his seat steady.

Their horse was a docile creature, and he stepped into a reluctant walk. Still, Felicity's heels slammed away, and Will grew even harder despite himself, the feel of her tight body writhing over him more than he could bear. She slammed her heels and the horse broke into a sluggish trot.

Will groaned, fighting to keep ahold of himself. His fingers gripped her soft flesh, and a distant part of himself worried he clung too hard. But she gasped her pleasure, tangling her fingers hard in his hair.

He was losing control. Needed to keep control. This was implausible, unimaginable.

"We must . . ." he began, and then realized he'd forgotten what he was going to say. It was as if a madness was overtaking him. He was deep in her, so deep.

She grew still, and he watched. Fascinated, reverent, he watched as her face grew flushed. Her eyelids flickered shut and her breathing hitched, halted. And then she shouted her climax.

"Will!" she cried, and it echoed through the valley. Somewhere in the back of his mind he knew they needed to be careful.

"We must," he began again, but was unable to speak, so instead put his fingers over her mouth to quiet her. He slowed the horse to a walk, and began to move in and out of her, in time to the gait of the horse.

Felicity bit his fingertip. She opened her eyes, catching and holding his gaze as she sucked his finger in and out of her mouth. Her tongue was rough, her cheek smooth, and Will fought his own climax as memories of his cock in her mouth jerked his body.

She was going to be the death of him. This gorgeous, shocking, unexpected gift would be the death of him, and he'd go a happy man.

Felicity sagged in his arms, her hips rocking in an exaggerated sway. Inhaling sharply, she ground against him, and he could tell she was winding up once more. He felt a rush of her wetness. Her body stilled, and he knew she was close.

He pulled his finger from her lips. He could wait no longer. Clamping his mouth over hers, he took her breath with a kiss as he shot himself into her, riding Felicity as she came in waves over him.

Chapter 28

They'd arrived at the Cameron clan's Tor Castle. Laird Ewen Cameron was huge, with black hair and blue eyes and the chiseled look of a romance novel cover model. But it was the ginormous sword poking up from between his shoulders that currently held her attention.

"He's not going to try and use that on Will, is he?" Felicity's eyes shifted from the laird, to his wife, and back again.

"My husband likes to carry a big stick."

"Uh-huh." Felicity eyed Lily Cameron, noting the toddler's pudgy hand held in hers, the baby on her hip, and poor thing, the belly ready to burst with her third. "I'll say he does," she blurted without thinking.

But instead of laughing, Lily narrowed her eyes thoughtfully. Even after Felicity turned away, she sensed the woman assessing her, could see her poufy white-blonde hair out of the corner of her eye.

"Och," Will gave a good-natured growl, "I've known Ewen since he was a stripling. If he tries to move on me, he knows I'll give him a sound thrashing."

Ewen's deep voice exploded into laughter. "Have a care,

Rollo, or I'll use your wee staff to skewer you and eat you for supper. Now come. We've much to discuss. Lily can show your woman around."

His woman? A Neanderthal and his baby-machine wife. Great. Where the hell had Will taken her?

She gave Rollo her best please-don't-abandon me look, but he just smiled in return, traipsing off with Ewen, and leaving her with the blonde and the two kids.

Felicity realized Lily was still watching her, light dancing in her eyes. *What's her deal?*

The laird's wife giggled and said, "My husband can be an acquired taste."

Felicity could only stare dumbly. *American accent?* Recovering, she asked, "You're not from around here, are you?"

"No." Lily smiled at her. "And I could tell from the get-go that you're definitely not either." She hiked the baby higher up on her hip. The kid seemed huge already. If the size of the laird was any indication, the woman was going to need some serious chiropractics when all this baby making was done. "Now come on," Lily said. "I'll have one of the maids show you your room."

"Uhh . . ." *Oh goody*, she thought. More household staff for her to be nervous around. More impenetrable accents and strange looks.

"Ah." Lily gave her a quick nod. "Got it. Let me just drop the rug rats with Kat, and I'll show you around myself."

It was when Lily took extra time to carefully explain the finer points of castle plumbing that Felicity finally began to relax. Who'd have thought a castle would have such a cool little stone toilet? Once you got used to the freezing air blowing on your bum, that is.

By the time Lily dug up an old gown for her to borrow, the two of them were chatting as if they were old friends. "Seriously," Lily said, pushing the gown into Felicity's hands. She rubbed her belly, adding, "I'm not going to be fitting into any real clothes anytime soon."

"Well, *seriously*," Felicity mimicked the other woman's

word with a smile, "I don't see how *I'm* going to fit into this
either." Smoothing the dress out on the bed, Felicity tucked
at the bosom, creating imaginary darts. "If you haven't noticed, you've got a lot more going on upstairs than I do."

Lily giggled, then asked, "East Coast or West?"

"Excuse me?" Felicity spun, staring at the woman. Will
had alluded to other women traveling back in time. Could
this be one of them? "What did you just say?"

"Will didn't know about me, did he? No, he wouldn't
have," Lily mused, answering her own question. "I think it's
been years since he and Ewen have seen each other. Well,
if Will didn't already know where I'm from, my husband's
probably telling him right now. Over a whisky, if I know my
Ewen."

"I'm sorry," Felicity said tentatively, sitting down on the
bed. She'd felt an instant connection with this woman, almost like she recognized Lily. But actually meeting another
woman from her place, her time, would be too much to ask.
"Are you saying what I think you're saying?"

"No, *I'm* sorry." Lily smiled. Supporting the small of her
back, she eased herself onto the bed next to Felicity. "I'm
getting way ahead of myself. Where exactly are you from?"

"I . . ." Felicity faltered, unsure of how to respond. "I'm
from Glasgow."

"If you're from Glasgow, then my name's Britney
Spears."

An incredulous laugh burst from Felicity. She *never*
would've guessed it'd ever feel so fantastic to hear the name
Britney Spears.

"You don't think I could pass?" Lily picked up a swath of
her hair, studying it. "I guess my hair is a little too curly. And
I'd never be able to do the—what is it—a Louisiana accent?
I'm a Cali girl after all."

"Oh, California!" Felicity exclaimed, her eyes wide. "Really? Me too."

"Yep," Lily said, her voice growing wistful. "San Fran,
baby. Late nineties. And what I wouldn't do for an avocado
right about now. You?"

"I can't believe this is happening. I live . . . I *lived* there too. In the Mission."

"Crazy . . ." Lily shook her head, marveling. "I always wondered when we'd meet someone else. There was another, Robert, Ewen's foster brother." Lily's smile faded, and her voice grew subdued. "He died. Though lately we've been talking about the whole time travel thing. It seems like there must be some way to . . . Well, that's a whole other story." Lily brightened her features. "You still haven't told me, *when* are you from?"

"A little later than you. But not by much." Felicity's initial surprise was waning, replaced by an absurd pang of jealousy. *She* wanted to be the only one whose love was so great and so perfect the universe sent her back in time for it. "Did you make a wish to get here?"

"Wish?" Lily tilted her head, confused. "No way. I . . . sort of . . . fell here. Through the labyrinth. Wait, did you come through the maze too?"

"Maze?"

"Long story."

"Oh." *A maze.* Felicity hadn't needed a gimmick. She'd made a wish, and the universe had delivered Felicity directly to her One True Love. The thought perked her back up. "You could say I wished for him."

"You wished to come here?" Lily laughed. "Then I guess you weren't as freaked out as I was."

"Not really, actually. Tell me," Felicity said, pinning the laird's wife with a serious look. "What did you do to get Ewen to let you stay?"

"What?"

"How'd you convince him? To let you stay in the past."

"We reached a point where . . ." Lily blushed crimson. "Well, I don't think he'd have let me leave if I tried." She gave a little grinning shrug that was like a dagger in Felicity's chest.

Ewen loved Lily. Wouldn't let her go.

Sadness and desolation swamped her. Why wouldn't Will want her to stay too?

"But . . ." Felicity hesitated. "It seems so dangerous here. Aren't you scared? Like, aren't you afraid to be pregnant in the past?"

She could tell she hit a nerve somewhere. She saw the flicker of it in Lily's eye, and it made her feel a little guilty. But all the laird's wife said was, "When you love someone, I guess it conquers all fear."

Lily studied Felicity, as if seeing her anew. "Why?" she asked. "Are *you* scared to be here?"

Felicity was grateful they were interrupted by a knock on the door and a teenage boy bursting into the room. A handsome kid with the devil in his eye. The spitting image of Ewen.

"Da's looking for you." Though he was speaking to Lily, the boy's gaze didn't budge from Felicity.

"Is he now? It's not simply that you wanted to meet our new guest?" Lily winked at him. He screwed up his face, looking as though he were trying to summon lasers from his eyes with which to melt her. She grew very formal, and said, "Felicity, this is our son John."

"Pleased, mum." He gave a curt bow, then turned back to Lily. "But Da *is* looking for you," he said, before racing from the room, cheeks blazing red.

Lily giggled. "We don't get much new blood around here. You've stirred up quite a lot of buzz. Though I'm sure Will tells you all the time how pretty you are."

Felicity promptly ran through her memories, cataloguing what Will had told her when, and decided she might just have to cast bait for a *pretty* compliment. She could use one of those at the moment.

"Speaking of pretty," Felicity said, "you look way too young to have a son John's age."

"I'm not his biological mom. Ewen was a widower when I met him."

"Really?" *Odd.* Did that mean Ewen really was Lily's One True Love, or really wasn't? "You'll have to tell me the whole story while we go find the guys."

"The guys," Lily muttered, taking her arm. "It's *so* nice having someone to talk to like this."

Felicity felt another stab of guilt over her competitive thoughts. Lily was a total sweetheart, and Ewen was clearly hot in a brooding sort of way.

But no man was as great as her Will. They were meant for each other. In her mind, no other relationship could compete with theirs.

Felicity frowned. She had only a matter of time now in which to convince *him* of that fact.

Chapter 29

Felicity walked down the empty corridor, headed back to her room. Lily had promised to arrange her a bath, and she was desperately looking forward to the prospect.

The other rooms were empty and the doors were all open, but for one, pulled to, and she heard the low rumble of Ewen's voice from behind it. His tone was easy and relaxed, interspersed with a decidedly more feminine voice. The laird and his wife, talking in the library.

She was about to pass right by, when mention of her name stopped Felicity in her tracks.

"Felicity, yes," Lily said in answer to an indistinct question. With a quick glance up and down the hallway, Felicity edged along the wall to listen. "I got the impression Rollo doesn't want her to stay," the laird's wife added.

"Did the woman say as much?" The voice was clearly Ewen's.

"No." Lily's voice was subdued, and Felicity leaned her ear closer to the cracked door. "But a woman can tell."

"Oh can she?" Ewen chuckled. "Well, as it happens, I ken Rollo's mind, and you speak truly."

Felicity's mouth went dry. The men had discussed her?

"You mean he's *making* her leave?"

"Aye."

"Aye?" Lily asked incredulously. "Come *on*, Ewen. You know I need more details than *aye*. Didn't you see how googly-eyed Will is for her? He's obviously totally in love with her."

Felicity gave a little nod. *Yeah*, she thought. *Totally in love.*

She heard another low chuckle. "I can't speak to the man's eyes, but aye, you have the right of it. Will is clearly besotted. But it doesn't matter."

A chill swept Felicity, turning her blood to ice.

"How can being in love not matter?" Lily sounded crestfallen.

"Rollo speaks of a debt he owes, and nothing comes between Will and his duty."

"A debt . . . like he owes money?"

"Och, lass, no. He's . . ." Ewen paused, considering his words. "The man is a staunch Royalist. Simply because the battles have subsided does not mean the Royalists aren't fighting on, behind the scenes. Rollo owes his fellows a debt, and if there's one thing I've learned about the man, it's that he doesn't go back on his word."

"But . . . that's horrible. You have to talk to him."

"I have. And I plan on helping him."

Anger tightened Felicity's chest. The fates conspired against her, and now this man too? What had she ever done to Ewen?

"What?" Lily's voice was a low hiss.

"Aye. I'll show him the maze."

"But . . . but that's for Robert. We're building it to try and save Robbie."

"Why not for the woman too?"

"Ewen, have a heart," she said in a lowered voice. Felicity heard rustling. It seemed Lily was about to bust out the feminine wiles on her husband. "Come on, honey, why can't she just stay with us? She'll be safe here."

Go, Lily! Her new best friend.

"It has naught to do with my heart, lass. Rollo's brother is out for blood, and by now most of Perthshire will think her a witch. Soon, Rollo himself will be called to help men who rally in secret for the King. He finds himself in a dangerous business . . ." Ewen let the words—and their obvious implication—hang.

Dread stole the breath from her lungs. She had to leave to save her own life. Will's honor made him stay, even though he'd likely be killed. The laird was saying as much.

"If she were to stay and something came to pass," he went on, "Felicity would be left alone. And all the stone in Tor Castle wouldn't be able to protect her."

"But," Lily protested, "you know how life is here. Once they part, they'll probably never see each other again."

"Aye. Mayhap." There was another rustling, then Ewen's voice again, soft and low. "Och, Lil'. Such emotion on your bonny face. I'll never understand the quick tears of a woman."

"I know." Lily's voice was a barely audible murmur now. "It's the damned hormones."

"I ken what'll smooth the sadness from your brow."

"You can't mean . . ."

"Oh aye. I can mean. And I do. I've told you before," he said. "A laird's wife has duties."

"But Ewen, I'm about to burst." Lily's giggle was an arrow straight to Felicity's heart.

Felicity began to back away. Though she didn't know Ewen, it didn't take a rocket scientist to hear the masculine intent in his voice. She spun, taking the cold slate stones at a jog.

Ewen's voice resounded at her back. "Aye," he was telling his wife. "They say 'twill make the babe come faster."

But those weren't the words Felicity heard. It was Ewen's pronouncement about Will, about his dedication to duty, which echoed in her mind.

Because Felicity had also learned well. William Rollo would never go back on his word. Will would stay where he was, forsaking all else, forfeiting his life to keep a promise to a friend.

❁

Felicity slipped below the surface of the bathwater, letting the hollow nothingness of underwater fill her ears. But not even the sound of oblivion could erase the chatter in her head. She exhaled slowly, and tiny bubbles blipped to the surface.

The room was dark, candles and firelight chasing away only the most meager of shadows. She kept her eyes shut in the blackness, focusing her other senses outward. The water was soft on her mouth and soothing on eyes that still ached from recent tears.

Her hands traced along her bent knees, to her belly. She felt full there, and contemplated the firm swell between the jut of her hipbones.

Drifting up her chest, she let her fingers pause idly on her breasts, the flesh cool and lightly pebbled where they emerged from the water.

Felicity reached to her hair, floating in the tub like fronds of algae, silken and weightless. Her scalp was tight, aggressively cleaned from a brick of soap that had smelled faintly of pine.

Pushing her feet against the foot of the metal tub, she slid back up. Inhaled deeply. Her room smelled of lavender and mustiness, and her lungs clenched briefly in protest.

The maids had startled her when they'd knocked on her door, bearing the huge copper basin and buckets of hot water. She didn't know why she should be surprised. Lily seemed on top of everything, and Felicity didn't see why her bath would be the thing to fall by the wayside.

She was grateful for the tub, but though it soothed her body, it wasn't doing much to lift her melancholy spirits.

She hadn't been able to wrap her mind around it, but hearing someone else speak the words had brought the truth home. Will had work to do. Dangerous work involving kings and intrigues.

There was no place for her.

Not because Will didn't want her, but because Will might not return alive.

She refused to think on it. Tried instead to be a purely sensory being, all thought pushed from her mind.

Slowly, she traced back down her chest, back over her abdomen, and tucked a finger between her legs.

The tender flesh there, though wet, wasn't slick, and water rocked over her breastbone as she adjusted, canting her knees, gingerly nestling within the delicate folds of skin.

She touched and explored, lazily waiting for nerves to awaken, wanting to feel some inner fire crackling to life. Patiently, she touched and waited, but her body wouldn't rouse.

Already she belonged to Will, her whole body his and his alone. And she thought the loneliness of it would drown her more surely that any water could.

"May I help you with that?"

She gasped in surprise, sending water sloshing onto the floor with a dull slap. It was Rollo, she sensed him now behind her. Saw his shadow flickering low along the wall.

"How'd you get in?"

His laugh was low. "I'm a man driven."

She didn't turn to face him. Somehow she felt too nervous, and so Felicity stared forward, listening to him walk slowly to her.

The familiar click and shuffle of his gait kindled something deep within her that none of her own touches had been able to stir. "Deprivation makes a man clever."

A little thrill rippled through her. "You're feeling deprived?"

"Aye." Will pulled a stool close to the tub. His movements were unhurried, deliberate. "And a man with needs knows no obstacles." He sat facing her. Laid his cane at his feet. His eyes roved shamelessly over her naked body. "And I need *you*, Felicity."

Her skin shivered tight at the sound of desire, husky in his voice.

"Wash yourself," he commanded.

"What?"

A wicked look creased the corners of his eyes. "I want to see you wash yourself."

The smile she gave him was low-key. She was sad, but she'd never turn Will away. "You think I'm dirty?"

"Och, woman, not dirty enough." Raising his brows, he gestured to the soap. "But for now, I'd watch you in your bath."

She rubbed and turned the soap between her palms. The scent of pine drifted to her, fresh and vaguely citric. Her melancholy muted into something more poignant, more languorous.

His stare was steady on her, brow furrowed with intensity. Felicity let the soap slip from her fingers and began to lather up each arm, holding Will's gaze all the while.

She rubbed lazy circles along her collarbones, between her breasts, over her abdomen, and back up again. The suds were thick in her palms now, and her hands glided easily over her skin.

Will tensed, a barely perceptible movement recognizable only by a lover. She knew she was driving him mad, and her own desire speared her through. An aching swamped her, at her chest, between her legs. He was sending her back. The knowledge charged the moment.

Her eyes flicked to his kilt. She saw he was aroused and it gratified her.

Slowly, she brought her hands to her breasts. Cupping them, she circled her thumbs over her nipples. They were beaded tight. Her whole body, tight. Poised and open for him.

Her lips parted. Watching him watch her stoked Felicity's desire. Will's eyes were hooded, his expression veiled in the shadows. He was so tall and handsome, like a fallen angel come to take her, to bear her off to some dark paradise.

Her heart beat shallowly, the heat of her want, the heat of the water, making her light-headed. She felt suddenly desperate for him to hold her, to anchor her. But he just watched, still as granite, his eyes smoldering and dark in the candlelight.

She slipped her hands from her breasts. Skimmed her palms along her belly to her legs. Spreading her bent knees, she stroked her hands down the inside of her thighs. An inadvertent moan escaped her, so hungry was she for the touch of his skin on hers.

Will moved then. Sudden like a panther, he leapt for her. His mouth claimed hers. He tasted of whisky, and the ghost of a beard was rough on her chin. His hands were hot on her shoulders, her body chilled where the damp skin had been exposed to air.

"You're so bloody gorgeous," he rasped between kisses. "It's unbearable." His mouth moved to her neck, nibbled and kissed. "I can't bear it." His kisses trailed higher, and he whispered in her ear. "My body can't bear to watch you. I have to touch you. So lovely, Felicity."

"So . . ." she began tentatively, lifting her chin to urge his kisses lower. Will's words awed and pleased her, and she recalled her conversation with Lily. "So, you really think I'm pretty?"

"Och," he growled, pulling his face from hers. Bathwater rocked and spilled from the tub. "You speak of *pretty*?" His shirt had gotten soaked, and water dripped steadily from his arms back into the tub.

Cupping her cheeks in his hands, he said fiercely, "Aye, you're pretty, and more than pretty. You're exquisite. The fairest creature ever who lived. Pretty indeed, my Felicity," he said, raining light kisses along her face. "My bonny, sweet love."

He released her. Reached for the large linen square that was her towel.

"Come then," he said. Will pulled her easily from the bath and situated her on his lap, tenderly drying and wrapping her in the towel as they sat on the stool.

How many more moments like this would they share? She couldn't bear it, couldn't bear the sadness. She placed her hands over his where they tenderly cupped her cheeks.

"I love you, you know. The fates sent me here, to you. I know you don't believe that. But I'm here now, and I love you. And in the end, that's all that matters. Being together is what's right. *We're* right. Back in my own time, I was so lost. But you've shown me so much. Like . . . like being with the horses. I'm actually good at that. For the first time, I'm good at something that also gives me such joy. My life is so much richer here. So much richer with you."

"Aye, love. As mine is, with you." His voice was hoarse with pain, with want. "Would that we'd both been born in some other time, some other place. Sometimes I think I'll not survive your leaving. That the moment we part will be the moment I breathe my last."

She shivered.

"Och, love, you're cold." He kissed her gently on each cheek, on her mouth, and then swept his hands along the thin towel to dry her.

She sensed an infinitesimal change in his breathing. Gradually his movements slowed, became more focused. A hand that had patted her dry, chafed now, rubbing teasing circles over the points of her breasts under the coarse fabric.

"I think I'm dry," she whispered weakly, standing and letting the towel fall to the ground. "And this is way too scratchy," she added, tugging at the thick layers of wool he wore. Unknotting the thong at his shoulder, she pulled his plaid from him. Peeled off his wet shirt.

"Come back." His words sounded pained, giving voice to something more far-reaching than what they were sharing in that moment. He pulled her down to straddle his legs. Will didn't enter her, and she felt the heavy weight of him brush against her leg.

"Don't go to the King," she whispered, stroking her palm over his broad, smooth chest. "Stay with me. We can run away."

"You know I would." He shut his eyes, breathing in deep. "But you know I cannot."

They were together now. He was by her side, right then,

and she'd regret wasting a minute of their remaining time together.

Felicity hitched her hips closer, seeking him out. "Be with me, Will. I want you."

He kissed slowly along her neck, traced his finger and his tongue along her collarbone as if he'd memorize her.

"I want you, Felicity. I've always wanted you." He kissed his way down her throat, took a breast in his mouth, sucked and teased with teeth and tongue. She felt empty and needful, wanting only for him to fill her.

Tracing his hands along her thighs, Will brought his fingers to her, stroking where water still dampened the hair between her legs.

"Now," she moaned. "I need you. Now."

"Aye," he said between gritted teeth. He lifted Felicity onto him and glided into her. "Now."

She planted her feet on the ground and began to move, tilting and rocking, bringing him in and out. But Will stopped her. Gripping her hips, he drove himself into her and held Felicity tight to him.

Holding her hips immobile, Will ground her pelvis against his. A pleasure so acute swamped her, she dropped her head to his shoulder, letting him rub and grind her against his body.

"Yes," she whispered. Felicity trembled, barely holding on. He kept her there, in a place just beyond fulfillment, shifting inside, yet not moving from her.

Will raked a hand through her hair and cupped her head, tilting it to face him. He brought his mouth to hers for a fierce kiss.

And then neither could hold on, and he kept her clutched hard and close through their climax.

Felicity, rooted to her Will.

Chapter 30

"And you're certain this woman is trustworthy?" Will asked, leaning on his cane as if it were a stake he'd planted defiantly in the ground. They stood outside the low cave, and Felicity was finding the stare-off between him and Ewen fascinating.

Will's face was furrowed, and it made her love him all the more. She knew it was partly wariness she saw mapped there. But physical pain was there too. She recognized it, bracketing his mouth. They'd had to tie off their ponies, and the tightly winding path they'd taken the rest of the way couldn't have been easy for him.

"Och, Rollo." Ewen raked a hand through his hair. "Trust me when I tell you, the witch Gormshuil is the only way. Though, as long as I live, I'll find the whole business difficult to fathom."

"You and me both," Felicity chimed in. That other women had traveled back in time? So strange—and kind of annoying. She'd wanted to think she was special.

Her eyes went to Will. He was watching her, an unreadable look on his face. Her Viking. She'd wished for her one and only love, and she'd been sent straight to this man.

No, she decided. She *was* special. What they shared was special. It was a relationship decreed by the fates.

She thought of those other women and frowned. They all got to stay in the past, regardless of the dangers. Why not her?

"How can we be certain Felicity will be safe?" Will asked, not taking his eyes from her.

"It seems like you're unsure," she said, realizing her opportunity. "So we'd best just head back. Who knows *who* this witch might be?" she mused dramatically. "Better to be safe than sorry. And," she added, turning her attention to Ewen, "we should probably go soon. Lily is looking pretty far along. You must hate to leave her when the baby could come, like, any minute now."

Will's eyes narrowed. "Nice try, love."

"Indeed," Ewen added. "And to answer your question, *I* know who this woman might be. Gormshuil is trustworthy, and she will help."

The Cameron laird led them into the cave. It took a minute for Felicity's eyes to adjust to the darkness and to the cloud of pipe smoke that drifted languidly through the air like incense.

"Come, come," someone called from the shadows. The voice cracked, the timbre that of an old woman, yet something stronger ran through the sound, something tensile, as if girded by fiber or tendon.

Felicity stepped closer and the woman came into view. Gormshuil was smaller than the sound of her voice. She was wizened, with paper-thin skin and a watery gaze, and yet Felicity saw at once the ghost of the young woman she'd been. Petite, with wide, round eyes. She somehow knew at once that a man had loved this woman.

Gormshuil cackled. "I see you too, girl."

A shiver ran up her spine.

Felicity felt her legs moving, drawn to her. She walked to Gormshuil, sat by her side. Patting Felicity's leg, the witch tittered again, and for a moment she sounded almost youthful.

Some deep-rooted tension unclenched, and Felicity

sighed. The woman's touch made her feel tingly and at ease. She inhaled deeply, and the sensation spread. She wondered distantly just what it might be the woman was smoking.

"You know," Felicity blurted out, "I'm kind of like a witch too." She felt warm, and a little buzzed.

"Are you now?" she heard someone ask. It was Ewen, chuckling.

"You have such a deep voice," Felicity marveled, turning to the laird.

"You're no witch." There was steel in Will's tone, and it stung her. She'd only ever heard him use that voice with other people. "Do not share such thoughts again," he commanded. "Ever, with anyone."

His words were like a gust of cold air in her muzzy brain. "Don't get testy," she said. She felt more alert, wakened from her haze.

"You make a mistake," the witch warned.

"I know." Felicity scowled in Will's direction. "Tell him, not me."

"You'll regret leaving your man. And," Gormshuil said with a nod to Will, "you'll regret letting her go. Mark me. 'Tis a grave error you make." Her eyes flashed to Felicity's belly. "Especially with the child."

"I knew it!" Felicity exclaimed. She'd noticed her belly had grown thicker. *Pregnant*, she thought, beaming. A baby. Of course. They had been doing it like a couple of bunnies, after all.

"Now I *can't* leave," she told him triumphantly.

"Now more than ever you must," he replied quietly.

"This is"—Ewen hesitated—"better discussed later, I think." He turned to Gormshuil. "Will requires not your judgment, but your instruction. You helped me once, saw fit to let me make my own decision. I ask that you do no less for my friend."

Gormshuil sucked on her pipe. The stem clacked dully between her teeth, sending up a fresh plume of gray smoke. "So it shall be," the old woman said in a voice suddenly thin with age. "I shall help your friend."

She tugged a small pouch from her belt. A leather thong

tied it shut, and Gormshuil bit the strip between her teeth, pulling it open. A small mound of dried, crumbled leaves spilled into her palm.

A low droning began to reverberate off the cave walls. Felicity realized it was Gormshuil. She'd begun to chant. Foreign words, sounding strange and thick, as if from the back of her tongue.

Felicity looked to Will. His eyes cut to her, as if he'd felt her gaze on him. She wanted a smile, a nod, but he simply sat stiff and erect, the look on his face unreadable.

There was a rapid movement on the edge of her vision. The witch had thrown something on the fire. The flames bloomed, swelling to life like a cresting wave, crackling angrily and spewing gray smoke through the cavern.

She felt ill from the stench of it. *Pregnant*, she thought. She was pregnant and nauseous. She swallowed hard.

Her mind grew muddled. She tried to focus on the woman's ceremony, but her mind spun away, thoughts slipping like sand through her fingers.

She clung to the sight of Will. They were having a baby. He was going to be a father. He couldn't let her go now. The thought transfixed her, a lone spotlight as her conscious mind meandered through the fog, Gormshuil's chanting drifting over her like so much pipe smoke.

The witch clapped her hands. Felicity's eyes snapped to her, finding Gormshuil staring. Smoke hung in the air, reddening the woman's pale eyes, making them seem rheumy and ancient. "I see the way, girl."

The witch turned her attention to Will. Her voice was stern as she intoned, "Heed me, William Rollo. If this woman leaves, she will never return. She shall be lost to this time forever. *Cho fad's a bhios muir a'bualadh ri lic.* As long as sea beats on stone. Lost, to us, forever."

Tears stung Felicity's eyes, anguish and fear stealing the breath from her lungs. She looked at Will. Surely he'd fight this. He'd change his mind. She peered at him through the smoke, but all she saw was the face of a war hero. Grim and still as he'd ever been.

The woman's voice keened from the shadows. *"Sìth do d'annam, is Clach air do Chàrn."*

"A proverb, lass. For you." It was the Cameron chief, his voice low and kind. "The witch bids peace to thy soul, and a stone to thy cairn."

❀

They journeyed back to Tor Castle in tense silence, Ewen having made it clear he'd tolerate no lovers' quarrels in his presence.

The thought that he might be embroiled in something so banal as a lovers' quarrel thrilled and gutted Will in equal measure.

The enforced silence was just as well. He needed to think. That Felicity carried his child rocked him.

It was a miracle. How strange and wondrous to think on what they'd created. Would the child have hair dark like his, and her brightly chattering ways? Would he or she be good with horses; be tall like him, or petite like her?

He fought the impulse to see it as a sign that she'd been right all along, that they were destined to be together. Was sending Felicity back still the right course? That his seed had quickened so soon in her belly sowed doubt in his mind.

He knew now they were meant to be together. It was the *staying* together that seemed impossible. Danger was all around. From Roundheads and witch-hunters. From his own family, God spare him.

He owed the Sealed Knot men a favor. It would surely be a dangerous errand, a fool's errand, him likely paying his debt to them with his life. If something happened to him, how would Felicity manage alone, with a child?

And yet.

A baby. *His* baby. He'd never imagined he'd have a family of his own. He thought of his father, of all they'd shared. Of how great an impact he'd had on Will's life. How much the man had formed him, taught him.

If he said good-bye to Felicity, he'd never know the other side of that relationship, would never be a parent to a child.

He'd never teach his son or daughter to ride, never share that great gift his father had given him.

How could he survive with his child out there, somewhere, growing up without him? He couldn't bear not being with Felicity, not seeing her become a mother.

Not seeing her become his wife.

For that's what a child meant. Will was already her husband in his heart. A child was simply proof of that love.

He watched her, riding on the road back to Tor Castle. Watched as she stroked her belly, regularly reaching down to rub circles where their baby grew, some new inner radiance brightening her already too lovely face.

She thought this news would mean she'd be able to stay. And though his heart protested, he knew that, now more than ever, she needed to leave.

His brother had made it his lifelong goal to destroy anything Will had ever loved. If a young Jamie would maim a boy and his pony, what would he do to Will's child now that he'd grown into a man desperate and bent on revenge?

Will's own father hadn't been able to protect him, and from his very own son. How could Will be assured that he'd be able to protect his own child?

Will had no choice. He'd have Felicity and their baby safe.

And he knew now it would kill him to do so.

That he'd never lay eyes on his child was a crushing loss. It would be the single greatest tragedy of his life. Second only to saying good-bye to Felicity.

The ride was a blur, silent and anguished. Seeing Felicity's newfound joy, his pain redoubled. His love for her would grow on, in this child she carried. And sending them away would destroy him.

They arrived, and a letter awaited him. Ewen left them, going straight to check on Lily. But Will opened the envelope immediately, standing there in the entryway.

"Who's it from?" Felicity shrugged off her cloak, handed it to a maid. "Who even knows we're here?"

She felt light and giddy, and in the way of all great moods, she had the sense that everything was now going to go her way. She was sure the letter bear some additional bit of amazing news. Like Jamie was apologizing, or maybe the whole king thing was settled.

"What's it say, Will?"

"It looks to be two letters, actually," Will muttered.

"Are they both to you?" She craned her neck to get a better look. "Why don't you open the other one?"

"It's not to me."

"What do you mean it's not to you? Who's it to?"

"Och, woman," he snapped. "Please give me a moment."

She'd been riding so high, his brusque tone came as a shock. "Ouch," she mumbled, feeling herself deflate.

"Och," he growled again. "I'm sorry, love." He looked at her, and his expression startled her. There was a blankness there, a deadness in his eyes. "'Tis only . . . this is happening sooner than I'd expected."

"What is?" she asked quietly. "What's going on?"

He sighed. "The letter. It's from Ormonde. A summons from the Sealed Knot men," he said, showing her the opened letter. "And"—he gestured to the elaborately sealed envelope—"a message for the King."

"The King?" she asked, taken aback. "What do they need to write to the King about?"

"Cromwell." Will was remote, his mind seeming to whir on other things. "He's dead."

"Wow . . . well . . . that's a good thing, right?"

"His son Richard has been named his successor. Be it one Cromwell or another," Will mused distractedly, "time will tell what that means for Charles."

"But what does this all have to do with you?"

"Don't you see?" He pinned her with his gaze, his attention clicking back to the moment. "The Sealed Knot asks that I be the one to deliver word to the King."

"I . . . I'm still not getting it. Where is he? I thought the King was—"

"In Belgium? Aye." Will crumpled his letter in his fist.

"He's in exile, in Bruges. And I'm to deliver this message to him."

"Oh." It finally hit home. Will had to leave, to see the King. In Belgium. "Well, I'll just go too. I've never been there before."

"The only place you're going is back to your own time." He stared at the King's letter in his hand, his face a hard mask. "This has become far too dangerous. My brother, witch-hunters . . . they are nothing compared to this. Cromwell's spies hope to intercept just this sort of correspondence. To capture and kill those who carry it."

She'd been feeling so joyful, and the intensity of her emotions took a pendulum swing to anger. "So you're still going to send me back."

"That's why we came," he told her, subdued. "To get instructions from Cameron's witch."

"But we just found out I'm pregnant. You're going to let me go even though I'm pregnant?" He simply nodded, and so she pressed, "So you're just going to say good-bye. Even though *I'm carrying your baby*. How can you do that?"

"I do it to save you."

"I don't get it," she snapped. "I don't get how all these other women are allowed to stay here. Lily, Maggie, whatever the hell their names are. Why can't *I* stay?"

"It's not safe for you."

"Ewen let Lily stay! She's even had babies, and she's still fine."

"Ewen is chief of his clan," he said evenly. "Who am I? I'm not even an eldest son. Jamie won't rest until he sees you dead. And a child of mine? Even worse. He'll rally religious zealots, Parliamentarians, my old Covenanter enemies, he'll use all at his disposal to see me . . . to see *us* destroyed. I cannot see you and a baby . . ."

He shut his eyes as if to gather himself. When he opened them, the man she knew had retreated, and before her stood the stoic William Rollo once more. It made her unutterably sad. "I cannot see you and our baby in danger. I love you, Felicity, and this is the only way I know to protect you."

"You could come with me then."

"No." The foyer was dim, and torchlight flickered on the edges of his features. A handsome face, through some strange alchemy turned to steel. "I can't. I have obligations. I made a promise. I must see the King restored."

"Seriously, Will." She was grasping at straws. "Listen, England had a queen when I left. They've got princes coming out of their ears over there. The monarchy was alive and well. Your work is as good as done."

"I would," he began, looking pained. "I would go with you. But I made a promise, and I am a man of my word."

"How'd they even know how to find you?"

"The Sealed Knot men can't be underestimated."

"Well they sure found you mighty fast."

"Perhaps I'd mentioned to Ormonde that we were traveling to Lochaber."

"*Perhaps* you'd mentioned it," she said testily. She put a hand up to silence whatever excuse he was about to give her. "Whatever. I get it. There's no convincing you. It's bye-bye Felicity. The noble hero is gallivanting off into the sunset and certain death."

Her voice cracked on those last words. Anger and confusion and grief clawed at her, paralyzing her thoughts, freezing her tongue in her mouth.

And, for the first time in a very long time, Felicity was silenced.

Chapter 31

Will came for her in the night. Though they'd been given separate rooms, he'd come for her every night as if it were the most natural thing in the world.

But this night was different. This night she knew would be their last.

She lay there, silently, wondering if he'd know she was really awake. She feigned sleep, but her anger she didn't have to pretend.

But she needed him. She loved Will, more desperately than ever. She needed him near, and so she lay still, listening as he unlatched the door, slowly pushed it open, walked to her bed.

She heard the shuffle and light tap of his cane, and the sounds seared her. Ran her through. He was gorgeous and noble. Thoughtful, brilliant, kind, and brave. But it was Will's vulnerability that she loved most of all.

She heard him pause. He stood by her bed, not making a sound. She was terrified he'd leave. Terrified Will might turn and go, forever.

Felicity considered saying something, but stayed mute. She'd already said it all. There was nothing left to say.

There was the heavy sound of wool falling to the floor. *His plaid.* Relief burst through her, a tingling cascade across her chest. She realized she'd been holding her breath.

She felt the skim of bed linens against her skin, and moved just the slightest fraction over, making room.

Felicity lay on her side, her back to him. Still she pretended sleep, but wondered who she was kidding. She was naked. Waiting.

She felt the mattress give with his weight. It was stuffed with dried heather and made a light crunching sound as he lay next to her.

Did he think she was asleep? Surely he could tell from her breathing that she wasn't. She wondered what he would do. Would he wake her? How much did he want her?

"Speak to me, love," he whispered into the darkness.

She lay still, listening to the rasp of his breathing. Though he wasn't touching her, his body radiated warmth along her back.

He pulled the bed linens up, sliding them carefully over her shoulder. Tucking his finger under her hair, he slid the mass of it from where it had tangled at her neck. There was another rustle, a hit of chill air, and warmth again as she sensed his arm under the covers.

"We part tomorrow." He reached for her, and his fingers scorched her like a burn. "It will be the end of my world." His hand stroked along her side, tracking a slow curve from hip, sloping to waist, up along her ribs, and back again. "I will be as a dead man, Felicity. A man without his heart."

Her breath hitched and she struggled not to speak. Bottled-up emotion clutched at her throat, aching with her unshed tears.

"I want you." The husky tremble in his voice made her shiver.

She wanted him too. Had never stopped wanting him.

He stroked up and down the side of her body.

Is this it?

Would this be the last time they'd ever be together? Felicity thought maybe she should turn around. Grab him, and shout, and make it memorable. But she could only lie there, stricken by her pain.

"Say something," he whispered.

But there was too much to say. Nothing more she could say.

She thought for a moment, maybe if she didn't have sex with him . . . Maybe it wouldn't be good-bye until they did.

But she couldn't play those games. She had to be with him, one more time. Will was so perfect, it was impossible for her to resist when offered.

"I feel as though you've left me already."

She couldn't stop herself. Her breath hiccupped, and she curled in more tightly on herself. It was unbearable. *Leaving him.*

"Och, love." His whisper was unsteady, unbearably tender. "Do you cry?"

His body melded to hers. Hot flesh along her back. Muscle, the light bristle of hair, his hardness. "Please." She felt his mouth at her shoulder. "Say something."

Will's touch was tentative, reaching around to cup her breast. She nudged her hips back, letting him know it was all right.

His hand stroked to her thigh. She shifted her leg, resting it over his.

He slipped into her from behind.

The last time.

He didn't move at first. She wasn't sure when he'd started to move. He went so slowly. Every motion, quiet tenderness. Every moment to be savored.

The last time I'll feel him.

She'd truly believed she was his. Til this very last moment, she'd held out hope. But hope had faded to despair. She'd thought Will was the one, and yet Gormshuil had told her, if she left, she'd never return.

Looking back now, she wondered, had they always been saying good-bye? Somehow, from the start, their time together had never fully been their own. Always anchored in place and time, they'd never been free to be lovers, carefree and easy.

"My love," he murmured simply.

She felt her body coiling. Building. She wouldn't cry out.

My last time.

Felicity gasped as her climax slammed into her. She wanted to scream, to moan and shout. To shout at Will, at the fates conspiring against them. But she stayed silent, biting her lips to swallow her cries.

Will held her tight. She felt a tear in the corner of her eye. It spilled to her nose, hovered there, and then drifted down. She shut her eyes tight, willing sleep to take her.

This last sleep by Will's side.

Chapter 32

Though they traveled now on separate horses, the memory of their ride together, on a single mount with her body pressed close, crushed him.

Such memories pierced Will, buffeting him in the silence. Each was a tiny flame that had sputtered to life in his heart, lit by Felicity. And now he would feel them wink out, one by one, until slowly he'd be extinguished.

They traversed Cameron lands, across emerald green glens and over tangled Highland hills, toward the spot where they'd mark out the labyrinth.

Will adjusted himself on the saddle, adjusted his sporran. The crude map folded inside weighed on him more than the heaviest physical burden.

"From what Ewen told me, it isn't far now," he said, trying for the thousandth time to talk to Felicity.

Please say something.

"We'll not need to build the maze, of course," Rollo continued. Felicity had fallen behind a few paces, and he slowed his horse to let her catch up. "This Gormshuil claims the power lies in the star map itself, which Ewen has already begun to etch into a stone that will someday be the heart of the labyrinth. He and Lily dream of saving one whom he called brother. A man named Robert who took a bullet for the laird."

Please speak to me.

"This paper I carry bears the pattern in its entirety. The witch claims you need only place it over the stone and trace it with your finger."

She didn't even nod her acknowledgment. Her silence gutted him.

Past conversations poured through his mind. Why had he not treasured every single one? He regretted any times he might have dismissed her, hushed her. All he wanted now was to hear Felicity's every thought.

"The witch promises, if you trace the lines just so, you will go to the correct place in time. I wish there were some way to return you to your exact location, but Gormshuil knows only the magic of the maze, and unfortunately the maze is in Scotland."

Why won't she speak? The total absence of Felicity's easy chatter was a shock to his system. Like being deprived of air he hadn't realized he was relying on to survive.

"That is a concern to me, though she does assure me of your safety otherwise."

Felicity pulled her horse to an abrupt halt, the reins wound tight around her fists, and swung her head to look at him. Her eyes were swollen and red, and such explicit evidence of her pain stung like an accusation.

"Safe?" she croaked. "Yeah, my heart feels real safe in your care, Will." She turned away, scrubbing at her face.

Her words lashed him, and Will reminded himself he was doing the right thing. Felicity was better off sad and alone, than dead.

"Love—"

"Don't *love* me," she snapped, and he thought himself a pathetic sot, for even angry words from her were better than none at all. "I don't think you know what love is."

"You are wrong," he said, his voice a tight rasp. Felicity,

who felt so quickly and lightly, who blithely moved her way through the world, she had no idea what depths he plumbed. How powerful love became when forged by darkness and loss. "I am desperately in love with you."

"It'd only be desperate if I didn't love you back."

He shuddered an inhale. Would that he could stay with her for always. "You don't understand. My world doesn't allow for feelings. Has never allowed for them."

"Then come to my world, with me."

"Could I, I would go with you. In a moment, I would go with you, follow you to the ends of the earth. God help me, Felicity, I dream of going with you. But what kind of man would I be if I abandoned my responsibilities here?"

Sensing his angst, Will's horse skittered, fighting to trot. He eased his seat, slowing the animal. "Felicity, don't you see? You've made me a better man. But there is a debt I owe here. You've made me a better man, and I can't dishonor that gift by going back on my word."

He let the words hang, then added quietly, "I am a man of my word. And I keep my promises."

"Then promise to find me." Her voice was small, so timid and small and unlike Felicity it shattered him.

"I cannot," he whispered.

"Why not?"

Because I'll likely be dead. "Because it would be a vow I don't know that I could keep."

She looked away, staring sightlessly into space. Will sat, the silence torturing him. He couldn't think what more to say, and so let the horses resume walking.

Their journey had grown gradually more difficult. Low braes had risen into steeper hills, the smooth, green glens replaced by land more tangled and ragged.

"There," Will said, seeing their destination. Looming like a scar in the earth, in the greens and reds of gorse and bracken, stood a wall of cold, gray granite.

"The path forks and narrows," he recited, "in the shadow of a granite crag. That's the spot Cameron described."

Pulling his horse to a stop, he pounded life back into his legs, preparing to dismount.

Trembling, Felicity forced air in and out of her lungs. It was time.

She watched Will punching at his legs, just the way she'd told him not to do. But now she was too tired to say anything, and instead just watched, sadly remembering their first carriage ride so long ago, when their time together had still been ahead of them. She wondered if there was something she should've done differently.

He was off his horse, making his way to her. The land fought him, thick and tangled with life, ferns and bulrush challenging his every step. But he came to her, raised his hands up to her, and she let him ease her from the saddle.

The feel of his strong grip on her waist stung fresh tears in her eyes. He brought his thumb to smudge them from her cheeks, and she flinched away. These tears were only the beginning, and she'd let them flow.

"We'll place the pattern over the rock," he said, opening his sporran. He unfolded the paper tucked there. It bore a crude map of lines and dots.

How odd, she thought. *The secrets of the universe etched just there, on some old scrap of paper.* There was no going back now, and it made her feel dead inside.

"The labyrinth itself matters not." His eyes went from the paper to her. "They build the maze merely to obscure the map, which will someday lie hidden at its center. This"—his hand tightened on the sheet—"is what holds the power."

They walked to the rock face. Though the sun still had a couple hours left in the sky, the high granite wall obscured it, casting them in cool shadow.

She saw the spot. A curve in the wall. A niche in the rock, and a stone tablet within.

This is it. And then, a sudden shrill at the edges of thought: *Is it safe?* She pushed the thought away, letting fear and grief blank her mind.

Her surliness seemed a stupid thing now, a ridiculous,

tragic waste of their time together, and Felicity grabbed him
tight.

He responded at once to her touch, wrapping a strong
arm around her. "Och, love," he whispered in her hair as he
leaned to kiss the top of her head. "My heart and soul go
through that rock with you. You leave only the shell of me
behind."

They approached, and she saw where the laird had begun
to chisel lines in the stone tablet. They would place the map
over the stone, as if it were tracing paper.

She stopped in her tracks. Afraid now, and uncertain.

"If it's the map that's so important . . ." she hesitated,
cleared her throat. She stared at the paper in his hand. "Why
can't I just draw that anywhere and disappear through time?
I don't get why you're so sure this will work."

"There is some magic held by this very rock." He stared
at it, brow furrowed. "Some magic spoken, some talisman
cast. The witch claims you must leave from just here."

She trembled fiercely now, and he supported her as they
walked the final steps to the stone. Icy perspiration prickled
along her body. Her breathing and heartbeat felt shallow, and
she thought that maybe if she passed out, she might prolong
their time together just a little bit more.

But she didn't pass out. Events marched forward.

She stood before the rock and Will put his hands on hers.
Together they smoothed the sheet over the stone.

"Wait," Felicity said. Will stood behind her, and she
craned her neck to look at him.

She memorized his features. Would she see them someday on the child she carried? Thick brown hair. Hazel eyes
that looked brown in the shadows. Those sharp, strong lines
of his cheek and jaw.

Could she grab his hands, grab Will tight and pull him
through with her? Wouldn't Livvie just die to meet him?

Livvie. She'd see her aunt soon. And yet the thought just
made Felicity sad. She wasn't ready.

"Is this it?" she asked, realizing that a part of her had
been waiting for something else to happen. Some interven-

ing force that would keep her by Will's side. The fates had sent her here, where were they now?

A cascade of small rocks spilled from overhead. Slivers of shale bit into her exposed skin, and Will pulled Felicity to him, covering her head with his own.

They both looked up. A rider stood on the rise above.

Cold dread crushed her.

Jamie.

Will shaded his eyes, glued to his brother overhead. Finally, he asked, "How did you find me?"

"It's easier than you'd think, getting folk to talk. Be it bribe or blade, there's always a way to loosen tongues." Jamie's horse pranced nervously, and a shower of gravel rained from the high ridge. "'Twas a crofter who sold you out just now." Jamie shrugged. "These Camerons are a stubborn lot. This one was forced to pay in blood."

Will's brother was lit from behind, and when his lips peeled into a smile, the dramatic shadows transformed his face into a sinister mask. "Paid in blood," Jamie added, "as your woman will also pay."

"*My woman* has done nothing," Will snarled, stepping in front of Felicity to guard her at his back.

"To the contrary. Any woman who lies with you is soiled. That is crime enough." Jamie's hand went to the broadsword at his side. "And now she will pay, and I will enjoy having you watch."

There was shuffling, and Felicity saw the heads of two other horses, tossing just in view. Jamie had brought friends.

Will must have spotted them too. He turned to face her. His attention only on her.

She saw the intensity in his eyes and she knew. The fates weren't intervening to save her. Jamie's appearance was a shove further down this path of no return. She whimpered simply, "No."

"I love you, Felicity." Will's voice was hoarse with emotion as he turned her to face the stone once again.

She stood limply, yet between Will at her back and her

legs locked under her, somehow Felicity remained propped upright.

No. The thought was tiny. The events unfolding around her were too big, too inexorable to stop. There was no fighting it now.

But she'd been so positive she was his. She couldn't go through. The witch said she'd never come back.

He took her arm in his hand.

No.

Distantly she heard the scuffle of horses along the ridge overhead.

Will began to draw her finger over the marks.

Her hand was cold and limp in his. She couldn't accept this. The blood drained from her head, and she felt clammy and woozy.

There was the dull patter of gravel falling at their feet. A hollow laugh from above.

Her arm started to buzz.

This was it. It was happening.

"I can't live without you." Her voice hitched, tears streaming down her face.

"Go around," came a shout from above. More rock rained down. "This way, you fools." Jamie's voice, moving along the ridge.

Will worked faster. Her finger grew hot.

She was suddenly so heavy. Gravity pulled at her, making it hard to stand. She tried to lean back into Will, but he held her hard and apart.

Her free hand flailed behind her. She could grab him, take him with her. But she was weak now, and her hand met only air.

"Good-bye to you, love." Will's voice cracked. She felt his rough kiss on the back of her head. "Good-bye to my heart."

She tried to speak, but her body was numb, immobile. She wondered if she traveled already. Was this what it would feel like?

The sound of horses came from behind.

Vertigo whirred in her head as she sank out of control. She wanted to cry for help, but couldn't. Her body was deadened. *Not right.*

She couldn't breathe now, and panic spiked through her. Tried to inhale, tried to move. *Frozen.* She was terrified now, terrified of the cold that was pulling her down.

Strange, disjointed laughter came from behind, so surreal.

Felicity felt Will's hands on her shoulders. Such sweet relief flooded her. She was dying and he would pull her back, would save her from this darkness.

But then he pushed. Will shoved her down and through, and in that moment, it was a betrayal, shattering her heart.

Finally sound came from her throat, as if she surfaced from the paralysis of a nightmare. Felicity screamed, and the noise was engulfed by the whirl of stars around her.

Chapter 33

The growl ripped from Will's throat. It was a feral noise, rabid and fierce. The sound of his soul being ripped from his body, as he watched his Felicity, so terrified and vulnerable, torn from him forever.

He spun from that accursed star chart, turning to face Jamie's men. He'd heard their approach, worried they'd reach him before he could push Felicity through to safety.

Will despised them, hated Jamie with everything he had. They'd forced his hand, forced him to push Felicity so violently away. He'd seen the shock of it on her face, the heartbreak and the betrayal.

They didn't get a proper good-bye. His final sight of her, simply the last of her beautiful blonde hair getting sucked into a terrifying maw of black nothingness.

The image would haunt him the rest of his days.

He sized them up in a heartbeat. Two men charging on foot. His cowardly brother still watching from the ridge overhead.

Will didn't even deign to pull his sword from where it was hidden in the length of his cane.

The first man rushed at him like an ass, but Will stood still as a rock. He held his cane steady, tilting his wrist up at the last moment, extending it straight out from his body. The man leapt for him with dagger and targe, but Rollo simply jabbed him in the gut, followed by a strike to the groin.

His opponent fell to the ground retching, and Will tossed the cane up, catching and swinging it back down in a single fluid movement. He struck the handle against the man's temple, stilling Jamie's hired half-wit forever.

The second one came fast on his heels, charging Rollo with his broadsword extended. Will scowled to see the elaborate gilded basket hilt that guarded the man's hand. The blood of Royalists had paid for that gilt.

He tossed his cane up, grabbing high along the length of it. Just as the swordsman lunged, Will pivoted sideways, hooking the cane's handle on the man's bicep, and reaping his arm down.

The man stumbled and Will struck him in the small of the back, hammered once on the back of his neck, and then on the kidneys. The man fell down, but Will swung up, striking him in the throat.

It felt good, this savagery. But it wasn't enough. Nothing would ever be enough to atone for his and Felicity's final farewell.

His opponent choked his last, a grotesque wheezing at Will's back. But the man was already forgotten as Rollo looked up at his brother, waiting on horseback along the top of the ridge.

"Can't fight your own battles?" Will shouted up. Loathing seethed from his voice.

"Can't fight like a normal man?" Jamie countered, with a scornful nod to Will's cane.

Will's eyes scanned quickly, searching out the mounts of the hired men. Two stout ponies grazed idly, at the base of the hill.

He made a soft whickering noise. One of the ponies twitched an ear, and then lifted his head to look at him. Will clicked his tongue again. The beast seemed to think on it, then heaved his body into a slow walk.

Will met the animal halfway. Grabbing the reins, he hauled himself easily onto the saddle. Leaning high on the pony's neck, he kicked into an abrupt canter.

Jamie waited for him at the top of the rise. "Oh, Willie," he hooted, greeting him with laughter. "This is too rich! You on a pony once more." Jamie's horse, a big bay, skittered beneath him. "How about we take care of your other leg, little brother?"

"I'd get ahold of your mount, Jamie," he said nonchalantly. "The beast seems too much for you."

Jamie merely hissed in response. He drew his sword and, swatting it on his horse's rump, charged.

"You always did charge too soon," Will muttered, coolly sizing up his brother. Jamie swung his sword wildly, keeping his other hand fisted tight in his reins.

His eyes narrowed, watching Jamie flail so. Will was a trained cavalryman. A lifetime of riding and decades of pain had forged his muscles. Misshapen they might be, but Will's legs were steel. He calmly knotted his reins, settling them high on the pony's neck. Unlike his brother, Will would have two hands with which to fight.

His brother raced along the ridge, but Rollo kept a quiet seat on his own mount, keeping the creature placid despite the warhorse headed straight for them.

"Always with the same error," Will shouted. He slid his cane through his fist to grip it at the base.

Jamie was on him in seconds, charging wildly.

Will ducked back, but not enough to completely dodge the shallow slice of his brother's blade. He withstood the attack, had braced for it, knowing it would come. The price of his own strike.

"It's the mistake you made at the Tower." Will flexed, and with a nudge of his left leg, the pony spun in a tight circle to face Jamie. "And you make it now," he gritted, extending from his saddle despite the bloody track blooming along his chest. Leaning out, Will charged, hooking his brother's arm with the handle of his cane.

Though Will didn't tear Jamie from the saddle as he'd intended, his brother slid halfway off.

"The same errors," Will said, unsheathing his blade.

Jamie scrambled wildly, and the sight was disturbingly satisfying. Will wouldn't kill his brother, but it didn't mean he didn't want to see the devil suffer.

"In battle as in life, eh, Jamie?" He tucked the shell of his cane under his thigh. "Impatient," he snarled, leaning once more from the pony. He slapped Jamie with the flat of his blade, his intention to pummel, not kill. "Foolhardy." Another slap, to the shoulder. "Impulsive." Again, the flat of the blade, this time to Jamie's face.

Will would never recover from his broken heart, but the smack of steel on his brother's flesh did much to appease. A red haze overtook him, his rage wiping out all thought. He continued to strike at him, beating him down and down again.

The big bay reared, and Jamie slipped from his saddle.

"Weak," Will spat. It felt good to see Jamie helpless on the ground, as he'd lain helpless so many decades past. But the satisfaction tasted bitter on his tongue, like raw spirits that turned belly to bile. "You're weak. Rolling in the dirt like a coward."

Jamie scrambled to his knees. Though close to the ledge, his eyes were only on the tremendous warhorse looming over him. "Damn you," he hissed, not taking his gaze from the spooked horse. "You're the weak one. Feeble Willie."

Will stared as the horse reared again, nearly trampling Jamie. Detached, he wondered at the morbid and poetic justice of it.

The animal bucked and started, and Jamie scrambled backwards.

Rollo heard the shocked shout at the same moment he saw Jamie's body lurch. His legs had slipped over the edge and he clung to the lip of the ridge, feet kicking wildly in the air.

Will stared, for a moment dumbfounded. And then there was a moment of total clarity. He could let his brother fall to his death.

This man who'd maimed him, who'd spent a lifetime fighting against all Will believed in. Jamie had destroyed everything he'd ever loved, had forced Felicity from his life.

But even as he had the thought, Will knew. He was incapable of letting his brother die.

Will dropped from the pony. Using his sword for a walking stick, he went to Jamie, looked over the ledge at the valley below. There was a drop to a sharp slope. A man could survive the fall, but it wouldn't be pleasant.

Jamie frantically clawed at dirt and rocks, trying to find purchase along the ridge.

Will knelt, awkward for a moment, then sat, grabbing for his brother's hand. "Take it."

Jamie swatted at the proffered hand, lunging instead for an unearthed root. "I'd rather die than take your help."

"I may despise you," Will said evenly, "but I'll not let you die."

"I'll not see you win." Jamie looked down, estimating the drop. A narrow ledge seven feet down, then a rocky slope to the bottom. "This isn't the last of it," he snarled. And then he let go.

Fascinated, horrified, Will watched his brother drop hard, scramble vainly for purchase, then slide down. Scree and gravel sped his descent, sounding a hollow noise that echoed in the valley. He careened faster and faster.

"Bloody fool," Will muttered, shaking his head with loathing. "Bloody bastard." He remounted, driving his pony along the ridge then back down the slope.

Though Jamie lay limp at the base of the hill, Rollo's approach was tentative. Leave it to his brother to feign injury, then spring at the last moment to attempt a deathblow.

But as he got closer, Will knew. He knew before he dismounted, before he reached the body, knew even before he saw the blood matting his brother's hair and the dark crimson shimmering on the stones.

Jamie was dead.

He inhaled. Waited for emotions to come. He braced for some feeling to slam into him, filling him with relief, or rage, or regret. But nothing came.

Will simply stood and stared at the body of James Rollo.

He had a job still to do. And all he felt was empty.

Chapter 34

She landed hard, rocks digging into her hands and knees.

It took Felicity a moment to realize what had happened. Was she still traveling? She stared at her hands. Her hair spilled over them, fingers clawing at dirt and moss-covered stone, her nails dirty half-moons.

She was breathing now, and it was a relief. She swallowed, shook her head. Where was she?

Felicity looked up and cried out a short, sharp shriek. Gone was the green and shadowed serenity of the Highland woods. Walls of dark, spiky leaves rose high all around. Purple flowers reached for her, drooping from their vines. Berries dangled there too, their ripeness an obscene, dull black.

She fell to her bottom and scrambled backwards. Her back struck a dense wall of foliage and she screamed again.

The maze, she told herself, trying to calm her pounding heart. This would be the maze.

Felicity looked up. The stone tablet was there.

Will.

"No!" Bounding to her feet, she slammed her hands on the stone. "Where are you?" she cried.

The star chart was fully etched in the granite now. The stone was dull, aged. It had been there for hundreds of years. Ewen had finished his maze, and he'd be long dead.

She was pierced by anguish. Her Will. Dead now, for hundreds of years.

Staccato sobs shrieked from her. She rubbed and traced the fine lines and points, over and over, until her fingertips were raw. "Where are you?" she cried again.

She wanted Will. She wanted to go back. She didn't care if it killed her. Jamie and those men had come for them, and she belonged near him. She'd die by his side.

She slapped and drew along the stone tablet, but it was dead under her hands. Dead and cold and lifeless, and Felicity stumbled back, falling to the ground in tears.

She hadn't said good-bye. She'd never see him again. Would never touch him, or hear him, or see Will again.

A breeze rustled along the top of the hedge. She shivered. The labyrinth was like a live thing that she needed to flee. It felt ancient. Moss grew thick underfoot, untouched for how many years?

She was back in modern time now. Her Viking, centuries away.

At least she hoped she was in modern time. Panic dumped adrenaline through her veins. What if she'd traveled to the wrong time? What if she couldn't find Livvie?

She needed to find her aunt. She needed to get out of the maze. She needed to call Livvie. All Felicity wanted to do was hear her voice.

She stood, got her bearings. She was in a small cul-de-sac, at the head of which was a single opening. Trying not to touch any of those hideous leaves or berries, she peeked through. Though Felicity knew what she'd see, knew she'd find herself in a labyrinth, the sight still startled her.

Dark green walls pressed in, curving and opening onto shadows. Her heart gave a sharp kick in her chest. She needed to get the hell out of there.

Livvie. She was so numb, that lone thought was like a lifeline. She'd get out of there and find a phone to call Livvie.

Pure animal panic emptied her mind, and Felicity let her feet take her where they would. Blindly, she turned corner after corner, trying not to think about those purple flowers reaching for her, brushing against her skin like a touch from beyond. She hunched through each doorway, relying on some instinctual part of her to lead her to the light.

The leaves grew a brighter green as she went, the maze gradually opening to allow the sun's fingers to wend their way in. Fresh air was sweet in her lungs, and Felicity realized the maze was at her back.

She stumbled forward, looking for landmarks to place herself. Fresh tears stung. *Will.* They'd stood together just here. How many minutes ago, how many centuries?

Had he died here? Her throat closed, her grief a constant ache lodged just there.

Phone. I need a phone, she thought, as she began to jog. Hiking her long skirts high, she jogged away from the maze, welcoming the stitch in her side and the burn in her chest.

She galloped down a hill she remembered climbing with Will, and it pushed her harder. Her leather slippers were soaked through, and they made a dull slapping as she raced across a damp, green glen, desperate now to hear Livia's voice.

Felicity didn't know how far or how long she'd been going when signs of life began to pierce her consciousness. A distant lowing. The bleat of a sheep.

A car horn.

She broke into a run.

A narrow street wound at the base of a valley, and she ran to it, hypnotized by the sight of small, boxy cars winding in the distance. A dingy, squared-off truck. Some white, compact Eurocar.

She slowed, mesmerized. The sight of modern amenities wasn't the relief she'd thought it might be, and the notion rocked her.

She just wanted Will.

She scrubbed her arm along her face, wiping the damp from her cheeks and eyes, and made her way onto the road.

Felicity stood in the middle, ready to flag down a car. Some-one might hit her and, at that moment, she didn't really care.

It was a blue minivan that stopped. A startling number of people stared at her from inside. Car exhaust filled her lungs, and it was a smell both familiar and yet so jarringly foreign and wrong.

Idling, the driver rolled down his window. "Are you okay?"

A rear window rolled down. "Do you need help?"

"There's room," came from somewhere in the car. "She can fit."

"Did you have an accident?" the driver asked.

"She looks sick or something," a woman's voice said.

"Yeah, like from one of those zombie movies." Laughter. "You're not going to eat us, are you?"

She was pummeled by questions, all of them surreal and meaningless after what she'd just been through. It took a mo-ment to register that they spoke with American accents. The sound was so recognizable on such a deep-seated level, Fe-licity didn't immediately recognize the anomaly.

They grew quiet, watching her. A window rolled back up. *They must think I'm crazy.* She didn't want them to drive away, and so she ventured a weak smile.

The driver was quick to smile in return, and tried one more time to connect. "Did you just come from some sort of Renaissance Faire or something?"

She struggled to make meaning without context. A woman in the backseat was eyeing Felicity's dress, and it finally clicked. *The period clothing.*

"Yes." She took a deep breath. "I did. But . . . but my car broke down and I need a phone."

"There's a phone down the road a ways," the driver said.

A door opened to the backseat. "Hop in," a woman told her.

And Felicity got in the car, every moment, every mile tak-ing her further from her Viking.

Chapter 35

Will had arrived well past midnight. And though he lay, weary and warm, in the bed of his childhood, he found no comfort there.

He thought about Felicity. Always it was Felicity. Falling asleep at night, upon waking, in his dreams. She was ever in his thoughts.

Dawn crept through cracks in the thick draperies. He needed to rise. He must tell his parents of the death of their son.

But the thought of rolling from his bed, placing his feet on the floor, and hauling the weight of his body onto sore legs overwhelmed him.

He reached down, rubbing life into his knee. Winter's chill reached his bones with an acute ache, his joints like shards of broken glass that barely fit together.

Felicity would have rubbed his legs. She'd have stolen thoughts of pain from his mind.

Felicity. He hoped desperately she'd survived the journey. That she'd been able to find her way home and was safely reunited with her aunt. But he couldn't think on that. He needed to push such thoughts from his mind, save them for the wee, cold hours of the night.

He had a job to do. He'd tell his parents about their eldest son, and then tell them their youngest traveled off in duty to his king, perhaps never to return alive.

Despondent, Will stood. The stone floor was bitter cold, and pain crackled up his calves like the sharp fracturing of ice on a thawing loch. He embraced the sensation, willed it to steal the conscious thought from his mind, if only for a moment.

He unfurled his plaid, stabbed by the inevitable memories of Felicity. Of her playful and curious ways.

As he dressed, he pictured her, draping the heavy swath of wool over herself. How many times had her pale, tender hands pushed this plaid from his body? Not enough.

He grabbed his sporran. He remembered her teasing. Was there anything in his life untouched by her?

Buckling it on, he thought of the Fool card, still tucked away. He now understood the message sent to him from the universe. He was that fool.

Will cursed himself. He needed to seek out his father before he grew any more piteous and self-abasing.

He found the man in his favorite spot in the garden, settled in a chair beneath a great, towering birch. "Och," Will muttered, seeing that nobody had thought to cover the man's legs despite the merciless chill in the air. "Do all here think only of themselves?"

He retrieved a blanket from a garden bench. It had been left out, forgotten, and Will shook the damp and leaves from it. "Damp wool's better than none at all, eh, Da?" he said, draping it over his father's legs.

The old man looked up, greeting his son with a wavering smile. His father seemed stronger somehow, his eyes clearer, his expression more sure.

"You look fine," Will said. He smiled back at his father, thinking it was his first since he'd said good-bye to Felicity.

His father's eyes darted around, brow furrowing.

"Looking for Felicity, are you?" Will didn't wait for a response. He knew how she'd touched his father, and so broke the first of much news. "Aye, she's left me. It was too dangerous for her here."

Will faltered. He wandered to the old birch and began to pick idly at the silvery bark. "Did she tell you everything? About where she was from?"

He turned to face his father, who watched intently. The lines at his brow and the confusion in his eyes gave Will the answer.

"Aye," Will said. "She'd not have." Sighing, he brushed the dirt from his hands. "Felicity was from very far away, Da. I'll not be seeing her again."

His father opened his mouth as if to speak, but Will couldn't bear a moment more on the topic, and so said abruptly, "I've news. Of Jamie."

"Why do you speak to your father?" His mother's voice was shrill in counterpoint to the tranquility of the garden.

"Why would I not speak to my father?" Will countered. He knew full well his mother's meaning, but still, he'd make the shrew speak the words.

She merely glowered.

"My father is as aware as you or I."

"No indeed," she snapped pertly. "Your father is dead to us." She pointed to her husband. "That man is not—"

"*Ist*," his father hissed. It was a word commanding silence, and yet it came thick on his tongue, easily mistaken for the sibilance of a senile man.

"He speaks," Rollo told her.

"He spits. He spits and sputters like a dotard, and it disgusts me."

"Aye, you prefer your men younger, don't you, Mother?"

"Why are you even here?" Her skirts crinkled as she whirled on him. "Trouble follows you. You're cursed."

"I'm here to deliver word of your favorite son."

Startled, she looked at him blankly. His mother had made her preference clear when he'd been but a child. Jamie's death would crush her.

His heart had closed to his mother years ago, and yet he'd not relish delivering the news.

"Jamie is dead."

"You killed him," she shrieked.

"No," Will said simply. "Jamie killed himself."

"My son would do no such thing."

"It's your son's choices that killed him."

His mother stalked to him. Her face was an icy mask, her obsidian eyes tightened into slits. She'd been a rare beauty in her day. Tall and dark, and the odd thought struck him how beautiful she'd remained through the years.

Beautiful and elegant, a queen carved of ice. And he wanted naught to do with her.

"Get out," she hissed, pointing a long, thin finger accusingly at him. "It's the inheritance, isn't it? You just want to be the eldest. You never could accept Jamie's precedence. He was always the stronger boy, he outranked you, out*manned* you."

"Til the very end, my brother acted less than a man," Will said, his tone dangerously quiet.

"He married, at least." The disgust that flickered in her eyes startled him. "Unlike you. So stubbornly aberrant you were. And when you finally bring a woman home, it's some . . . some deviant, with her strange—"

"Ennn . . . nough."

Father.

Lady Rollo's head spun to gape at her husband, and his eyes snared her as if she were a pinned butterfly.

There was a curious absence of emotion on his father's face. His eyes bore the blank look of a disciplining parent grown weary of an unruly child. "I know . . ." He gathered himself, swallowed, then continued, "What . . . goes . . . on."

"No," she gasped. "It can't be."

Will walked to put a hand on his father's shoulder. "I imagine there will be changes, Mother."

His mother screamed, as if she'd seen a ghost. She turned and ran, shrieking for her maid.

"I imagine she'll have a bag packed and in the carriage before we're even back inside." Will watched his mother sweep up the stairs, disappearing into the shadows of Duncrub. The sight made him sad. Such waste, all around.

He felt his father's eyes on him. "She'll . . . not want."

"Aye, I imagine she'll be away to my aunt's."

His father closed his eyes in agreement.

"And if I know you, she'll have an allowance and will have her fill of gowns and callers as before."

The older man gave a slight shrug.

It stung to see his father cuckolded so. "How can you—"

"No," his father interrupted. "Pity not. Her money," he said, and Will knew he referred to the fortune that his mother had brought to their union. "My choice."

The older man shut his eyes for a moment, suddenly looking so tired. Just when Will thought he'd drifted off, his father spoke again, his message clear. "The lass. Go to her."

Even though he knew it impossible, the thought thrilled him. Will let the prospect shiver along his spine before he crushed it from his mind. "I cannot. It's impossible. And besides, to go to Felicity would mean good-bye forever."

"Go." The man's voice was as clear and steady as it had been when Will was a child.

"There is something I must do," he explained. "For the King. It's . . . dangerous business."

His father gave an uneven nod. "Send word. After." He'd worry for his son, but as he'd done Will's entire life, he'd delude himself about the true nature of the situation. Will knew he might not return, but his father would never entertain such a notion. "Then, Felicity," the man added. He stumbled on her name, a jumble of sounds on his tongue.

Will caught the dart of his father's eyes across the garden. And the unsettling truth of things came into focus.

"You speak well, Da. You've been practicing. With her, I'll wager," Will said, nodding to a woman watching and waiting patiently at the edge of the lawn. She'd been his father's maid for as long as he could remember.

Will's eyes narrowed. Was there no honor to be had? Who

had strayed first, his father or his mother? He looked away from the woman, dispelling what was a distasteful thought. He'd rather not sully his mind contemplating the deceits of bored nobility. Even if they were his own parents.

He'd remember his father as the man he'd been to him. Thoughtful, loving. "This is good-bye then," Will said.

"A parent's lot." The older man inhaled sharply. Grief etched the corners of his eyes. "To part."

"I thank you, Father."

"Be safe," he said with a nod. "And go to her."

Chapter 36

It was a weird experience, driving with Americans. Recognizing her accent, they peppered her with questions, which she answered in as few words as possible.

It was nice to feel recognized, to be immersed once more in such benign familiarity, and she realized she'd missed modern people, *her* people.

And yet, she also hadn't. Not really. Her mind kept going to Will. Her place, with Will.

It was a short drive to the tourist shop. Tour buses skewed at odd angles along the edges of a sprawling, unevenly paved parking lot. Scotland's Pride Woolen Mill was huge, and Felicity fought off a vague sense of alarm at the sight.

Tourists milled in front of the store, drinking coffee in white paper cups and pulling disposable treasures from their bags to show their friends.

Felicity stared in awed silence, and then sensed the quiet hum of expectation in the car. She was supposed to get out.

"Just there," the driver urged her, pointing to a bright red phone booth on the far edge of the lot.

"Are you sure you're going to be okay?" the woman next to her asked.

Felicity managed a nod and scooted out the door. She made herself place one foot in front of the other.

Livvie. Livvie. Livvie.

Strangely, her legs were juiced with adrenaline, and by the time she reached the booth, they were weak and quivery. She grabbed the receiver, fingers poised over the dial. Her hands were shaking, and it took her a moment to remember what to do.

Operator.

She pressed Zero. Nothing. She jiggled the hook, pressed random buttons, a spurt of panic making her movements abrupt.

Weird, she thought distantly, as the foreign dial tone hummed to life.

The rest came to her by rote. Collect to Los Angeles, to her aunt's house.

Voice mail.

Her heart sank. Something niggled at the back of her mind, and on a hunch, Felicity tried again. Collect to her apartment in San Francisco.

Livvie picked up on the second ring.

"Baby!" her aunt exclaimed. And then, in a conspiratorial tone, she asked, "Where did you get off to last night? You little minx, I see you did the Tarot. Did my candle work for you? Are you calling from Mister Right's apartment?"

Last night?

It took a moment for Felicity to make sense of Livvie's words. Had it only been last night?

"I . . . Yes, Liv." Felicity rested her head against the glass wall of the phone booth. She'd hoped her aunt's voice would be a balm, but she felt more overwhelmed than ever.

Last night. Did that mean Will was out there, trapped in some excruciatingly slow unfurling of time?

"I did meet someone." Her voice hitched, and she braced herself. There would be no hiding her anguish from her aunt.

"Are you crying? Did he hurt you? The bastard. What did he do to you? Did you go out to a bar? You know I hate those types you meet in bars."

"No." She numbly repeated the events of the past months. "I went back in time. I was in the past. In old Scotland."

"Are you okay?" Liv's voice was instantly grave. "This guy didn't give you anything, did he? I've heard about the drugs some men slip into girls' drinks—"

"No, Livvie," she said, tears pricking through her daze. "I was back in time. The man I met was wonderful."

"Did you have . . . a dream?"

"No. I really was there." She scrubbed at her face, willing Livvie to just believe her. Felicity didn't have the energy to try and convince anybody of anything. "It was your candle. I made a wish on it. I asked the universe to send me a Viking."

"You met a Viking? How far back did you travel?" Livia was silent for a moment. "I *told* you that's a good candle."

"No, he wasn't a real Viking." Felicity wiped her eyes through a breathy, grateful laugh. Leave it to Aunt Liv to believe her immediately. "I just called him that. It was the 1600s."

Fresh anguish choked her. *Will. Where are you, Will Rollo?* "His name is . . . was Norse."

Of all things to share, why was she telling her aunt that? Suddenly it was the little details that seemed the most profound, and the biggest ones the most inconsequential.

Livia was blessedly silent on the other end of the line. She would let Felicity tell her story in whatever order and however slowly she needed.

Breathing deeply, Felicity gathered herself, her emotions alternating between anguished and anesthetized. "I was there for ages. His name is Will." She paused, fighting not to break down. "William Rollo. I love him. He's the only man for me. The universe sent me to him. And Livvie, he loved me too. We're . . ." She swallowed hard. *Breathe.* "We're having a baby. I'm pregnant."

Livia screamed. "No shit, honey! That is fantastic!"

"Do you believe me?" Felicity asked hesitantly.

"Of course I believe you. What a silly question. Now when can I meet Mister Viking Hottie?" The glee in Livia's voice was torture.

"I left him in the past."

"You did what?"

She closed her eyes. Just thinking about it brought a fresh stab of pain. "I met a witch. She helped me get back to this time."

"You silly, silly girl." Liv's voice was low, and it sent goose bumps rippling across Felicity's skin. "You make a wish, get sent to your true love. You get this gift, this huge, amazing, wonderful gift from the universe, and you *throw it away?*"

Livvie grew quiet. Only the sound of her breathing echoed over the phone. "You have to go back," she stated with finality.

Felicity was taken aback. It was the harshest her aunt had ever spoken to her. The shock of it got her tears to stop.

"I can't. I'll never be able to go back." She couldn't process it all, and so repeated Will's reasoning by rote. "It's a dangerous time. I was kidnapped. People thought I was a witch. His brother tried to kill us. Staying wasn't sensible."

"Screw sensible." Livia was outraged. "When have I ever taught you to be sensible?"

"I was in danger."

"But not from your Viking."

"Of course not, no," Felicity murmured. She sighed, sad to her bones. "Not my Viking. He protects me."

"Well, then he'll protect you when you go back to him."

"I can't though. The witch said I'd never be able to go back."

"*Can't . . . never . . .* What did I teach you?" Livvie's tone gentled. "Honey, you need to try."

"There's a maze," Felicity said hesitantly. "I could try that again. But . . . it's so dangerous there."

"We can put people on the moon, surely you can find a little modern ingenuity to protect you."

"You won't miss me?"

"Of course I'll miss you, you silly *chit*." Livia paused on the word, as if waiting for some reaction. "Isn't that how they speak back then?"

"Yeah, kind of." Felicity laughed, a giddy, tension-relieving giggle. "What I can understand anyway."

"Then we have to get you back. I'll come help you. Where are you?"

"I'm in Scotland."

"Good heavens, of course you are." Her aunt gave a sharp sniffle, and Felicity thought how hard it would be for Liv to say good-bye to her only niece forever, and by telephone, of all things. "Then you'll just need to hang up this phone, and go back to that maze, and figure out a way to get back to him."

"I love you, Liv." She shut her eyes, wishing she could give her aunt just one more hug. But Felicity knew, if she could choose only one person to have near for the rest of her life, it was Will whom she'd hold close. "Thank you."

"For what, dear? Now," Livvie added quickly, "just hang up the phone and figure out a way to go be with your Viking. And, Felicity?"

"Yes?"

"I love you too, dear."

Felicity was no longer trembling when she hung up the phone. The numbness had cleared, and she forced herself to hold onto hope, willing her resolve to push the sadness away.

She knew they were meant to be together. She'd find a way. Figure out how to protect herself and them if it meant tromping into that silly tourist shop and getting her hands on the best reproduction claymore Scotland's Pride Woolen Mill had to offer.

Because, Felicity decided, she'd stay by Will's side. No matter what.

Chapter 37

London, 1659

"Massey has been captured," Ormonde said, scanning the pub nervously. His voice was hushed, even though they sat in what was the primary Royalist outpost in Croydon.

Though in the shadows, Will saw the intent clear in his friend's eyes. "I see where this leads. But I fulfilled my promise. I delivered your letter. I bore tidings of Cromwell's death, returned the King's own correspondence back to you. My debt is paid, to you, to the Sealed Knot."

"And a fine job you did," Ormonde replied smoothly. "I hear the King is fond of you."

"Mm-hm." Will was too jaded to take the bait.

"It seems Charles took a liking to you from the very first," Ormonde continued. "You met years ago, when he was first crowned at Scone Palace."

Will gave a cynical shake of his head, remembering. "He says he's fond of Perthshire."

"Is that so?" Ormonde laughed and poured himself a finger more whisky. "And an honor it will be for you to attend Charles when he returns once more."

"I care naught for court. I'll not be there."

Ormonde leaned back in his chair. Crossing his arms, he studied his friend. "So morbid you are, William." Realization narrowed his eyes. "It's that woman."

"Aye," Will replied, a challenge in his voice.

"She's a strange bird."

He swung his cane, quick as a musket flash, touching it to Ormonde's throat. "I am not in the mood, friend."

"Easy." The redheaded man leaned away from the tip of Rollo's cane. "I meant nothing by it. Such a puzzle you are." Ormonde raised his glass to his lips, took a thoughtful sip. "So just summon her. You can both come to court. Lord knows it's well past time for you to take a wife."

"She's gone . . . to a place from which she cannot return."

"How terribly gloomy." Ormonde leaned onto the table, steepling his fingers. "Fine, then. I'll bite. Why not simply go to her?"

Will was silent for a moment. He decided there was no harm in telling the truth, a partial truth at least. "She's too far away. In America."

Ormonde spat the whisky from his mouth. "You jest."

"When have you known me to jest?"

"When have I known you to brood over a blonde?"

"That's enough." Will saw what his friend was about. Ormonde was trying to take his mind from the issue at hand. But he wouldn't be diverted. "I'll speak no more about Felicity this night."

His friend pretended to nose his drink, but Will saw the machinations at work. "Say it, Ormonde. Tell me your real purpose. Why am I sitting here with a belly full of whisky?"

"Massey," Ormonde conceded. "He was captured in Gloucester, by the militia. It seems he planned a wee uprising that didn't sit well."

"That makes how many arrests for the man?" Will asked dismissively. "He's been taken more times than a South Bank whore."

"This is serious, Will. They plan to bring him to the Tower."

"I've pulled my last man from the Tower," Will snapped. When Ormonde didn't reply, Rollo shook his head, in disbelief of what he saw coming. "Surely you have men closer to Gloucester than we are here. What of Oxford? Doesn't the Sealed Knot have men in Oxford who could rescue him?"

"None as good as you, Will. And Massey's not in the Tower yet. He's still held in Gloucester. Child's play for a man of your talents."

"Your flattery may amuse, but it does naught to convince."

Ormonde remained deathly silent, clearly thinking his uncharacteristic gravity would be the thing to convince Will.

"Massey will be fine," Rollo said. "I've not enough fingers to count the times that man has escaped imprisonment."

"This is different." Ormonde raised his glass to drink, then put it down, thinking better of it. "Our enemies have become aware of his value. Massey joined Charles in exile. Became his pet."

"I thought the King preferred spaniels," Will replied dryly, referring to Charles's famous hounds.

"Aye," Ormonde laughed, unable to maintain his somber mask for long. "A nasty wee rat of a creature."

Rollo ignored the jest. "Why didn't the man just stay with Charles in exile?"

"We all have work to do *here*. We're close, Will. So close." Shoving glasses aside, Ormonde leaned in, elbows on the table. "England is in chaos. The army despises Richard Cromwell, they rally against him, call him Tumbledown Dick."

"I heard it was Queen Dick," Will muttered. "So, if you foment enough unrest . . ."

"The people will see the need to reinstate their king," Ormonde finished for him. "Tumbledown Dick"—Ormonde gave a sly smile—"is close to resigning."

"Because the army won't follow him?"

"Precisely. And while Parliament and the army argue . . ."

"The King shall make his glorious return," Will concluded. He spun his glass around and around on the table. "And Massey is key to this unrest."

"Aye. Massey is a key player. We have momentum, Will. There are few men I'd entrust with such a mission. We need you. Just once more."

Rollo nodded somberly, thinking he'd heard that line before. He studied his friend across the table. Wild red hair and the bright eyes of a boy. His friend needed him.

Will had nothing but his friends now. Felicity was never coming back. His love, gone from him forever. Without her, he had nothing left to live for.

"We need you, Will. Please, help us this one last time. And then you can go to her. Go to America."

"I cannot."

"Why not?"

"It's impossible."

"Impossible for *you*?" Ormonde raised his brows, confounded. "Why?"

Why indeed? Will tried to formulate an answer.

His father's words came to him. *Go to her.*

And why not try? He'd likely not make it. He could die in the attempt. But death would be preferable to this grieving that choked him day and night.

"It's not as though you'd be the first Scotsman to cross an ocean. Or . . ." Ormonde's eyes lit. "Is it that you're afraid of the sailing?"

"I am not afraid of sailing."

"Good then." The redheaded man smiled. "Then you'll not be minding our plan."

Will's eyes narrowed.

"To save Massey," Ormonde clarified.

"You've a plan already?" He canted his head in disbelief. "I've been taken."

His friend chuckled. "We sail around. To the mouth of the Severn."

"No boats," Will snapped. "I will help you, but there will be no boats."

"We ease along the passage," Ormonde continued, ignoring him, "like the Viking ships of old. Come, now." He shot Rollo a broad and challenging grin. "Your woman did call you a Viking, did she not?"

Chapter 38

The small fishing boat was cold, wet, and dark, and Will regretted that nobody was there to witness the scowl he wore openly on his face.

He despised boats.

"Far cry from a Viking," he muttered. He sat on the floor of the hull, his back against the hard bench. The position did much to conceal him from view, but it did naught to soothe the ache from his bones.

The militia held Massey on a modest, twelve-oar birlinn. They'd boarded and would surely launch soon, and Will wondered just what was taking Ormonde so long.

The wait was interminable, and unfortunately it was giving him way too much time to think. Already his mind drifted to the future. Will kept reminding himself that anything less than total focus on the task at hand was dangerous, but thoughts of Felicity were irresistible.

Because he was going to find her.

Now that the notion had taken root, he was a man determined. As unlikely as it seemed, he would see her again. He adjusted his sporran in the darkness, thinking of the tattered star chart he still carried there. He'd return to the maze, go through himself, and he didn't care if it killed him in the effort. Because if he couldn't be with Felicity, he'd rather be dead.

Will had once thought it'd be the errand he ran for the Sealed Knot men that would kill him. But his father's words resonated. *Go to her.* And the possibility would have to keep him alive, through just one more intrigue.

He wondered where she was. Wondered if he'd be successful, and where, or when, he would land. Would she have had their baby? Would he come upon her moments after she'd traveled back, or would he discover Felicity as an old woman?

He cared not. He simply wanted *her.*

Which meant he needed to survive the night.

And, curse it, Ormonde had convinced him of the damned boat. The Gloucester militia was shorthanded, and so transported their captive to the Parliamentary soldiers by water. A rescue by boat only made sense.

Which is why he found himself bobbing like some dour, godforsaken seabird in the waters just beyond Sharpness Dock.

Ormonde was ashore, where Rollo wished he were. The plan, for his friend to create a diversion, drawing the militiamen from the water. Will would've liked to join him on land, but the choice of roles was clear.

If they chase me, I can run. Ormonde's words echoed in his head. His friend was fleet of foot, and without the aid of a horse, Will wasn't fleet of anything.

His friend had spoken the words, then sensing the gaffe, had played it off. Said he'd taken the part of a crazed monk in their last outing, and now it was Will's turn to have the more distasteful of jobs.

But Will knew. Though he could create a diversion, he was a cripple. The militia would run him to ground as surely as hounds did a fox.

And it redoubled his purpose. Although he reminded himself he needed to stay safe, as ever before he felt the need, like a primal urge in the recesses of his psyche, to prove himself.

A shot fired. He was roused and ready, a kick of nervous energy making his body hot despite the brisk breeze off the river.

It was time.

Another loud crack sounded, followed by flashes of signal fire in the distance. Ormonde had set numerous flares, each using a variation of the delayed saltpeter and paper fuse that had worked for them before. The effect was that a dozen men approached, instead of Ormonde's one.

Men shouted from the deck of the militia birlinn. Will heard distant splashes as they left their boat to investigate. The night was clear and cold, and the sound was vivid, carrying to him over the water.

There were more shouts, this time from the dock.

The diversion was working. They were abandoning their prisoner, for the moment. Will hoped they hadn't left more than one man to guard him.

Will pulled himself up onto the bench. The chill had locked his muscles, and the movement sent shards of glass shattering from his calves up his spine. Grimacing, he flexed, inhaled deeply, and exhaled, trying to breathe out the shock of pain.

He eased his oars into the water and began to row. *Boats.* He glowered. *Despise them.*

He pulled ashore not ten yards from the birlinn. Holding onto the side of his boat, Will clambered over, using his arms to ease into water up to his thighs. He had to let go for the final drop, and stumbled when his feet hit the soft silt of the river bottom.

A spike of rage hit him, more visceral than any icy water. He gathered himself, grateful none were there to witness the clownish lack of dignity.

He heard a distant gunshot. Ormonde, doing his job. Time for Will to do his.

Bracing himself, he waded to the birlinn. He carried an old cane, carved of oak, the strongest of Scottish wood. It was more a staff than a mere cane, with a hefty crook for a handle. It would be his ticket onboard.

He stood in the shadow of the birlinn. The smooth, low hull blocked the night's chill wind, but it also blocked the moon from his line of sight. Will waited, letting his eyes adjust, opening his ears to the activity on deck.

It was silent, but for the sounds men made. A clearing throat, a low cough. One guard then, he estimated. Two wouldn't be able to resist talking.

He had to act fast. Until he was onboard, he'd be unacceptably vulnerable to attack from above. Reaching his cane up, Will hooked the thick crook over the lip of the vessel. He dried his palms one last time on the shoulders of his coat, and climbed fist-over-fist up the length of oak.

As silently as he could, he gripped one hand then another on the lip of the birlinn. The guard caught sight of Will just as he was shimmying over.

By the time he fell hard onto the floor of the hull, the guard was on him, pistol cocked.

"Damn," Will muttered. He hadn't bargained on a loaded gun. He rolled to the side. Gunpowder might trump steel, but no aim compared to a dagger's. Rollo had his *sgian dubh* pulled from his sock in an instant, and he lashed, slicing just above the man's heel.

Will felt as much as heard the hideous pop as the tendon snapped in two, and the man shrieked, crumpling to the ground.

It was quick work from there, Will driven to haste by the need to silence the man's hysterical cries.

"Very impressive." It was Massey's voice, speaking in a hush from the rear of the vessel. There was a rustling, then he added, "If you'd be so kind, I have been trussed and tethered like a sheep for the shearing."

"A moment," Will gritted out, pulling himself to standing. He unhooked the cane from the boat, grateful that, even after all the commotion, the thing still hung there.

"Ah," Massey exclaimed, his voice a bright little pop of sound. "You're the cripple."

Will hissed a response, cleaning his blade on the dead man's sleeve.

"Rollo, is it?"

"Aye."

"You seem quite deft with that stave of yours. I've heard of your exploits." He squinted, trying to study Will's legs in the darkness. "Good on you, to make the best of your infirmities."

He shuffled toward Massey, his legs unsteady on the gently pitching deck. *Boats.* Will glowered. *Loathe them.*

"They say you've got quite the knack for cavalry fighting," Massey continued, shaking his head in awe. "But how you manage to seat your horse. It's a marvel."

Will grunted, slicing through the man's bonds, and decided to let tense silence be his response. He needed to listen for the militiamen's return. But mostly he was finding Massey irksome.

"Well," Massey said, rubbing his freed wrists. "I thank you—"

"*Ist,*" Will hushed him with an iron grip on his shoulder. He'd heard a faraway shot. "They return. We must make haste now."

"But of course," Massey replied in a stage whisper. "It puts me in mind of the time I escaped from the Tower. Wriggled my way up the fireplace like a damned chimney boy." Chuckling, he followed Will up and over the side of the boat.

"Oh Lord help us," Massey exclaimed, "this is bitter cold." He waded behind Will in an ungainly return to the fishing boat. "The only flaw in a tidy plan, I say. I hear you've also helped a man escape from the Tower. Our Ormonde, in fact."

"Our Ormonde is out there"—Rollo nodded into the night—"risking his hide for *you.* So I'll ask again that you hold . . . your . . . tongue." His tone brooked no response.

The men clambered into the small boat. It bobbed and rocked with the weight. Finally it settled, the only sound the dull slap of water against the hull.

The coast was ragged, and the plan was to shelter in a nearby cove, keeping out of the moonlight, waiting for Ormonde to return overland. Will rowed in silence, with Massey watching him all the while, a tidy, peevish smile curving his lips.

Just when Will began to wonder where Ormonde was, there was the crack of multiple gunshots. They exploded in rapid succession—too rapid to all be his friend.

Massey studied the spit of land edging the cove. "We should—" he began, then flicked his eyes to Will's legs. It was the briefest of glances, but it didn't go unnoticed. "I should investigate," he amended. "Something's amiss."

"Go," Will told him through clenched teeth. If Massey thought he was incapable of saving Ormonde, let him. Will would beat him to it, doubling back by boat.

His oars were in the water before Massey had even gotten his footing on land. Will pulled hard, putting his back and aching legs into it, his face grimacing with the effort.

Jamie was dead, and yet still he felt this maddening need to prove something.

With only one man's weight on board, it was a quick return to the other side of the river. He opened his ears to the night, trying to hear beyond the heavy slap of water on the hull and the rhythmic splish of his rowing. Sensing activity on the riverbank, Will dragged his oars, slowing his boat to a stop.

A shout rose from near the dock. Then Ormonde's voice pealed above the din, theatrically loud. "You *three* vagabonds, you'll not stop me, even though *I'm bound*."

Will laughed low to himself. It seemed the more perilous the situation, the more humor his friend brought to bear. But still, Ormonde's message was clear. He was trussed, captured by three men.

Will rowed closer, pulling along the far side of the militia boat. He'd need to intervene before they got back onboard their birlinn. Somehow disable the three men and save Ormonde.

With naught but his cane and a dagger.

His eyes creased in thought. There wouldn't be much time. He just needed to plunge in and hope a strategy made itself clear.

Will slid back into the icy water, and it was oddly warming on his cold, wet clothing. Scowling, he trudged the shallow river, casting his mind open for a plan. The silt was thick, and it fought his every step like a bog. *So damnably slow*, he thought. And then the idea struck.

All men move slowly in the water.

Will had been cursing it, but really, this hateful river was the great equalizer. It mattered not that he was crippled. *Every* man who tried to move in shallow water would be rendered a lumbering fool.

Ducking out of sight, he waited, assessing their location. Birlinns were low and light—it was what enabled them to move easily through shallow water—and this one hugged close to shore. The militiamen would need to push it back into the water, with a man at the rear to guide it.

He waited, knowing what would come, and finally he heard it. Someone approached from the rear of the boat. The man cursed low to himself, about the cold and the muck, completely unaware of what lurked for him in the water.

Will sank to his knees. Though he canted his chin up, the river swayed and splashed lazily, tasting soft and muddy at his mouth. Water seeped under his collar and sucked the heat from his chest, but focus made him immune to the cold.

He eased his cane underwater, stretching it out along the river bottom.

There was splashing, another curse, and the man came into view. Will's sight was accustomed, but this man moved from moonlight to shadows, and it took him a moment to adjust.

Holding tight to the base of his cane, Will sucked in a breath and slipped beneath the surface. Blackness and silence engulfed him. Steadying himself, he dug one hand into the slime of the river bottom and extended the cane before him with the other. The water fought his every movement, and he flexed his wrist, fighting to keep the handle from skimming into the silt.

He swung, pushing the cane in a sluggish arc through the water. The crook struck the man's ankle, and Will gave a quick, sharp tug.

The man fell into the water with a shout and a splash. Will came up for air, distantly aware of the change in the other men's voices. He had but a moment to silence this one before he let out a call of alarm.

He went under again, dragging the man's foot to him. Will grabbed the man's thigh, pinned flailing hands beneath his feet. And then Rollo drowned him.

It seemed to take forever for him to thrash his last. The two of them struck an obscenely intimate pose, this stranger's body writhing beneath him, the water's resistance choreographing a languorous dance. Will's hand tangled in the man's hair, holding him under while he tilted his own chin up for precious sips of air. Until finally, blessedly, the man flinched, and grew still.

He didn't have a moment to savor his victory. Hearing the commotion, the other men called to their fellow.

Someone was making a clumsy approach from around the back, and Will kept his eyes trained on the rear of the birlinn. Which meant he didn't sense the man behind him until he felt the knife on his throat.

"What have we got here?" a voice hissed in his ear.

Anger, clear and lightning bright, was his only response. *Felicity*. He needed to live for Felicity.

Will grabbed the man's knife hand, securing it. With a growl, he slammed his elbow back, catching the man in the gut. His attacker stumbled back. Will stood, pivoted, watching in slow motion as his attacker arced his blade arm back up.

Forget the blade. Fight the man.

Will made a fist, his every ounce of desire to see Felicity a tidal wave driving his punch. His right fist slammed into the man's jaw. Immediately, Will torqued his torso, catching the man's cheek with his left. He swung up, his right fist connecting with the man's chin.

The militiaman wavered, gave an uneven shake to his head, and then collapsed into the river.

The third and last man approached fast at Will's back, and he spun to face him, just in time to see Ormond hobbling behind, arms still trussed at his back. His friend dove for the militiaman, slamming awkwardly into him, both falling with a splash into the river.

Ormonde struggled to stand but his feet kept sliding on the viscous muck of the river bottom. His trussed hands made his body awkward, and his head slipped below the surface of the freezing water. He bobbed up, inhaled sharply, and disappeared again.

The militiaman had recovered from his fall and stalked toward Will, Ormonde ready to drown if he didn't act fast.

Rollo reached down, his frozen fingers fumbling along his calf. His dagger. He gripped it, careful to keep ahold of the wet hilt. Standing tall, he took the blade of the *sgian dubh* between his thumb and fingers, and threw.

The man teetered, clawing at the knife stuck in his throat, and then disappeared into the black water.

Will stumbled, leaping for his friend. Hooking his hand under Ormonde's arm, he pulled him to standing.

"That was quite a pretty throw," Ormonde said, steadying himself. He feigned nonchalance, but Will heard the relief in his voice.

"MacColla's woman showed me the trick." Will stood behind him, studying his wrists. The knots were tight, the bonds cloth, not rope.

"Good Lord," Ormonde exclaimed. "You're better men than I with these . . . *uncommon* women of yours."

Will laughed low, picking at the knots. The water had made them tenacious, and he leaned down to tear the fabric with his teeth. "I seem to always be saving your hide," he grumbled, then spat a thread from his tongue.

"It's the hair, Will." Ormonde shook out his arms, and gestured to his bright red curls, dusky brown in the moonlight. "I stand out."

"Then how did you manage not to get shot?" Rollo asked, eyeing his friend for injuries. "Such fireworks. The Gloucester militia must've expelled their munitions stores for the next month."

"Stand out I may," Ormonde assured him, "but I am also quite wily."

"I see." Will chuckled. "Or the militiamen are blind in the dark, more like."

There was a light splashing along the bank, and, locking eyes, both men froze. Turning in unison, they poised for attack. But it was only Massey, chest heaving with exertion, peering into the darkness of the river. "Oh," he said simply, seeing Ormonde standing shoulder to shoulder with Will.

Will smiled. Massey's single "oh" spoke volumes. He turned his attention to the water, scudding his feet along the riverbed.

"Is this what you're looking for?" Ormonde slipped under to dig in the silt, coming back up with Will's muddied staff. "You took a great risk, helping us," he said, dashing the water from his face. "You have my gratitude. And it seems it is I who owe you now."

Will raised his hands in protest. "Och, please man, let's just call the tally even."

The two men laughed low. "Now go, friend," Ormonde said, handing Rollo his cane. "You've done enough. Go to your woman."

"*Now* you'd have me leave?" Tugging his wet collar from where it clung at his neck, Will shook his head. "Soaked, cold, and disarmed? Thank you, no." He shivered, looking downriver to where the fishing boat bobbed near the dock. "We'll take that tub down to Bristol and part ways there. I might hate sailing, but it'll be the fastest way between here and Lochaber."

Ormonde laughed, clapped Will on the back, then shuddered as a sudden chill seized him. "Good Lord, man," he said, a smile still on his face. "Lochaber? You must really love this woman."

"Aye," Will said simply. "Love her I do."

Chapter 39

Will stood before the stone tablet, cane forgotten at his feet. He turned the star chart in his hands, careful not to tear the tattered paper. It had gotten a thorough soaking in the river, and some of the lines and dots had bled into formless clouds of gray ink.

He placed it over the stone. Rotated it, studying the map from a different angle.

He needed to be certain. He'd have only one chance to go to Felicity, and he hoped he knew what he was doing.

"The hubris of youth!" a voice cackled, and even before he spun to see, he knew he'd find the old witch Gormshuil there.

"Took you longer than I'd thought," she said. She walked toward him, her approach along the path almost leisurely. The morning sun cut through the trees at a sharp angle, turning her gray braid into a white rope hanging over her shoulder. Though long, the wiry wisps didn't do much to conceal her pale scalp.

"You're a stubborn one, William Rollo." Gormshuil stopped, standing in front of him, sucking thoughtfully at her teeth. She smelled of earth and cherry-sweet smoke. "Who knows where you'd end up without my help?" she scolded, snatching the chart from his hands.

"What have you done?" She muttered and shook her head, studying the chart. Her features danced a medley of expressions: grunted annoyance, to anxious confusion, to squawks of impish humor.

"I kept it as safely as I could," Will said, his tone uncharacteristically hesitant.

"Let's pray you're able to mind your own self better than you did this wee scrap." Gormshuil's eyes were the white blue of a hazy sky, and they hardened on him. "Do you know what it is you attempt?"

"Aye, of course—"

"*Ist*, boy, and listen. Do you know where it is you go? Your woman's world is not your world."

"Felicity *is* my world," he answered quickly and surely.

"I pray you're correct." Gormshuil chewed thoughtfully at her lip. "Because I don't know that you'll ever be able to return."

"I don't want to return," he said, and he meant it.

He thought on his family. Jamie was dead, and his mother might as well be. Will would mourn his father, but if the attentions of one attractive, older maid were any indication, the man was recovering just fine.

And though Will would miss his friends, he'd not miss how their obsessions had a way of drawing him in. He'd given his all to help MacColla, to help Graham. He loved those men like brothers, and would do it all again, but they lived on, with their own concerns and loves. While Will was left always alone, in the wake of the lives of others.

And then there was Ormonde. Will gave a fond and knowing chuckle. God love him, but the man was like the tides, pulling all under and down, to the neglect of anyone else's desires but his own.

He considered his country. Oliver Cromwell was dead, and his son Richard ousted from power. Charles II was well on his way to being restored as king.

No, he thought. He knew exactly what world he was leaving. "I know what I do," he told the woman. "And I ask that you help me."

She studied him silently, then with a sly smile and a brisk nod, Gormshuil returned the star chart to the granite tablet.

She licked her thumb, smudging at some of the lines on the page. "You'll do like so," she told him. Her finger was wrinkled and thin, the pad of her fingertip flattened with age, but it moved fluidly over the paper, gracefully outlining shapes on the chart. "Trace thus."

Goose bumps pebbled his skin with the sensation that he glimpsed some deeper geometry, some overreaching structure to the universe.

"Clear your mind," she snapped, and Will wondered if the witch had read his thoughts. "Reason not, Will Rollo. Keep your thoughts a tranquil pool. Felicity the only ripple on its surface."

Dozens of questions gnawed at the edges of his brain, and he fought them all. Inner calm had always been, for him, hard-won. He wanted to ask just one more thing, but before he had a moment to seize on a single question, Gormshuil gave a sharp sniff and rolled her eyes back in her head.

"Now," she hissed. "Off with you, now." She wheezed a long exhale. "Go."

The witch's hands gripped his upper arms, turning him to face the tablet. Though an old woman, her grip was strong, and those long, bony fingers cut into him like talons.

"For her, time has slowed," she intoned. "But it's not stopped. She, a lone candle among millions. If you want to find the woman you seek, you must go. Now."

He hadn't considered he might travel forward in time, only to not find her. Panic seized him. He gripped the stone, anchoring the paper to the tablet with one hand.

The other flitted over the chart in rapid movements that felt almost automatic, remembered somehow. His arms were numb where Gormshuil gripped him, and he wondered distantly if she weren't transmitting some secret magic through her touch.

The buzzing began at his feet, a warmth at the soles, as if he were being permanently rift from the earth. It intensified, crackled up his legs, molten heat locking his limbs.

Is this what Felicity had felt? *God, no.* Had he made her do this, made her feel such pain?

His legs, they were on fire now, and blooming into a pain beyond comprehension. Such pain, as if he were dissolving, a man carved of wax, melting to the ground.

Always, it came down to his accursed legs. With that thought, an alarm sounded. The witch said he must be a calm pool, and he tried desperately to blank his mind. But his thoughts kept returning to his legs.

His damned cane. He'd need his cane. But Will was already being sucked under. Immobilized now, but for a finger still moving over the paper, pure instinct driving his gestures.

Black seeped in at the edges of his vision, the world closing and tunneling until there was only the paper before him.

Light and sound screeched in his head. Blinding, numbing, deafening sensation. His head whirling, his body a raw nerve, unable to break free.

And then Will's body slammed to the earth.

It took him a moment to realize the cool moss beneath his hands. To realize the stone cutting into his cheek.

Felicity. Where was she?

Had he traveled? Was she there?

Will raised his head, darting his eyes, making sense of his dim surroundings. Ghastly walls of leaves and berries rose all around. It was belladonna, bearing deadly Devil's Cherries, their color the rich and repugnant purple of a vicious bruise.

The labyrinth. He was in the maze. It closed around him, like some malignant prison hemming him in. Keeping him from Felicity.

Felicity.

He must find her. *One among millions*, the witch had said. His mind blanked, all thought dumping from his brain but for the single image of Felicity. She was the only thing that existed, the only thing that mattered.

Frantic, Will scrambled forward. He scrambled on hands and knees, scrambled into a lope, and then into a run. He raced through the maze, his body careering off the soft and obscene give of the labyrinth walls. He moved like a drunken man, a possessed man. Frantic only to find Felicity.

He vaulted from the opening of the maze, and ran. Breath filled his lungs, the air suddenly fresher, clearer. His legs pulsed and his chest swelled, and he wondered at the strange sensations.

Will skidded to a halt. His legs.

He doubled over, hands on thighs, panting for breath.

His legs, they were straight and strong.

The maze had transformed him. A man whole once more. And all because of Felicity.

There was a strange sound from faraway, rising over the hill as surely as pipes on the eve of battle.

He sprang back into a run. Felicity had been right. They were destined to be together. Steely determination drove him hard, his arms and legs pumping.

He crested the hill to see a street winding at the base of the valley. And there were vehicles there, moving so fast along, so foreign and so unfathomable. He realized they must be the car that Felicity had told him about—a carriage of steel requiring no horse.

He grinned broadly, and a laugh erupted from deep in his soul. What a place of miracles this was.

Will bounded down the hill and stopped on the side of the road, panting and marveling. He thought he must look a crazed man.

A car slowed, then stopped beside him. Will knew he should be wary, but the open smile of its driver put him at his ease.

"Are you from the Renaissance Faire too?" the man asked.

Will leaned closer, trying to make sense of his accent. He shrugged his confusion.

A glass pane at the rear of the car rolled down. "Hey,"

a woman said, leaning out. "Where'd you guys find those clothes? They're awesome. So realistic."

Will looked blankly. What to say? His Felicity, *a lone candle among millions*. He wondered if these people might be able to help. "Have you seen—"

"The woman in lavender?" she finished for him.

"The blonde," the driver stated. "Are you missing a pretty blonde?"

"Aye." Will tried to temper his sudden joy in front of these strangers. "I'm looking for that woman."

"Hop in, dude."

The door was barely closed behind him when the driver took off. Will barked out a laugh despite himself, to feel his body jolt so in space. It was exhilarating, this speeding carriage.

"Man, your friend was in some rough shape." It was the person seated next to the driver who spoke.

"Is Felicity safe?" Will asked quickly, fear hardening his voice to steel.

"Easy, cowboy." The driver chuckled. "She's fine."

"A little on the emotional side, though," the woman said. Will had settled himself next to her, crushing himself as much as possible along the door so as not to press up against her so intimately. "Did you have a fight or something?"

"That explains it," the driver said.

"Ohhhh," another said, "now I get it."

"She seemed pretty bummed out," the woman added.

"Man," the other chimed in, "I wouldn't want to be you."

"There she is." The driver pointed to a figure walking along the side of the road. It was a woman, in a lavender gown, scrubbing at her face. "That's your friend, right?"

"Good Lord, is she carrying a sword?"

"Watch out, dude, looks like she bought a claymore."

"Out," Will gritted. He jiggled the door handle. "I must get out."

"Whoa." The driver screeched to a halt. "You've gotta wait til I stop."

Will spilled from the car. He shouted for her, ran to her. His Felicity. He couldn't reach her soon enough.

She saw him, and momentary bewilderment flickered into joy.

He pumped his legs harder, elation swelling in his chest. His body slammed into hers, and he swept her up at once into an embrace. Will swung her around and around, laughing and kissing her all over.

"How . . . ?" She studied him, tears marking thin paths down her dirty cheeks. "And your legs," she shouted, realizing suddenly.

"I couldn't be without you," he told her. His eyes consumed her, so lovely, so right, in her soiled and tattered dress. For the first time in his life, Will knew perfect joy. "And so I came to be with you. If you'll have me."

"Oh yes, Will." She stood on her toes, whispering her words on his lips. "I'll have you."

Epilogue

The dew was cool on Felicity's bare feet. The grass sounded a tiny squeak every time Will spun her before him. His hand was strong and sure at her waist, the other warm and enveloping hers.

Her heart filled to watch him, to watch his smile. These days, a smile lit Will's features more often than not. He was so handsome in the moonlight, laughing low, twirling her, lifting her.

Her Viking loved to dance.

And they danced now under the stars. Their favorite thing, stealing this time alone together. The children asleep, their only music the rustle and squeak of dewy grass and the faraway bleat of their neighbor's sheep.

They'd chosen to stay in Scotland, in Perthshire, in a country cottage on land that rolled gently to the banks of the River Tay. Duncrub Castle was only a memory now, but they still loved to sneak away when they could, for a quick tumble along their Roman road.

Felicity loved Scotland, where never before had she felt

so truly, deeply at home. At first, she'd worried what Livia would think.

But that was before she'd realized her aunt had long harbored fantasies of finding herself some brawny, gray-bearded blacksmith. And though Livvie had yet to encounter just the right candidate, she seemed to be enjoying the hunt, making her way from isle to isle in the Hebrides.

She thought she heard something. Putting her hand on Will's shoulder, she stilled him. They locked eyes. Speaking wasn't necessary; he'd know what she was doing.

Their youngest was just shy of a year old, and Felicity was still getting used to the fact that she no longer needed to be on call all night, through the night.

They paused, and while she listened, Will kissed her. His mouth was warm and soft on her neck, her jaw, her ear. "Baby Olivia sleeps yet, love," he whispered to her. He unbuttoned her sweater, roving his hand under her shirt. His skin was hot on her cool breast. "But I find myself feeling very awake at present," Will murmured, nipping at her ear.

"I'm sorry I'm so nervous." She tangled her fingers in his hair, and it was the only invitation he needed.

"Not too nervous," Will told her, and he reached a hand around her back. Clutching her bottom, he pulled her closer to him.

He was hard for her, and she giggled, flush with pleasure. He seemed always ready for her.

"You're perfect with them," he said, referring to their three sleeping kids. "The greatest mother I could imagine."

"Your mom didn't exactly set a stellar example."

"No indeed," he said with a low laugh. His kisses stilled. He pulled from her, tracing her hair from her cheek, tucking it behind her ear. "I wonder what came of them."

Felicity knew he referred to his parents. Though folk like the Campbells and MacDonalds lit the pages of history books like major constellations, there was not so much about

Clan Rollo. They'd tried researching, but hadn't been able to find much beyond dates of birth and death, and some of Will's own exploits on the battlefield.

They'd found all kinds of stuff about Ewen Cameron, though. Some of the poems written for him had made Felicity roll her eyes. But mostly they made her smile with the memory of him. She was happy he'd lived a good, long life.

"Do you think Ewen did it?" she asked abruptly. "Went back and saved Robert, I mean?"

"Well," he mused, "the labyrinth is certainly there, as we both well know." Resting his elbows on her shoulders, he stretched his arms around her, hands clasped thoughtfully. "Aye, lass. If I know the laird Cameron, I think he'd have found a way to save his foster brother. The man did live til the age of ninety, so whatever he did, he managed to survive it."

"And with well over a dozen kids too." Felicity shook her head, exaggerated dismay on her face. "God, Lily . . . That poor woman."

They shared a laugh, and she watched her husband, watched as those chiseled features softened, his hazel eyes looking to someplace faraway.

"Do you miss it?" she asked quietly. "Old Scotland, I mean?"

"Och," he smiled. His eyes scanned around them, taking in the world they'd built together. A cottage, land, trees. She traveled twice a week into Perth, where she was studying to be a veterinarian. They had a paddock full of horses, and Will had a rich life as a horse breeder, and, she believed, the best kids' riding instructor in the Highlands. "I love our life," he told her.

Cupping her chin, he added, "You forget what gifts your modern age gives. Here, where the water runs, but the blood does not. So, no, lass." He smiled. "I don't miss it one wee bit."

He spun her suddenly, and she yelped in surprise. Will reeled her to him, dipped her, and stole a quick kiss.

He pulled Felicity back up, keeping her tucked close. "My life is where you are. You, my delight. And besides, love," he said, giving Felicity a loving little swat to her rump. "I find you to be a very bonny dancer."

They laughed, and kissed, and Will and Felicity walked arm in arm back inside, to peek at the kids one last time for the night.

Author's Note

Compared to the histories of my previous heroes, there is next to nothing written about William Rollo. We do know that he was "lame," though I haven't been able to uncover how or why. We also know that he was a gifted cavalry soldier who fought closely with his friend James Graham.

He had an older brother, James Rollo, who truly did go from James Graham's sister to Campbell's. I couldn't find many facts about the eldest Rollo son beyond that, but you can imagine just how irresistible I found that nugget alone.

Perthshire does indeed bear traces of the ancient Romans, including a road and marching camps. And a monument to Maggie Wall still stands outside the village of Dunning.

In fact, it's estimated that at least fifteen hundred people were executed for witchcraft in Scotland during three peak periods: the 1590s, 1640s, and 1660s. A young, zealous minister named Alexander Robertson was responsible for many accusations, though his heyday was in the early 1660s, postdating my story by a few years.

The Sealed Knot society did exist, plotting in secret for the restoration of the King. Though we don't know for sure if James Butler, the Marquis of Ormonde, was a member, he did conspire on a number of occasions with Royalist agitators. Though he wasn't in the Tower in 1658, that year found him narrowly escaping capture by Cromwell's agents.

Edward Massey was indeed a trusted ally of Charles II, and he also escaped imprisonment at least twice: once from the Tower of London by climbing from a chimney and then from the Gloucester militia who'd discovered him plotting an insurrection.

I blurred my timing by a few months. The fact is, there was no single dramatic event that precipitated Charles's return to the throne. And you can imagine how we authors hate not having Dramatic Events! This is how I came to incorporate Massey's story.

As for the Parliamentarians, in what was a surprising turn, Richard Cromwell took over as Lord Protector after his father, the infamous Oliver Cromwell, died in 1658. Richard was indeed known as "Tumbledown Dick," or "Queen Dick." Under pressure from an army that despised him, he resigned in May 1659. This predates the real Massey's capture and escape, which took place in July of that same year.

And finally, Dear Reader, you'll please forgive me the following. As a result of Will's relative obscurity, I didn't have a full picture of his life when I began writing. I managed to unearth tidbits as I went along, discovering to my dismay that I inadvertently changed some pretty big elements in history from the start.

First and foremost, I was well into the book before I discovered that it was Rollo's brother who bore the title of Lord. And moreover, Will had been captured on the field at Philiphaugh, fighting with Graham. (Readers of *Sword of the Highlands* will recall a critical moment for Rollo in this very battle.) He was later hanged, his charge that he refused to betray his friend, warning Graham of imminent danger instead of assassinating him as he'd been ordered.

A testament to the lack of hard facts about Rollo can be gleaned from the following. He is a minor character in a love story entitled *And No Quarter: Being the Chronicle of the Wars of Montrose As Seen by Martin Somers, Adjutant of Women in O'Cahan's Regiment*, written by Maurice Walsh and published in 1937. The Dunning Parish Historical Society tells me that this book, though fiction, was used as a standard history textbook in Scottish schools for many years.

The Historical Society has one more book on hand. Dating from the nineteenth century, it refers to William Rollo as a "man of excellent parts and unblemished reputation." And that's truth enough for this author.

You'll find additional details, images, and more strapping Highland heroes at my Web site, VeronicaWolff.com.

Turn the page for a preview of the new
historical romance by Veronica Wolff

Devil and the Deep Blue Sea

Coming Fall 2010 from Berkley Sensation!

Chapter 1

Marjorie skittered down the steep path, purposely descending too quickly to think. The specter of Dunnottar Castle felt heavy over her shoulder, looming in near-ruin high atop Dunnottar Rock, a massive stone plinth that punched free of Scotland's northeastern coast like a gargantuan fist. Waves roiled and licked at its base far below. Chilled, she clambered even faster, skidding and galloping downhill, unsure whether she was fleeing closer to or farther from that grim mountain of rubble the MacAlpins called home.

She shook her head. She'd sworn not to think on it.

She'd done entirely too much thinking already. Much to her uncle's consternation, she'd chosen her gray mare, not his carriage, for her ride from Aberdeen. She'd realized too late that the daylong ride offered her altogether too much time to brood over what felt like a lifetime of missteps. And she hoped she wasn't about to make the grandest, most humiliating one of all.

She was going to see Cormac.

Whenever she'd thought of it—and she'd thought of little else on her interminable ride—she'd turn her horse around and head straight back to home. But then those same thoughts of him would have her spinning that mare right around again, until her horse tossed its head, surly from the constant tugging and turning.

She reached the bottom of the hill, where the knotted grass turned rocky, its greens and browns giving way to the reds and grays of the pebbled shore. The beach curved like a thin scimitar around the bay, its far side concealed from view by the ragged hillocks and blades of rock that limned the shore as though the land only reluctantly surrendered to the sea.

Marjorie slid the leather slippers from her feet and set them carefully down. She wriggled her toes, leaning against the swell of land by her side. The pebbles blanketing the shore were large and rounded, and looked warmed by the late afternoon sun. She stepped forward, moving slowly now. The water between the stones was cold, but their smooth tops were not, and they sounded a soothing clack with each step.

She was close. She could feel it.

Cormac. *He* was close. Amidst the gentle slapping of the waves and the sultry brine in the air, she sensed him.

She'd not needed to stop in at Dunnottar to ask his siblings where to find him. She and Cormac had known each other since birth, and Marjorie had spent every one of her twenty-three years feeling as though she were tied to him in some mysterious and inextricable way. Though they hadn't spoken in what felt like a lifetime, she'd spared not a penny nor her pride to glean word of him, writing to his sisters for news, aching for rare glimpses of him through the years.

She'd offered up the prayers of a wretched soul when he'd gone off to war, and then prayers of thanks when he returned home whole. And God help her the relief she felt knowing he'd never married. She couldn't have borne the thought of another woman in Cormac's arms.

No, Marjorie knew. Alone by the sea was exactly where she'd find him.

She screwed her face, shutting her eyes tight. There were many things she knew.

She knew that Cormac blamed her. To this day, he blamed her, just as she blamed herself for the foolish, girlish dare that had ripped Aidan from their lives. Because of her silliness, the MacAlpin family had lost a son and brother that day. And Marjorie had lost more still than that: She'd also lost Cormac.

She froze again. What was she thinking? She couldn't do this. She couldn't bear to see him.

But she couldn't bear not to.

The draw was too powerful to resist. Her feet stepped inexorably forward before her mind had a chance to stop them. She told herself she had no other choice. Events in her life had led her just there. She needed help, and Cormac was the only man with skills enough to come to her aid.

The hillock at her side dropped away, revealing the far edge of the beach. Revealing Cormac.

His shirtless back was to her, his *breacan feile* slapping at his legs in the wind. He was hauling in his nets. A fisherman now, as his sister had said. Hand over hand, the flex of muscle in his arms and back was visible even from a distance.

Gasping, Marjorie stumbled back a step, leaning into the rocks for support. She'd told herself she came because he could help her. But she knew in that instant the real reason she'd come: The only place for her in this treacherous world stood just there, down the beach. *Cormac.*

She'd willingly suffer his blame, suffer his indifference; yet still, like the embers from a long-banked fire, she knew Cormac would give her solace, despite himself.

She hadn't moved, hadn't spoken, but he turned, as though he'd felt her there. Her hand went to her chest, reminding her heart to beat, her lungs to draw breath.

He turned again, abruptly, and tears stung her eyes. Would he spurn her?

But she saw he merely bent to gather his nets, dragging them farther up the shore where he carefully spread them out.

Relief flooded her. She scrubbed at her face, gathering herself, and tucked errant wisps of hair behind her ears. She knew it was purely a nervous gesture; the strong sea wind would only whip her curls free again.

She tempered herself. This meeting would not go well if she were this vulnerable from the start. But of course she was this vulnerable, she thought with a heavy heart, considering all that had recently come to pass.

She took a deep breath. He'd seen her. She couldn't go back now.

Marjorie picked her way toward him. He stood still as granite, waiting for her, watching her. His dark hair blew in the wind, and his brow was furrowed. Was he upset to see her? Simply thoughtful?

Suddenly, she regretted the absence of her slippers. She loved the sensation of the smooth rocks beneath her feet, but now felt somehow naked without every stitch of her clothing. She fisted her hands in her skirts. She imagined she'd always been sort of naked before Cormac, and there was nothing that could truly ever conceal her. He was the only one who'd ever been able to read her soul, laid bare in her eyes.

He was silent and still. What would he see in her eyes now?

She felt as though she'd forgotten how to walk. She made herself stand tall, focused on placing one foot in front of the other, but she felt awkward and ungainly, unbearably self-aware as she made her way to him. *Lift the foot, place it down, lift and down.*

Her brain spun with frantic thoughts. Who would be first to speak? She'd sought *him* out; the initial greeting would fall to her. It would fall to the woman, to *her*, to chatter with ease. She could ask after his family. Would inquire as to the day's catch.

He was not ten paces away. He was tall, but with a man's body now, broad with muscles carved from hauling nets, from firing guns. That last gave her pause. She spotted the fine sheen of scars on his forearm, a sliver of a scar on his brow. He'd been long at war. What kind of a man would he have become?

Inhaling deeply, she let her eyes linger over his face. She

was close enough to see the color of his eyes. Blue-gray, like the sea. Her heart sped. She forced herself to step closer.

She'd been unable to summon an exact picture of him in her thoughts, but now that he stood before her, his face was as familiar to her as her own. There was Cormac's strong, square jaw. The long fringe of dark lashes. But he was somehow foreign, too. The boy had become a man. A vague crook had appeared in his nose, and she wondered what long-ago break had put it there. Where had *she* been the moment it happened, what had *she* been doing while he'd been living his life?

She stopped an arm's length from him. Intensity radiated from him like the sun's glare off the sea.

Her throat clenched. She couldn't do it. What had she been thinking?

He blamed her still. He didn't want to speak to her. He didn't welcome the sight of her.

The silence was shrill between them. She swallowed hard, wondering how best to get herself out of there. How to gracefully back out, to never, *ever* see him again.

For Davie. She had to do this for Davie. That thought alone kept her anchored in place.

Cormac opened his mouth to speak, and she held her breath.

"Ree," he whispered, in the voice of a man. "Aw, Ree, lass."

Her every muscle slackened. Her fear, her disquiet, stripped away, leaving Marjorie raw before him. Hot tears came quick, blurring her vision.

"Cormac," she gasped. "It's happened again."

Chapter 2

Cormac heard the hollow clack of rocks shifting behind him. Years of savage training had attuned his senses, sensitized them, rendering him as acute as any predator. The merest rustle could sound at his back, and pure instinct flared, making him ready to fight, or to kill.

He'd spun, but it was her. *Marjorie*. The sight of her was a punch in the sternum.

She was his guilty pleasure. Through the years, he'd hold himself off, until he could bear it no longer, then he'd allow himself to ask after her, or more delicious still, find an excuse to travel to Aberdeen and the promise of a chance glimpse or two. To his family he feigned casual disinterest, but Cormac felt certain the world saw through his mask to the anguish beneath.

He should've saved Aidan that day. If he'd been stronger, less clumsy and inept, he could've fought to save him. But like a fool he'd gotten himself stuck in a damned chimney flue. He'd borne the shame of it every day since. His stupidity had lost him his twin, and his grieving mother hadn't survived the year. Two losses on his head, all before his ninth birthday.

The third loss, though, the crushing blow, was the loss of this woman who approached him now. This fine and beautiful creature whom he'd never deserve.

He suspected Marjorie saw more in him than his shame, but he could not. He was beyond feeling love, or joy, and he'd sealed that fate when he'd gone off to war, craving battles like a parched man does water, baptizing himself in blood. But rather than washing his soul clean, the blood of others had only stained it blacker.

Marjorie grew closer, gliding across the rocky beach as though it were a ballroom. She held her head high, and her long golden brown curls whipped in the wind. The ache in his chest turned sharp, from the punch of a fist to the twist of a knife.

Rarely did he truly *see* anyone anymore. All faces looked the same to Cormac. All, except for hers. She emerged from the world's meaningless bustle as a goddess would a frieze.

Marjorie was close enough now that he could see her eyes. He'd been seeing them in his dreams for years. He'd convinced himself it was merely a last remaining boyish fancy that had embellished his memories, but he knew now he'd been wrong. Her eyes were as brilliant as he'd remembered. They were wide, a rare blue that had always reminded him of the petals of *barraisd*. Her eyes, like the flower, were impossibly vivid and bright.

"Ree," he heard himself whisper. And with that, a veil cleared from before those startling eyes. He saw her pain, and it sliced through his armor as easily as a blade between ribs. "Aw, Ree, lass."

"Cormac, it's happened again."

He understood at once, and fought the urge to reach for her. "Tell me."

"I live with Uncle now, in the old town house." She paused, the memory of that house and that day hanging between them. "I've been helping tend the children at the Saint Machar poorhouse."

He nodded, even though he already knew where she lived

and how she'd been spending her time. She'd been battling her own demons, just as he had.

He wanted to give her some reassurance, but instead felt his eyes narrow. He cursed himself. Perhaps he'd never remember how regular folk acted, how they comforted, how they smiled.

"I was with Davie—" Her voice caught.

Jealousy spiked his veins like acid. Had Marjorie come to him to discuss another man? Rage overcame him, then disbelief. He waited for Marjorie's explanation in pained silence.

"I was with a boy named Davie," she began again, "down by the docks. He's a wee lad, just five, and clings to my skirts like a limpet, he does."

Cormac's chest eased, and he realized he'd been holding his breath.

Marjorie peered at him for a moment, a curious look in her eyes. "I had business in Castlegate," she continued, "and so gave him a bawbee for some food. The baker had a pan of rowies hot from the oven . . ." Her voice drifted off.

Dread lanced him, and for a moment, Cormac knew what it was to be a feeling man again, instead of the brittle husk he'd become. He hardened his stance. "And?" His voice came out harsher than he'd intended, his battle to remain remote making his voice sound a snarl.

Marjorie looked down. "And he never came back to me," she finished quietly.

He forced a casual shrug. "Maybe he ran off. He's just a boy after all." But even as he said it, Cormac knew. No boy in their right mind would tear themselves from the skirts of the fine Marjorie Keith.

"No," she said simply. She collected herself, inhaling deeply. "I know him. He'd not run off. And . . . there have been rumors . . ."

Cormac regretted it, but there was nothing for it. Marjorie deserved to hear the truth. "Not rumors, Ree. Fact. Parliament decreed long ago that able-bodied poor found idling be gathered and claimed as property."

"Like Aidan?" Her voice was barely a murmur.

He set his jaw. "Aye. Precisely like that."

She wiped a tear from her cheek, and Cormac fisted his hands at his sides. He would not—*could* not—comfort her. " 'Tis a cruel world, Ree. There are even some who say the poor lads are the better for it, breathing the fresh air of the Indies, or the Americas, rather than—"

"Rather than climbing chimneys?" she asked coldly, putting a fine point on both their pain. At his nod, she blanched, and then darted her eyes down to stare at her foot as she toed a rock. "It's horrible. How can men do that, and to children?"

"Aye, man is horrible." He'd seen it firsthand. *He'd* done horrible things.

As if she'd read his thoughts, she reached for him. The touch of Marjorie's hand on his arm was light, but it was as though lightning cracked, splitting his heart wide open. Her touch shattered him, exposing the pale, bleak creature hidden at his core.

In that instant, he was vulnerable. Alone, and aching with yearning.

He looked at her fingers wrapped around his forearm, and a lifetime of want burst to the fore. His eyes rose to find her gaze on him. He'd loved her so. The sight of her reminded him of all he'd lost. Of all he was missing.

Cormac stiffened. He let his mind rove to a dangerous place. One where he eased Marjorie down to take her along the rocks, running his hands over her body, through her hair. She'd let him; he saw it in her eyes. He could bury himself in her, forget it all. She'd absolve him of his pain.

His eyes clenched shut as he let that pain roil through him. He couldn't touch her. He wasn't the man she needed. He could never be good enough for one like Ree.

Cormac turned to heave a basket of fish higher up the shore. "Forget the boy, Marjorie."

He set his haul down with force, his eyes shut in a grimace. He'd never used such a tone with her. Hadn't called her by her full name in he knew not how long. But he couldn't help that the world was a cruel place.

"Marjorie!" his youngest sister shouted from up the beach.

Cormac busied himself with his nets. He heard a rustling as Bridget enthusiastically embraced her.

"Marjorie," Bridget exclaimed, breathless. "Where have you been hiding yourself? Cormac was asking after you just the other day."

He scowled, untangling and smoothing the twine webbing, even though the nets were already in impeccable shape. If he could, he'd tan his sister's meddlesome hide.

Bridget trilled merrily on. Cormac could hear from the laughter in her voice that she knew she'd gotten under his skin. "Truly, Marjorie, it distresses me what a stranger you've become. You'll stay for a time with us, of course."

Cormac winced. "She'll not want to bed down in our pile of rubble," he said, not looking up from his work.

"Cormac MacAlpin!" Bridget leaned down to swat his shoulder. "It's not so grim as all that. Come"—she linked arms with Marjorie—"and be welcome at Dunnottar Castle."

He rose slowly, meeting Marjorie's gaze. They locked eyes and, for a blessed instant, the rest of the world fell away. He lost himself, the past, his pain, drowned in vivid blue.

She blinked, and something shifted in her gaze. Cormac swore he felt it shimmer like electricity across his skin. Marjorie narrowed her eyes, assuming a look, *her* look, the one she used to get before issuing one of her infamous dares. That glint aimed straight for him, and Cormac braced.

Marjorie patted his sister's hand, her gaze never leaving his. "Thank you, Bridget. I look forward to my stay."

Enter the rich world of
historical romance
with Berkley Books.

Lynn Kurland

Patricia Potter

Betina Krahn

Jodi Thomas

Anne Gracie

Love is timeless.
penguin.com

M9G0907